Richard Denning was born in Ilkeston in Derbyshire and lives in Sutton Coldfield in the West Midlands, where he works as a General Practitioner.

He is married and has two children. He has always been fascinated by historical settings as well as horror and fantasy. Other than writing, his main interests are games of all types. He is the designer of a board game based on the Great Fire of London and others. He is also the director of the UK's Largest Hobby Games Convention.

You can find out more about Richard and his work on his website: www.richarddenning.co.uk

I0544849

Also by the Richard Denning

Northern Crown Series
(Historical fiction)
1.The Amber Treasure
2.Child of Loki
3.Princes in Exile

Hourglass Institute Series
(Young Adult Science Fiction)
1.Tomorrow's Guardian
2. Yesterday's Treasures
3. Today's Sacrifice

The Praesidium Series
(Historical Fantasy)
The Last Seal

The Nine World Series
(Historical Fantasy)
1.Shield Maiden
2. The Catacombs of Vanaheim

Yesterday's Treasures

by

Richard Denning

Written by Richard Denning
© Copyright 2011 Richard Denning
First published 2011
ISBN: 978-0-9564835-8-4
Published by Mercia Books

Book Jacket design and layout by Cathy Helms
www.avalongraphics.org
Copy-editing and proof reading by Jo Field.
jo.field3@btinternet.com

Author website:
www.richarddenning.co.uk
Publisher website:
www.merciabooks.co.uk

For Jane, Helen and Matthew

CHAPTER ONE
THE FORT

The bronze gun barrel loomed over the narrow strip of water, keeping a silent watch upon the straits it had once, long ago, been positioned here to guard. Thomas Oakley peered down its length, imagining for a moment that he was a gunner aiming at a distant target. Then he turned and gazed along the fort's battlements, which stood like silent sentinels upon the coast. 'Fort Belam' - that was the name of the place. His dad had fancied coming here when he saw it in a holiday brochure.

"It's an old fort built back in Napoleonic times to keep an eye out for a French invasion," he'd explained to the rest of the family. "Been turned into a holiday camp now with cottages and apartments. Fancy going there this summer?"

The suggestion had not been enthusiastically received. Tom's sister, Emma, wanted to stay at Centre Parks and Tom and his mother both preferred the idea of an 'all inclusive' vacation in Corfu, but his dad, having lost his job that spring, had only just got a new one. Money was tight, so a cottage in North Wales was where they went.

In the end, it was not as bad as it had sounded. The weather was a bit mixed, but when it was dry there were beaches not far away, a number of towns with amusement arcades, interesting shops and castles to visit. Nearby, the mountains of Snowdonia

1

loomed over the skyline. Tom had to admit that he certainly needed a break. The year so far had involved some unpleasant, dangerous adventures and he had been quite ready for - and had enjoyed - the two weeks they had spent at the fort: two weeks of peace and quiet with no complications.

No complications, that was, until a moment ago.

Tomorrow they were going home and in a couple of days the new school term would start so, after lunch, his mum, dad and sister had gone to nearby Caernarfon to buy some souvenirs and presents. Tom had turned down the offer, fancying instead a few hours alone in the cottage and a final look around the fort.

Bringing his camera with him he had strolled along the battlements, stopping every so often to take a photo of a cannon, the fort, Anglesey across the bay in one direction and the distant mountains in the other. On the top of the fort a Union Flag fluttered in the breeze and he snapped that. Then he checked the image in the small screen on the back.

What he saw when it came into view made him stare in amazement.

"Uh?" he muttered as he studied the picture, which clearly showed a flagpole with a flag hanging on the top. However, this was not the familiar red and blue crosses on a white background that he expected to see, but an altogether different flag: one with three broad stripes of red, white and blue. It was the tricolour of France!

He peered up at the standard that flapped about in the gentle wind coming in off the Irish Sea. It was, without a doubt, still the Union Flag. Baffled, he turned his head to glance around the fort, but he could not see a second flagpole anywhere nearby.

"That's stupid!" he muttered. Then he slapped his forehead and smiled. This image was obviously an earlier photo left on the memory card from another day. He checked the image date and time and then frowned when he saw that the date it recorded was today and it had been taken only a few minutes before.

Shaking his head, he looked back at the flagpole and gaped as he now saw the French flag up there, where moments before he was certain it had been the British one. Behind him he heard footsteps coming closer, so he looked around but there was no one in sight. As he stood and stared at the empty battlements he felt something brush past his right arm and heard the footsteps pass on by.

"Oh flip!" he muttered to himself. The guide book had mentioned a ghost that was supposed to haunt the battlements but, like all visitors, Tom had dismissed the story. Was whatever it was that had just brushed past him a ghost? A chill passed down his spine and he felt goose pimples creep along his arms.

"Come on Tom!" he chided himself. "There are no such things as ghosts." Feeling not quite certain that he actually believed this, he decided to go back to the cottage. He walked a few paces towards the stone steps that ran down inside the fort to ground level.

"*Garçon, arrêtes-toi!*"

The order was bellowed from behind him. Tom's heart seemed to leap in his chest and he spun around. He gulped as he saw he was gazing right down the end of a gun barrel. Not a modern gun, like a shotgun or rifle, but an old-fashioned one: a musket. That was frightening enough, but even more terrifying was the man holding the musket. His face was scarred on the right cheek as well as above the left eye, and he leered at Tom with a dangerous expression that threatened violence. He was in uniform: a blue jacket and white trousers. On his head he wore an odd hat - tall, round and black with a brass plate bearing the number

3

31 and a green pompom on the front.

Tom stared at him for a moment, and then slowly he relaxed. This was no ghost. He knew who this was - or rather what kind of man he was. He grinned, feeling a bit sheepish. "You're a re-enactor aren't you? You here to re-fight a battle or something? I've seen that kind of thing before."

"*Comment t'appeles-tu?*" The man demanded.

Tom smiled. "Oh, I get it; you like to play the role. OK then, Je m'appelle Tom Oakley. *J'ai douze ans...*"

"*Es-tu un espion?*"

"What ... I mean, *Je ne vous comprend pas,*" Tom said, forehead wrinkling under the effort of remembering his French lessons. It was no good though: he had no idea what 'espion' meant.

"He said are you a spy?" another very heavily accented voice replied, but this time in English and coming from behind Tom. He turned around and saw another man in similar uniform, although smarter looking and adorned with some gold braid - an officer perhaps. This man was brandishing a long curving sabre in one hand and a pistol in the other.

"Well, are you?" he asked, pointing the sword at Tom.

"Say, you guys really take the part seriously, I'll give you that. So then, when is the battle? I would love to see it. Only we go home tonight and I think ..." He trailed off as he noticed the officer shaking his head.

"I am afraid you will not be going anywhere mon ami unless it is the cells. Now, speak: what is all this about a battle? Is the English army finally coming to face us? Or are the mountain rebels planning an attack on this fort? Mon Dieu but I dearly hope so ... we will teach them a lesson for that raid on Conwy last month. I will have half a dozen strung up by nightfall if they come here."

4

"I ... what?" Tom asked, now utterly confused.

"Come with me!" The man ordered and turned to walk towards the steps.

"Wait ... this is fun and all, but joking aside, I was on my way back to my cottage. Look, if we are still about, we will come and see the battle."

The officer glared back at Tom.

"*Vite, maintenant!*" he shouted and Tom was suddenly and violently thrust along the battlements by the other man - the one with the musket.

"*Wait ... wait ...*" Tom stuttered, then a terrible thought dawned upon him. That French flag above this Welsh fort, these men dressed as French soldiers from the Napoleonic wars of two hundred years ago and what the officer had said offhand about rebels in the mountains and a raid on Conwy: all these facts fell into place and he suddenly realised where he was.

"Oh God, this is the Twisted Reality isn't it?"

The only answer was a puzzled glance from the officer and another painful shove from behind, but Tom knew he was right. The Twisted Reality: a world parallel to Tom's, but where history often took different paths. He had been here before, earlier in the year and visited Britain in the twenty-first century: but it had been a Britain where the Nazis had won World War Two. Now, he seemed to be there again, but at an earlier date when the French under Napoleon had invaded and occupied at least part of the country. So, how did he get here? A third shove from the musket butt told him that it did not matter, at least not for the moment: what mattered was to get away.

He needed to find a place to get his bearings and then he could transport himself back to his world. He stumbled along a few feet until he was just behind the officer, then took off and barging past him, landed on the top step and careered down them, two at a time.

There was a loud bang from behind. Glancing over his shoulder, Tom saw a cloud of smoke around the soldier's musket. Having discharged his weapon and missed, the Frenchman was quickly fastening a bayonet to the end of the musket as he scuttled after his quarry.

Tom carried on down the steps and landed with a crunch on the packed earth of the fort interior. Thirty yards away were the fort gates - both open and apparently unguarded. Tom made for them but after ten strides stopped in his tracks. The gates were open because a horseman was coming through them. The man wore a green jacket and a shiny brass helmet and he sat on a huge, dark brown horse. His eyes narrowed as he took in the sight of the officer and soldier chasing after Tom. He drew his sword with a metallic swish and dug in his heels. The horse leapt forward at a gallop, heading straight for Tom.

Behind, the soldiers had almost caught up with him. Desperately, Tom reached out in his mind for the Map - the connection he had with the world about him and the tool by which he could transport himself anywhere. But in his panic he could not focus on it. The thundering beast charged down upon him and the cavalryman's sword arm went back, ready to strike down and cut him to pieces.

Tom closed his eyes and waited for the blow!

CHAPTER TWO
MUD

It seemed as if time was stretching out. Tom waited: his eyes closed, his heart pounding in terror. Every second that passed appeared to last an eternity. Surely the sword would slice into him at any moment, or he would feel the terrible agony of a pistol shot, the stabbing pain from the bayonet? Yet the blows never came. Tom kept his eyes squeezed tightly shut for a full minute before, very slowly, he opened one and peeked. He relaxed when he saw there was no horse, no cavalryman, musketeer or officer. He glanced up at the flag pole and was relieved to see the Union Flag hanging there. Of the soldiers who had attacked him, there was no indication they had ever been here. There was, however, a group of tourists staring at him from over near the entrance. He waved back vaguely and staggered away towards the private path leading to his family's rented cottage.

He unlocked the door and then just stood in the hallway for a few minutes, feeling confused, disorientated and with his vision a bit blurred. After a while he pottered down to the bathroom and splashed some cold water on his face. Finally he looked at his reflection in the mirror. A boy with brown eyes and jet black hair stared back at him.

"What on earth was that about?" he asked himself.

It had been, without a doubt, a very strange occurrence, but not the strangest he had ever experienced. He thought back over the previous twelve months or so. First there had been the dreams: last year he had dreamt he was Edward, a British soldier in the Zulu War, about to be killed by fierce Zulu warriors. Then, just a few months later, he had dreamt he was a girl named Mary, about to burn to death in the Great Fire of London. After that had been the dream about Charlie, a sailor drowning on a sinking submarine in World War Two. Dreams can be peculiar, but the oddest thing about these was that they were true. These people really existed and the dreams had led to him getting involved in an astonishing adventure.

Not long before his twelfth birthday, Tom Oakley had discovered that he had extraordinary powers enabling him to travel through time and space. He had rescued these three people of his dreams moments before their deaths and brought them back to the present day. That had proved to be just the start of his adventures because then, evil and powerful men had tried to use him to change the world. They had come from another Earth in a world that was parallel to but very different from his own, and they had tried to coerce Tom into helping them conquer his world, promising him unimaginable power. Fleetingly, he had been tempted but then, risking his life and those of his family, he had refused and defeated his enemies. It was that other world, he now realised, that he had just inadvertently revisited. But how?

Tom wandered through to his room and lay down on the bed, thinking back over the terrible adventure of a few months ago. Together with his new friends, Edward, Mary and Charlie, who each had powers similar to his own, Tom had saved his family and the world as well. He had been helped by Professor Neoptolemas, who was in charge of the Hourglass Institute – a secret

8

organisation dedicated to protecting Earth's history from villains and opportunists. Villains like Captain Joseph Redfeld, who had come from that parallel world Tom knew as the 'Twisted Reality', and who strove to bend history to their will. Opportunists like ... well, like his friend, the Welsh time traveller, Septimus Mason, who worked for the Professor – or kind of did. He was a mercenary and usually made a living stealing historical artefacts from the past and selling them in the present.

They had each wanted Tom to use his powers as they used their own. At first, Tom had wanted to lose his ability to move through time – Septimus called it 'Walking' - and be just an ordinary schoolboy, as he had been before all this started, but in the end, not long after his twelfth birthday, he had chosen to join the Institute, to help the Professor and to become *Custos crastinos* – 'Tomorrow's Guardian'.

That had been a few weeks ago, just before the summer holidays. Now it was almost the beginning of September. The summer had passed quietly and although Tom had visited the Professor he was left to enjoy the holiday. He was due back at school in only a couple of days and had hoped for a normal beginning to the year.

Then, out of the blue, today's adventure had happened. Without trying to, he had Walked to the Twisted Reality as well as travelling back two hundred years and he had almost been killed. So then, what did it mean?

There was another question. Why now? Why at this time?

Time?

What time was it? Tom rolled over and reached out to his bedside table. On it was a brass alarm clock, sitting on three little legs. He picked it up and looked at the clock face. Its silver arms showed that it was half past one. As the second hand ticked slowly around its circuit, Tom thought about what to do. His parents and his sister were on their little shopping trip and had promised to call Tom on his mobile when leaving Caernarfon so he could put some pizzas in the oven. That was still likely to be a few hours away, which meant he had some time to kill and a puzzle to solve. In other words, it was time to visit the Professor.

He put the clock back down and picked up his mobile phone, located a stored number under the initials PN and hit the call button.

"Hourglass Institute. Good afternoon. How may I help you?" Tom heard the polite but stilted voice of Mr Phelps, the Professor's secretary.

"Mr Phelps, it's Tom: Tom Oakley. I need to talk to the Professor straightaway."

Tom could almost feel the irritation through the phone. Mr Phelps liked order. He liked diaries and appointments. Tom rarely followed his rules.

"You are going to tell me that you have had one of your dreams or adventures or something like that, aren't you?"

"How did you know?"

"The Professor said he was expecting you to call. He also said I was to fit you in as soon as you did."

That was odd, thought Tom. "How did the Professor know I would call?"

"He said that if you asked me this, I was to say that there are some reasons why he is a professor, young man."

Tom grinned; Mr Phelps sounded almost like Neoptolemas when he said those words.

"OK then, I'm on my way," Tom said, calling off.

In his mind, Tom pictured his Map: it was a map of Britain and a bit like looking at a Google satellite map. On it he lo-

10

cated North Wales and then zoomed in until he could see the fort. Now, he zoomed back out and panned across the country: southwards until he reached London. Closer in he went until he could see Hyde Park and there, just north of the Park, was a series of small streets lined with Regency-era houses, each with black painted iron railings outside. In his mind, Tom was now inside the house, then inside the study where he expected the old man would be sitting behind his desk.

"Walk now!" Tom whispered and he was off, moving along the route he imagined, getting nearer and nearer to London. This was one of the talents he had – the ability to travel to any place he wished. All he need do was to imagine the Map in his head and he would be there in a few moments. Once Septimus had taught him how to do it, it had been as easy as stepping on an escalator to whizz up to the next floor in a shopping centre. Despite his earlier hesitation in the fort, Tom had got used to the effortless ease of Walking, which is why he was taken by total surprise when, a few moments later, everything went wrong.

He suddenly felt dizzy. In his mind the Map seemed to spin and he felt himself hurtling off course.

"Help!" he shouted, although here, in that strange space outside the world which he occupied when Walking – that void of nothingness – he knew that no one would hear. He suddenly lurched to the left and was flung forwards.

"Help me!" he shouted again, despite himself.

Suddenly, he reappeared back in the real world.

He just had time to register that it was night time when he realised that he had materialised three feet off the ground. Giving a yelp of panic, he fell and landed in a puddle of icy cold water that seemed to have filled a large saucer-shaped depression in a patch of muddy ground. The water was deeper than he expected

11

and his head went under the surface. As he plunged down, his arms floundered around, searching for something to latch on to. His outstretched hand found a long and narrow object embedded in the muddy slime at the bottom of the pool – it felt like a stick. It was quite heavy and one end was bent at an angle to the main part. He pulled on it and found that it came up out of the sludge.

He kicked hard against the bottom of the pool and now he was rising up towards the surface. He emerged into the air and gave a gasp as he breathed in. Then he coughed and spat out a mouthful of muddy water. He kicked again and used one hand to paddle across to the side of the pool, where he pulled himself up out of the water and then lay panting on a little beach of mud that ran around the top of the saucer.

In the distance, Tom heard a sudden boom, then another and a moment later the night sky seemed to light up.

'Great; thunder and lightning! Probably means a storm is coming. That's all I need, I'm soaked already,' Tom thought. Ah well, he would just catch his breath for a moment, work out where he was and then he would be on his way.

As he lay there, he examined the strange shaped stick he had found. In the dim light cast from the sliver of moonlight above him, he could see that the stick had various metal knobs and projections around the angle. Then it struck him what he had found. It was a gun – some sort of rifle.

What was it doing in this pool of water? Was it a murder weapon? Maybe he should call the police. Tom pulled out his mobile phone; slid down the cover and then shook it to clear out the water. Anxious that the plunge would have harmed it, he was relieved when he saw that the phone display was still visible. The bright light from the screen illuminated the depression and lit up his face. He checked the display.

"Rats, no signal! I must be well off course."

So, where was he? He reached out for the Map in his head. But when he did, it was as if he was looking at a compass that someone was moving over a magnet in a physics experiment at school. Just in the same way that the needle would then spin and shake erratically, so now the Map was rotating violently.

Tom let go of his link to the Map and instead tried the Clock. In his mind he now had an image of that brass alarm clock beside his bed. This was how he moved through time: how he could Walk to other years and visit places in the past. All he needed to do now was to move the hands in his head and he would make it day time and then he could see where he was. Yet, when he tried this he found that the Clock was going wild, too. The hands seemed to be spinning in opposite directions to each other and when he tried to link to it, he felt as if he was going to be sick.

He let go of both images and tried to figure out what was going on. The Clock and the Map were there alright, but he could not use them – at least not for the moment. So then, he must walk – the ordinary way – and find out where he was and then phone for help.

Tom stood up. About twenty yards away there seemed to be a barbed wire fence. Maybe there was a farm over there. He clambered up out of the dip in the ground and started in that direction. As he did so there was a shout from near the wire. A moment later there was a popping sound then something like a firework flew high into the sky and exploded. The area around Tom was now illuminated by a bright light.

He then heard a word ringing out through the night.

"Offenes feuer!"

Tom knew that last word. It was German for ...

Oh heck ... it was German for fire!

There was a crack of gunshot and the rifle that Tom was holding was knocked violently out of his hand. Another crack and the ground near his feet suddenly exploded as mud flew up into the air.

Tom turned and jumped back into the icy water. Just as he did so, he heard a mechanical 'rat-a-tat-tat' sound from over near the fence and the edge of the crater was struck by dozens of bullets one after the other. It seemed that someone was firing a machine gun at him.

"Help me!" Tom shouted.

Boom!

There was a shattering explosion just over the lip of the depression where Tom was hiding. Soil was flung high into the air and came raining back to earth. Tom risked a glance over the top and saw another huge hole in the ground. He could now make out that there were in fact dozens more stretching as far as he could see. A bullet whizzed by just a few inches away and Tom ducked back down into what he now knew was a shell hole.

You fool, Thomas Oakley, he thought to himself. He was not sure what had gone wrong but somehow he had ended up not in London in the present day but – he now knew where and when - he was in France or Belgium in something like 1916.

He was right in the middle of No Man's Land, near the German trenches and around him World War I was being fought!

There was another huge boom nearby as something like a hand grenade exploded, deafening him for a moment.

"Help me!" Tom shouted again.

CHAPTER THREE
IN THE NICK OF TIME

Desperate to escape, Tom again reached out for the Map and Clock but found they were still behaving erratically. The Map was now moving back and forth between the North Pole and the middle of the Atlantic Ocean whilst the Clock's hands were spinning backwards. He still could not control either and without them he was trapped here, on the Somme or Paschendale or wherever it was, in the middle of the First World War.

What could be causing these problems? Was he ill? Was he losing his talents after all, even though he had recently chosen to keep them? Or was something else going on?

While he was pondering this he noticed that the machine gun and rifle fire had dropped off and no one was throwing grenades anymore. He was just beginning to feel relieved when he heard a whispered conversation and it was coming closer.

"*Schnell, schnell. Der Englande ist in der granattrichter. Kommen sie!*"

That did not sound good. Tom's German was woefully lacking, but he knew *schnell* meant quick and he concluded that *granattrichter* meant shell hole. It sounded horribly like they were coming out of their trench to look for him.

'What do I do?' he thought, panicking. Maybe get out of the hole, give himself up and hope they did not shoot him as a spy

15

before he could Walk away. Maybe he should get out of the hole on the other side – the British or French side. Then again, if the French or British caught him, would they be any less likely to shoot him? He would still be coming from the direction of the enemy lines, wouldn't he?

Paralyzed by uncertainty, Tom peered over the lip of the crater and gasped as he counted six soldiers coming towards him across No Man's Land. They were dressed in grey uniforms along with steel helmets and they carried rifles fixed with fearsomely sharp looking bayonets. Even more frightening: they were only a few yards away.

Ducking back down Tom almost jumped out of his skin as someone tapped him on the shoulder. He spun round, crying out with relief as he recognised Septimus Mason and behind him, Edward Dyson.

"Odd place for a holiday, Tommy boy!" Septimus said, hunkering down beside him.

"I never thought I'd say this, but am I glad to see you!" Tom's grin turned into a grimace. "Septimus, help me please. I can't Walk! Please get me out of here," he pleaded. Glancing back the other way, he could just see the tips of the German bayonets visible over the rim of the crater. The answering grin on the Welshman's face dropped as he now also spotted them. With a nod at Edward, he reached out to grasp Tom's outstretched hand just as a head popped up over the top of the crater. In a split second, half a dozen rifles were levelled at the three of them.

"*Halt! Händehoch!*" shouted one of the soldiers.

"Hands high?" drawled Septimus. "I don't think so, boyo. Sorry to dash but we're in a bit of a hurry." As he spoke, Septimus Walked them out of the crater and away, moving forward almost a hundred years and across the English Channel. A moment later they appeared in front of a park bench in Hyde Park. Tom was momentarily blinded because in stark contrast to the darkness they had just left, the Park was bathed in the bright sunshine of a beautiful late-summer's day. Squinting as his eyes adjusted to the daylight he saw Charlie Hawker and Mary Brown waiting on the bench, both looking anxiously at him and the others.

At once, Mary jumped to her feet and bustled over to him. "Are you hurt, Master Thomas?" she asked in a small voice.

"I'm fine, Mary ... no harm done. Just a bit dizzy, that's all," he replied, as he slumped down onto the grass beside the bench. Septimus collapsed next to him, both of them dripping with wet mud from the shell hole.

"What a dreadful place!" Edward muttered, squelching across to sit down on the bench next to Charlie.

Septimus shrugged, "Oh I don't know, Hyde Park isn't all that bad," he commented with a straight face.

Edward gave him a weary look. "Not the Park! That place we were just at. I read about it in the Professor's library: Ypres wasn't it? Truly awful to think of men being trapped there for years on end," he shuddered.

"I had an uncle who died at Ypres and my dad was injured on the Somme," Charlie muttered. "Never spoke about it afterwards, but everyone knew how horrible it was." He peered at Tom. "Why *on earth* did you go there, Tom?"

Tom hesitated. He was not sure himself what had happened. Tentatively and fearful of what he might find, he reached out for both the Clock and the Map and discovered that they had calmed down now. The frantic spinning and agitated movement had ceased and he could connect easily with both of them. He frowned. "I don't know ... I got confused, I guess. It's been a

17

while since I Walked any distance. Just went off course, that's all."

He saw the others exchange doubtful glances. He could understand why: earlier in the year he had always been the one to lead them across time and around the world; he had never made a mistake before.

"Do you feel ill, Master Thomas?" Mary asked - both her expression and tone betraying her concern.

Tom looked up at the girl and sighed. Mary was once a maid in the baker's house on Pudding Lane, before he and Septimus rescued her at the start of the Great Fire of London in 1666. Since then, despite Tom's best efforts, she seemed to think of him as more a master than a friend.

"Mary, I keep telling you to call me Tom or Thomas - Tommy even, but not Master," he pleaded.

Mary nodded obediently but did not reply.

"Well, Tommy boy, do you feel ill?" Septimus asked.

Tom shook his head. "I had some dodgy curry a week or so back and got Delhi belly afterwards for a few days, but no, I feel fine now."

Still studying him as though he was a science project, Septimus looked doubtful.

Tom held up his hands in surrender. "Look, I'll talk to the Prof about it when I can, OK?"

Now it was Edward who spoke. "If you can get to talk to him."

"What is that supposed to mean?" Tom stared up at his friend.

"He means that all summer - since that fight at Tintagel -the Prof has been avoiding us," Charlie answered.

"Charlie speaks truthfully," Mary said. "I have wanted to speak to him myself, but he is never there. Or if he is, Mr Phelps says he is too busy."

"Well, I need to talk to him right now. Come on, let's go." Tom got to his feet and headed across the grass.

As they strolled through Hyde Park, past the Serpentine and the lawns filled with tourists and office workers on their lunch breaks, Tom turned to Mary to ask a question niggling him. "What did you want to talk to the Professor about, Mary?

Mary gave him a sharp look and hesitated before answering. "I ... er ... Master ... sorry, Thomas, I do not wish to speak about it."

"Is everything alright? You're not worried about anything are you?"

Mary did not reply and they walked along in silence for a few moments until she stopped to gaze at a businessman who was sitting in a deckchair reading a copy of *The Times*. At last, hurrying on by, she spoke. "Thomas, I find that I keep asking myself the question: 'What am I doing here?'"

"I thought we had talked this all through earlier in the summer. You felt that you had a purpose – that, er ... God wants you to be here helping the Professor," Tom said, feeling a little uncomfortable, but understanding that for Mary, with her godly seventeenth century upbringing, this was entirely natural.

Mary looked at Tom and her expression was now bleak. She tossed back her head to clear the hair from her eyes and then answered. "Yes, I did say that at the time, but now I'm not so sure."

"Why? What do you mean?"

Mary stopped walking and again looked around at the people in their teeming hundreds dotted all over the Park. Her expression was full of distrust; even of fear.

"I just don't feel as though I belong here, Master Thomas. Maybe ... maybe I did what I was supposed to do when I helped at Tintagel. Perhaps that was God's purpose for me and now I

19

should go home."

"Home? You mean to 1666?"

Mary nodded.

"Mary, this is madness!" Tom gasped.

"I think..."

"Mary, you *can't* go back," Tom cut across her. "You know what the Professor said. According to the history books, you died in the fire. If you go back and survive, that might have a huge effect on the future ... on our own past. Who knows who you might meet – who your children would be and what they would do?"

"Yes, I know."

"So what are you saying?"

"I am saying that I do not feel I belong in this time. It is frightening and I have no place here. I cheated death - maybe I should go back and die in my own time as I was meant to."

"Mary ... I," Tom was not sure what to say, and before he could think of anything, Septimus shouted from up ahead.

"Come on you two, catch up!"

Tom turned to say something more to Mary, but she sped on past him. He hurried after her and drew level with Septimus, who was talking to Charlie as they strolled along, side by side. Mary, hanging her head, walked beside them. Edward was striding ahead on his own.

"... maybe a couple of thousand quid if you know where to go," Septimus was saying, in response to some question of Charlie's.

"What, per vase?"

Septimus nodded.

"That's fantastic. Will you help me? Can you teach me to Walk through time on my own so I can get into that business?"

Septimus shook his head. "I work for the Professor now. I gave up the freelance stuff a few weeks ago, soon after Tintagel."

"Why is that Septimus? What happened?" asked Tom, falling into step with them. This was news: in the past, the Welshman had made a career out of peddling and stealing items from across time.

Septimus shrugged, but did not reply. Charlie, however, pursued his previous line of enquiry. "Ah come on, Septimus, you must have contacts – folk you know who would help me."

His face clouding at the question, Septimus shook his head. "Charlie, why not work for the Prof? He pays well enough," was his only answer.

"But there is serious money in the freelance work," Charlie protested.

"Admitted ... but the Prof's work is more important, don't you agree?"

Although what he said might be true, Tom detected a note of regret in the way Septimus said it. Charlie did not answer and Tom noted the greedy expression on his face. So then, Charlie wanted to do what Septimus once did: be an adventurer and freelance mercenary, using his talents to travel back and forth through time. Ironic that it was Septimus who was trying to talk him out of it.

Tom walked on past the three of them and caught up with Edward. "Seems that you have all been busy thinking about your future plans whilst I've been in Wales," he muttered.

"Mary and Charlie have certainly," Edward shrugged nonchalantly.

"What about Septimus: what's the deal there?"

Edward twisted his neck to glance back at the Welshman. "I can't say much. Only that a few days after Tintagel - once he had healed up from that pistol wound he took fighting Redfeld - he went off somewhere. He said he had a job to do and was gone for a month. A couple of weeks ago he turned up in a terrible state and went straight in to see the Professor. Would not speak of what he'd been up to, but he looked dreadful and was clearly distraught. Since then, he says he has given up his mercenary activities for good."

"I wonder what happened."

"Indeed." Again Edward just shrugged, so Tom changed the subject.

"How about you?"

"I made my choice only a day or two after we met, Thomas," Edward replied, his voice sounding a little tense. "I elected to work for the Professor, if you recall."

"Yes you did, but you seem to have something on your mind."

"I have no problems. I wait for orders and obey them," Edward replied, still not looking at Tom.

"You mean like just now, when I called the Professor and said I was coming and then didn't turn up. So the Prof sent you and Septimus to find me. You used that talent of yours to track me?"

Edward grunted an assent: tracking was one of the Victorian officer's most useful abilities. Tom likened it to a dog following a scent. Once Edward had met a Walker – someone who could travel through time – he could follow them wherever they went, even into the past.

"So then, come on, Edward. Tell me what is going on!"

After some hesitation, Edward said shortly, "It's the Professor."

"What about him?"

"These last few weeks he has been rather inaccessible and when he does agree to see me, the meetings are brief. He just

22

gives me orders and finishes the interview without giving me a chance to speak."

"You're saying he seems to be avoiding you?"

Edward nodded.

"That is what's upsetting you?"

"Well, yes. I still have much I want to learn and find out about this world he had you bring me to: about my talents and what I can do with them. It's just ... irritating, that's all."

Tom sighed. It seemed that nothing stayed the same forever. He had assumed his companions would be just as they were when he had left them, but their lives had moved on, as had his own. These four were now very different to when they had first met, but they were still his friends and they all appeared to have their own problems. Edward was sulking about the Professor not finding time for him; Charlie was looking to take up Septimus' morally questionable line of work, which the Welshman himself seemed to have given up on for some mysterious reason. And as for Mary – well, clearly she felt like a fish out of water and was talking about going back to accept her fate.

Then there was himself, Tom thought ruefully. What happened when he had tried to Walk today was frightening. To lose control like that was disturbing. What was more upsetting was that he had no idea what had caused it. Was it linked to that encounter with the French soldiers from the Twisted Reality? He had hoped that in defeating Redfeld at Tintagel and blasting him back through the portal to his own world - quite possibly killing him in the process - he was done with all that. If that was not so, Tom needed to find out what was going on and then discover what to do about it. It was a grim prospect, and as they entered the front door of the Hourglass Institute, he wondered what other complications the next few days would bring.

CHAPTER FOUR
NEW JOB

Mr Phelps examined Tom and his companions from the far side of his meticulously tidy desk. Tom was still wet, following his drenching in that muddy shell hole, and was very dirty. He was aware that water was dripping from his sodden clothes onto the desk. A few drops splashed onto the diary in which Mr Phelps recorded all meetings and the daily comings and goings at the Institute, as well as the Professor's appointments. Without taking his eyes off the soggy schoolboy for even a moment, Mr Phelps wrinkled his nose, lifted his phone and spoke one word into it.

"Towels!"

Only a few moments later, a door behind Tom opened and one of the staff emerged and offered Tom, Septimus and Edward each a large, fluffy warm towel.

Tom dried his hair and then put the towel down on the desk. Mr Phelps' eyes bulged as he whipped his diary out of the way. He stood, holding it like a mother with a baby, glaring in irritation. Then he pointed at the far door.

"The Professor will see you now," he muttered. Then, as they all moved towards the door, he added: "Just make sure you don't drip over his papers!"

Tom knocked on the door.

24

The Professor's voice barked out from inside the study, "Come in!"

Turning the brass door handle, Tom entered the room. Professor Neoptolemas was not sitting behind his desk as usual but was in one of two large leather armchairs, which stood on either side of the empty fireplace. On the table between them was a steaming tea pot, a bowl of sugar lumps, a milk jug, a collection of empty cups and saucers and a plate of custard creams. Sipping at his cup, the Professor gestured to Tom and the men to each bring forward an upright chair from near his desk; Mary he waved over to the vacant armchair.

As Tom sat down he realised that the Professor did not look his usual dapper self. In the past he was always alert and remarkably spry for someone whom, Tom had always assumed, was in his early eighties. Today, the man looked frankly tired: his suit was crumpled as if he had slept in it the night before and yet his face was pale and his eyes red and bleary, as if he had in fact had no sleep at all.

"Are you alright, Professor?" Tom asked, concerned.

"I have been better, Thomas. Tea, anyone?"

Septimus and Edward accepted and the Professor sorted out two spare cups and saucers.

"Is something the matter?" Tom asked again, shaking his head at the offer. The Professor stopped pouring the tea to look up at him.

"My dear boy, I run an organisation dedicated to preserving history from villains and rogues. Something is almost always the matter."

"Well I guess so... but you look knackered, er ... tired out I mean."

"Tommy's right, Prof. You look exhausted," said Septimus,

taking his cup of tea.

Neoptolemas took off his glasses, rubbed his eyes and yawned. He flashed them a bashful look and shrugged. "I will acknowledge that I have had something on my mind. But that can wait for now. So, young man, tell me about your day so far. You have had a strange experience, am I right?"

"Before I do, can you tell me how you knew about me having one?"

"Mr Phelps told me."

Tom shook his head. "But you knew before then, Professor. That is, I mean, it seemed that you were expecting me to call you, as if you already knew something was going to happen."

The Professor shrugged. "Intuition. There are ..." he started to say, but Tom interrupted him.

"Yes, I know ... there are reasons why you are a professor!"

"Quite." The Professor answered, with the merest glint of amusement in his eyes.

As he was obviously not going to say any more, Tom proceeded to describe the events at the fort. "And that was when I decided to phone the Institute," he finished. Leaving the matter of the disorientating journey to one side for the moment, he added, "Now, I am certain I have not seen any of these people before, but I am worried that Redfeld or Thielmann are behind it and if so, that Captain Redfeld is not dead as we had hoped."

Septimus looked thoughtful. "And is trying to find a way back to our reality like before, you mean?"

Tom nodded.

"I would not put it past him," the Welshman commented, "although I can't quite see what he gains in transporting Napoleonic French Infantry to the twenty-first century."

"Well, maybe not, but who, then?"

26

"The Custodian, mayhap," Mary suggested.

There was silence as they all pondered the possibility. The Custodian was in charge of the Directorate: the strange inhabitants of that void between the Twisted Reality and Tom's world who, from the confines of what they had come to know as 'The Office', monitored the Flow of Time and strove constantly to maintain a status quo between the worlds.

"That seems most unlikely," Edward observed, sipping at his tea before continuing. "I mean to say, from what we know about him, he wants to prevent interference between the realities, not cause it."

"Maybe," Tom agreed, "but if you remember, he allowed Redfeld to wipe out my family and at one point, was hoping I would be out of the picture, too - just because I disturbed his precious 'balance'! And although in the end we came to what could be described as a truce, I'm not certain how long that might last."

Tom paused and looked round at their attentive faces, all except Neoptolemas, who, his shoulders hunched, was staring at the empty fireplace. "Even so," Edward went on, "the point remains that whilst the Custodian and his Directorate have the power to intervene, I am fairly sure that transporting men from one reality to another is not something they would readily contemplate."

"So what is causing it, and why in Wales?" Charlie asked, reaching forward to seize a custard cream. "Don't mind if I eat this do you, Prof?" he mumbled around a mouthful of biscuit.

The Professor looked away from the fireplace and glared at the sailor as if he did mind, but he made no objection. Instead he replied, "It is not just in Wales. One of the reasons I lost sleep last night was because we have been getting reports of similar events from all over the world." He gestured at a pile of papers sitting on his desk.

Septimus leapt up from his chair and walked across to the desk to look at the papers. After a moment he chortled, "Good grief! According to this report, the Test Match at the Oval was interrupted when a Spitfire fighter plane materialised in the middle of the pitch ..."

"Yes, a shame that," the Professor muttered. "England were(was?) 250 for 2 at the time and going well."

With a wry grin, Septimus picked up another sheet of paper and burst out laughing. "This one says the American President was naked and about to take a shower when an entire women's hockey team suddenly appeared in the room with him ..."

"Cor! Lucky man," Charlie said with a whistle.

"... but they vanished before his security team could seize them."

"Not so lucky then." Charlie clowned a grimace of dismay.

"It's no laughing matter, Hawker," the Professor snapped, frowning in disapproval.

Septimus flipped through the sheets. "There's more – hey, listen to this ..."

"Oh, many more," the Professor cut across him, sighing heavily. "In the last 48 hours, cavemen have been seen in the Vatican, a Roman gladiator turned up in a school in Tunisia, and a Mongol horde tried to assault the Great Wall in China. All of them just vanished moments after appearing."

There was a stunned silence.

"So, what is going on Professor?" Tom asked after a moment.

The old man shook his head. "I don't know ... I am still trying to establish a feel for the scope of it all. Give me a little time to work it out."

Tom nodded. "Well then, let me tell you about what happened after I had phoned Mr Phelps ..." he went on to describe how he had been disorientated and confused and had ended up in the middle of a battlefield.

The Professor sat back and listened. After Tom had finished he did not speak for a while. Finally he drew a deep breath. "Tom, this is worrying news. What you describe is most unusual. Maybe you were just out of practice or else...."

Tom sat forward, suddenly anxious. "Or else what?"

"I have only heard of it happening a couple of times before but ... but a very few Walkers have sometimes lost their talents, as if some illness had destroyed their ability to Walk. We were never able to get to the bottom of it."

Tom was shocked. A few months ago he had yearned to be plain Tom Oakley, the schoolboy. Now, since he had decided to use his abilities to Walk and help the Professor, the thought of not being able to travel to other times and places ... well, it was just too horrible to contemplate.

"Can you not do something to help Master Thomas, Professor?" Mary asked.

Tom looked up hopefully at the Professor, but the old man's expression was doubtful. "I will try ... look, Thomas, it may be nothing. You may be tired or there could be another explanation."

"Like what?" Tom demanded.

"We'll find out ... but not right now! There is another matter that I need you all to investigate."   With this abrupt change of subject, the Professor jumped to his feet and marched across to the desk. He leant over and scooped up a sheet of paper, examined it and then returned to his chair. He glanced at Tom, who was still feeling upset and unsure of himself. His expression must have betrayed this because the Professor sighed and then reached across to place a hand on his arm.

"Thomas, I promise I will fix the problem. But be patient; you need to trust me again as you did before. Acorns, remember?"

Tom nodded. The Professor had once before used the analogy about tiny acorns growing into big oak trees to explain that everything has a habit of coming right in the end. "Yes, Professor, I do trust you."

Neoptolemas gave a kindly smile. Then he removed and polished his spectacles, popped them back on his nose, glanced up at the five of them and after clearing his throat, began speaking.

"This is a letter I received this morning. I am going to read it to you, as it explains what I need you to do. It is dated yesterday and comes from the Department of Prehistory at the British Museum. It is addressed to me personally, at this Institute.

Dear Sir,

Forgive my writing to you without any introduction but I have a matter of the utmost importance that I wish to discuss with you. I understand from colleagues that they have consulted you on matters of unusual historical and archaeological phenomena in the past and that you are also employed by the government about matters which ordinary academics cannot resolve. I have such a matter to bring to your attention.

I do not wish to go into details in this letter, but I have a cuneiform engraving I need you to see. It dates to the 29th century BC and was found in an excavation in Syria.

There is perhaps nothing remarkable about that, but believe me when I say that when you see this engraving you will feel otherwise.

Perhaps you or one of your representatives would come over tomorrow and see for yourselves?

Yours faithfully,

Dr Paulo Midas PhD, MIFA

The Professor passed the letter to Septimus to look at.

"What's MIFA stand for?" Tom asked.

"Member of the Institute of Field Archaeologists," the Professor said absently.

"What's a cuneiform engraving when it's at home?" Charlie asked, helping himself to another custard cream.

"It's the oldest form of writing; older even than Egyptian Hieroglyphs. Goes right back to the first cities in the Middle East. They used it to record things like how much someone had to pay someone else," Edward said, looking over Septimus' shoulder and displaying his extensive knowledge, the result of many hours spent in the Institute's library.

Looking slightly taken aback, the Professor nodded. "That's right, Lieutenant."

"Sort of an ancient I.O.U then?" Charlie suggested.

"Yes," Neoptolemas answered, "something like that."

"Sir, may I ask a question?" Edward asked, sounding somewhat stiff and formal.

"Of course, Lieutenant," the Professor replied; if he had noticed Edward's icy manner, he did not remark on it.

"Who exactly is Dr Midas and what do we know about him?"

In reply, the Professor opened up a file on his desk and handed Edward a sheet of paper. "This is a biographical note compiled on Dr Paulo Midas by Mr Phelps."

Edward glanced at it and then read out loud: "Born April 18th, 1965, Island of Rhodes. Attended Thessalonica University, where he gained his doctorate in Archaeology. Worked on archaeological digs in Israel, Syria, and Iran and is on a sabbatical in the UK. Accepted as a member of the IFA in 2005 and has been lecturing at the British Museum on his discoveries and cuneiform engravings."

"So, to summarise," said Charlie, "you are saying that if there is something strange going on with one of these engravings, he sounds like the man to tell us?"

"It would seem so." Neoptolemas looked around at them all. "So, please can you go and meet Dr Midas? Give him my compliments and say you are there to make a preliminary visit and establish what is going on. Then report back to me."

Edward looked up sharply. "Sir? Are we to understand that you are not going?"

The Professor shook his head. "No, Lieutenant, I am busy with something here. Maybe another day ..."

Edward nodded and handing back the letter, said no more.

Tom, who had been following the conversation intently, asked, "Do you believe this cuneiform business might be connected in some way to the other strange occurrences, Professor?"

Neoptolemas gazed at Tom for a moment, as if about to say something, then shrugged. He looked so weary and distracted that Tom did not press for an answer. He exchanged a worried glance with Septimus, who said brightly, "Right then, lads and lassie, shall we be getting on with it? Do we Walk or ..."

Hesitant to test his talents again so soon, Tom said, "No, if you don't mind, let's not. It isn't very far."

So they rode the underground for the short journey to Russell Square and then followed the signs to the British Museum. Tom had never been there before. His first sight of the building as he walked through the wrought iron gates made him stop and look up in appreciation at the vast columns and huge steps that comprised the entrance.

"Wow!" he breathed. "Now that is impressive!"

"Who lives in this palace?" Mary gaped, awestruck.

"No one: it's a museum," Tom answered.

"A museum? What's that?"

"Ah yes," Septimus intervened, "a little after your time, Mary. Museums are places for storing collections of more or less anything of interest: could be stuffed animals, rocks, clocks, manuscripts from ancient times ..."

Mary's brow creased in a puzzled frown. "But why would anyone do that?"

"Maybe that's a question for Dr Midas when we meet him. Shall we proceed?" he replied.

Looking confused, Mary walked ahead of them.

Tom raised a querying eyebrow at Septimus. "What was that all about?"

"Seems a bit muddled, doesn't she," Charlie remarked.

"As I said, museums were pretty much unheard of in her time, certainly to an ordinary housemaid in a baker's shop," Septimus grinned. "The British Museum was the first to open to the public and it wasn't founded until the middle of the 18th Century."

"1753, to be precise," Edward commented, which effectively silenced them. They walked on up the steps, between the pillars and in through the front door. In the reception area Septimus strolled across to the desk and asked for Dr Midas.

"He is expecting us," the Welshman added.

Some minutes later, a broad-shouldered man wearing a tweed jacket, a shirt open at the neck and dark green trousers approached them. He wore thick rimmed spectacles, had a heavy black beard that reminded Tom of pictures he had seen of American Civil War generals, and was around the same age as Septimus. He examined them all with a slightly nervous expression.

"Professor Neoptolemas is not with you?" he asked them. His voice was thickly accented, yet clear and easy to understand for a native Greek speaker speaking English, thought Tom.

"No," Edward replied with a hint of sarcasm, "he is very busy apparently."

Septimus glanced at Edward and spoke quickly. "But he asked us to come in his place, Doctor, and make a preliminary assessment."

Dr Midas looked somewhat irritated at this news but after a moment he smiled. "No matter; let us proceed. Come with me please," he said.

"What exactly is the concern you have, Doctor?" Septimus asked as he walked along beside Midas.

"Easier to show you than tell you: this way."

Midas led the way through the museum. They first walked out into a bright, central courtyard, past the circular reading room of the original British Library and into the Hall of Antiquities, their footsteps echoing on the polished floor.

"I study ancient languages such as hieroglyphics, Sanskrit and so on. Consider this for a moment."

They had stopped in front of a huge blue-black stone, surrounded by a gaggle of excited tourists. Tom noticed the stone had three distinct languages engraved upon it. A label proclaimed it was...

"The Rosetta Stone, am I correct?" Edward asked.

"Yes indeed, young man."

"You have seen it before?" Tom looked at Edward in surprise.

"Yes, as a youth in this very museum. The place has changed a bit since then, mind you," he added, glancing around.

"So then, behold the Rosetta Stone: the defining object in the research of ancient languages," said Midas. "See, it has the same text in ancient Greek, demotic and hieroglyphics. Because archaeologists knew ancient Greek they could eventually decipher the other languages. Quite inspired it was."

34

Her mouth still agape at the strange sights around her, Mary cast an anxious look at Tom, who reassured her with a smile.

"Now, come this way," Midas instructed them, walking away from the stone. "The Rosetta Stone and every other piece of ancient script and engraving in this building – which, counting those NOT on public display, runs to thousands - all share one feature: the writing or images engraved upon them never change."

Tom frowned, well of course they didn't! He wondered why Midas had said something so obvious, but with that enigmatic comment, the Doctor was already leading them up some stairs to the first floor, past a crowded room full of yet more tourists staring at Egyptian mummies in glass cases, and then off down a side gallery to where dozens of stone tablets were displayed. They all had lines and scratches on them that looked a little like tick marks.

"This is cuneiform: the oldest written language. Some of these tablets have images on – see, like that one." Midas pointed at a tablet with the picture of what looked like a king or at least a very important person sitting at a table. "Others are just written script. Not one of the tablets in this room is less than three thousand years old. Now, look at this one."

He pointed at an oval-shaped tablet of sand-coloured rock. They all moved closer to get a better view. At first the markings around the edge looked like the tick marks on any of the other tablets and were arranged around an indistinct central image. Tom thought it had just been poorly drawn or maybe damaged.

Then, as he tried to focus on it, the lines seemed to blur and merge into each other. They changed shape, curving and coiling around until he was seeing characters written not in ancient cuneiform, a language which, according to Dr Midas, had not been used in two thousand years, but in the letters and numbers used in Britain, as well as the rest of the western world today.

"What on earth?" Charlie asked.

"You see it, too?" Midas said in a hushed voice.

They all nodded, watching the letters change form and shape before their eyes.

Now, as they looked on, the image at the centre of the tablet began to sharpen and become more defined. A long cigar shape stretched across the tablet, beneath which was a slightly rounded rectangle. Now, two fin-like triangles emerged from one end of the cigar shape. Next, they could see lines running down the length of the cigar and from top to bottom.

Finally, a word and a series of numbers appeared in the mess of letters swirling round each other beneath the image.

Tom squinted at these for a moment and opened his mouth to ask a question, but Septimus beat him to it.

"Dr Midas, when did you say this tablet dated to?"

"Around 2900 BC."

They all stared at him and then back at the impossible tablet, with the impossible words.

The writing now said:

LZ 129 Hindenburg May 6th 1937

CHAPTER FIVE
THE BLACK ROBES

For a moment no-one spoke. Then there was a sudden clamour from the direction of the doorway leading back to the Egyptian Hall, as a tour party emerged, led by a guide.

"This chamber contains examples of the earliest writings in any language ..." the tour guide started to explain, breaking the silence that had descended on Tom and his friends as they stared open-mouthed at the tablet.

"Many of these engravings date to before the time of the Great Pyramids and were used to record trade dealings and commercial activities, treaties and the laws of the kingdoms ..." the tour guide's voice droned on, all the time coming closer.

Tom watched the party, a few students, but mainly tourists by the look of them, who trailed along behind the aged guide. Some were bored, others clearly fascinated, but one thing united them all. As they walked past, glancing this way and that at the tablets the guide pointed out, not a single one of them remarked on the engraving that Midas had brought the stunned members of the Hourglass Institute here to see. Surely these people could not fail to register how unusual it was, thought Tom.

The guide stopped briefly, right beside the Doctor, nodded at him vaguely and then pointed at a triangular fragment only inches away from the tablet. "This is a fascinating item. It is actually a precise recipe for a type of bread that was being ordered for a feast to take place in honour of King Alcalamite III of Syria. It seems the King had a liking for barley in his bread and made sure the baker knew about it!" He acknowledged the titters from the crowd with a tired smile then said, "Let us move on," and led his party out of the chamber and on towards the Persian collection.

Looking after them, Charlie whistled and shook his head.

"How odd," remarked Edward, his eyebrows drawn together in a perplexed frown, "it is as if they did not notice the tablet at all."

"That's because they didn't," Midas said in a taut undertone. "I have asked many passing visitors, as well as members of staff who work in this Department, and not one of them could confirm what you and I can see."

Mary looked back at the engraving. "It is indeed strange they did not see that which was plain as day in front of them. Even I can see that it is unusual, but I do not understand what this is," she pointed at the cigar shape, "or what the letters mean ... H-I-N ..." she read out loud, clumsily pronouncing the first few syllables then frowning as she struggled with the rest of the word. She gave up and turned away, red-faced.

"You're not the only one, Mary," Tom reassured. "I don't know what it is, either." That was not quite true, but he knew Mary had never learned to read in her old life, and although Edward had tried to teach her the basic letters of the alphabet, she could not yet cope with anything complex. He beamed at her and she shot him a grateful smile.

"It says 'Hindenburg'," Septimus explained. "THE Hindenburg: it was a German passenger airship."

"You mean, like the advertising blimps they have at some

sports matches these days?" Tom asked, recalling one he had seen flying over Twickenham when he and his dad had been watching a Rugby International on TV.

"Yes, but much bigger. Airships had cabins and a bar, dining areas, a reading room and so on," Septimus said. "For a while people thought they would replace planes. They were certainly far more comfortable and luxurious. But then there were several accidents and finally the Hindenburg disaster, which was huge."

"Airship ...? Blimp ...?" Mary tried out the words, her face blank with incomprehension as she looked from Septimus to Tom.

"Ah! I remember it now," Charlie muttered. "It was about six years ago, so that would be, er, let me think, 1937. It was all over the newsreels at the time: The Hindenburg was flying to America, past New York to its airfield. As it tried to land it caught fire and lots of folk died but some got off, I think."

Septimus coughed and tilted his head towards Dr Midas, who was staring at Charlie as if he was mad.

"1937 was a good deal more than six years ago, young man," the doctor frowned.

"Oh ... er yes, right," Charlie muttered, "I mean of course that I read something about it six years ago."

"Ah," Midas raised his eyebrows and gave a curt not, but did not look convinced.

Tom looked away to hide a smile. Only a few months before, he and Septimus had gone back to 1943 to rescue Charlie from a sinking submarine, so for him, 1937 still felt like only six years ago.

"So then," Tom quickly changed the subject, "what is it doing on a stone tablet supposedly five thousand years old?"

"It must be a fraud or a hoax." Charlie said. "How much did you pay for it, Doc?"

"Nothing - I dug it up in Syria and I assure you that nothing had disturbed that site for countless years. From the characteristics of the letters, as well as the dating of some organic material we found embedded in them - seeds and so forth - the tablet is five thousand years old."

"Impossible!" Edward said.

"Irrefutable!" Midas replied, his beard bristling slightly.

"Very well then," said Tom hurriedly, glaring at Edward, "if what you say is true, the Professor does need to see this."

Midas' face flushed a deep red. "That is why I called you and I resent the implication that I am not being truthful," he said tersely.

"He didn't mean it like that, Doctor, please don't be offended. It is just that ..." Tom's efforts to placate Midas were interrupted by more footsteps approaching the entrance to the chamber. This time, however, they did not belong to a tour guide or more tourists, but eight identically dressed figures.

Each of them wore a black hooded robe, the hoods thrown up to hide their faces. On their chests was the image of a crown picked out in silver. The figures halted momentarily when they saw Tom and his friends, then they spread out and came forward again. As they did so, they reached inside their sleeves, pulled out long, sharp daggers and held them menacingly as they closed in. Two of the robed figures stepped ahead of the rest - one tall and broad-shouldered, the other shorter. They had a whispered conversation before the tall one continued to advance.

"Who are you blokes?" Charlie said loudly, adding in an undertone to Tom, "They look a mite cross, mate, best get ready to Walk."

"We have come for the tablet: give it to us at once," the leading figure demanded, his voice oddly stilted, almost a monotone. Tom wondered if they were on drugs and it seemed the same thought had occurred to Septimus.

"Well I agree, you do sound like you are on medication of one sort or another, but we don't have any pills on us boyo," the Welshman replied. "Nice outfits, by the way. What are you, street players - what do you call yourselves," he grinned. "No ... let me guess, would it be 'The Black Robes' by any chance?"

"Do not treat us like fools," the leader hissed. "You know of what I speak. We will take it now. You can either give it to us ... or you can die and we will take it anyway. Your choice."

"I'm afraid that won't be possible. You see, our employer wishes to see the tablet," Septimus said calmly, "but you Black Robes can buy some nice replicas of the Rosetta Stone in the Museum shop. Make really nice prezzies they would, too!"

"Kill! Kill them all," the leader shouted, his voice suddenly animated. The Black Robes came on again and moved in to attack.

"Time for a little rumble," Charlie said with a grin, cracking his knuckles and rolling up his sleeves.

Three of the Black Robes, including the leader, made a beeline for Charlie and Dr Midas, whilst another four spread out on either side of Edward and Septimus. The shorter figure hung back and watched the exit behind them.

Spoiling for a fight, Charlie moved to stand between Midas and his assailants and bringing his fists up into a boxer's stance he waited, his face challenging and determined as he taunted, "Fancy me, do you?"

The Black Robes' leader snorted and lunged at Charlie, the point of the dagger aimed for his throat. It never reached its in-

41

tended target because at that moment, Charlie moved. This was not just a matter of dodging or weaving out of the way of the blade. For, whilst Charlie was not as talented as Tom or Edward when it came to Walking through time, in a fight he was unbeatable. This was because his talent was to make hundreds of minute little jumps from one spot to another, only inches away. Taken one after the other in rapid succession, it looked like the flickering of strobe lighting. His attacker seemed to be moving in slow motion, whilst Charlie danced around him in a blur of movement, all the time watching for a chance to finish the fight. The man he was fighting sliced his knife back and forth through the air, stabbing wildly to his left and to his right, always where Charlie had been for a brief moment but never lingered. Then, like a flash of lightning, one of Charlie's fists emerged from the whirlwind and connected with the man's jaw. His head tilted backwards, eyes rolled upwards and he gently keeled over and landed with a crunch on the tiled floor. Charlie, with a satisfied smirk, spat on his hands and turned to deal with the next assailant.

Meanwhile, the group of four advanced on Dr Midas. Septimus passed to their left and Edward to their right, whilst Tom pulled Mary and the Doctor back out of the way.

Septimus Walked a few feet and appeared behind one of his opponents. He slammed his foot hard into the back of his assailant's right knee and the Black Robe's leg collapsed under him. As he fell, he managed to stab backwards and the point of his dagger slashed open the front of Septimus' shirt.

"I say, boyo, watch the clothes - acquired these from Savile Row, I did. They'd have been expensive if I'd paid for them!" Septimus complained, and booted the man in the small of the back.

42

With the first man floundering on the ground, the Welshman gave his attention to another, who had spun round and was backing away towards the glass cabinets so that there was no space for Septimus to appear behind him. They watched each other warily for a few moments.

On the other side of Charlie, Edward had not tried to Walk like Septimus because the shorter Black Robe was close behind him by the door and there was not enough room. Instead, he allowed the men to advance at him. One of them stabbed towards his belly. Edward permitted him to come on and then sidestepped, so the dagger passed harmlessly by. He then stuck out his leg, seized the man's arm and slammed it down hard on his knee. The Black Robe shouted in agony as with a loud crack, a bone in his forearm snapped. Whimpering, he dropped the dagger and fell to his knees, clutching his arm and holding it close to his body.

Watching the fight, Tom saw that the second Black Robe had tugged back his hood revealing his face, which was distorted into a snarl as he advanced on Edward. Tom's eyes widened as he saw a silver chain glinting about the Black Robe's neck. From it hung a large, lustrous pearl, which seemed oddly feminine and out of place, but just then the man lunged forward and the pendant was lost from view. He threw his dagger at Edward and it flew like a missile straight at the lieutenant's head. His eyes sparking with fear, Edward tried desperately to dodge out of the way, but Tom, watching in horror, knew he was too late.

The blade never reached him.

Mary had jumped forward, and flinging her arms outwards so that she resembled an Evangelist preacher, she yelled, "WALL!"

In the air, just inches from Edward's nose, there appeared a barely perceptible shimmer of light. The dagger hit the almost

43

invisible barrier and stuck in it, quivering. Tom breathed a sigh of relief: this was Mary's particular talent, for although she could not Walk as the others did, she had the ability to manipulate Time, freezing it to create walls and barriers. It was a gift that had saved their lives on several occasions, not least when they had first rescued her from the Great Fire of London and brought her back to the present day. It was this talent that she used now - freezing time within the barrier so it moved at a much slower rate. It was enough to hold the dagger suspended in the air for a few moments, but it took all her strength to keep it there.

In the centre of the fight, Charlie was still outnumbered two to one. A Black Robe lunged at him and again Charlie easily avoided the weapon, but while he was distracted, the second man skipped on past him and ran at Midas, lifting the dagger ready to strike.

Tom stepped quickly to the Doctor's side and reaching out with one hand, placed it on his shoulder, preparing to Walk them both out of the way.

"Get behind me lad!" Midas shouted, pushing him away just as Tom started to Walk. He let go of Midas and tumbled backwards out of the doorway to the next chamber, where he collided with a group of teenagers, knocking several of them down in a heap of arms and legs.

"Oi! Wot yer doing mate?" One of the boys said, struggling to his feet and shoving Tom away.

"Sorry!" Tom managed to get out and then staggered back towards Midas. The Black Robe had now reached him. Tom braced himself and Walked, intending to appear next to Midas, grab him and then pull him out of the room: maybe back to the Institute.

It was then that it all went wrong again.

Tom appeared, not in the room of ancient engravings, but on top of a huge stone lion in the Persian collection. He teetered on the lion for a moment then, head spinning and vision blurred, he fell from the twenty-foot high statue towards the stone floor below.

As he fell he managed to Walk again. This time, at least, he appeared in the correct room, but unfortunately he materialised two feet above one of the display cabinets containing various stone engravings. With a yelp he fell down onto the glass, smashing and splintering the panels.

Somewhere an alarm started ringing, activated by the breaking of the glass. Tom rolled off the shattered cabinet and tumbled down, landing on his feet. He rubbed his fingers in his eyes to clear his sight and looked about. He was standing near Septimus' opponent, who had turned round to stare at him. The man stabbed out with his dagger. Tom jumped away as the dagger point nicked him on the arm. The Black Robe made to stab again, but this time Septimus appeared, winded his opponent with a punch to the solar plexus and then brought his knee up to connect with the man's chin, knocking him out cold.

"You OK, Tommy boy? You seem a bit out of touch today. Best keep out of the way, eh?"

Midas was now backing away from the Black Robe who had reached him. The man seized his shirt and pulled the doctor towards him. The other hand went back, ready to thrust the blade up under his ribs.

Septimus jumped forward and whilst he was still in the air, Walked the ten feet between himself and Midas, appearing right behind the Black Robe. The momentum of the jump was still with him and so he collided with the man's legs, whipping them out from under him. With a cry of outrage, the Black Robe stum-

45

bled backwards over the Welshman. As he fell in a scrunch of broken glass he jabbed the blade at Midas, who in desperation flung up an arm to defend himself. The knife cut open his forearm, but was deflected away and being knocked out of the assailant's hand it skidded with a clatter across the floor.

Suddenly, from the doorway behind Midas, a half dozen burly security guards ran into the room.

"Right, that's it," one of them shouted. "We are calling the police. Just drop the knives!"

Lurking by the other door, the short black-robed lookout gestured at his companions and let out a long, low whistle, whereupon, those still on their feet scuttled over, picked up the two who were unconscious and dragged them backwards to the door.

At that moment, Mary lowered her arms and gave a low sigh. The dagger entrapped in the barrier fell to the floor, bounced and skittered away.

As the guards stared at it in astonishment, the Black Robe's leader turned to face Tom and his friends. "We will have the tablet ... mark my words," he sneered.

He stretched out his arm and placed a hand on the lookout's shoulder. The others did likewise. Then, with a pop, they vanished.

"My God!" Charlie exclaimed. "They were Walkers!"

CHAPTER SIX
STONE TABLET

"What on earth is going on here?" The security guard's eyes bulged as he stared at the spot the Black Robes had occupied only moments before.

Dr Midas, still holding his bleeding arm, moved to speak to him. "This party is with me. I am Dr Midas - attached to the Museum on a temporary basis. See here," he let go of his arm and fumbled in his pocket for a pass, dripping blood on the tiled floor.

The security guard snatched it out of his hand, examined it suspiciously for a moment before nodding and passing it back. "You ought to get that arm seen to, sir." He looked round at Tom and his friends. "That group in black clothes - what about them then?"

"Nothing to do with us," Midas assured him. "Seemed like a bunch of fanatics. I assume they are some organisation that believes in the return of historical artefacts to their original owners."

"But they just ... disappeared!" The guard gazed at the door. "They were right there and just ... vanished."

"A clever trick - maybe done with mirrors," Septimus suggested, adding with a laugh, "I mean, it's not like they could really disappear, is it?"

The guard looked uncertain and then started to smile. "No, I expect you are right. Maybe I should have kept off the beer last night, eh lads?" He turned to grin at his underlings. "Right then - get after them! And switch that flipping alarm off!"

Sniggering, the other guards bustled past Tom and his friends and out of the far door. A moment after they had gone the alarm bell stopped ringing. The silence came as a welcome relief.

The guard looked down at the shattered glass and spots of blood on the floor, then turned to look back at Midas. "So, Doctor, do you need any help?"

"Yes, I think I need stitches. Maybe you could arrange transport to hospital? I will come to your office in a moment, just let me say goodbye to my little tour group here."

"Of course, sir, right away." The guard strode away, talking into his radio. "I need a driver to take a man to St Thomas's. Yes, that's right. And while you're about it, send someone into Antiquities to clean up the mess. We'll need to rope it off ..."

When the guard's voice had faded down the corridor, Midas turned a pale face towards Tom and his friends. "They really did disappear, didn't they? And don't bother to deny it," he said in a shaky voice. "Something strange is going on here. Then again, I suppose I already knew that," he added, nodding towards the tablet.

He stepped across to the cabinet that Tom had narrowly missed when he fell, and retrieved from his pocket a long chain attached to a set of brass keys. Selecting one that looked a little like an Allen Key, he inserted it into a keyhole at the end of the cabinet, twisted it and then pulled the glass door open.

With his good hand he removed the stone tablet from its mounting and paused to examine it. "This is the heart of the mystery. Whoever the black-robed visitors were, they want it. This

48

stone engraving was created more than four thousand years ago and yet it now contains the image of an object from only eighty years ago. Furthermore, the writing changes if you study it long enough. There have been other images too, but they only started coming up a few days ago and before today, only I could see them. Until you came along I thought I was going mad."

"What other images?" Septimus asked. "Did you see other words as well?"

Midas nodded. "At first the images were blurred and indistinct. So was the writing, but I could see they were different shapes. They changed over a few days, sometimes fading, sometimes coming back - I tell you, I have hardly slept since it started - and each time they changed, I recorded the images and the writing in my notebooks. However," he eyed the engraving, "over the last twelve hours this shape has been the one that has dominated. This morning it became sharp and clear the longer I looked at it, although it must have faded when I took my eyes off it because then - just as now - it came back, only slowly."

"Are you saying it is actually responding to your gaze?" Septimus asked.

"It certainly seems that way."

"Sir, where did you record this information?" Edward asked.

"Like I said, in my notebooks, which are in my office on the third floor."

"Could we ..." Edward was interrupted by the sound of a polite cough. The security guard had reappeared at the end of the room, together with a man wearing overalls and carrying a bucket, broom and mop. Looking up, Tom saw that while they had been talking, the doorways had been roped off.

The guard unhooked the thick white rope at one end and held it open. "We have a car ready now to take you to the hospital, Dr

49

Midas, would you like to follow me?"

Midas nodded at him and turning to Septimus, handed him the tablet. "Take this to your Professor. Ask him to examine it and to get back in touch soon. As soon as my wound has been seen to, I will get my notebooks and send them on to the Institute."

"OK Doc." Septimus took the tablet carefully. "We will report back to you once we have spoken to the Professor. Shall we contact you here?"

"Yes, I will return to the Museum as soon as I can."

Skirting the cleaner with an apologetic smile, Midas went off with the guard.

"Right then, back to the Institute," said Septimus to the others. "Anyone got a carrier bag?"

"I have, Master," said Mary, blushing as she pulled a folded Harrods bag from the pocket of her jeans.

"Clever girl," Septimus grinned, "been shopping I see." Folding the distinctive green bag round the tablet, he tucked it under his arm. "I think we had better take a cab, Tommy here is a wee bit off balance today."

Tom grimaced but did not argue. Instead he forlornly followed the others back through the Museum and out into the street. They hailed a cab and headed to the Institute, spoke briefly with Mr Phelps, and then went straight into the Professor's study.

"Ah, you're back," Neoptolemas said, as they filed through the door.

Immediately unwrapping the stone tablet, Septimus laid it on the desk.

An eager expression leapt to the Professor's face as he picked up the engraved stone and studied it for a few moments before his eyes suddenly widened. He snatched a magnifying glass off his desk and bent over to peer closely at one corner of the tablet.

There was a hushed silence in the room, broken only by muttered exclamations and incomprehensible and highly technical words uttered under his breath by the Professor. Finally, the old man sat back in his chair and stared at them all.

"My word," he said at last.

"Professor, whatever is the matter?" Mary asked.

Tom leant over and peered at the tablet. The image of the Hindenburg was now sharp and clear, as were the letters underneath. Furthermore, another line of numbers and letters had become visible beneath the date:

19.23 to 19.27 EDT

It was a time period, but what did it mean? Tom looked up at the Professor, who stared at each of them in turn.

"Tell me how this appeared when you first saw it and what Dr Midas said about it."

Septimus related Midas' account of the tablet's finding and origin, and the fact that he alone of the museum staff seemed to be able to see the strange changes to the tablet, and even more strange, that it appeared to react when he looked at it.

The Professor nodded. "That being the case, I think we need another conversation with Dr Midas when he returns from the hospital."

"Why is that?" Tom asked.

"The tablet shows where to find certain objects of great importance. The objects are hidden in different geographical locations and in varying dates and times."

Tom looked at the image of the airship. "May 6th, 1937, be-

51

tween 19.23 and 19.27 - that's er ..." he stumbled whilst trying to remember the twenty-four hour clock.

"Between twenty-three minutes and twenty-seven minutes past seven in the evening," Charlie came to his rescue.

"But what does it mean?" Mary asked.

"It means that something important was present aboard the Hindenburg between those times, I assume. But what exactly?" Septimus asked, locking his gaze on the Professor.

"It means something else as well," the Professor said, ignoring or at least not answering the question. He lifted the slab up and held it so they could each see the airship.

"You all can see this can't you?"

"Of course we can, Prof, we're not blind," Charlie answered for them.

"Indeed, but dozens of members of staff, as well as thousands of tourists who each day visit the museum are, apparently, blind. Blind at least about what we can all see quite clearly."

They pondered this for the moment.

"So ... mayhap ... mayhap the tablet cannot be read ... leastways not in the way we read it, by someone who is not a Walker," Mary said in a quiet voice.

The Professor nodded. "So ..." he said, encouraging her to go on with this line of thought.

"So ... so that means that Dr Midas ..." she hesitated.

"Yes?"

"Is a Walker!"

"Well done, Mary." The Professor leant back in the chair and smiled. "Which is why you need to go and talk to him, find out more about him and get your hands on those notes."

"That may have to wait until tomorrow - he is in the hospital," Septimus observed.

Following the conversation intently, Tom was distracted when his mobile rang out. He pulled it out of his pocket, checked the sender and said, "Sorry, I have to take this, it's my mum."

"Tom?" her voice said in his ear.

"Yes, Mum."

"We are on the way back. Be there in fifteen minutes. Can you put the pizza on?"

"Er ... yeah sure mum."

"Is anything up?"

"No ... no I am fine. See you soon."

He rang off. Disoriented, it took Tom a moment to remember that his family were (was?) still in Wales, which is where he was supposed to be. That was always the problem with Walking, there were times when he didn't know if he was coming or going. It felt as if days had passed since he had seen the French soldiers, then landed in that shell-hole, but in fact it was only hours. He looked at the Professor and grimaced. "Well, I have to go. Tomorrow I will be back at home. Mum and Dad are at work and my sister is going away with the Brownies so I won't have any problem coming. I'll be here about ten, then?"

"Very well, Thomas," the Professor said kindly.

Tom stood up and prepared to Walk, but then hesitated, feeling suddenly uncertain about it. "Septimus, sorry, but can you give me a lift back to the Fort?"

"Sure Tommy, no problem," the Welshman answered cheerfully. His frown suggested, however, that he was concerned. As Septimus placed a hand on his shoulder, Tom caught the others exchanging troubled glances and realised that Septimus was not alone in worrying about him.

Walking Tom back to the fort, Septimus strolled with him to the cottage then said goodbye, declining the invitation to come in for a cup of tea. "See you on the morrow, Tommy boy," and with a wave he was gone.

Around him the Fort, having closed for the night, was quiet and to Tom eerie. He risked an anxious glance up at the battlements but found them deserted. Feeling suddenly exposed and a little lonely, Tom went indoors. There he turned on the oven and got the pizza out of the fridge, opened the door and slid it onto a metal tray in the oven. That job done, he went into his room and began packing his bag for the journey home. A few minutes later he heard the car pull up outside the cottage and his mother's voice calling out to him.

After a quick tea, with his sister talking non-stop about the shopping trip, they cleaned the cottage, loaded the car and departed for home. Tom sat in the back beside Emma, still prattling on about Caernarfon, and after a few miles found himself drifting off to sleep. For the first time in weeks he was aware that he was dreaming, but this was not the same as for normal people. For Tom, it could be like Walking – he called it 'dream-walking' - when he travelled into the mind of another person and for a brief period actually became that person. This was how it had all started just before his eleventh birthday about eighteen months ago. Even before he knew he was a Walker, Tom had dreamed of Edward and known he was in mortal peril. Soon afterwards the same thing had happened with Mary and then Charlie. It seemed that strong emotions and vibrant thoughts echoed across the years and even from one reality to another so that Tom could relive them, experience them and at times be terrified by them, for always either he himself or the person in his dream was in grave danger.

This time the journey was a long one; far back to ancient times...

CHAPTER SEVEN
TITUS AND KNOSSOS

*T*om ... *no, not Tom, for now he was Titus, tugged off his bronze helmet and ran his fingers through his mousey brown hair as he gazed up the rock-strewn path. The trail curved around a slab-like hill upon which stood the Temple: a temple once built to honour the great God, Zeus – but now in the hands of his former friend, Knossos and the Cult, who worshipped him like a god. As a result, it was known for hundreds of miles around as the Temple of Knossos.*

He squinted up at the building silhouetted against the bright sun that blazed in the perfect blue sky. He could make out the huge sloped roof supported by thirty vast stone pillars as wide and as tall as the largest of tree trunks. There, on the front of the temple, an image of Zeus had been chipped away and was replaced by a carving in the shape of a huge crown. It was a crown that all men knew and all men feared: the Crown of Knossos.

The real Crown – a bronze and silver treasure adorned by an emerald gem of surpassing beauty - was what Titus had come to destroy this day, along with its owner, if needs be.

He turned and looked back down the trail. The warriors who were his escort had reached him and now stood in column awaiting his orders: thirty soldiers under an officer named Xanthus, from the nearby city of Elis. The elders of the city knew of the threat Knossos posed and had placed this company under Titus' command for this mission. The unfriendly glances from amongst the ranks suggested that many of them wondered who this young upstart was and why he was giving the orders.

Titus waved at the company's officer, indicating that he should let the soldiers rest for a moment. Xanthus, a scarred veteran with greying hair, was almost fifty, yet he seemed untouched by the march so far. Titus had found the climb from the city on this roasting hot day exhausting, but the officer and his men did not seem to have noticed it. As they stood or crouched, drank from waterskins and removed their own helmets, Titus studied them.

Each man was strong and fit, and wore a bronze breast plate shaped like the chest of a muscular athlete fastened to his body with leather straps. Titus had refused the armour – he was not trained to move freely in it and he needed to be unencumbered for what he must do – but he had accepted the offer of a helmet. These helmets were also bronze and had long cheek plates to protect the face. On the top were elaborate red and white striped plumes, running from front to back. All the soldiers had huge circular shields decorated by a galloping white horse, the symbol of the city, and were armed with long spears and short stabbing swords. Despite the heat, Titus shivered at the sight. These men were killers, but at least they were on his side. He needed all the help he could obtain today, even the blessings of the gods, for the enemy they faced was all powerful.

Enemy? Yes indeed, Knossos was the enemy and yet even now Titus felt a tinge of regret. Had Knossos and he not grown up as friends? Had they not been inseparable through childhood? Yet now, with the benefit of hindsight, when he thought back over the years, Titus could see signs of the troubles that were to come. He had always been that little bit faster than Knossos in a race; that little bit more able at philosophy and mathematics. Just a hint of jealousy had taken root in those childhood days. But it was once they discovered their astonishing talents that the

56

problems had really begun. As they passed into manhood at the age of thirteen, they had found that with just their thoughts they could move great distances and even travel to other times and eras. These rare abilities had made them sought after by the rulers of the Greek city states and in time, although few men knew it, they had become the saviours of Greece itself, for had they not together defeated Hyperion, Coeus and their brothers and wrenched arcane secrets from them?

As they explored their new found powers, their philosophies had diverged. Titus saw the opportunity to explore the great mysteries of the universe. Knossos, however, saw in these powers the chance to dominate mankind. He yearned to use them to take his place amongst the gods and in time became convinced that he actually was a god. He gathered a group of followers about him – the Cult of Knossos - and they worshipped him. This was not enough for him, however, because he saw that in the rest of humanity there was no respect and adoration for him – only fear. This was unacceptable to Knossos and so he had created the Crown – a device to focus and direct his powers and use them to mould reality to his own desires. With the Crown, Knossos had already destroyed an army sent to oppose him and had subdued all the surrounding land. Only Titus had been strong enough to contain Knossos and now he was coming to finish the job.

Titus looked back up at the sky. The sun was almost at its highest point. Noon was the time Knossos would do what he planned and so noon was when Titus must stop him.

"Get your men ready, Captain Xanthus; it is time," Titus ordered. The officer nodded and gruffly barked out his commands.

"Right men, form up three files wide. It's double time up this hill. Remember our orders: no one in the Cult survives. Understood?"

"Yes sir!" bellowed the warriors. Titus grimaced but not at the noise. The Cult must have seen them coming from far away, so surprise was not an option. No, it was the thought of the killing they - he

- must do this day that appalled him. Then he turned to look back up at the Temple. There on the hill top far above he could see a single figure in a black robe. The sunlight caught something metal on his head and the reflection was blinding. It was Knossos. Titus reached out with his mind in an effort to detect Knossos using the Crown against them, but felt nothing. A moment later the man was gone. Titus slapped on his helmet firmly. With a determined yank on the chin strap, he fastened it to his head and set off after the column of soldiers – already fifty paces up the track. Time for remorse could come later: today he had a job to do.

The trail wound almost a complete circuit around the hill before it reached the plateau upon which the Temple was built. At the point where the track joined the hilltop it was only three men wide and here the Cult members, commonly called the 'Black Robes' because of their macabre choice of clothing, had constructed a barricade. They had over-turned a cart and then piled barrels and crates of supplies around and on top of it. A dozen men in long black robes - each with the hood pulled up over his head and with the symbol of a silver crown emblazoned on his chest – stood at the barricade. They were armed with spears and swords. Meanwhile, on each side of the barricade and lining the edge of the plateau so they could peer down at Titus and his men, half a dozen more were deployed. These men had slings and a large pile of stones each. The Cult was well prepared for them and this attack was going to be costly.

"Form up! Shields at the ready. Fast march: let's go!" Xanthus yelled and then turned back to Titus. "Stay here, sir, let my men do their job and we will get you inside," the officer instructed, and although his words were polite enough there was something in the tone of his voice that said 'keep out of the way- we don't need civilians cluttering things up.' Some of Xanthus' men heard it too and sniggered at Titus.

He nodded and ignored the slur. He did not mind. Let them use their valour. He had other tools at his disposal.

The company marched up the hill as one body, curving around the trail like a snake: a snake of bronze and leather. As they marched, their heavy sandals stomped down on the hard packed earth and crunched against the stones and pebbles, throwing up a small cloud of dust in passing. At the top of the hill, Knossos' men waited for them.

When they closed to within fifty paces of the black-robed enemy, the air was suddenly full of a high pitched whirling sound – a little like a swarm of hornets. Titus could see that the half dozen slingers on either side of the barricade were spinning the slings around their heads. A moment later they released their missiles and the stones flew straight and true towards the soldiers. With a noise like hail stones on a tile roof, most stones deflected off the shields and helmets of the soldiers, but within the column there was a sudden scream of agony. As the soldiers marched on they stepped over the crumpled body of one of their comrades who was rolled up clutching his leg. It was gushing with blood, the shin bone clearly shattered. Another volley was released and another man fell, this time with a wound to the forehead. The man lay still. Was he dead? Titus, moving up slowly behind the warriors, could not tell.

The soldiers left their injured behind and marched on through the storm of stones until they reached the barricade. The first rank tried to clamber over the cart, but to do so they had to lower their shields. The Cult members leant forward to thrust and stab with spear and sword. Two of the leading warriors fell dead, and then another was felled by a sling stone smashing hard into his temple.

"Keep attacking, get over the cart. Keep moving!" Xanthus bellowed and climbed up the cart so he now stood upon it. He drew his sword and hacked to his left and right killing two of the Cultists. Then, a spear caught him in the thigh and he tumbled back, landing on two of his own men. The men scrambled to their feet, slipped hands under his shoulders and tugged him back to the rear.

The shower of stones was continuing unabated and the warriors had so far failed to get over the cart. Xanthus staggered to his feet and leant against one of his men. He glanced at the barricade and then at the slingers and shook his head.

"Fall back, fall back!" he commanded and his men started to retreat slowly, shields still held high to deflect the missiles until well out of range. Xanthus, one hand held over the bleeding wound on his leg, stood looking back up at the barricade. The Black Robes were jeering and taunting them and Xanthus' face grew dark with fury, but he turned away and seeing Titus standing on the trail, yelled, "Why did you come on this expedition? You brought no weapons or armour save that helmet. What did you hope to achieve?"

Xanthus' men said nothing but stared stony-faced at Titus: angry at this young man who was unhurt whilst most of them were bleeding from more than one wound. Titus walked past the captain without a word and for a few seconds studied the barricade and the slingers on either side, before tilting his head to fix the officer with an intense stare.

"Captain, I don't need weapons, but please believe me when I say that I am still your best hope of getting into that Temple." He pointed up the trail, past the bodies of three of Xanthus' men and beyond the Black Robes, to the huge structure that loomed over them all.

The soldiers jeered, but Xanthus did not. He frowned. "You? What can you do," he asked scathingly. "I still do not know why the elders placed me under your command in this attack on Knossos."

"What do you know of Knossos, Captain?" Titus said, coming back to stand close to the older man.

Xanthus blinked. "Oh, I've heard the old wives' tales: Knossos is a god who they say was thrown out of Olympus. Others say Knossos is a sorcerer with powers greater than any man. It is all nonsense and hot air, I tell you. I've never seen any sorcery and the gods keep themselves

60

to themselves if you ask me. I'm just a warrior with a sword, but I reckon it will kill him, same as any man!"

"Knossos is no god, Captain," Titus shrugged, "but he is a sorcerer and has been to places you would never imagine."

"What?" Xanthus started to smirk, but something in Titus' expression stopped him. "You are serious aren't you?"

His steady gaze on the captain's disbelieving face, Titus nodded.

"So it's true then? He is the most powerful sorcerer ever?"

Titus laughed. "No Captain, he is not."

The captain's brows drew together in a perplexed frown. "So who is, then?"

Titus smiled and patted him on the back. "My dear Xanthus, I am!"

Xanthus blinked again but before he could reply Titus carried on talking.

"So, what we will do is this. I am going to take two or three of your men up to the top of the hill and behind the sling shot men on the left there. We will deal with them and then move to the barricade. Once you see us up there, attack again. The diversion should be enough for your attack to succeed this time."

The captain's expression changed to one of incredulity, clearly thinking that in the heat of battle, Titus had gone mad. "And how will you get my men up there?" he asked in a tired voice, as though humouring a child.

"Don't worry; it will be as easy as .... as easy as walking."

"Walking?"

"That's what I said."

Xanthus shook his head. "I'm sorry, sir, but I cannot throw my men's lives away on the whim of a deranged civilian."

"May I remind you, Captain, that civilian or no, you are under my command and the penalty for mutiny is death?"

For a moment Xanthus stared at Titus in disbelief then snapped to

61

attention, "Yes, sir." He turned to his men. "Three volunteers for a dangerous mission!" he bellowed.

A few moments later, three burly giants were standing around Titus.

"Gentlemen. Put your hands on my shoulders," he instructed.

"What?" the largest of the warriors grunted.

"You deaf or something, Argonus? Put your grubby little hands on the gentleman's shoulder," Xanthus ordered.

The three warriors glanced at each other warily, but each reached over and placed one sweaty hand on Titus' shoulders.

"Take a deep breath; we are going for a ride."

An instant later, Titus and his three companions appeared with a pop on the top of the hilltop, right behind a half dozen Black Robes. Argonus and both his companions screamed in absolute terror, startling the sling shot men.

The Cultists and the three warriors stared at each other in disbelief and stood in stunned silence for a moment.

"Well now," Titus muttered to himself, "I think that went well."

"Charge!" shouted Xanthus from down the track and the other twenty of his men still on their feet hurtled back up towards the barricade. Meanwhile, on top of the hill, Argonus and his companions, on hearing their captain's voice, stirred from their surprise and fell upon the unarmed and un-armoured Black Robes. Titus moved towards the barricade where several of the swordsmen were advancing on him. He held up his hands, palms outwards towards the approaching enemy.

"Come no closer or you will die!" he shouted at them. The Cultists sneered at him from under their black hoods and came on waving their swords back and forth.

"So be it, I warned you!" Titus said and then thrust his hands forward with a single muttered word: "Age."

All three of the Cultists halted abruptly and screamed in agony.

62

Their hands went to their heads. In an instant their hair grew white, teeth cracked, blackened and fell out, their nails grew longer and - most horrific of all - their skin wrinkled, dried, and then fell from their still living limbs. A moment later they were mere corpses, dried and shrivelled like mummies on the ground.

"Great Zeus and Hades!" swore Argonus, who was now standing next to Titus, his sword glistening with blood, his face rigid with horror.

"You do not need to fear me, Argonus." Titus looked at him for a moment and then back at the bodies. "Gods forgive me, but I must do what has to be done. Come on!" He moved on towards the barricade. Xanthus and his soldiers had reached it now and were clambering up it again. This time, however, they met no resistance. The Black Robes on the barricade had seen what Titus had done to their comrades and a look of sheer terror flashed upon their faces. A moment later and they and the remaining sling shot men were running towards the Temple and the promise of safety it offered.

Xanthus heaved himself over the cart and dropped down the other side with a groan of pain. He limped over to Titus and nodded at him.

"Well done, sir, I owe you an apology," he said, in a tone full of respect and awe. "Now what?" he added.

Titus nodded towards the pillars behind him. "The Temple. Be careful though: Knossos will not give in easily."

They were at the side of the Temple. Here a line of a dozen pillars ran the length of the building supporting the vast sloping roof. Titus and his men cautiously approached a gap between the pillars and peered inside. Torches burned in sconces fixed to the inside of each pillar and cast a flickering light that fought with the shadows created by pillar and roof. Here, out of the direct sunlight, the air was cooler. In front of them they could see the main structure – a long rectangular building stretching to their left and right. Xanthus led the way to the left – towards the entrance at the far end.

Suddenly, there was a shout and a dozen Black Robes hurtled out of the shadows at the base of one of the pillars and attacked them. The air was full of the clang of sword against sword; then screams as men on both sides fell injured or dead. Their cries echoed around this outer chamber as if they were in an underground cave. Finally, the remaining Cultists ran and Argonus led three warriors in pursuit whilst Xanthus and Titus led the rest of the company towards the entrance.

When they reached the front doors they found them wide open and the ante-chamber within empty, save for a brazier burning with bright blue and yellow flames. Separated by flickering torches, murals of Zeus and others gods decorated the walls. Someone had painted the symbol of a crown across the murals, defacing and defiling the holy place. Xanthus looked grim and a determined expression came on his face as he strode across the room to reach the interior doors leading to the main chamber of the Temple.

As he reached the halfway point he stopped abruptly, as though he had walked into a barrier – an invisible wall stretching across the chamber. He rebounded off this obstacle and landed hard and flat on his back. He winced and groaned, then swore as several of his men rushed to pick him up.

"What in the name of the gods was that?" he asked, wiping blood from his nose.

Titus came forward and explored the extent of this barrier that no one could see. He felt from left to right, testing its resistance and strength.

"Knossos has done this. He has created this wall by freezing the passage of the moments within it."

Xanthus looked confused and Titus opened his mouth to elaborate, but then shook his head. "It is too complicated a thing to explain right now. I will try and do so later – if we live ..." He hesitated because they could all feel something in the stone beneath them: a rhythmic pounding – maybe the stamping of feet, perhaps the banging of a drum.

They looked through the barrier towards the doors that opened into the inner chamber.

"How is it we can see through this wall Knossos has made?" Xanthus asked, peering into the gloom of that inner sanctum. Titus shrugged.

"Because Knossos permits it to be so. He allows light and sound to pass out but nothing to pass in."

"Why would he do that?"

"Because he is a show off, Captain. He wants us to see his moment of triumph."

"Hah, hah, haaah!" the laughter echoed from within the inner chamber. They all stared that way, straining to pick out any details. However, they could see nothing. Out of the darkness a hoarse, rasping, almost whispered voice emerged.

"Titus is correct, Captain. I wish you to see this moment: to realise that I have won. More than that, I wish Titus to know that I, Knossos, have defeated him. Then, with that knowledge gnawing at your insides, you will all perish."

There was another loud boom of a drum echoing out of the chamber and all at once a dozen torches flamed into light and – at last – they could see the interior of that room.

The inner sanctum was a long rectangular chamber heading away from them. It was lined with more pillars along the sides, each mounted with a torch, which together illuminated the room. Between each pillar stood a pair of Black Robes armed with spears and swords, their hoods pulled up to obscure their faces. At the far end of the stone chamber a huge statue of the God Zeus sat in majesty on a throne. Again, as with the carvings on the temple exterior and the murals in the anteroom, this statue had been defaced and the features hacked and chipped away. A black robe had been thrown around its shoulders and a crown made from the branches of an olive tree woven around its head.

In front of the statue was a large stone slab, which was the Temple's altar. Standing on the far side of the altar and facing towards the doorway was a man. He too wore a black robe, but his hood was thrown back to reveal his face – a man the same age as Titus, with olive green eyes and charcoal black hair. His eyes stared at them with an intense, greedy expression, but the most striking feature of all was perched on the top of his head. It was the Crown of Knossos.

The Crown was wrought from bronze and silver: a wide band of bronze encircled the rim and silver, emerging from the top, was moulded in a lattice-like structure to form a single projection. At its pinnacle, mounted in interwoven tendrils of silver, was an astonishingly beautiful emerald gem the size of a man's clenched fist.

Knossos lifted his hands and closed his eyes. He was muttering under his breath. The words grew louder and louder until they could hear him first speak and then shout them: one phrase, repeated over and over again. One sentence chanted with increasing volume and intensity. Words that – Titus knew – Knossos was using to focus his own mind, his own talents, via the Crown and through it, to magnify the power he now used.

"No will, no world but mine! No will, no world but mine! No will, no world but mine! ..." he chanted.

There, in the anteroom, Titus became aware that the chamber around them was darkening. Beyond the invisible barrier the inner sanctum was still brightly lit, but here the light was growing faint. No - more than that. It was not just the torches that were dimming: it was as if the walls, ceiling and floor were fading from view.

"Sir! sir ... what is happening?" Xanthus asked, for the first time an edge of panic in his gruff voice.

Titus glanced at him and then at the room.

"Sir?"

"It's Knossos! He is using the Crown to project his will. He is chang-

ing the world."

"Into what?"

"Into a world in which he alone is God. Captain, unless we get inside this barrier and stop him in the next few minutes, everything outside the barrier will cease to have ever existed. A new world, in Knossos' own image will replace it. A world in which all men worship him."

"What are we going to do?"

Titus shrugged. "I don't know ... I have an idea but ... but..."

"Come on man! We must act now!"Xanthus shouted above the chanting, the gruffness back.

"Yes, yes I know but ..."

"But what?"

"But, I am ... afraid ..."

CHAPTER EIGHT
THE CROWN OF KNOSSOS

"Tom!" a distant voice shouted, "Tom," it repeated. He jerked awake and stared blankly at his surroundings, which came slowly into focus. He was in the back of the family car and they were parked on the street in front of their house. Outside it was dark: night time. He blinked and for a moment, saw imprinted on the back of his eyelids the shining emerald on top of that crown. Then, when he opened his eyes, it was gone.

"Dad?" he asked vaguely.

In the driver's seat, his father turned and gave him a penetrating stare. "You all right?" When Tom did not answer he added, "Come on son, we're home. Time for bed I think. It was a long journey, it's after eleven and we are all tired out. Mum will take Emma to the Brownies' day out in the morning and I will be at work, so we will leave you in bed, OK?"

Tom nodded and dragged himself out of his seat, into the house and up to his room. Only vaguely aware of taking off his clothes, he tumbled into bed. This time - mercifully - there was no dream, just blissful darkness.

Bright sunlight was flooding in through his bedroom window when he was woken by his mobile phone ringing. Tumbling out of bed, he scavenged around the room until he located the device in his jeans, which he had flung onto his chair the previous night.

"Hello."

"Tommy?" a voice asked.

"Yes?"

"Tommy, it's Septimus. It's 10.15 and you are not here yet. Do you want me to come get you?"

Tom blinked. 10.15? Why had his alarm not gone off? He turned to look at his desk, but saw that the clock was not there. Now he recalled that it had been packed in his bag - which was probably still in the back of the car where he had left it.

"Sorry, I overslept. Give me a few minutes and I will be there."

"You sure you can do it alone?" Septimus asked tentatively.

Tom thought about that but when he reached out in his mind to touch the Map and the Clock, found that both were present and behaving as they should. "No, I'm cool, Septimus. See you in five."

He rang off and pulled on his clothes, stopping only to clean his teeth. Then he Walked to the Institute and found himself a few moments later strolling into the Professor's study. As he entered the room, mumbling an apology, he saw that Septimus was perched on the desk, deep in conversation on the phone. Neoptolemas was sitting in his usual chair and seated opposite him, Tom's three friends were listening to Septimus.

"When will that be ... half an hour? Oh, an hour ....Very well can you let the Doctor know that his associates at the Hourglass Institute will be coming to visit him later? We are ... most concerned about his health and would like to see if he is in need of anything," the Welshman said. There was a pause as the person on the phone responded to this and then Septimus continued.

"Oh, I am sure he will see us. Let him know and if it is not convenient we can always come away ... yes, all right ... thank you very much."

He replaced the handset and nodded at Tom. "Hi Tommy boy. Right then, I think we had better be going soon. First though, I have some questions for you, Professor."

"Very well." The old man pressed his fingertips together and nodded for Septimus to continue.

"Well firstly, who were those men in black robes and why were they after the tablet? What is the tablet and why is it telling us something important is hidden on this airship?"

The Professor opened his mouth to reply, but Tom jumped in first. "I think you need to hear about my dream first ..." he began.

Aware of how significant such dreams had been only a few months before, they all listened intently as he related how he had become the man, Titus; about his attempt to destroy the Crown and his relationship with this figure, Knossos. When he had finally finished the extraordinary tale, Tom noticed that Edward was frowning.

"What is it?"

"You say that this man, Titus, was alive in ancient times in Greece?"

Tom nodded.

"So then, how was it that you were able to understand what everyone was saying?" Edward asked.

"Well I..." Tom started to say and then stumbled. How did he understand what they were saying, he wondered?

"It did not strike me as odd last night, but I honestly have no idea ..." Tom replied. "Do you?" he added, throwing the Professor a questioning glance.

The old man appeared to ponder the puzzle for a moment before responding. "We really do not understand how your dreams work, Thomas, but I would surmise that as you seem to

70

actually assume the identity of the man ... or woman," he added, looking at Mary, "about whom you are dreaming, that you then see the world through their eyes and think about the world through their mind. Language is all part of that so I don't think it is such a puzzle, really."

"But I don't speak Greek," Tom objected.

"No, but Titus did, so you could."

"I suppose you must be right." Tom shrugged. "Anyway, I should have come straight here last night but I was exhausted and just crashed," he said.

"That's all right, Tommy," Septimus said and then turned to the Professor. "You know, Prof, this all rings a bell. Can't quite place it yet but there is something about that name ... Knossos. Something very old and very important..." the Welshman's voice trailed off. Tom looked up to see that he was staring at the Professor and following his gaze, saw that the old man's expression had changed to one of abject horror. He was bent over the tablet and studying it intently.

For a full five minutes, all the while muttering under his breath, he remained looking at the stone. "It cannot be can it ... mind you, the cuneiform appears authentic for the period ... it might be a clever forgery ... no ... no ... it's genuine," he mumbled and finally slumped back against his chair and stared at them each in turn.

"What is it Professor?" Edward asked.

"Prof?" Septimus joined in.

Neoptolemas was looking even paler than he had the day before. Finally, he took a deep breath and tapping the magnifying glass a few times with his fingers, said, "I am sorry to say that if my suspicions are correct, this stone tablet is the most dangerous object in the world. Or rather, I should say, part of one of the

71

most dangerous objects in the world."

There was a moment's stunned silence, broken by Charlie. "It's just a slab of clay, Prof..." he started to say, but broke off when he saw the Professor's expression. The old man's face was the colour of ash, his eyes black and foreboding.

"No, it is not just that!" he snapped. "It is in fact far more than just that. Please give me a little while to study the tablet before I answer your questions. Just believe me when I say that we must find out more about Dr Midas and this artefact. I need to see those notebooks of his, or at least a copy of them and then ... then you are going on a journey. It will be dangerous, but it is important." He took off his spectacles, polished them on the handkerchief in his breast pocket, perched them back on the end of his nose and peered over the top of them at the five Walkers. Finally, he cleared his throat and in a doom-laden voice said, "More than just important: it is vital."

Again there was a stunned silence, this time broken by Mary. "Where?" she asked in a small voice, "where are we going?"

The Professor gestured towards the image on the stone tablet that lay on his desk.

"You're not serious!" Septimus said after a pause.

"I am afraid I think it might be necessary."

"But ... the Hindenburg? You do realise it exploded."

"Actually, it was more the case that it was incinerated," Neoptolemas said slightly pedantically.

"Oh, that makes all the difference then," Septimus muttered dryly. The Professor flashed him an apologetic glance.

"I am sorry. But you must trust that I will act for what is best and will not risk you on some whim. Just please go and talk to Dr Midas. I will make a quick study of this tablet and then come to find you at the Museum."

"OK then, in that case," Tom said, reaching out both arms, "would anyone like a lift to the Museum?"

Warily they all looked at him and then at each other, a little doubtful at the offer.

Tom scowled at them: no doubt images of him depositing them on top of Big Ben or in the Thames was floating into their minds. "Look," he protested, "I'm fine - I got here this morning, didn't I?"

With some reluctance, they all reached out to touch his arm or shoulder. Tom now closed his eyes and brought the Map into focus. There it was, clear and strong; he found the street that he was in (on?) and then panned across London to locate the British Museum. Then he Walked them all there. In just a moment, they were stepping out of the air just a few paces from the entrance and behind the huge pillars. Fortunately, nobody appeared to notice and even if they had, would not have believed their eyes, thought Tom. "See, I told you it would all be fine," he said, as they entered the impressive portico.

Dr Midas' departmental office was on the third floor, behind a plain door marked 'Staff Only' and the security guard, whom they had met the previous day, escorted them through it and down a maze of corridors to a lift, which took them up to the office of Dr Midas. Through the open door they saw the Doctor, who was sitting at a desk, one arm in a bandage, examining photographs of the stone tablet.

Septimus gave a light tap on the door. "Good morning Doctor, we are back."

The Greek archaeologist's eyes snapped up and he stared at them for an instant before recognition shone across his face.

"Ah, my new friends. See how the doctors have ... how do you say ... 'patched me up'." He lifted the bandaged arm slightly and smiled at them.

"How are you feeling, Dr Midas?" Edward asked.

"Well enough. It was not a large wound and I heal remarkably quickly. So, then, what did your Professor make of my little tablet?"

"He has not yet told us," said Edward, "but he does think it is very important. He has asked to see your notebooks - the ones where you recorded the other locations and times."

Dr Midas looked appalled. (I think apologetic would be a better choice over appalled) "I am sorry to disappoint you. I was going call you today and let you know. Only, what with the police coming over and then having to talk to the Museum's insurance company, I'm afraid it must have slipped my mind."

Edward looked puzzled. "Sir, I don't follow, what are you saying?"

Midas pointed at the window in the corner of the room. Tom could see that it had been smashed and was hanging open.

"What happened?" Mary and Charlie asked in unison.

"The Museum was broken into last night. Or rather, my room was broken into. But see," he gestured at his desk, "the computer is still here. So it seems the burglars were not merely after valuables. I am afraid to say that they appear to have been interested only in my notebooks: they are all missing, every single one."

Septimus whistled. "Ah well, never mind. Perhaps you can recall the dates you recorded?" he asked hopefully.

"I can remember some details," Dr Midas said, shaking his head, "but not the exact times. Sorry..."

"Do you think it was those black-robed thugs from last night, Doctor?" Charlie asked, moving to examine the shattered window.

74

Midas frowned. "I don't know who it was, but it seems likely doesn't it?"

"Not sure that it does," Septimus shrugged.

"Because they were Walkers you mean," Tom put in. "Why go to the trouble of breaking in when they could have just appeared here?"

"I don't understand." Dr Midas looked sharply at Tom. "Walkers - one of you mentioned that word before, yesterday in fact. What do you mean by it?"

"Oops, sorry Septimus, " Tom apologized, aware that he had maybe let out something best kept secret.

"Don't be sorry, boyo, I was about to ah ... educate the Doctor a little about us. But before I do, I should emphasize that the burglary is not your fault, Dr Midas. We have the tablet at least. The Professor might have made some sense of it by now. He is coming over soon."

"Excellent," Midas replied, a smile coming to his lips. "It will be wonderful to meet the great man. But, er ... what did you mean by 'educate me'? And would you like some tea and biscuits while we wait?" he added.

"Yes please," Charlie answered at once.

"You will get fat!" Mary hissed. (scolded might be better than hissed)

"I'm a growing boy," Charlie insisted.

"That is what I am afraid of" She cast him a baleful stare.

"No thank you, Doctor." Septimus glared at Charlie, who looked disappointed. "But we would like to ask some questions and maybe answer yours."

"Very well; go ahead, be my guest."

"The Professor believes that only a certain type of person can see the images on that tablet and read the text."

Dr Midas nodded and picked up one of the photographs he had been looking at. "That is what I have been saying. Look at these photos. See how the tablet is plain - just with cuneiform writing and nothing else on it?"

"Yes," the Welshman replied, picking up and studying the photographs. The others crowded round to look over his shoulder.

"They were taken when the image of the airship was very clear," Midas said. "I could see it distinctly and I wanted to prove it to a colleague, so I took these shots. See how not one of them shows any sign of what we all saw yesterday?"

"I am not surprised, Doctor." Septimus replaced the photos on the desk.

"Really?"

"Yes. Can I ask why it was that you approached the Institute?"

"The sponsor of the dig suggested you."

"Oh? Who was that then?" Charlie butted in.

Dr Midas frowned. "This is going to sound strange, but I don't know him. The University was funded to do the dig by some company who said they were happy to support us and stay at arm's length. I only ever spoke on the phone to them, but no more than that."

Septimus raised an eyebrow. "That does seem odd."

"Universities can't afford to be too fussy, especially during these tight financial times," Midas said, arching his fingers and examining the Welshman as though expecting him to make a critical remark.

"I guess so," Septimus shrugged, "but how did this company recommend our involvement?"

"Well, when I called the sponsor of the dig and commented about what I was seeing on the tablet, he was the one man who did not dismiss me out of hand. He suggested I see you because he said he had heard that you people have experience with the extraordinary, the unusual and the downright bizarre."

Tom, who had been watching Midas closely, said, "It was more than that though, wasn't it, Doctor?"

"Yes, you are right. I hesitate to say it, but the rumours about you suggest that some of you can … well, that you can travel back in time and that is how some of the mysteries of the past have been solved – from information your agency has gathered. Nonsense, of course." He gave a weak laugh.

"Not nonsense, but fact, Doctor. We call it 'Walking' and refer to ourselves as 'Walkers'. Walking through time, you see," Septimus said.

Midas' mouth fell open. "You mean it's true ...?" He gazed at them for a moment then appeared to collect himself. Closing his mouth, he nodded. "Ah ... I see now where the term comes from."

"Indeed," Septimus said. "Now: here is the thing. The Professor believes that the tablet is special and that it can only be read – I mean properly read – by someone who is a Walker. Which, you see, means …"

"That I too am a Walker," Midas said calmly.

"You do not seem surprised," Edward remarked.

Midas shook his head. "I am not … not really. I had no idea it was possible to actually travel through time, but I have been aware that strange things happen to me. That somehow, I am different to other men. I could always detect exactly where to dig on a site to find the ancient artefacts. My colleagues say I have a knack …a talent for it. Now I see they were right..."

"Is that how you found the tablet?" Septimus cut across him.

Midas nodded, but after a moment shrugged. "Sort of - the dig site was selected by our sponsor. He funded our work providing we dug in certain locations. You know what these corporations are like. Probably thought we would find gold or something. Once we were on the site, though, they stopped interfering. Good thing too, because right from the first day we arrived I could feel there was something unique and remarkable there: it was as if I was drawn to the location. It did not take long to dig down and find the tablet, but as we carefully removed the layers of earth above it, each moment seemed to take an eternity, until finally it was revealed."

"Can you Walk? Travel in time I mean," Tom asked.

"I have never tried, will you show me how?" Sitting up eagerly, Midas looked so like a puppy begging for a treat that Tom found it hard not to laugh.

"Maybe, if there is time later."

Midas slumped back down, slightly disappointed. Then he brightened up and winked at Charlie. "How about that cup of tea and biscuits now?"

"That would be wonderful, Dr Midas," came a voice from the doorway. "Two lumps of sugar for me if you please."

Professor Neoptolemas stood there with what looked like a rolled up poster under one arm and carrying a metal strongbox. He strolled in and walked up to Dr Midas.

"Permit me to introduce myself. I am…"

"Professor Neoptolemas I presume," Midas interrupted, rising and after a moment, offering his hand for the Professor to shake.

"That is correct. Now, I am in a position to explain to you the significance of the stone tablet." He dropped the poster on a chair and placed the strongbox carefully on a table pushed up against the wall. "Gather round, everyone," he said, opening the lid of the strongbox and removing the tablet.

As everyone crowded round the table, Neoptolemas indicated the image of the Hindenburg, etched clearly on its surface. "Before I do, Doctor, could you help me with a minor translation. Can you read this name here?" He pointed to a corner of the tablet.

Midas lifted up his thick glasses and focused his green eyes on the engraving. "Knossos ... it says Knossos."

Tom leaned forward to look, his heart hammering in his chest. Knossos, his old friend turned enemy. No, not his; Titus's.

"Knossos," Septimus repeated, looking distant as if he was struggling to recall a fact.

The Professor nodded and took the tablet back. "Well then ... this is basically a map. It reveals the locations of historical artefacts, which each comprise just a part of a much larger treasure."

"What treasure?" asked Charlie, his face lighting up. "Is it valuable?"

"Infinitely so, Mr Hawker, but not just in the way you mean."

"You mean it is one of those cultural treasures - important painting, statue - that kind of thing, but not worth much in terms of actual cash?"

"It is not something to which it would be appropriate to attempt to attach a value," the Professor frowned. "You really are sounding more and more like Mr Mason, Hawker."

"Heh!" Septimus complained, stirring from his contemplation.

"My apologies," Neoptolemas said, "I am straying from the point."

"Which is?" the Welshman prompted.

"The point I was making is that the artefact I refer to is probably the most powerful single item in the universe and it was

79

thought lost five thousand years ago!"

"You don't mean ... the Crown of Knossos?" Septimus asked and then snapped his fingers. "Ah, now I remember who Knossos was!"

"I am impressed, Mr Mason. Are you saying you had heard of the Crown before Tom related to us his dream?"

"Oh, I know about most lost treasures," said Septimus airily. "I keep my eye on rumours and legends - after all Professor, it used to be my bread and butter."

"So what do you know of it?"

The Welshman was silent for a few minutes, as though drawing together the facts in his mind. Midas went back to his desk and clicked the intercom. Tom heard him asking for a tray of tea and biscuits for his six visitors. Septimus moved away from the table and perched on the desk while the others each found a chair. The Professor almost sat on his rolled up poster, but Tom grabbed it just as Neoptolemas was lowering his backside. "Oh, thank you, Thomas," he said absently.

Handing it to the old man, Tom wondered what it contained and was about to ask, but Septimus had proceeded to talk.

"OK, so what I know is this: the Crown was made by some ancient Greek guy called Knossos. He used to be a Walker of great power. It went to his head though and one day he went mad and tried to destroy the world. Something went wrong and Knossos and his followers were swept into oblivion and the Crown destroyed and lost forever. It is thought to have been a good thing."

"Why?" Tom asked, thinking that Septimus had said nothing new – it was what he had told them all earlier this morning – except he had not known the bit about being swept into oblivion. The image of a temple and a man wearing a bronze and silver

80

crown with an enormous emerald, popped into his mind.

"Because," the Professor answered, "the Crown could be used to focus the raw power of a Walker and channel it. It could magnify the talents they had and be used to manipulate reality. In effect, when in possession of the Crown, Walkers can change the world in any way they want."

"So the tablet is..." Tom started to say. He was interrupted by a knock on the door.

Midas jumped up to answer it and a member of staff entered, pushing a trolley laden with tea things. "Ah, splendid," Midas beamed. "We will help ourselves, thank you.

"You were saying, Professor," he prompted when they were alone again, at the same time sorting everyone out with a cup of tea and handing out the biscuits.

"Er ... yes, it's a map: a map that seems to have come into being when the Crown was - supposedly - destroyed."

"So are you saying it wasn't destroyed then?" Edward asked.

The Professor nodded. "Apparently not. This tablet reveals that the Crown was clever. It split itself into several parts and hid itself in different locations."

"It was clever? You speak as if the thing was alive," Edward pointed out.

"In a way, it is. It was built to channel and enhance a man's thoughts and his mental energy. But the evidence is that it absorbed some of that energy and in the end, it became semi-sentient. That is to say, it developed a sort of consciousness all of its own. Maybe that is why Knossos went mad. Or maybe he was mad already. Anyway, the legend is that it split itself into many parts and then it made this map to point the way to where and when the parts are to be found."

"Where?" Charlie asked, spraying biscuit crumbs, his eyes

gleaming in anticipation.

"When?" Midas asked, ignoring Charlie. "What do you mean by that, Professor?"

"I mean that the tablet split itself not just across different physical locations but across time. Remember the date and time reference under the Hindenburg?" He pointed to the writing. "That tells us that part of the Crown is present on the Hindenburg, only during those brief moments. I suspect the other parts are similarly placed and restricted as to when we can collect them. Unfortunately, I gather we have lost your notebooks, Doctor. Your notes may have helped us. As it is, I believe we will only find out where to find the other parts when the first part is retrieved. Or perhaps the first part will reveal the whereabouts of the second – and so on."

"A bit like a treasure hunt, with clues and things," said Tom. His dad used to enjoy the ones run by the Rotary Club.

"Indeed," the Professor said, but did not smile.

"Maybe we should just leave the artefact alone. If we don't go and we destroy or hide this tablet, can we not prevent the Crown ever being found?" Edward suggested.

Mary was nodding. "It sounds evil and dangerous. Why try to find it? Why not leave it lost?"

"Who do you think those men in black robes were?" the Professor asked quietly.

"The Cult of Knossos," Tom suggested. "They were the same in the dream."

"That makes sense actually Professor," Septimus said. "They wore an image of a crown and one of them was a Walker, at least one - probably more ... oh blast!"

"What?" Edward asked.

The Professor answered for him. "As Mr Mason says, they

were Walkers, so if one of them got a look at the tablet during the fight, he would have seen the inscription and will know as much as we do. Furthermore, if they have the Doctor's notebooks ..." his voice trailed away as the implications sank home.

"Besides which," said Septimus, "if the first part points to the second, if they get there first, they could locate all the parts with or without the notebooks."

"Precisely." Neoptolemas sighed. "It goes without saying that if they are the Cult of Knossos, somehow here in the present day, and they are actively seeking the Crown, then I am afraid their intention will be to use it to destroy or change the world."

"So then, as you said, we must go and get it," Septimus concluded, "and before they do!"

"Get what? What is it we are looking for exactly?" Tom asked.

"Look at the tablet," the Professor instructed, "it may answer your question."

They all got up and moved to the table to stare down at the stone. The airship was there, with the date and time below, but Tom could see nothing else, until he realised that what he had taken to be an outline or frame around the entire image was in fact another shape. A series of linked circles, like a necklace or...

"It looks like a string of pearls," Tom suggested, surprised.

The Professor nodded. "Yes. According to the inscriptions in cuneiform, the Crown manifests itself as different objects. But I believe that during this brief window of time a string of pearls will become the Crown - or part of it any way. If we can take it at that time and Walk it forward to today, it will stay as a fragment. If we fail, the moment will pass and as you know, we cannot revisit the same time again."

"Why not?" asked Midas.

"It is a basic fact of time travel, Doctor," the Professor said.

"You cannot go twice to the same moment of time at the same location. It is, quite simply, impossible."

Charlie frowned. "Well the pearls must have got onto the airship in the first place, presumably round some rich woman's neck. Can we not go further back and steal them before they even get on the Hindenburg, and then hide them somewhere and wait for the right window of time?"

The Professor shook his head. "No, because the space and time co-ordinates are linked together. It must be those pearls on that particular airship at that precise time."

There was a pause before Septimus spoke, his forehead wrinkled in an almost comical expression of dismay. "So, we have to visit the Hindenburg on the night it was destroyed by fire and retrieve a string of pearls from one of the guests, and do so during a five minute window, which straddles the time the fire started?"

"That summarises the situation very well, Mr Mason."

"I really do need to consider the direction my career is going!" Septimus winked at Tom and added, "OK then, when do we start?"

CHAPTER NINE
THE PLAN

The Professor picked up the tablet and placed it back in the strongbox, which he now closed. Then, upon the table, he spread out the rolled up poster he had been carrying, revealing it to be a large printed image. It showed a schematic of the Hindenburg, including various cut outs and cross sections as well as a deck plan. Tom studied it hard - committing it to memory - for he was sure he would need this knowledge again soon. The Professor glanced up to make sure each of them was paying attention and began talking.

"The LZ 129 Hindenburg airship completed construction in 1936 and her first flight was on March 4th that year. She was 804 feet long, with a diameter of 135 feet, and a total gas capacity of just over 7,000,000 cubic feet of hydrogen. Along with her sister ship, LZ 130, she remains the largest object ever to have flown, being some five times as long as a modern jumbo jet."

"Good grief!" Edward said.

"Indeed, it is impressive. When she flew over cities like New York and Berlin, folk would stop their cars and get out to stare at her. She was truly vast.

"So then, to the details," the Professor went on. "The framework of the ship was constructed from triangular duralumin girders forming fifteen main rings and dozens of secondary rings, with other longitudinal struts connecting them." Neoptolemas paused for breath, glanced at Mary's perplexed features, shrugged and ploughed on.

"It was between these rings and girders that the gas cells were positioned. The vessel was propelled by four 1320 horsepower Daimler Benz engines, positioned in engine cars protruding on either side of the main structure: two towards the front and two further to the rear," He pointed at pods that could be seen on the plan. As he did so, Charlie let out an enormous yawn and the Professor glared at him.

"I apologise if you find all this less than exciting, Mr Hawker. However, in a very real sense, your life may depend on this information, so you may wish to pay attention. That is, unless you wish to be incinerated in only a few minutes' time."

Charlie blinked, appeared to consider this possibility and was suddenly sitting bolt upright, staring at the plan. "Sorry, Prof. I'm all ears."

"Very good. Well, as I was saying, the engines combined to produce a cruising speed of 125 Km/h which meant they could get across the Atlantic in about three days - impressive when you consider that most sea going vessels of the day took over a week and remembering that transatlantic flights by passenger aircraft were not yet commonplace."

He tapped the poster with his fingertips. "Now, the ship was controlled from a control car under the forward keel. Crew and passenger accommodation was provided on two decks. The larger A-deck contained twenty-eight twin passenger cabins, a dining room, passenger lounge and two long promenades from where you could see outside the vessel."

"Wow. Sure sounds like it would beat being crammed into your seat on a budget flight to Spain," Tom muttered, thinking back to his last trip in an airplane the year before.

The Professor smiled. "Oh indeed - these airships were the height of luxury."

"Until you got fried," Edward murmured with a grimace. Charlie snorted.

With a stern look at them both over his spectacles, the Professor cleared his throat and continued. "B-deck, meanwhile, was smaller and was below A-deck. It housed the crew quarters, as well as being connected to the interior passages of the airship." The Professor now pointed out gangways running through the superstructure. "Via these, you could reach the engine cars and the control cars, as well as the gas cells, should any maintenance be necessary. There was also a smoking room on B-deck."

"Wait a moment," Tom said, "a smoking room? On an airship filled with hydrogen? That's just asking for trouble. Was that why she burnt?"

The Professor shook his head. "No it wasn't, actually - but I will come to that in a moment. The smoking room had carefully controlled airlocks to make sure it was a self-contained area. But in an age when most adults smoked it was a necessity and apparently a very popular room."

"Next door to the bar, I see," Septimus observed, pointing at the plans. "Probably another popular room." He grinned at Charlie.

"Yes, I expect so," the Professor agreed. "So then, that is the layout. On May 6th, when the disaster occurred, there were thirty-six passengers and sixty-one crew members on board: thirteen of the former and twenty-two of the latter perished."

"What happened, Professor?" Edward asked. "What went wrong?"

"Well, that day conditions had been poor over Lakehurst Naval

Airfield - where the Hindenburg moored - and in fact the captain had taken her for an unscheduled tour down the US coast while he waited for a message to say it was safe to land. He returned in the early evening around seven, and started to manoeuvre to approach the mooring mast."

The old man paused and pointed at the plans. "Several witnesses report the outer skin of the airship bulging and flapping up here - just in front of the rear fin. A few moments later, flames were spotted there. They spread quickly, from one gas cell to the next. The ship tipped backwards onto its stern and a flume of burning gas erupted upwards as far as the bow ... incinerating her. The entire episode took less than a minute."

There was a hushed silence for a moment before Charlie spoke. "I heard about this of course, when I was a lad, but what I never understood is how anyone managed to escape."

The Professor shrugged. "Luck, mostly. Crew located near exit points, passengers standing at the promenade widows - almost all of these got away. Passengers in their cabins, crew deep in the interior spaces or those at the bow end did not, poor souls."

"You were going to tell us why it caught fire, Professor," Tom prompted.

"Was I? Ah, yes." Neoptolemas nodded absently. "There were many theories, Thomas, from Nazi sabotage to a build-up of static electricity and even a lightning strike, but nothing was ever proved. There's a book on the disaster in my library if you're interested."

"So then, Professor, do we have any idea where this string of pearls might be?" Edward asked, bringing them all back to the matter in hand.

"Yes, I had Sebastian in the IT department pull up details of the insurance claims after the incident. Two of the ladies on board who survived made a claim for missing pearls. None of the relatives of those who died made any such claim. We must hope that they would have known about them and assume there were only the two sets of pearls aboard."

"Bit of a long shot, isn't it?" Edward remarked, his face grim.

The Professor nodded. "Yes, but we can only work with the information we have, Lieutenant. Now, according to the details of the claim, Baroness Von Wilmer had placed her pearls into the keeping of the Hindenburg's captain and they were in the ship's safe in the crew quarters, whilst Frau Denitz kept hers in her cabin." He pointed at the plans. "Just here: cabin 17."

"The Baronesses' were probably worth more ..." Charlie mused.

"Indeed, but the Knossos Crown would not be concerned with wealth or value. The worthy Frau Denitz's jewellery might just as easily be the fragment we seek," the Professor suggested.

"It seems to me - and I speak as a total novice, you will comprehend - that you need to go and get both necklaces," Dr Midas said.

Mary looked up at him in surprise. "You seem to have accepted all this very easily, Doctor. I hope you do not mind my saying," she added hastily.

Midas shrugged. "Let's just say that it makes an awful lot of sense to me now. It explains all sorts of strange events that I have experienced."

"He has an advantage over you," Tom whispered to Mary. giving her a nudge. "He never thought he was a witch!"

She giggled. "You mean a warlock, Master," she quipped.

Tom was about to reply, but the Professor treated them both to one of his stern glances.

"Well then," Septimus said, playing thoughtfully with his

short goatee beard, "how do we get on board the airship in precisely the right place at the crucial time?" His eyes narrowed and he looked at Tom. "I suppose we could Walk back to when she was being fitted out and try to get a tracker on her ..."

"A tracker?" Charlie asked.

"Yes, it's a bit like a GPS bug the police use to pinpoint the exact locations of individuals or vehicles," Septimus explained, "except that the Institute's trackers work through time. They send out signals that a Walker can latch on to and then guide him to it. That was how Tom and I found your sinking U-boat in the middle of the ocean and were able to rescue you, Charlie."

"And there was me thinking it was simply because Tom was brilliant." Charlie grinned.

"It is an interesting notion, Septimus," the Professor broke in, "except that the Hindenburg's home base was Frankfurt in Nazi Germany. Do you fancy smuggling the tracker on board her whilst she's moored there?"

Septimus shook his head. "Er no ... that would not be my first choice."

"Surely we don't need to," Edward pointed out. "We have a precise time that the Hindenburg came in over Lakehurst and we know when the fire began. We get to the naval base a little before the airship arrives and we hop on board - somewhere in the superstructure. Then we go into B-deck and whilst one of us searches the safe, the others can go up to the passenger deck and try the cabins."

"It's a plan, BUT there is one issue," Septimus said, hesitating and glancing at Tom.

Tom grimaced. He knew what Septimus was reluctant to say. Of them all, Septimus and Edward could Walk individually to the date and time of the disaster, but only Tom could take all of the others along too: it was his unique talent. They could not hope to remain undetected for very long on a vessel with only sixty crew and passengers. So they needed to arrive on board at a point in time very close to the disaster, find the pearls within a few brief minutes, and get away before the airship went up in flames. It was a tricky assignment at the best of times. Only Tom had the ability to guide them all to the Hindenburg - to get them into the vessel and then get them away from the disaster. Providing ... providing that whatever had caused the problems of the previous day did not recur.

"I ... I think I am OK, Septimus," Tom said. "Yes, I feel fine. Not sure what caused that earlier, but I am sure I can do this."

"Good ... good. It is as I had hoped," the Professor said, looking oddly smug. Tom wondered what he meant by that but before he could ask, the Professor had continued.

"Very well then, good luck. Erm ... Dr Midas, I wonder if I might keep the tablet for a while? I think with further study it will reveal more to me."

Midas looked doubtful for a moment and then nodded. "Of course, Professor. Please let me know anything you discover."

"Naturally I will," the Professor said. He picked up the strongbox then turned away and in an instant he had vanished.

"Good lord!" Midas said after a moment, still staring at the spot where Neoptolemas had stood. "So then, boy," he swung round to direct his gaze at Tom, "when will you and your companions attempt this daring mission?" (He swung round to direct his gaze at Tom. "So then, boy, when will you and your companions attempt this daring mission?"

Tom looked at his friends and back at the doctor. "Oh, now seems like a good time," he said, glancing around the room at the others.

Everyone nodded. "Right then, hang on to me. Here we go!"

CHAPTER TEN
HINDENBERG

Tom stretched out both his arms. Edward and Charlie each placed a hand on one and Mary and Septimus on the other. In his mind Tom brought up the Map. He scrolled across it to find the eastern seaboard of the United States. Once there, he located the naval base at Lakehurst. He focused upon it and Walked in that direction. As he moved, he brought into his mind an image of the Clock - his brass alarm clock that had once belonged to his father. He spun the timepiece's hands backwards, moving them faster and faster until he knew he had reached the target date, and as he did, he Walked them all back through time to May 6th, 1937, a few minutes before seven p.m. local time.

They materialised in the gap between a warehouse and some packing cases. Septimus popped up to take a look over the top of one and glanced about, then turned and beckoned for Tom to join him. Tom peered carefully round a box labelled 'J.P. Sutton - Machine Tools'. Beyond the cases, and only a few feet in front of them, was a wire fence about twelve feet high and through it he spotted two enormous hangers running off to their right. Ahead and to the left was a large open space with marked out runways and a windsock fluttering in the breeze. On the far side of the landing field, more huge hangars loomed. To their left and about two hundred yards away, in the middle of the large open landing field, was a tall structure made of steel girders. Much like the Eifel Tower, but actually shaped a bit like a rocket, it rose to a point high above them.

"I have been here before," the Welshman whispered. "A few years prior to today, in fact; I was ... ahem, borrowing some secret plans. Anyway, according to memory, those hangers house the airships when they are not in flight." Septimus pointed at the vast buildings. "The Americans had several naval airships based here I believe, as well as it being the landing field for the Hindenburg. Now, look over there everyone," he gestured.

They all stared at the huge tower.

"That's the airship mooring mast. When the Hindenburg arrives, it will come in and descend so that it is level with the top of the tower. It will then dock with it and be winched down to ground level. That at least is the plan. Of course, that never actually happens, because, whilst the ship is approaching the tower, the disaster occurs and she burns and crashes."

"Good Lord, there she is!" Charlie exclaimed.

They turned to see the airship approaching from behind them: an impossibly large cigar-shaped balloon hundreds of feet above them, but still vast, casting a giant shadow over the airfield. She was a metallic blue colour all over, with the exception of the glass windows in the control car at the front and the promenade windows of the passenger deck at the thing's belly. Prominently displayed were red and black swastika flags, painted onto the fish-like fins projecting out of her rear end. Eerily, her approach was almost silent.

Tom heard a loud sob and turned to see Mary staring up at the Hindenburg, one hand over her mouth and the other clutching at Septimus. "I am frightened, Mr Mason. What demons drive that creature, what magic can make it fly?"

93

"Mary, don't get upset. It is a thing; a machine that men make. There is no monster within it - just engines," Septimus explained, but Tom could see Mary was far from convinced and she kept on staring at the airship as it moved by. Did she see it as yet more evidence of incomprehensible things beyond her time – a time she was perhaps never meant to see? Exchanging worried glances with Edward and Charlie, Tom placed his arm around her waist and gave her a comforting squeeze. He could feel her whole body trembling and knew she was struggling not to weep.

"Mary, you don't have to come. You can stay here and we'll pick you up later."

"No, Master," she said firmly, letting go of Septimus and dashing a hand across her face, clearly making an effort to re-gain her composure. "Forgive a moment's weakness. I will be fine now, I swear it."

Relieved to feel that she was no longer shaking, Tom gave her an encouraging smile and withdrew his arm.

The Hindenburg was still high up and well above the moor-ing tower. As it passed over the top, it turned to the north and then to the west and now Tom could see that it was descending slowly as it curved around and began to come back towards the east - back towards them and the tower.

Septimus checked his watch. "Right, it's about fifteen minutes before the disaster. Time to get on board. Tom, take us into the superstructure near the crew compartment's access door to the aft gangway."

Tom nodded and tried to hide the doubts he was feeling. He was glad he had taken careful notice of the Professor's plans, but had he paid enough attention to the details? What if he got it wrong? One of them could end up outside the airship or inside one of the gas cells. Then, of course, it was not just a question of recalling the layout correctly. If whatever had afflicted him the previous day happened again, they might all end up in the middle of the sea for all he knew. The lives of his friends were in his hands and the enormity of the responsibility made him falter.

"OK Tom?" Septimus hissed(whispered). "No time to hang about, boyo!"

Shaking his head in an effort to dismiss his gnawing anxieties, Tom frowned in concentration. They had only minutes on this job and he had to get it right. In his mind he brought up the Map and then, having made sure he was anchored to the location at Lakehurst, he superimposed the floor plan of the airship, orientating it in his mind so it matched the alignment of the real ship above them. There, just behind the hatch into B-deck, was a corridor. But it was a narrow space, only wide enough for one person, so with a hurried explanation, Tom had his companions form up in single file then positioned himself in the middle of the line. He nodded to the others and they reached out to touch his outstretched arms. Then, with a final nod, he Walked them away.

They materialised in the corridor running along the keel of the airship, which was formed within a triangle of steel girders. A narrow gangway led in two directions within the triangle, whilst outside the girders there were huge sheets of whitish canvas. Tom realised after a moment that these were the gas cells and that he and his friends were surrounded by thousands of tons of hydrogen: the gas that fuelled the sun. A single spark might turn it all into an inferno. He gulped and looked along the walkway.

From one direction down the corridor, the whirl and clunk of machinery could be heard. "Generator room in the heart of the ship: that's aft of the cabins. Come on, this way," Septimus muttered and led them in a single file away from the generators. On either side of them they now saw a series of cabin doors. Septimus held his finger to his lips to keep them quiet and hissed (whispered) two words, "Crew quarters," before carrying on along the corridor.

Beyond the crew quarters, a large steel door blocked their path: the rear hatch leading into B-deck.

Septimus looked round to check they were all still with him and glancing at Tom, he raised a questioning eyebrow and tapped his watch.

"It is now seven-fifteen local time," Tom said. "Assuming the Professor knows what he is talking about and the stone tablet is also correct, then these pearls we are after will begin to change into the fragment of the Crown in eight minutes. The fire starts in, er ... ten and then in two minutes more, the ship is destroyed."

"Right then. Charlie, Mary and I will try to get into the Captain's safe. Tom, you and Edward go to the passenger cabins and look for the pearls there. If we fail to find them, we meet up here in ten minutes. All clear?"

"As mud!" muttered Charlie.

"Excellent," replied Septimus. "Right, let's go!"

Cautiously, Septimus opened the hatch and peered around it. Beyond the doorway, the corridor extended forwards about fifty feet before ending at another hatchway. More doors led off the passageway on either side. Septimus allowed Mary and Charlie to pass by him into the corridor. He went to follow them then suddenly he slapped his forehead, turned around to face Tom and Edward and frowning, pointed up at the ceiling.

"Damn!" he exclaimed. "I just remembered that you can't get to the stairs from here without going through the Purser's cabin and the bar. The bar is through the smoking room airlock and

96

will be manned by the barman. You two are going to have to Walk up through the ceiling."

Tom nodded and imagined the plan of the airship in his mind. Directly above them he could picture the hallway at the top of the stairs from B-deck, which was the entrance to the passenger cabins. "Ten feet straight up," he instructed his companion. Edward nodded and they both Walked to the landing.

On either side of them, stairs led downwards. Beyond these were doors to the dining room on one side of the ship, and the passenger lounge on the other. Directly in front of them, two corridors ran between the passenger cabins. A moment after they had appeared, a smartly dressed man in a jacket and tie strolled out of one of the corridors, examining a camera he was holding. He pushed past with barely a glance and then turned to take a second look at them.

"*Guten Abend, wie heissen Sie?*"

"*Er, Ich heisse Herr Edward Dyson,*" Edward said in hesitant German.

"Ah, you are American? Why have I not seen you before?" the stranger asked, switching to English.

"English, actually but we have both been ill, only just come out of our cabin."

The German gentleman looked doubtful at that answer, but shrugged and walked on towards the lounge. "Well, we are just landing," he said over his shoulder, "so I would hurry yourselves: you don't want to miss that, do you?"

After he had gone, Tom let out the breath he had been holding and Edward nodded at him. "Phew, I thought he might raise the alarm. Come on, let's go - we can't have long now."

"Just nine minutes to go," said Tom, turning to peer towards the cabins. "Which corridor?"

Edward shrugged and then rushed across to one of the openings and glanced along it, his gaze taking in the nearest of the doors on one side and then the one opposite it. "We want number 17, don't we? These are 1 and 14, so not this corridor," he announced, moving to the other entrance. "Here's 15 to 28. Come on, it's this way."

Tom ran after his friend, counting off the cabins as he passed them: "15 ... 16 ..."

"Ah, 17, this is it," Edward announced, giving a gentle tap on the door, his ear pressed against the polished wood. "Thank goodness, no one there," he said after a moment, his hand twisting the doorknob. "Blast! Locked," he muttered and then stepped back, steadied himself and hurtled into the door like a rugby forward, putting his weight behind his right shoulder. With a great crack followed by a splintering sound, the door was knocked back off its hinges.

"You don't think it might have been easier to Walk?" Tom muttered with a wry grin.

Edward shrugged and just smiled. "Maybe ... but it wouldn't have been as much fun."

Beyond the shattered doorway the cabin was tiny: only six feet long by about five feet wide. On their left they could see a wash basin and a curtain that led to a small closet. Ahead of them was a fold-down table and a stool. Finally, on the right, was a bunk bed, complete with a ladder leading to the upper bunk. On the lower bunk, Tom spotted a suitcase.

Edward had seen it too and tried the catches. "Locked!" he grunted. "Try checking the closet, hurry we have only eight more minutes," he added, pulling out a penknife and flicking out a blade.

Tom poked his head through the curtain, but the shelving

inside was bare. Frau Denitz had obviously packed her clothes away in the case.

Edward, meanwhile, had pushed the point of the blade behind the lock and twisted. With a snap the catch flew open. He repeated this manoeuvre on the other side then he tipped the case upside down. Shirts and blouses, trousers and skirts fell out of the case and tumbled on to the blanket covering the lower bunk. Two small boxes fell out as well: one bouncing on the bed to land on the floor. Tom bent over to retrieve that one, opening it hopefully, but then grimaced when it turned out to contain only a fountain pen. Edward opened the other to reveal a string of shiny and very beautiful white pearls. Tom grabbed the jewellery and grinned at Edward.

"Eureka! Found it!" Tom said. "Quick, let's go."

He turned to exit the cabin and then froze, for there, in the corridor outside, stood a man. He was somewhat older than the young lieutenant - perhaps about the same age as Septimus - clean shaven but with a shock of red hair. He wore army style canvas trousers and a Chelsea football top. There were two striking things about him, other than his hair. Firstly, the football shirt was from the recent 2009 to 2010 football season and secondly, he was holding a pistol.

"I'll 'ave that mate!" he said, speaking with a London accent, cocking the revolver and pointing it at Tom.

CHAPTER ELEVEN
ROLF LAPACE

Edward Walked: vanishing from where he stood next to Tom and appearing in the corridor beside the stranger, his fist going back, ready to land a punch on the redhead's face. Edward blinked, gasping as he saw the man was no longer there, but had vanished the instant Edward materialised.

Tom was about to join Edward when he felt a pistol barrel dig into the back of his neck. With a chill he realised the man was now right behind him and that he too was a Walker.

"Nice try, sunshine!" said a voice in Tom's ear. Reaching over, the redhead seized the string of pearls and with a pop, was gone.

Edward slammed his fist against the wall in frustration. "Damned cheek! Who the devil was that chap?"

"I have no idea, but he's got the pearls and it's less than two minutes before they become the fragment." Tom frowned as a thought occurred to him. "Tell you what though, whoever he is, if like us he's after the Crown, he won't leave until the fragment appears."

Edward closed his eyes and screwed up his face in concentration then nodded. "You are quite right, Tom. He is still on board. He is ... oh my ... he's in the Captain's cabin!"

Tom's eyes widened. "The others: come on, let's go!" he yelled and without waiting for Edward, he Walked down through the vessel to the keel corridor near the bow of the airship, above the control car and just outside the Captain's cabin.

As they materialised, Edward gave a cry of alarm, seized Tom and yanked him sideways. An instant later, Septimus tumbled out of the doorway, blood streaming from his nose. Without hesitation, Edward rushed into the room, followed by a slightly more reluctant Tom, to find themselves face to face with two huge men.

Both were at least six foot six inches tall, bald-headed, wore boiler suits and appeared to be identical twins. One of them, his face bearing a scar above the right eyebrow, had presumably just punched Septimus, for the other had Charlie in an arm lock around his neck and was squeezing the sailor's throat. Charlie was clawing at the man's hands, choking and struggling to get free. A third man - the redhead in the Chelsea shirt, who was clearly the leader of the trio - was pointing his gun at a terrified Mary, who stood cowering beside the Captain's desk.

As Tom and Edward burst into the cabin, the redhead swung the pistol round to cover them and in that instant, Tom saw that the door of the safe was hanging open, its contents strewn across the desk. Amongst them was a jewellery case.

"Now now, gentlemen, no need to take any risks." The leader waved the gun from Tom to Edward. "We all want to get off this airship alive, don't we?" He glanced at the huge twins. "Orme, get the pearls!"

The big man with the scarred face grunted and stepped towards the desk, but at that moment, Mary lunged for the jewellery case. The leader swung the pistol back and again the silenced weapon pointed at the girl.

"Don't try my patience, lass. I warn you: I will shoot if I must," the man threatened, frowning as Mary flung her arms upwards and screamed, *"Wall!"* There was a flash of light and surrounding her now was a shimmering shield of frozen time.

"Nice trick, lass!" the leader said and with a mocking grin he Walked, appeared on top of the desk and pushed Mary roughly to the ground, the shield disintegrating as she fell. Seizing the jewellery case, her assailant jumped down and an instant later, the gun was once more pointing first at Tom then at Edward. They exchanged a despairing glance: they had not had a chance to move; Charlie was still struggling and gasping for breath ... and the seconds were ticking away.

"Right! Orme, Jez, we have them both. Back to location Y," the redhead ordered and the three of them were gone.

Septimus staggered back into the room, blood still streaming from his nose, whilst Edward ran over and helped Mary to her feet. Charlie stood coughing, one hand massaging his bruised throat.

"Where are they?" Septimus asked, turning to Edward.

"Gone ... to the rear of the airship," Edward shouted. "Around ring 62, I think."

"What do we do now?" Charlie gasped.

"Get us after them, Tom!" Septimus snapped.

"It is only seconds before the pearls ... whichever set it is, becomes the fragment," Tom warned. As he spoke, the sound of bellowed orders and the clattering of running feet echoed through the open doorway as a group of men hurtled down the corridor towards the front of the ship.

Septimus leapt to the opening and quickly closed the door, but stood holding the handle in case anyone should try to enter. Whoever they were though, they did not stop at the Captain's cabin, but carried right on by. "Those are crewmen, running towards the bow to help straighten up the Hindenburg," he ex-

102

plained. "The Captain had some difficulty keeping it straight and he used their weight to level it out. That was only just before the fire. In other words, we don't have long: come on Tom, NOW!"

Tom Walked them all back through the ship to the corridor near ring 62. It ran into a dead end just behind them - the very rear of the ship. On either side of them were long, white, oval-shaped canisters the size of coffins - ballast tanks, Tom thought. Above them, a ladder ran vertically up through the ship between the gas cells. A few rungs up the ladder, still holding his pistol and pointing it at them, was the red-headed man in the Chelsea shirt. Higher up the twins were hanging on to the ladder, each holding out a single set of the pearls they had stolen.

"Just stay there, Septimus," said the redhead. "No need for a fuss. I only need a few seconds more."

Tom gaped at Septimus: the fact that this man knew the Welshman by name came as a great surprise and not just to Tom, judging by the shocked faces of his companions. They all turned to look at Septimus.

The Welshman paid them no heed. Glaring up at the stranger, his face twisting with outrage, he spoke at last. "Damn you, Rolf Lapace! I thought we agreed to keep out of each other's way."

The other man snorted. "Yes, well, IF you recall the conversation, what we actually agreed was to avoid competing for the same contract. It seems that you and I are working for different employers who are apparently both interested in the same item just now. I appear to have possession of that item - one of these," he gestured at the two sets of pearls dangling above his head. "We will see which one in a moment - so don't try anything stupid. I would hate to have to shoot an old pal! It might cause an explosion," he said, laughing.

103

"Keep him talking, I'll get up there," Tom whispered to Septimus and he slid back behind the Welshman and out of sight. Then, as he Walked, he felt Mary slip her hand onto his elbow. They materialised side by side on the ladder, directly above the uppermost one of the big brutes - the scar-faced one: Orme, thought Tom; the lower one must be Jez.

When they appeared, both he and Mary clamped one hand onto a rung to steady themselves. The sudden noise drew Orme's attention and he glanced up at them, but not quickly enough to prevent Mary from reaching down to grab the pearls. He swayed, almost overbalancing, slack mouth falling open in his brutish, unintelligent features.

"Boss!" Orme's very deep voice boomed.

Lapace looked up to where Tom and Mary balanced precariously on the ladder. He whipped the pistol round and without hesitation fired a shot. The bullet missed Mary by an inch and there was a ping as it ricocheted off the rung next to her head and flew away.

"Lapace, you fool!" Septimus yelled, "The whole ship is full of hydrogen!"

As if in response to those words, there was a muffled explosion above them. Tom glanced upwards. The ladder upon which he, Mary, Lapace and his grunts clung ran up above his head, emerging in another corridor - the axial one that ran though the very centre of the airship. Another ladder ran up again from there to the top of the airship and ended at a ventilation shaft that led out onto the external surface. There - high up at the top of the Hindenburg - a gas cell had been punctured and, as Tom looked on with horror, it suddenly erupted into flames.

"Oh, my God!" he yelled as the fire spread down towards them.

Still clutching the string of pearls, Mary held out her hand and grunted in concentration. Just as she had done once before in Pudding Lane, she held the flames at bay. However, the fire in 1666 had not been fuelled by thousands of tons of hydrogen. Sweat collected in beads on her forehead as she struggled to contain the ball shaped inferno that threatened to expand and incinerate them along with the ship.

Biting his lip, Tom stood as if paralysed, watching whilst the fireball glowed and flickered, like a miniature sun that would devour the Hindenburg in just a few brief moments. In the last few months he had faced death on more than one occasion, but never had it been more terrifying.

Just then he heard a new sound: a strange screeching, like someone running their nails down a blackboard. Distracted by the fiery globe only thirty feet above his head, it took Tom a moment to realise the sound was coming from below, not above. He glanced down and saw that the string of pearls in the hands of Orme's brother, Jez, was glowing intensely. All eyes were drawn to it as the sounds and the glowing lights seemed to reach a crescendo. Then Tom saw that Jez no longer held a string of pearls, but instead he now clutched a shard of metal. Tom recognised it instantly as a piece of an ornate crown: the Crown from his dream.

"Sorry lass," Lapace drawled, "bad luck and all, but it looks like you've got the wrong one there," he taunted. "Let's go boys!"

The three of them vanished away from the Hindenburg, leaving Mary holding a string of beads; just an ordinary set of pearls. She was pale as snow, her brows drawn together as she swayed on the ladder, her strength almost at an end. The fireball began to inch towards them.

"Blast!" Septimus cursed.

"They are not on board anymore," Edward shouted up. "Maybe I can track them, and we can follow?"

"I can't hold it any longer!" Mary cried. She slumped exhausted into a dead faint, letting go of the ladder and tumbling away. Tom reached out and seized her with one hand as she fell, but her weight jerked him off the ladder. They both landed in a crumpled heap in the keel corridor.

Above them there was a detonation. The entire ship shook with the violence of it, throwing them all off their feet. As they struggled back upright, the fire erupted forwards through the gas cells and down towards them. Then the Hindenburg lurched and tilted backwards onto its tail.

The sudden movement of the airship saved their lives, removing them from the worst effects of the blast. The five of them tumbled to the dead end of the keel corridor, rolling over each other and ending up as a mass of arms and legs, with Tom buried underneath them all. Mary came to with a groan then screamed.

Charlie, on top of the heap, seized Tom's arm. "Tom, get us away now! For God's sake NOW!" he yelled, as the heat around them grew fierce and fire proceeded to incinerate the great vessel.

Tom closed his eyes and just Walked. Anywhere, any time was better than here and now, but as he Walked them all away, he realised that, as once before, the Map was spinning and the Clock's hands were rotating erratically: he had no control over where they were going. They all cried out in panic as they hurtled through the void, still an entangled ball of limbs.

"Concentrate, Tom, *concentrate!*" Septimus yelled.

"I can't!" Tom shouted back, panicking now.

"Yes you can, lad. Just focus on the Map. Focus on one point on it - Hyde Park. Find the Serpentine and get us there."

"I ... I ... OK, I will try!" Tom stammered. He tried to block out everything else and just find the lake in the Park. There: he had it. Now, just go there and try and get the date right.

"Go - go now!" he shouted and suddenly, with nauseating abruptness, they hurtled out of the void and landed with a mighty splash right in the centre of the Serpentine.

There followed a few moments of paddling and splashing around as they swam to the side of the lake and, to the amusement of city workers and some French tourists, they emerged, dripping on the grass.

After he had caught his breath, Septimus turned to Tom and said, "OK, I'll admit it: I did say 'find the Serpentine'. But I didn't expect you to land us right in it, boyo!

CHAPTER TWELVE
NEW GIRL

Afraid to rely on Tom, everyone returned on foot to the Institute, squelching up the road in their sodden clothes with Tom bringing up the rear. He stomped along, head down, puzzled about how he had lost control of the Map and the Clock and wondering if he dare trust his talents again.

Despite his initial attempt at humour when they had climbed out of the Serpentine, Septimus walked along stony-faced and did not respond when Edward asked him who Lapace was. Mary remained silent, but Tom noticed that she shivered as she walked. He was certain it was not because of the plunge into the lake, for the afternoon was warm and their clothes were drying quickly. Her eyes looked wild, as if she was reliving the last few moments of the Hindenburg. It must have brought back horrifying memories, Tom thought. Was she thinking back to the fire that had almost killed her in 1666? It seemed likely.

Of them all, Charlie, meanwhile, remained quite cheerful. As they crossed Bayswater Road and passed along the road leading to the Institute, he also asked Septimus about Lapace. Septimus refused to speak at first, but as they entered the Institute, Charlie persisted with his questioning.

"He seemed to know you well, that Rolf Lapace. Old business partner was he? Is he in your line of work? I mean, did you work together on different projects? So who is he really, Septimus?"

Finally, Septimus gave in and turned to face Charlie as they stood in Mr Phelps' office, waiting to go into the Professor's study.

"I told you before, Charlie, I work for the Professor now. I'm not in that line of business anymore."

"Aw, come on man, throw me a bone here. Give me something to go on."

Septimus looked at him. "Like what?"

"Well, how do you get into it? How do you contact folk who will pay you for this stuff?"

"Leave it alone, Charlie. I am not going to make it easy for you," Septimus yelled, stalking off to the corner of the room.

Charlie threw up his hands. "Maybe I will ask Lapace then!" he shouted after Septimus.

"Suit yourself," the Welshman retorted as Mr Phelps opened the door to the study.

A moment later they were standing in front of the Professor and reporting a failure.

"What do you mean - someone else got it!" the Professor boomed at them from behind his desk. "Who ... who has got it?" Startled by this uncharacteristic outburst, they all stood in chastened silence, exchanging nervous glances with each other.

"Well? I'm waiting. What happened?"

Tom frowned: he could not remember Neoptolemas ever being so agitated. He was always the calm one, which made this behaviour so surprising. What on earth had got into him?

Septimus slumped down in a chair by the desk and sighed. "It was Lapace. Rolf Lapace."

The Professor's eyes seemed to bulge at the name. "Lapace was on the Hindenburg? He took the Crown fragment?"

Running his fingers through his hair, Septimus nodded. "The man seems to have a second sight when it comes to treasure," he said gloomily.

The Professor stared at him. "Maybe, or maybe someone told him about it?"

"What are you suggesting, Professor? Do you think I would betray you?"

"You were his partner for a long time, Mr Mason. It would not be so unlikely."

"I told you before, Prof - I keep telling everyone - I don't do that anymore and certainly not with Rolf."

The Professor snorted, his mouth twisted into a disbelieving sneer. Tom glanced at him again. What was up with the old man?

"You expect me to believe that?" Neoptolemas asked scathingly. "Time was that Mason and Lapace were the names to call upon if you wanted anything found. The stories of your deeds can still be heard wherever Walkers gather: Mason and Lapace retrieved the lost works of Aristotle from the Great Library of Alexandria. Mason and Lapace located Atlantis. I even heard it said that Mason and Lapace spent an hour on Apollo 13 without being spotted by any of the crew."

Septimus shrugged at that and winked at Tom. "Did that for a bet," he muttered.

"So then, you can see how one could believe that if your old partner popped up and asked for help, you might just betray us for a cut."

"No!" Septimus insisted.

"Oh, leave him be, sir, please leave him alone!" Mary cried out, and they all turned in surprise to look at her. "If he said he did not do this, I believe him."

"Well now, Miss Brown." Neoptolemas raised his eyebrows and gazed at her over the top of his spectacles for a moment then added, "How can you be so certain?"

Flushing under the old man's scrutiny, Mary threw a pointed glance at Septimus.

Tom, who had been watching the Welshman closely, saw him give an almost imperceptible shake of his head. Mary looked quickly away. "I just believe him, that's all," she mumbled, staring at the floor.

Breaking the awkward silence that followed, Edward said quietly, "Is it possible that someone else hired Lapace?"

"Like who?" Tom asked absently, still wondering about the unspoken signal that had passed between Septimus and Mary, which no one else appeared to have noticed.

"Well, we know the Black Robes are out there somewhere. Maybe one of them did?"

"Maybe, Lieutenant," the Professor shrugged. "It's possible I suppose," he conceded.

"Yes, well I also think we should investigate Dr Midas a little more," Edward suggested.

"Ah: as it happens, I thought so too, so I have already looked into his credentials and have satisfied myself that he is everything he says he is," the Professor said dismissively.

"But sir, maybe we should look into him a little more," Edward pressed.

"No. Do not waste your time, Lieutenant!"

"Oh, it is no bother, I assure you."

"I said no!" the Professor snapped. "Are you questioning my judgement, Lieutenant?"

Edward blinked and looked hurt. "No sir, of course not."

Perhaps aware that he had been rather harsh, the Professor

took a deep breath and spoke more softly. "I am sorry, Edward, but you must realise that events are gathering pace and we cannot afford to duplicate our efforts. We must focus on locating the fragments of the Crown as quickly as possible."

"Why do you say events are gathering pace, Professor?" Mary enquired.

In response, the old man picked up a sheet of paper from his desk. "There are yet more reports of incursions from other time periods - or even from the Twisted Reality. This one states that Prime Minister's question time was today interrupted by a Roman dressed in a toga, who materialised in the chamber of the House of Commons, assaulted the Speaker and vanished during the subsequent chase through the division lobby."

"Livened up proceedings in Parliament, I should think," Septimus observed with a wry grin.

Charlie snorted; Edward looked scandalised. The Professor ignored them both, but Tom was sure he saw a twinkle in the old man's eyes as he shuffled the papers on his desk. "Maybe so," he said, "but that is not all: a Scottish couple who visited the Tower of London yesterday are now claiming compensation for the violent behaviour of a group of re-enactors. They insist they met a lady dressed in Tudor-era clothing purporting to be Queen Elizabeth I. She was accompanied by a party of soldiers armed with pikes, who tried to have the couple arrested for treason on the grounds that they were spies working for the Queen's cousin, Mary Queen of Scots."

"Not re-enactors I'm guessing," Tom grimaced.

"No, but like you assumed at Fort Belam, Tom, the couple believed these people were just a costume group, until one of the soldiers actually walloped them both in the stomach with the shaft of his pike. As on the other occasions, the whole party disappeared before they could be arrested. Nobody can explain it, but the media are assuming the Scottish tourists interrupted an imaginative, if somewhat misguided, attempt to steal the Crown Jewels."

"Do you still have no idea what is causing these incidents, Professor?" Tom asked.

Neoptolemas shook his head. "I am sorry to say no ... or not for certain. But I have a few suspicions that they are connected in some fashion with the Crown's reappearance. This is why we must locate all the other parts quickly and cannot waste time on side investigations." He directed his gaze at Edward. "Do you understand me?"

Edward nodded. "Of course I do, sir," he replied, "now that you have taken the time to explain it."

Although his tone was calm, Tom felt there was a message hidden in his terse response: a hint of criticism that the Professor had not given Edward his full confidence.

"So what is the plan, then?" Tom asked, keen to change the subject.

The Professor opened his desk drawer and took out a cloth-covered object, which he unwrapped to reveal the tablet. The image of the Hindenburg had vanished. In its place was a blurred, rather fuzzy shape that Tom could not make out.

"It seems the next fragment is revealing itself. I suggest we get some rest and I contact you tomorrow or the day after when we know what it is."

They got to their feet and started moving towards the door.

"Mr Hawker, please stay behind a moment," the Professor called after them, halting Charlie in his tracks.

Edward turned back in the doorway and seemed about to say something then appeared to change his mind, shutting the door behind them and leaving Charlie and the Professor alone.

Septimus muttered that he was going off to have a cup of tea and pushing past Mary, disappeared through the doors to the kitchens. Tom, intrigued by her staunch defence of the Welshman, followed the girl into the hallway.

"How come you were so certain that Septimus had not been in touch with Lapace?" he asked her.

Mary shook her head. "Sorry Master Thomas, I can't tell you. I made a promise not to," she said, and walked towards the stairs leading to the bedrooms.

Tom wandered back to where Edward was staring into space just outside the Professor's door, eyed by the ever-vigilant Mr Phelps.

"You alright?" Tom asked.

"I am not sure what is wrong with the Professor, but he does not seem to trust me anymore." Edward both looked and sounded glum.

"Surely not!" Tom exclaimed, feeling sorry for his friend. "I admit he is not exactly forthcoming, but he has a lot on his mind. Besides, it was Septimus he accused just now remember, not you."

Edward did not look convinced. "I am going for a walk," he grunted and stomped off towards the front door.

Tentatively, Tom reached out for the Map, but found to his relief that it was steady and behaving normally. He could hear the murmur of voices behind the Professor's closed door and leant towards it, wondering what the old man wanted with Charlie. Phelps looked up pointedly from his desk. Tom shrugged and moved away from the door, knowing he ought to get off home. It was evening now and the next day was a school day - the first day of term in fact. With a last glance at Phelps, he Walked to his bedroom, arriving back a little while before his parents came in from work, had a bath and then packed his schoolbag ready for the morning.

The next day, Tom opened the door to his new classroom at Parklands Comp and, not looking where he was heading, walked into the back of his old enemy, Kyle Rogers, who had been standing just inside the room. The red-faced bully spun round, eyes full of anger and left fist coming up to punch whoever dared to knock into him. Tom noticed that his right arm was still in a plaster cast and hanging in a sling: a souvenir of the last time they had met. When he saw Tom standing there, Kyle's eyes widened and he stepped backwards, the fist pulled hurriedly behind his back.

"Ah, Oakley, you alright mate?" the big lad said hesitantly.

Tom grunted and moved past him to where his best mates, Andy and James, were sitting at the back of the room.

Andy was shaking his head. "Tell you what, mate - I don't know what you've done to Rogers, but there are guys in our year who will pay for the secret."

"I really don't know why he treats me any differently to the rest of you," Tom lied and with a shrug glanced back at his erstwhile enemy.

Kyle Rogers was a thick-necked, broad-shouldered bully who had terrorised Tom as well as his friends, Andy, James and William, along with other boys in the class, but who suddenly seemed afraid of Tom. In fact Tom knew quite well what had changed Rogers' attitude towards him. When he had returned from his adventures at Tintagel at the end of last term, he had encountered Rogers and been forced to use his talents to avoid the boy's punches. Dodging out of the way he had Walked round Kyle, who in astonished disbelief had fallen, hit his elbow

115

on the curb and broken his arm.

Since that day, Kyle had avoided Tom and the two had not met over the summer holidays, although Tom had seen him once or twice in the street. The bigger lad had scuttled off down a side road, his eyes wide with fear. Now, he sat watching Tom warily from across the classroom. His puzzled expression suggested that he was still trying to work out Tom's secret: just how had he moved so fast and dodged the punches? More to the point; how was it that it was him and not Oakley who had ended up with a broken arm?

Reading the bully's chagrined expression with ease, Tom grinned. His train of thought was interrupted by a voice at his elbow.

"Excuse me, can I sit here?"

The voice belonged to a green-eyed girl with black hair that fell to her shoulders. She looked a little bit Mediterranean - like the Spanish girls Tom had seen the year before while on holiday. He thought her rather pretty - not that he would admit this to Andy or the others – and with studied nonchalance, he nodded vaguely and waved at the empty desk next to him.

"Sure, whatever. Help yourself," he mumbled, turning back to Andy who, he was annoyed to see, was winking at him.

"Hi there! My name is Andy," his friend said, smiling broadly at the new arrival. "Anything you need - anything at all - just ask me."

The girl glanced across at him and nodded, but Tom thought he saw a flash of irritation cross her face, although her reply was polite.

"I am ... pleased to meet you, Andy," she said. "I am Persephone. My family's not long moved here from London and we just opened a delicatessen on Market Street."

116

Her English was good but slightly accented. It sounded a little like the waitresses at the hotel that Tom and his family had stayed in a couple of years before in Cyprus.

"Persephone, eh? Nice name, I'm Andy ... oh, sorry, I've already told you that. This boy with the glasses is James and the redhead is William. Oh, and the chap next to you is Tom. So then, now we know each other, what are you doing Saturday?"

Embarrassed for his friend, Tom grimaced.

Persephone looked at Andy with an expression that suggested spending Saturday with him was definitely not on her list of things to do. "I have to help out in the shop," she muttered.

"Ah well, if you change your mind you know where to find me," Andy said with a grin.

The day plodded on through maths, geography and finally history. When the bell rang for home time, Tom and Andy drifted outside to find Persephone waiting there.

"I ... er, live close to you, Tom. Is there a short cut? Maybe we could walk along together and you can show me the way?"

"Erm ... yes ... sure," Tom muttered. Then it occurred to him that he had not told her where he lived so she must have taken the trouble to find out. Was she keen on him or something? The thought made him feel somewhat hot under the collar.

"He means that we would be delighted to see you home, Persephone," Andy said cheerfully.

"Oh, do you live near Tom as well?" the girl asked in a flat voice.

Andy nodded. "Yes, quite close," he answered and they started walking.

When they reached the end of Andy's road, he turned reluctantly away but then spun back to Persephone. "Would you like to come in for a drink?"

The girl shook her head. "No thank you, my house is this way, on past Tom's road."

"OK. See you tomorrow then, Tom," Andy said with a meaningful wink. As he turned away he gave Tom the thumbs up sign. Tom smiled weakly back. If Persephone really was keen on him then it was the first time a girl had ever paid him much interest and he felt suddenly nervous.

When he reached the next corner he stopped. "Er ... this is my street. Do you ... would you like a drink?" he asked.

"Yes, that would be nice."

"OK, well, just this way and I, er ...," he hesitated because he had just spotted Neoptolemas standing outside his front door. It had to be urgent; the Professor had never been to his home before.

"Wait a moment. It's my ... it's an old family friend. Let me see what he wants."

Feeling slightly irritated, Tom wandered up to the old man. "What is it, Prof? I am kind of busy," he said, then remembering who he was talking to, he stuttered, "Sorry Professor, that is, I ..."

The Professor smiled and turned to look at Persephone. "So I see. With your friend there? I must say she looks pretty. I won't be long though. It is a shame to keep the lady waiting and by the look of things she is the impatient sort. No doubt she wishes your attention. Ah, what it is to be young ..." he said wistfully.

Tom looked across at Persephone, who was standing just out of earshot about twenty feet away. She had a scowl on her face and was glaring at the Professor.

"Sorry, my dear!" Neoptolemas shouted, "I will not delay him long."

That did not seem to please Persephone because her eyes nar-

118

rowed even more.

"Well Prof, what is it?" Tom asked.

"The next fragment of the Crown has shown itself. It is the sword of Alexander the Great and was buried with him at his tomb in Egypt. The time window is for fifteen minutes between 6.30 and 6.45 on the 21st day of July in AD 365.

"Fine, when do we go?"

"Are you sure you can manage it?"

"Yes. I do not know what caused the problems before, but it seems to have settled again.

"Very well, if you're sure – come after school tomorrow. I want to get some more information. I will see you then. Tell me, Thomas, which is the way to the park? I fancy a walk."

"Over there." Tom pointed and stood for a moment, watching the old man wander away towards the park. He then turned back to apologise to Persephone, but much to his surprise, the girl was no longer there.

"Great," Tom thought, "the first girl to be interested in me and the flipping Professor turns up like a gooseberry!"

CHAPTER THIRTEEN
ALEX AGAIN

"We want Alex the Great's sword?" Septimus asked, as once more they were all gathered in the Professor's study. As well as Tom and his companions, the Professor had invited Dr Midas to attend the meeting and currently both men were poring over maps and documents on Neoptolemas' desk.

"That is correct, Mr Mason."

"Well then, I wish we had nicked it when we were in his camp a few months ago - would have saved all the bother now," Septimus commented, referring to the time that he, Tom and Mary had ended up getting captured by Greek soldiers in Ancient Persia.

The Professor shook his head. "I am afraid it would have done no good. Firstly, as you know, you have to remove the fragment, NOT the item it once was. That means being present in the exact time window the tablet specifies. Secondly, you met Alexander early in his campaigns to conquer Persia - some ten years before he died - and the truth is, we really have no way of knowing if it was the same sword."

"Indeed," Midas said, "it is likely in fact that the one he was buried with was a ceremonial blade made for the purpose. Quite often they were more elaborate than the functional weapons that a king would use in battle."

120

"So, what are we looking for?" Edward asked in a stiff voice. Tom glanced at him. He still seemed upset and the expression on his face when he looked at the Professor was rather cold, whilst when he regarded Dr Midas it was downright unfriendly. However, old habits die hard and the army officer was obviously trying to bury his feelings and looking to obey orders.

As before, the Professor seemed oblivious to Edward's mood. "Here is a reconstruction of what it should look like." He passed a black leather box across the desk.

Septimus took it and removed the lid. It turned out to be a carrying case containing a replica sword. The weapon had a short blade made from iron and engraved with an ornate inscription in gold leaf. The hilt was of bone and the gold-plated pommel was cast in the shape of a lion's head.

"We don't really know exactly what the sword looked like, but the Greeks used these short stabbing weapons called hoplites or Trojan swords, rather like the Roman gladius," Midas commented. "It seems likely that the weapon Alexander was buried with would have been more elaborate and some sort of decorative pommel is reasonable to assume."

"Very well," Edward commented as he in turn examined the blade and then passed it to Mary, "but where must we go to retrieve it?"

Mary took it from him gingerly and holding it at arm's length, studied it carefully, a mixture of awe and fear apparent on her tense face.

The Professor gestured at the pile of books and papers on his desk. "The tomb of Alexander is lost to history - although his body is thought to be in a church in Venice, while his sarcophagus remains in Egypt. In ancient times, Alexander was worshipped as a god and his tomb was a temple. We have records

121

here of what it was supposed to have looked like. There was a huge walled enclosure with impressive gates at the four compass points. It lay at the heart of the city of Alexandria, right next to the palace. The temple was thought to have possessed a pyramid-like roof over a colonnaded ground floor. Inside - probably below ground level and accessible via a staircase - was the actual chamber of the sarcophagus."

Neoptolemas held up a drawing and they each craned their necks to take a look. Tom noticed that even Charlie was attentive, so maybe the frightening experience on the Hindenburg had persuaded him the Professor's lectures were worth listening to. The image was a pen and ink sketch, showing a huge rectangular block of stone with letters engraved all around the sides.

"Originally the body of the King, dressed in his armour and with his sword by his side, was placed in a gold inner coffin that was moulded to fit his features. From all accounts, one of the Ptolemaic kings of Egypt melted the coffin down to pay for his army and later the Emperor Caligula stole Alexander's breast plate to use in a play."

"The thieving so-and-so's!" Septimus said with mock horror.

Charlie snorted and nudged him in the ribs, "You wishing you had got there first, eh?"

"Behave!" Septimus mumbled. "So, Prof; Doc, how do we find the tomb?"

"We have a few clues here." Midas held up a map. "This is a reconstruction of the ancient street plan drawn by an engineer called Mahmoud Bey in around 1866. See how the modern features in 1866 and the ancient roads are both visible. Now, this line," Midas pointed at a black line on the map, "marks the location of the medieval city walls. They were built centuries after Alexander's death of course, but are believed to have followed the line of the old enclosure and indeed, a small portion of the wall - a part thought to have belonged to the original enclosure - still exists in a modern-day garden: the Gardens of Shallalat. Both they and the wall survive from our target date."

"So, we find the wall, go back to 365 BC and then explore the enclosure. Inside there should be the tomb. At sunrise there is a chance it will be quiet, so we sneak in and do the dirty and get away. Should be a piece of cake or ... as it's Alex's tomb ... a dollop of hummus!" Septimus laughed, clapping his hands together. Charlie, Edward and Tom rolled their eyes and groaned.

"Whatever is the matter, Professor?" asked Mary, who had obviously noticed something in the Professor's expression. "It wasn't that bad a joke ... or is there something else?"

Looking up from studying the map, Tom saw that the old man was biting his lip. "You are perceptive, Miss Brown. There is indeed a problem and it has nothing to do with hummus!"

"Of course there is," Charlie said dryly, "should have realised there would be."

"One of the reasons why the tomb was lost to history is that sunrise on the 21st day of July in AD 365 was the time of a devastating earthquake, which caused widespread destruction to the eastern Mediterranean. We believe that much of the city was destroyed by the earthquake or the subsequent tsunami. It took years for them to dig down and retrieve the sarcophagus and not long afterwards the Christian church managed to outlaw the worship of Alexander. The body and sarcophagus pop up here and there over the years BUT the city was rebuilt and the tomb was probably broken down to provide stones for the reconstruction. That is why we don't know where it is."

"So, you are saying we have to turn up in the middle of an earthquake?" Tom asked, exchanging a wry glance with Charlie.

123

In response, Dr Midas and the Professor both nodded.

"Excellent!" Septimus said. "What a coincidence."

"Actually, I don't think it is," the Professor said.

"Why?" Dr Midas asked. Looking confused, he turned to face the older man. They all stared in silence at the Professor, who pressed his fingertips together, his face taking on a thoughtful expression, as though considering the question before replying. From outside, Tom could hear the distant hum of traffic beyond the garden. He turned his head to look out of the French windows: it was a grey, blustery day and a flurry of rain splattered against the glass. The leaves on the cherry tree were just beginning to turn, heralding the end of summer. Feeling slightly depressed, he brought his wandering attention back to the room as the Professor started to speak.

"The Crown is an artefact of immense power. Capable of great destruction - it can change the very nature of existence. I think that its individual fragments are themselves able to exert power and maybe even the treasures they once were. I believe the energy released when they manifest can cause disaster, such as what happened with the Hindenburg and perhaps also this earthquake."

"That does strike me as an illogical leap of reasoning, Professor. After all, it was Lapace who fired that pistol shot at Mary," Edward pointed out.

"Oh, I know he did. But he was close to the fragment at the time and who knows what influence it might have had," the old man mused, looking not at Edward, but at Tom.

"Well, whatever the cause it's time to go, I think," Tom said, feeling uncomfortable under the Professor's gaze. Was there something on the old man's mind - and if so, what?

"Can I enquire if Dr Midas is staying with you here?" Edward asked.

"Why do you ask?" The doctor stared at Edward, his eyebrow raised in query.

Edward shrugged. "Just wondering, that is all. These are dangerous times."

"You be about your task, Lieutenant, and let me concern myself with the doctor's safety," Neoptolemas said curtly.

Edward's face flushed as though he had been struck. "Very well, sir," he replied, turning away.

"You feel up to this, Tommy boy?" Septimus asked, placing a hand on Tom's arm.

Still puzzling over the Professor's cursory treatment of Edward, Tom nodded. "Yes, I'm fine. Felt a little dizzy first thing, but I have been fine all day in fact. Let's go." He held out his hands for them all to hold on to and reached out in his mind for the Map.

Tom took them first to the modern city of Alexandria. They appeared in the middle of the Gardens of Shallalat, which looked well maintained and orderly. Mown lawns lay between gravel walkways; neatly trimmed bushes and palm trees swayed gently in a breeze that carried the hint of sea air and gave welcome relief from the stultifying (did you mean to use stifling?) heat. Overhead the sky was devoid of clouds and the afternoon sun beat down mercilessly on their heads. Beyond the trees and bushes, blocks of flats rose skyward bearing crowns of TV aerials and mobile phone masts that sprouted out of the roofs like a forest. Further back were exotic looking minarets rising from a dozen mosques, their domes glinting in the sunlight. All around the outside of the gardens was the almost musical cacophony of cars, trucks and scooters making their way, horns blaring, through the traffic of the city. The Shallalat Gardens were a

125

small sanctuary within the urban sprawl - as if a fragment of Eden had somehow survived here and now fought against the modern world outside.

"Is that the wall?" Charlie asked after a moment. To their left was a small lake and beyond it, what looked like part of a ruined medieval castle. It was a stone tower about forty feet high, with crenellated battlements at the top, partially overgrown by the branches and leaves of a tree that emerged from somewhere within.

"I guess so - let's go," said Septimus, leading the way as they circled the lake to approach the tower.

"What do we do now? Do we stand next to it and move back in time?" Edward asked.

Septimus frowned. "There is the earthquake to worry about. If we appear when it is happening, we do not know where will be safe."

"We do know the tower survived though, do we not?" Mary pointed out.

"Yes, indeed. Good point, Mary. Maybe then, we go inside and find a way up to the roof."

Low down on one side of the ruins they found a doorway leading into a dark passage, giving access to the tower's interior. Above the opening was a notice in Arabic. Beneath it, written in English were the words: 'NO ENTRY; DANGER!'

Ignoring the sign, Septimus led the way and they filed in after him. Another archway leading off the passage opened into an almost pitch black room. Blinded after the bright sunlight, Tom could not see a thing and was relieved to hear the faint rattling of a box of matches. There was a sudden flare of light as Septimus struck a match and held the flame aloft, then swore as it burned his fingers.

"There, I see steps," Edward said, pointing at the corner of the room. Just before the match spluttered out and they were plunged back into darkness, they saw an ancient set of steps running around the interior of a stairwell, set into the tower wall.

Tom had a sudden thought and pulled out his iPod. The light from the screen cast an eerie glow around the tower's interior, but it was enough to guide them to the stairs. They proceeded to climb, hanging on to the crumbling masonry and placing their feet with care, emerging blinking into the bright daylight outside to find they were now behind the battlements, looking down on the lake.

"OK then," said Septimus, "back we go."

They all gathered around Tom, who closed his eyes and brought the Clock into his mind. Relieved to find it was behaving normally he Walked them back to 6.20 a.m. on 21st July 365 AD.

As they appeared, the city of Alexandria still lay around them, but it was utterly different to the one they had left behind. To begin with, the tower upon which they stood was now part of a long line of fortifications. High stone walls extended away in both directions to the north and south, running for about a hundred yards and then turning westward. From their vantage point they could see that the bulk of the city was made up of low rise, single- and double-storey clay houses all painted white; many had rooftop gardens. Between the houses, washing lines were suspended - mostly empty this early in the day. After the noise of twenty-first century traffic, the silence was weird.

"Gosh," Edward said, pointing northwards, "look at that!"

They followed his gaze: just north of the wall on which they stood, a palace lay amidst its own gardens - a spectacular building of many domes and towers - but it was not this to which the

lieutenant pointed. Beyond the palace lay the harbour of Alexandria, shielded from the sea by two breakwaters that reached
out like a pair of hands to envelope the crystal blue anchorage.

"Wow!" Tom murmured, for standing on the western tide
break, a huge tower loomed over the city. In terms of its size, it
was similar to the skyscrapers of twenty-first century New York.
Now that he thought about it, this was not such a bad comparison because it looked a little like the Empire State Building, with
a wide base and a narrow tower on top. At the very pinnacle of
the tower there was a sudden flash as a beam of light shot out in
an arc across the sea.

"That is the Pharos Lighthouse," Septimus said, in a tone of
quiet respect, "one of the seven wonders of the ancient world. It
is already some five hundred years old and does in fact survive
the earthquake to stand for another thousand years." He turned
to Tom and winked, "There you go, Tommy boy ... see all the
interesting places I bring you to!"

Tom nodded and stared in awe for a moment. Striking as it
was, however, it was not the lighthouse they were here to see.
Tom wrenched his gaze away and turned to the south west,
where another impressive sight presented itself.

The city wall extended to form a huge enclosure, about three
hundred paces from north to south and three times that from
west to east. Intermittently, gates bisected the wall and a criss-
cross of roads met in the large open space. Towards the eastern
end - near where they stood - was unmistakably the building
they had come to visit. It was as Midas and the Professor had
described it, with a pyramid roof and pillars around the outside.
Shading his eyes, Tom could see an entrance on the eastern side.

At that moment, without warning, he felt a faint vibration
in the stones under his feet. The shaking grew stronger, then

stronger still. There was an ominous rumbling from beneath the ground and suddenly the tower on which they stood seemed to leap about a foot into the air.

With a cry of alarm, Tom stepped over to grab hold of a pair of tooth-like crenels projecting up from the battlements. Mary screamed as she tumbled towards the open stairwell and Edward launched himself forward to seize her hands and pull her back up.

"Oops! Here it comes. Hang on everyone," Septimus yelled, grabbing hold of Charlie, who was teetering and about to fall.

Adjusting his grip on the two crenels, Tom held on tightly and peeked over the parapet between them. The city around the enclosure had suddenly come to life: people were emerging and rubbing at bleary eyes as they stumbled out onto rooftops to stand and stare, their confusion and fear apparent even from this distance. Another huge rumble emanated from deep under the earth and the tower started shaking violently back and forth, chips of masonry flying off the battlements in a cloud of stinging dust. Tom saw a huge crack appear in the side of a house nearby and heard terrified screams as it caved in, sending the family who had huddled together on the roof tumbling into the rubble. He had no time to see if they survived because at that moment Charlie shouted a warning and gestured wildly towards the lighthouse.

Beyond it, the calm waters of the Mediterranean had been stirred by the vast force of the earthquake beneath the ocean floor and now rose up in a massive tidal wave, some thirty feet high. A tsunami, with all the force and wrath of the sea behind it, rolled towards them. Even from this distance Tom could hear it roaring and thundering, like a herd of stampeding cattle or a charging regiment of cavalry – only more so. His heart thumping like a sledgehammer, he stared at it in morbid fascination as with effortless ease the water demolished everything in its path. Beneath his feet the ground jumped again.

"Hold on tight everyone," Septimus yelled, "this is going to be quite a ride!"

CHAPTER FOURTEEN
EARTHQUAKE

The light on top of the Pharos tower swayed this way and that as the earthquake shook the foundations of the lighthouse. The huge wave of water rushing in from the sea smashed against it and then surged around the ancient structure. Onward the wave came, crashing down onto the harbour with an ear-shattering boom. Ships at anchor were lifted high up into the sky and then tossed and spun around as if the sea was a juggler performing his act.

The wave rushed on inland, breaching the harbour walls and flooding the ancient city with seawater. Watching in helpless awe, Tom saw the crew of one fishing boat clinging desperately to their mast as it was thrown skyward. It came hurtling down to smash onto a roof top less than a hundred yards away. Amazingly the fishermen appeared to have survived their airborne adventure, but remained latched onto the mast as if not quite believing what had happened to them. The sea finally receded leaving no fewer than twenty ships similarly marooned, many with crew still in them now being rescued by the inhabitants of the houses on which they had landed.

Tom was just thinking that perhaps the earthquake had done its worst when there was another huge heave in the ground and the tower groaned again. Taken by surprise, he was thrown off

131

the battlement he was clinging to and hurtled straight into Charlie. In a tangle of limbs, the two of them rolled along the tower, crying out in terror as they scrabbled and clawed at the crumbling masonry, slid to the edge and tumbled over. Still entangled, they fell down onto the wall just beyond it. Then, with a crunch, the wall itself toppled over and disintegrated in a shower of stones and timber.

Desperately seizing hold of Charlie's ankle, Tom tried to Walk, but as he reached out for the Map he found the earthquake was affecting even that. It was moving erratically about so that he found it hard to pinpoint a position and when they materialised, although he had actually got them inside the enclosure, they were a terrifying ten feet above the ground. Before they had time to scream, they landed with a sickening bump in an ornamental flower bed, the soft earth and a large bush breaking their fall.

Tom coughed and choked as he tried to clear his lungs of the dust he had breathed in. Lying in a daze, he could hear the rumbling crash of collapsing buildings, the screams and cries of people trapped by rubble, and yet all around him the enclosure itself was strangely quiet and the ground, at least for the moment, had stopped shaking. Coming fully to his senses, he rolled over to look at Charlie, who lay motionless at his side. Tom gasped as he saw blood trickling down the sailor's face from a gash on his temple.

"Charlie!" He shook his friend's shoulder, relieved when, with a groan, Charlie opened his eyes, blinked and then sat up.

"Ouch!" he said, probing the wound with his fingertips, "that hurt."

"You OK?"

"I think so, but I took a whack from a falling stone I reckon." Charlie peered around. "Where are we exactly?"

132

"Erm ... somewhere in the enclosure." Tom looked up and gaped. Amazingly they had landed only fifty paces away from their objective. He nudged Charlie. "Look, over there; Alexander's tomb."

"That's handy." Charlie looked to where Tom pointed. "We can just stroll across, find the sword and get the hell out of here!"

"No, we can't."

"Why not?"

Not replying but instead, gesturing that Charlie should follow him, Tom crawled between some of the bushes until they were only about ten yards from the Tomb and near the edge of the shrubbery. He carefully bent one branch so they had a clear view of the entrance.

"Look again, Charlie. I caught a glimpse of these guys when we fell."

"Ah, I see what you mean," said Charlie, shading his eyes to peer at the tomb.

Six soldiers stood guarding the entrance, their heads turning this way and that as the noises of the earthquake and the screams of the Alexandrians came to them. One of them twisted around and gazed in their direction. Tom hunkered back down behind the bush and tugged at Charlie's sleeve. "Keep down. They'll be on the lookout for looters."

Tom eyed the soldiers, glad that he and Charlie were at least partially concealed by the low growing leafy shrubs in the border. The guards, looking ominously burly and battle fit, wore Roman legionnaire-style, segmented metal armour and helmets. Each man was armed with a spear and equipped with a large, blue-painted oval shield.

"Can't you just Walk us past them?" Charlie asked.

Tom shook his head. "No." He had already thought of that,

133

but he dare not just appear blindly inside the tomb. With no plan of the interior, he and Charlie could easily materialise inside a column! As he pondered what to do, a group of people came into their line of vision.

"Hang on a minute!" Charlie exclaimed. "What are *they* doing here?"

Screwing up his eyes, Tom gasped. There, walking bold as brass right up to the guards were Rolf Lapace, Orme and Jez, and another four men Tom had not seen before. Each of them had tossed a cloak around them to disguise their modern dress, although Tom could see trainers or boots peaking out beneath them. Lapace stepped forward and in a loud voice addressed the guards. *"Recedite, plebes! Gero rem imperialem."*

"What did he say?" Charlie asked.

"I don't know..." Tom started to say and then heard the sound of a branch snapping in the undergrowth behind them. His stomach clenched in fear as he swung round then he let out a deep breath as he saw Septimus, Edward and Mary, squirming along the ground towards them, their faces registering relief as they saw Tom was unharmed.

Septimus crouched down next to him. "We thought you two were a gonner when you disappeared like that, boyo," he murmured.

Mary, catching sight of Charlie's bleeding face, gasped and crawled on past Tom, rummaging in the pocket of her jeans for a handkerchief to stop the blood dripping.

They all froze as Lapace's voice shouted out again, *"Recedite, plebes! Gero rem imperialem."*

"Is that Latin? What's he saying?" Tom hissed.

"'Stand aside plebeians! I am on Imperial business," Edward translated and they all stared at him.

134

"Benefits of a public school education in the 1870s," he muttered with a shrug, "they concentrated on the Classics in my day ..."

"Hush," Septimus said. "Listen."

The guards were looking at each other and then suspiciously at Lapace. All took up battle stance, shields up, spears held forward at the ready.

"Etiam quod ego sum deus Jupiter," one of the guards shouted back; their officer, Tom assumed.

Edward snorted with laughter. "Ah, it seems the guards do not believe Mr Lapace. That one just said, 'Yes, and I am the God Jupiter!'"

The laughter died in his throat as Lapace shrugged off his cloak. His companions all did likewise. As the cloaks fell to the ground, Tom could see that Lapace and his men were armed with long, heavy looking pistols. No, not pistols; they were more like rifles. In fact they looked exactly like the tranquilizer guns he had seen on a TV programme about zoos: the sort hunters or vets use to capture, but not kill, animals.

Lapace smiled, lifted up his weapon, took casual aim and fired. The officer jumped back, dropped his shield and clapped a hand to his neck, blood trickling out between his fingers.

"That's a dart gun," Septimus breathed (whispered) as the officer shouted out something incoherent and then collapsed. "Lapace must've tipped the bolt with a knockout drug – hopefully not poison!"

Tom nodded: it was dangerous for Walkers to change the future; if Lapace or his men killed any of the guards it could have far-reaching effects – hence the use of darts rather than bullets. Tom wondered idly why Lapace had not done the same thing on the Hindenburg. Maybe the shock of realising his shot could have caused the disaster had prompted this more cautious approach today.

As their officer fell there was the briefest pause and then with an outraged roar the other guards attacked, levelling their spears and charging. Lapace's companions fired their weapons, but this time the guards were prepared and raised their shields so that the darts bounced harmlessly off them. Stabbing with their spears, they rushed Lapace and his men, pushing them back, but the guards were outnumbered and clearly frightened by the strange appearance of their foe, and as Tom watched they began to falter.

"Now's our chance, while they're all distracted," Septimus said, scuttling forward and waving at Tom and the others. "Come on, let's go."

He led them at a run towards the tomb and past the skirmishing men. They had almost reached the entrance when Septimus suddenly halted and swore.

"What is it?" Tom asked and peered past the Welshman.

There, blocking the doorway to the vault, were four men all dressed in identical grey lounge suits and ties, and each wearing a similar pair of dark sunglasses. They looked peculiarly out of place, akin to a group of businessmen, except that they stood menacingly side by side, more like the front row of a rugby scrum - and just as intimidating. Tom recognised the uniform: he had come up against men like these before. They seemed removed from the ongoing tragedy of the earthquake. The whole scene was completely surreal, thought Tom, who could hear distant sounds of terror and confusion from beyond the enclosure: horses neighing; the shouts and cries of local citizens and the desperate pleas of those who were trapped beneath collapsed buildings.

Glancing behind he saw that the fight had finished: all the guards had been beaten unconscious or lay groaning and holding broken limbs. One of Lapace's men was bleeding from a gash down his arm and another was bandaging him up. The other five, apparently unharmed, had roped the defeated guards securely together and were now stomping towards Tom and his friends, who were caught between Lapace's men and the row of suits.

Rolf Lapace strode forward, "Septimus, fancy seeing you," he smirked. "I will take it from here, mate. That sword is mine."

"Be my guest, Rolf old chap, but you might have to talk to those fellows first," Septimus pointed at the suits.

Lapace peered towards the entrance and then scowled, "Directorate men; here? Damn; what do they want?"

"Same thing we do, I would say," the Welshman answered.

For a moment they stood and considered the men in suits: the men of the Directorate - created to preserve the balance between parallel worlds. Earlier in the year, when Captain Redfeld, an evil officer from the Twisted Reality, had tried to invade Earth, the leader of the Directorate – a man of enormous power, known to Walkers as the 'Custodian' - had helped Tom defeat him. In doing so, the Custodian had made it clear that his sole concern was maintaining stability; he was not necessarily on Tom's side and might one day act against him; that in fact they might become enemies. Had that day already arrived, Tom wondered?

"Where is the Custodian?" Tom shouted out the question.

The men in suits did not reply but just stared blankly back, their faces devoid of emotion.

"Let us pass!" Tom ordered but there was still no response. Then the nearest of the grey-suited men shook his head and held up one hand, palm outwards.

"They have put up a wall to stop us Walking," Mary observed, tilting her head over on one side. "Why don't we just leave? If

137

the Directorate has the fragment won't it be alright?"

Septimus shook his head. "We don't know that for certain. We don't yet know enough about who is after the Crown and why," he added peering at Lapace. "The Professor wants the fragment and these guys are in the way so we have to go get it."

Tom's heart sank: they could not just Walk past the men in suits and anyway, given the darkness in the room beyond the door, he was still hesitant about materialising there. No, it was clear that somehow, they had to get past the Directorate by some other means.

"Well now," Lapace muttered, turning to look at Septimus, "it seems that we have a common obstacle in our way. Can we talk for a moment?"

"Do you expect us to trust you?" Edward retorted. "Last time we met you shot at Mary."

Lapace looked slightly embarrassed. "Yes, I am very sorry about that. I don't know what came over me. I only meant to threaten her with the gun, but it just seemed to go off."

Edward snorted, "I find that hard to believe."

"It's possible he speaks the truth," Mary said. "The Professor did say that the fragments might influence people and places."

Clearly unconvinced by the explanation, Edward frowned.

"There we are then," Lapace said. "I am glad we sorted that out. Now then, Septimus, shall we have that chat?"

Septimus bit his lip, seemed to consider refusal but finally nodded and followed Lapace off to one side.

Whilst they were talking, Tom turned to look at the enclosing wall that ran around the tomb. He could see at once that the earthquake had left huge gaps in it where weaker parts had tumbled over. Under his feet, he could feel another series of rumbles: gentler but still insistent and anxiously he inspected the tomb. According to the Professor and Dr Midas, Alexander's tomb was destroyed in this earthquake: some time in the next few minutes in fact. He wondered how long they had before the Crown of Knossos manifested and Alexander's sword was replaced by the fragment. Would that be before or after the temple's destruction? The Directorate men still stood like statues across the entrance. Barely discernible, the frozen wall shimmered faintly behind them.

Tom checked his contact with the Clock and found that now the intensity of the earthquake had died back a little he had control again over the Flow of Time. Over half an hour had passed since sunrise. In the next quarter of an hour the sword would become the fragment. Things were getting increasingly urgent and they had to make a move. He glanced across to where Septimus and Lapace were deep in conversation. Lapace was gesturing at the tomb and talking animatedly, whilst Septimus stood with his arms crossed and an expression like thunder on his face.

"What do you think they are discussing," Edward asked, ignoring the shattered walls and studying Septimus and Lapace.

"I imagine they are agreeing a deal," Tom suggested.

Edward grunted. "That is what I am afraid of."

A moment later Lapace and Septimus came back. "We have agreed to co-operate in getting to the sword," the Welshman told them with an apologetic grin.

"There is but one sword, Mr Mason. We cannot share it," Mary pointed out. Septimus did not answer and it was Lapace who responded.

"You are correct, lass. Whoever reaches the sword first can take it, but we will work together to get past the Directorate. Then," he added with a wink at Septimus, "it's every man ... or lady ... for themselves."

"Who are you working for, Lapace?" Tom demanded suddenly. "Who wants to get their hands on the fragments and what's in it for you?"

Lapace stared at Tom for a second then smirked at Septimus. "Can't you keep the young whippersnapper in his place?"

"Shut up Rolf." Septimus scowled at him. "Leave the boy alone." He shook his head at Tom. "Now is not the time, Tommy boy."

He and Lapace stood side by side facing the open doorway and the sombre guard of men in suits. Lapace's men moved to his side. Edward shrugged and wandered over with Charlie to stand next to Septimus. Mary and Tom held back for the moment; Tom, still bristling with anger, glowered at Lapace's back.

"Charge!" shouted Septimus and they surged forward towards the opening. The men in suits spread out as they awaited the attack, their movements slow and purposeful. As far as Tom could tell, none of them was armed.

Jez reached the 'suits' first and swung his enormous fist. As he connected with a suit's jaw, Jez gave a cry of agony and rolled away clutching his hand, which Tom could see was now twisted and deformed as though all his fingers were broken. What sort of men were these whose faces were like steel? More to the point, why were they here? Presumably because the Crown of Knossos threatened to upset the balance between this and other worlds, but surely the Custodian must know that Neoptolemas and the Institute were the good guys in all this? Was Lapace working for the Black Robes or perhaps someone in the Twisted Reality? Puzzled, his brain working overtime, Tom waited to see what would happen.

The rest of Lapace's mercenaries, Septimus, Charlie and Edward now reached their opponents, one of whom punched Orme on the chin. The big man's eyes crossed and he keeled over, out for the count. Charlie danced around his foe, making tiny Walks of just a foot here or inches there. The man he was fighting swung a fist wildly, but it failed to connect. Charlie jabbed a hand into where his opponent's kidneys should be then yelped and shook his hand, staring at the man in amazement. Watching, Tom concluded that the Directorate men's bodies were as steely as their faces. Clearly these were not normal beings and he began to wonder if they were some kind of sophisticated robot. Was the Custodian controlling them? If so, he had to be here somewhere – but where?

As the mercenaries started to go down, Septimus stared around at the carnage and shouted instructions, "Don't punch them and er ... don't get punched by them!"

"Very helpful," Edward said circling his man, but avoiding the fists, "but a bit late. Do you have any suggestions as to how to deal with these creatures?"

"Not immediately – no," Septimus replied, crouching low as a left hook swung over his head.

"Now I regret my humanitarian decision to bring tranquilizer pistols," Lapace muttered as he side-stepped a kick, adding, "oh, for a decent automatic pistol!"

"Oh well, in that case ..." Edward reached into his jacket and drew out his British Army revolver, cocked the hammer and then pulled the trigger. There was a loud 'Crack!' and the 'suit' recoiled, stumbled back a few feet and then came on again. Tom could see no blood, but the bullet had at least knocked the Directorate man back. "Try again!" he shouted, and keeping Mary behind him, moved closer to Edward.

The lieutenant did as he was told; there was another 'Crack!' and the suit was knocked down. He got up again but was staggering. 'Crack!' A third shot hammered into the suit, who this time stayed down.

There was now a gap in the Directorate line, but with the frozen wall they had erected behind them, no way through ... unless ... Tom turned to Mary about to ask if she could help, but she forestalled him.

"Yes, I can make us a door, but go quickly," she ordered, holding out her arms and frowning with concentration. "There; near the end."

Like a rip in gossamer a break appeared in the shimmer. Tom reached for Mary's hand and pulled her forward, seized Septimus' collar and Walked them both to the opening of the tomb.

From the entranceway they peered into the chamber beyond. Torches mounted on brackets and attached to the walls, which should have illuminated the chamber, had been extinguished, presumably by the priests the previous evening, and had not yet been re-lit. Nonetheless, the small amount of daylight penetrating the mausoleum cast a dim glow into the interior of the tomb and Tom could see elaborate hieroglyphics carved into the walls on all sides. Some of these depicted great battles; others, triumphant entries into cities; still more showed the construction of magnificent palaces and temples. It seemed that the life story of Alexander the Great was laid out for all to see in this, his final resting place. Impressive as it was, this was no time for sightseeing: they had only moments.

"There!" Septimus said, pointing downwards.

At first Tom could see nothing, but after a moment his eyes adjusted to the gloom and he could make out ...

"Stairs leading into the ground!" Mary announced voicing his thoughts.

"Yes," nodded Septimus, "Alex will be down there. Come on."

As they approached the stairs there was a faint rumble deep beneath their feet and the building around them shook violently, dust falling from the roof high above.

Tom checked the Clock and was alarmed to find that the sword would manifest as the fragment in less than three minutes. "Quickly, we don't have long!" he urged.

Septimus nodded and set off, hurtling down the stairs, his feet barely touching each step as he bounced along. Mary followed and Tom, pausing for a moment to catch his breath, brought up the rear. They came to a halt in a chamber about twenty feet by ten feet in size. Here there were lit torches in wall sconces, the flames sputtering and flickering, casting deep shadows.

In the exact centre of the vault stood a rectangular stone block like a sarcophagus, which Tom instantly recognised from the picture the Professor had shown them. Its sides were inscribed with more hieroglyphics as well as Greek script. The lid, however, had been removed and was leaning against the far wall next to a glass mummy case - the front half of one at least.

Leaning over the open Sarcophagus, looking down into it was ... the Custodian.

Tom felt a prickle of shock raising goosebumps on his arms: not because he was surprised to see the Custodian standing there - he had almost expected it - but because even though he knew the old man was identical to Professor Neoptolemas and knew why, the sight of him was still uncanny.

At the sound of them emerging from the stairway, the Custodian looked up and studied them for a moment. Then, he inclined his head in recognition.

"Thomas Oakley and companions I see."

Tom moved past Septimus and now he too could look down into the sarcophagus. He gave a little gasp as he saw the corpse

143

that lay there. The body had been mummified so that many of his features were preserved. When Tom had met Alexander in his camp as he prepared to conquer Persia, it was more than a decade before he died. Nevertheless, Tom recognised the King's face the moment he saw it. The body wore a leather and bronze breastplate, which was contoured like the muscles of a man's chest - presumably though, not the one he was buried in if the stories about Caligula stealing it were correct. Fresh flowers were strewn across the corpse, showing that the priests who maintained the tomb tended daily to the remains of the man they still treated as a god.

Then, Tom saw the sword they had come to find, still seated in its sheath alongside the body. It seemed that the Custodian had not yet touched it. That in itself was a puzzle but as soon as he spotted the sword, he realised something else was not quite as he expected it to be. For the sword was just that - it remained a sword. It had not yet changed into the fragment of the Crown. Yet, according to the tablet it should by now already have transformed. Why had it not done so? Tom inched closer and put his hand on the edge of the sarcophagus. The Custodian made no attempt to prevent him - he merely stood, motionless, watching Tom intently.

Septimus was next to him now and Tom glanced at him and rolled his eyes towards the sword. The Welshman nodded: he had seen it too.

Then, quick as a flash, Septimus reached in and pulled the sword from its sheath. He nodded apologetically to the corpse. "Sorry about this, mate, but you did try and have the three of us executed!"

The Custodian still did nothing, other than watch them without comment.

Suddenly, the whole building began to shake again, but this time the tremors grew increasingly powerful. There was a crack and a lump of masonry fell from the roof and shattered on the ground next to Mary, who cried out in alarm.

Then she pointed towards the blade in Septimus' hand. Even while the shaking around them grew steadily more and more violent, the sword had started to glow and then the same screeching sound they had heard on the Hindenburg emanated from it. A moment later, with a final burst of light, the sword was no more and Septimus was now holding a curved section of the Crown of Knossos. Smiling at Tom, he raised the segment up high over his head and cheered. At that very moment of triumph, he seemed to freeze on the spot as if he was playing a game of musical statues and the tune had stopped.

Tom glanced around him. The first thing he noticed was that the room had stopped shaking and the sounds and the sensation of tremors had ceased entirely. Indeed there was no sound at all. He looked over at his companions. Mary was frozen in the act of bending over to examine her bloodstained ankle where a moment before a fragment of falling stone had scratched her, whilst Septimus was standing with the fragment still held aloft and his mouth open in the middle of a celebration that Tom could not hear. Something like this had happened before: at Tintagel.

Grimacing, he spun round to glare at the Custodian. "You did this," he accused.

"I did indeed," the Custodian agreed.

"Why?"

"Because I want the fragment also."

"Then why did you not just take it?"

"Because I am NOT a Walker, at least not in the way you and your companions are, Thomas. I exist outside of time, as do my

Directorate. We can go where and when we will, we can even, as you know and can see, freeze time, but we are not mere Walkers."

"So?"

"Apparently, as the Crown was created by a Walker then it will only manifest to a Walker. I too touched it but nothing happened, so I had to wait until one of you came down here."

"You assumed a lot then. We might never have got past your Men in Suits."

"Oh, I was sure you would."

"Why?"

"You will have to work that out yourself one day. But shall I give you a clue?"

When Tom said nothing, the Custodian continued speaking. "How is it that you are unaffected by the temporal stasis I have created?"

"The what?"

The Custodian frowned as if struggling to put a complex concept into simpler words. "Why can you move and the others cannot?"

Tom blinked. "I... I assumed it was like Tintagel. You permitted me to move."

The Custodian shook his head. "Neither here, nor there, did I do so."

"Then how can I?"

"When you have resolved these questions, you will be closer to discovering what you are and what you can really do."

Tom shrugged. "Well then, if I can move, I can take this," he said, reaching out to seize the fragment.

Before his fingers were able to close on the Crown, a sudden overwhelming wave of nausea and vertigo came on him and he closed his eyes and held on to the side of the sarcophagus.

"What is going on," Tom asked opening his eyes and looking at the Custodian.

The Custodian moved round and pulled the fragment out of Septimus' hand. "That's another question for you to ponder, Thomas. Goodbye for now," he said, and vanished.

As he did so the violent vibrations returned and his companions were suddenly moving again, as if someone had paused a DVD and had just pressed play again.

"I have it!" shouted Septimus; then he stopped and stared stupidly at his empty hand. "I did have it ... where's it gone," he asked glancing around.

Before Tom could reply, more fragments of stone tumbled down from the roof above, then there was a huge boom and a massive chunk of stone broke off from the ceiling, blocking the stairway behind them. They were trapped and by the terrified, wild expressions on Septimus' and Mary's faces, both his companions had realised this as well. Another tremor followed and now the last torch in the room was knocked to the ground and went out, plunging them into darkness.

A scream rose in Tom's throat. They were now in a pitch dark room, with the roof above them about to collapse burying them under thousands of tons of stone!

CHAPTER FIFTEEN
THE TOMB

There was total darkness in the vault. All around them the very earth shook; quite the most terrifying experience Tom could recall, even worse than the Hindenburg and made doubly so by being unable to see what was going on. He expected at any moment that the roof would collapse and crush them. Next to him there was a sudden flare as Septimus lit another match.

Barely illuminated by the weak, flickering flame, Tom could see a huge crack that had appeared in the roof right above them. The room gave another judder and the crack widened.

"Quick, get us out of here!" Septimus shrieked. Tom nodded, placed one trembling hand on each of his companions and reached out for the Map. When he made contact with it he felt a wave of nausea just like before and the room seemed to spin around him. The Map was there, but once again he did not seem to be able to control it.

"I can't, Septimus ... I mean I don't know what is going wrong, but the Map is all over the place. I don't know where we will end up."

The match sputtered out leaving them in total blackness again. Septimus lit another then said, "Well, boyo, I can't help thinking that anywhere would be better than here!"

Above them there was another deafening boom as masonry

from the upper level fell and landed on the vault ceiling which, unable to hold the weight, gave way under the strain. Suddenly the air above them was full of falling blocks of stone and dust.

"*Shield!*" shouted Mary, throwing up her arms to create an invisible dome of frozen time. The rocks fell down onto it and bounced away from them, but more stone fell and now five thousand tons of cracked, twisted masonry was heaped up on the wall that Mary had created. The effort required to hold the stone up began to tell on Mary. Tom could see the sweat pouring off her, soaking through her shirt.

"Please Tom," she grunted, "I cannot hold it for long."

"Come on Tommy," Septimus urged, "get us away from here. Anywhere will do!"

Tom tried again: reaching out to the Map he attempted to focus on one point - any point. Then he found a location: the stone tower in the gardens, which still stood as a ruin in Tom's day and from where they had Walked. 'Get there', he urged himself, 'get anywhere but here.'

"Walk! Walk now!" Tom shouted and they were gone, mercifully away from that death trap. They materialised not on top of the tower, but in a ditch at its base - a ditch full of rotting vegetables, dead rats and assorted refuse from the nearby houses, which Tom chose not to examine too closely. He really did not care. Above them the sun shone and once again they could breathe the fresh, if somewhat tainted air, all of them coughing as they cleared their lungs of the debris and dust of the vault.

"Well done, boyo," Septimus gasped, wrinkling his nose and clapping Tom on the back, "that was by the seat of your pants, eh?" He grinned weakly. "Well done you too, Mary, for saving our bacon yet again."

She smiled at him, but said only, "We must find Edward and Charlie."

149

Finally they dragged themselves to their feet and looked about them. Nearby, the wall around the enclosure had fallen over and they could see the temple a couple of hundred paces away. Rather, they could see what was left of it; the roof had caved in and as they watched, more pillars and segments of the walls toppled and fell into the heap of stone, throwing up a thick cloud of dust.

"Well, goodbye Alex, my lad," Septimus said and then turned to the others. "Phew, glad we got out of there! What happened in there, Tom? I mean, one minute the old man was there and I was holding the sword and the next, both it and he had vanished. How'd he do that without me seeing?"

"It was the same as at Tintagel; it's like he can just freeze time for the people around him and then when he starts it again, it is so seamless they don't know anything has happened."

"But not you, I'm guessing?"

"No, not me, but I don't know why."

Septimus gave him a searching look, but said no more. The devastated city of Alexandria had fallen strangely quiet, aside from the intermittent sounds of collapsing masonry. Above them a flock of geese flew honking across a cloudless sky and fleetingly Tom wondered what their birds-eye view must show. He shivered, remembering all too vividly the aftermath of the Haiti earthquake that he had seen on TV.

Slipping and squelching out of the ditch, trying to avoid the flyblown rubbish that festered in the heat, they clambered over the ruined enclosure wall and walked across the gardens towards the temple, where Lapace and his men were in discussion with Edward and Charlie. Of the Men in Suits, there was no sign and Tom assumed they had left with the Custodian. As they approached, it was obvious that an argument was going on.

"We have to try and rescue them!" Edward was saying, pointing a finger at the wreck of Alexander's tomb.

Lapace was shaking his head. "Look I am sorry, I really am ... but we have no idea what is down there. We could Walk into a pile of rubble. We don't even know if Septimus and the others are alive."

Septimus crept up behind Lapace and poked him in the back. "Oh, we are alive, mate. You won't win your bet that way!"

Lapace spun round and glared at Septimus. "Should have known you would get away, you old rogue!"

Edward rushed over to Mary, his expression a mixture of relief and concern. "Are you alright?"

"Yes, Edward, I am fine. Thank you for asking."

"Tommy and I are fine too, boyo," Septimus announced with a smile.

Edward glanced at him. "The Crown?" he asked.

Septimus shook his head. "I had it and then I didn't," he frowned. "I think it was ..."

"The Custodian has it," Tom interrupted.

"Blast!" Lapace swore. "My employer is not going to be happy."

"So then, who are you working for, Rolf?" Septimus asked.

Lapace tapped his nose with one finger. "Oh come now, Septimus, you don't expect me to divulge confidential information like that do you?"

"Then perhaps you would tell us how you knew to come here at this time?" the Welshman persisted.

Ignoring his former partner, Lapace strolled across to Charlie. "It's time we left, but think about what I said. If you want to know more, you have my number." So saying, he clicked his fingers at Jez, Orme and the other mercenaries, and they were gone.

151

Tom and his friends were left standing beside the rubble of Alexander's tomb, while behind them, the trussed guards were moaning in fear and struggling against the rope that held them. "What did he mean by that, Charlie?" Septimus asked.

The sailor flushed and looked down at his feet. It was Edward who spoke for him.

"Charlie seems to have impressed Lapace," he answered. "It seems your former partner has offered him a job."

"What! Surely you can't be thinking of joining them, Charlie? Not after he shot at Mary and damned near killed the lot of us on the Hindenburg." Quivering with outrage, Septimus scowled at Charlie, who merely shrugged.

"He said he is sorry about that ... he was not sure how it happened. He reckons the Crown was to blame. Besides, you used to work with him; he can't be that bad," he added in a mumble.

"Well, he pulled the trigger!" Tom retorted.

"That's what I said," Edward agreed. Beside him, Mary nodded, frowning.

Charlie did not answer, but his expression was thoughtful as he looked at Mary.

"Well," Septimus said after a long silence, "I think we should get back to the Professor and tell him the bad news about the Crown. Our second failed assignment: we are starting to look a bit like amateurs!"

"What about the guards?" Edward gestured with his thumb at the terrified soldiers. "They're in a sorry state. At least two of them ought to have treatment and who knows when the priests will come back to the temple with everything that's going on in Alexandria today."

"Or even if; yes, I suppose we should at least release them," the Welshman agreed. "Poor chaps probably think we're gods."

He pulled a pocket knife from his belt and flicking it open, strode towards the guards. They shrank back, shrieking and babbling in Latin. Septimus bent down and sawed through the rope. "There you are lads; you should be able to get yourselves free in a minute or two." He backed away, called over his shoulder, "OK Tom, time to go. Do you think you can manage it?"

Tom thought about this. The Map and the Clock were both clear in his mind once more and the disorientation he had experienced in the tomb had gone again, but it was beginning to worry him that these problems were repeatedly happening at random moments. Nevertheless it seemed that he was still able to transport them all, so he kept his fears to himself and just nodded in response.

They reappeared in Mr Phelps' office and before he could stop them, Septimus had stepped across to the study and yanked open the Professor's door. Something that he saw there clearly shocked him because he just stood in the doorway, staring open-mouthed into the room beyond. Tom craned over the Welsh-man's shoulder to see what he was looking at and gawped. Behind him, Edward let out an indignant gasp, for there in the Professor's study, sitting opposite Neoptolemas, was none other than the Custodian.

Like two peas in a pod, both old men had turned at the noise of the door opening and for a long moment no one spoke. Recovering from the shock, Tom was first to break the silence.

"What on earth is he doing here, Professor? We just came to tell you that the Custodian has taken the fragment and here he is, about to have tea with you!" Tom spat the words out.

"Calm yourself, Thomas, please. The Custodian was just about to explain why he intervened in my reality," the Professor replied, casting an icy glare at his double.

153

The Custodian turned an expressionless stare on the astonished Walkers bunched in the doorway and then glared back at the Professor.

"How very inconvenient, Neoptolemas," he muttered. "What I have to tell you, I cannot say in front of these mortals."

"These are my Institute. I trust them."

"That is irrelevant. Trust is of no importance. Dismiss them at once!"

The Professor frowned, but eventually turned away and glanced at the doorway. "Gentleman, er ... and lady, please excuse us for a moment." He looked at them over his spectacles and wrinkled his nose. "You might take the opportunity to clean yourselves up a bit. There is the distinct aroma of rotting vegetables about you – and that's not the worst of it."

"Professor!" Tom protested.

"Please Thomas, just give us a moment."

Tom shrugged and backing away, closed the door and walking past the indignant Mr Phelps, trailed along with everyone else to the library where he threw himself into an arm chair. As far as he was concerned, this was no time to be having a wash!

"There you go - I told you that the Professor was up to something. Now he is even talking to the Custodian rather than us," Edward observed.

"Edward, I know that it is frustrating and I am angry too," Tom said, frowning, "but it seems to me that you are taking this personally. Even more than the rest of us I mean. Is there any reason why?"

Edward blinked and looked nonplussed by the question. "I don't know what you mean."

"Oh come on, boyo. The last few days all you have done is mope around and complain about the Professor," Septimus ob-

154

served.

"Got to say, he has a point," Charlie added. Mary nodded. Edward pouted for a minute and then shrugged.

"Ah, you may be right. But I don't understand it. Up until a few days ago the Professor was happy to talk to me whenever I wanted and he would often ask me in to discuss this problem or that. All of a sudden he is now avoiding me and won't confide in me at all. In fact, he seems downright short with me. I find it ... frustrating; that is all. Something is on his mind ... something he is not telling us, I am certain of it."

Tom scratched his head. "You may be right."

"So then ... should we ..." Septimus started to say then stopped.

"Should we what?" Mary prompted.

"I was going to say 'snoop'," the Welshman said, looking faintly embarrassed.

"You mean spy on the Professor?" Edward was outraged.

"Hold on a minute. You were the one who was saying the Prof was up to something," Charlie pointed out.

"Well yes, but to spy on your superior is not exactly cricket is it?"

"What's it got to do with cricket?" Mary enquired, her brow creased in a puzzled frown.

"It's just a saying, Mary," Tom explained. "He means it's not British ... um, not very sporting," he added, seeing Mary's puzzlement had not diminished.

"Ah, like cheating, you mean?"

"Sort of," Tom nodded.

"Cricket or not, that's all well and good." Septimus smirked at the affronted lieutenant. "So you don't want to know what's being said in that room, then?"

"Of course I want to know." Edward conceded.

"So what is it going to be, yes or no?"

Edward's face twisted with indecision, finally taking on a expression of determination. "No. It is no. Whatever he is doing, I have to trust him. I won't have anything to do with spying on him," the lieutenant answered stiffly, standing almost to attention.

"Very well, suit yourself. What about everyone else?"

"I'm in," Charlie said immediately.

"Mary?"

"I do not trust that Custodian, and it would not be the first time I have listened at a keyhole to find out what my master was saying."

"Miss Brown, really!" Edward was shocked.

A slight flush of pink staining her cheeks, Mary shrugged. "Such things were commonplace amongst servants in my day, Edward."

"Mine too, but that does not mean you have to follow their example," he said primly.

Septimus laughed. "I must say, Mary, you have just risen a few notches in my estimation." He winked at her and then turned to Tom. "Well? What about you?"

Tom pondered the question. He did trust the Professor and was aware the old man would play games to achieve his aims. Earlier in the summer they had all thought he was betraying them to their enemy, Captain Redfeld, but in the end it turned out that Neoptolemas was actually only pretending to cut a deal with him in order to save Tom and the world from Redfeld's evil intentions. So ... yes, he trusted the old man. But then again, whenever the Custodian and his Directorate were involved, Tom felt more uncertain. The Professor's double usually had plans that involved Tom in some way and if that was the case now, Tom needed to know.

"Yes, I agree to snoop. But I don't think we should all go and listen at the keyhole. Let me do it on my own," Tom said.

Edward glowered at him, saying, "If you are doing this, I will have nothing to do with it," and he stalked out of the door.

"Blimey! Does he need to be so Victorian?" Septimus muttered after he had left, then he turned to Tom. "Good luck boyo," he smiled.

"Thanks." Tom nodded. He concentrated on the Professor's study and Walked to a spot just outside the French doors. The evening was still warm and the doors were open a couple of inches to allow air to circulate.

He crouched low and held his hand over his mouth to conceal his breathing, wishing he had washed after all; even he could now smell the whiff of Alexandrian refuse rising off his clothes. Hopefully it would not drift in to assault the Professor's sensitive nostrils. On the other side of the doors there was silence and for a moment Tom was afraid his arrival had been detected, but then he heard the Custodian speaking.

"What have you told your minions about the dangers inherent in the Crown?"

"I have told them that if the Cult of Knossos find and unite the fragments they will use it to fulfil their master's last wish: to destroy the universe," the Professor replied.

"So, you have not told them everything. You must fear as I do, that there is a risk that more than just the Crown survived. That maybe HE survived?"

The Professor did not reply. Tom had the distinct impression that he was nodding in response to that question. But now Tom's mind was full of the image of that man in the dream and the determination in his eyes. Knossos: a man it seemed whose

157

mind was set on nothing less than the destruction of everything. What had occurred in the moments after Tom had woken? What exactly had happened when the Crown shattered ... and what had followed? Was it possible that what the Custodian was saying had come to pass? Could Knossos have survived that monumental encounter with Titus? Tom shuddered, bringing his attention back to the two identical old men.

"So, you are also aware that the Crown has chosen the Vessel," the Custodian was saying.

Tom heard the Professor sigh. "I am."

"You know who it will be, don't you?"

"I sensed it on him, but he knows nothing."

"I suggest you keep a close eye on him."

"I know my job, Custodian, but tell me now about your involvement in this. Why exactly did you take that fragment?" the Professor asked, moving on to the offensive.

There was a brief pause. Tom could feel a cramp starting in his left foot, but dared not move. He tried to block it out and concentrate on what the Custodian was now saying.

"A few days ago I became aware that what we had feared had come to pass. Some form of the consciousness embedded within the Crown survived the Event and lingers on. I felt it reaching out, trying to find all the fragments. It must not be permitted to reunite, brother."

"I know that," the Professor answered tersely. "I have felt the same sensation and dreamt the same dreams. No doubt the Colonel has as well."

Tom tensed: so Colonel Heinrich Theilmann was in on this too. Tom had seen him in the Twisted Realty. He was the third man in the triumvirate. The Professor had explained to Tom that they had once been only one man, but in the cataclysmic 'Event' that had split the universe into parallel worlds they too had been split, which was why the three of them were identical. It seemed they had been having dreams as well – the same dreams of Titus, Xanthus and Knossos? As far as Tom knew, that had not happened before. He thought only he had dreams where his unconscious mind Walked into other people's minds. So why were the Professor and his doubles dreaming now? This did explain, perhaps, why the old man was so tense. If he thought Knossos lived on and there was an even greater threat to the stability of their worlds than he had let on about, it was no wonder he was worried. The implications were horrific and Tom had a(to?) struggle not to cry out. Shifting his position very slightly to alleviate the cramp, he strained his ears to listen.

In the Professor's study, the Custodian continued with his explanation. "So, I decided that the best course of action was to find one of the fragments myself. Now I have one, I will not intervene if you choose to go after the others."

"What would be the point if you have one fragment? The Crown cannot be formed without all its parts. In any event, one of the parts has already been taken. Are you behind that too?"

There was another pause and Tom almost felt the Custodian staring at the Professor as he pointedly ignored the question. "Come now, brother, you and I both know that even if not united with the other parts, they could individually be used to distort time. You are aware that they each have a potent temporal field?"

"I am," was the short reply.

"Besides," the Custodian added, "you must know that the fragments have another significance that is more pertinent to your little domestic issues. Issues that may soon be of paramount importance - perhaps even more important than this present crisis."

159

Another pause but this time Tom felt it was Neoptolemas who was staring.

"If that is so, why would I go through with this?"

"Because you and I both know that the day will come when we need a potentate to stand alongside us," the Custodian said. "I am curious - have you told him, yet?"

"Is one potential apocalypse not enough for you, Custodian? Like to get started early on the next one, do you?"

"It is not that far away, brother."

The Professor sighed again. "He is still young. Can we not give him a little while?"

Tom felt a chilling tingle pass down his spine and the hairs standing up on his neck, despite the warmth of the westering sun shining directly onto his back. Were they talking about him, or one of the others? And what did they mean by 'a potentate'? He wrinkled his brow trying to remember the meaning of the word: could only come up with 'emperor or ruler', which seemed oddly out of context.

A third pause, this one much longer than before. Tom could hear the distant rumble of traffic and the hooting of horns on the Bayswater Road as the rush hour got underway. Finally the Custodian answered.

"Very well, a little while ... yes a little while. But not forever: we don't have forever. You say he is young, but remember how it was before, brother. His youth will not save him when the time comes. Your little schoolboy must be strong ... or he and everyone else will perish."

CHAPTER SIXTEEN
REVELATIONS

Tom staggered away from the patio doors and stared unseeing across the garden. What was going on? What was the Professor playing at? How was it that Neoptolemas had mentioned none of this to any of them? What was that about Knossos maybe surviving and what was the Vessel? What had the Custodian said: if he was not strong he could die? Why would he die? What had the old man meant by a potentate, anyway?

His head reeling with questions to which there seemed no logical answers, Tom leant against the garden wall and then slid down it. In the middle of the garden he could see the sundial. The sun's shadow was laid across it, showing the time. Suddenly, from out of nowhere, the words of an old hymn came to him: a hymn that Septimus had once sung to him when they stood together on the battlefield of Isandlwana; Tom's first assignment for the Institute.

'Crown Him the Lord of years, the Potentate of time, Creator of the rolling spheres, ineffably sublime.'

Potentate: the Custodian had used that word. It meant something like all powerful master. Was he talking about me? Tom thought. Surely not, and yet he had said 'schoolboy', so who else could it be?

Almost as if she was standing beside him, he heard his mother's voice in his head. She had once caught him listening out-side his sister's bedroom door when her friend was staying over. 'Eavesdroppers seldom hear good of themselves, Tom,' she had said. He did not think today's scenario was quite what his mum had had in mind, but even so, he began to regret snooping on the Professor. 'Ignorance is bliss', his father always said and he was probably right.

Tom wrestled with the problem of what to do now: should he speak to the Professor? Or the others? In any event, he had to say something to them. He Walked reluctantly back to the library.

"Well?" Charlie asked after Tom had appeared in front of them.

Tom stared at him unsure what to say. "I er ...," he began and then stumbled to a halt, flinging himself down in the nearest chair.

They all stared at him expectantly.

"Well?" Charlie repeated.

Unwilling to relate everything he had heard - at least not yet - Tom chose his words carefully.

"The Professor and the Custodian were discussing his taking of Alexander's sword and what he was doing there. The Custodian said he was making sure the Crown can't be made whole again by taking a piece and keeping it safe. He told the Professor that he had no interest in the other parts."

"Do you believe him?" Septimus asked.

Tom considered the question. "Do you?"

"Oddly enough ... yes," Septimus nodded. "The Custodian is actually quite straightforward. He acts to maintain the sta-tus quo and the balance between the realities. In this case, that means preventing the reforming of the Crown. If it needs all the parts and he has one of them, then that is 'job done' in his eyes."

"Well then, isn't it 'job done' for us as well?" Charlie suggested. "I mean, as long as we keep the parts separate and can be sure they don't come together, we don't need to hold them all ..."

He stopped speaking as they heard the creak of a floorboard from over near the door. The Professor was standing there, with Edward beside him. Tom wondered how long he had been there and if the old man was aware Tom had been spying on him. Had Edward told on them, he wondered before immediately dismissing the thought. No, he may be stuffy and old-fashioned, but Edward was not a telltale. In any event, if the Professor did know, there was no indication in his manner. Nor did he look at Tom, but at Charlie, whom he now addressed.

"I am sorry, Mr Hawker, but it is not as simple as that. I take it you were speculating what would happen if we simply sat back and allowed the other fragments to be found by the Cult of Knossos, the Directorate, or the mercenaries, " he added, his gaze flicking across to Septimus and then returning to Charlie. "Well, I am not content to allow that to happen. Firstly, we don't know who the mercenaries are working for and secondly, we cannot be certain that any one fragment is safe even if held by the Custodian."

"So then, we go after the other parts, sir?" Edward asked as he came into the room and sat down at a table.

The Professor nodded.

"Oh well." Septimus sighed. "Maybe it will be third time lucky. I have to tell you that I am getting mightily fed up with always coming in second in this race. This time we get the fragment. Where are we going next?"

"I will tell you that in a day or two. The tablet has not yet revealed the location."

The Professor turned towards the door and then glanced back

at Tom. "Thomas, come with me if you please."

Tom felt a jolt as if his heart had just leapt into his throat. All eyes turned to him and he saw Mary turn her mouth down in a grimace of sympathy. Getting up from his chair, he meekly nodded his assent. It felt like being hauled up in front of the headmaster at school.

Edward jumped to his feet, too. "Professor, may I come and speak to you?"

Without looking at him, Neoptolemas just shook his head. "Not at present, Lieutenant. Maybe later."

Edward scowled. "Professor, I must tell you something."

"I said not now."

The lieutenant persevered nonetheless. "But sir, please, it's about Dr Midas. I *have* to talk to you about him."

"No!"

"Damn it, Professor, this is urgent. I think Midas is a spy!"

The Professor spun around and glared at Edward. "You forget yourself!" he snapped. "What is more, young man, you are mistaken. I have the utmost confidence in Dr Midas. I will hear nothing to the contrary. Come Thomas!"

Tom followed the old man out of the room and before Edward could say another word the library door shut behind them. The Professor marched surprisingly briskly along the corridor, nodded at Mr Phelps and entered his study, closing the door as soon as Tom had followed him in.

"What was that all about, Prof?"

"Professor, Thomas! Just because Septimus is ill mannered, there is no need for you to emulate him," the old man snapped.

"Yes, yes, Professor." Tom waved his hands in agitation. "But Edward was trying to tell you something and you just cut him off. Don't you think he has a point about Dr Midas? Isn't it pos-

164

sible he might be a spy?"

The Professor sat back heavily in his chair, sighed and removed his glasses, which he tossed down on the desk next to the tablet.

"Thomas ... I am going to tell you something and you must promise not to tell anyone else. Not yet, anyway."

Tom shrugged. "OK, I guess."

"Is that a promise?"

"Yes Professor - I promise," Tom repeated.

"I believe the good lieutenant is actually completely correct that Dr Midas is a spy, although perhaps not in the way that he suspects."

"What?" Tom's mouth dropped open. "So why did you just cut him off like that?"

The Professor hesitated for a moment, picked up his glasses, polished them and popped them back on his nose before looking at Tom over the top of them.

"As I said, it may not be quite as straightforward as you might believe. You see, I don't think Midas is playing us false. That is to say, I think he is just what he appears to be - an archaeologist with a puzzle to solve."

What did the old man mean? Tom was now bewildered and his confusion must have shown on his face.

"I am sorry, Thomas; I am being obscure again aren't I?"

"You have got that right!"

"Someone paid for Dr Midas' expedition, this mysterious benefactor. The Black Robes most likely, possibly someone else. So, you see, because I need to find out who the doctor is actually working for, I decided to keep him close. As for Edward, the reason why I 'cut him off' - as you put it - is I that cannot trust Mr Dyson if he were to get too close to Dr Midas."

Tom blinked. Had Neoptolemas really just said that? "What? Edward – nah." He rested his hands flat on the desk, leaned forward and shook his head. "Not in a million years."

"Calm down, Thomas," the Professor held up his hands. "Oh don't misunderstand me, I'm not suggesting Edward would betray us deliberately, he is, without a doubt, the most honest man I know."

"Well then, what *are* you saying?"

"It is precisely because Edward is so honest that he cannot be the one to investigate Dr Midas. I want the doctor and whoever he is working for – even if he is unaware of it - to believe that I trust him completely, at least until I find out just who is behind all of this."

"But surely Edward could pretend ..." he stumbled to a halt, grimacing as he recalled how Edward had reacted to the thought of spying on the Professor. Maybe the old man had a point. Reluctantly he nodded.

"Exactly. Very well, now we have dealt with that issue, perhaps we can move on to matters you overheard when eavesdropping on the Custodian and me."

Tom's mouth dropped open. Struggling to compose himself, he cleared his throat. "Ah, yes ... sorry about that. It is just that you have been avoiding everyone - and particularly Edward - and we wanted to find out what was going on."

"I disapprove, Thomas, but I can't say I'm surprised. So then, you overheard some of our conversation. Do you have anything to ask?"

Tom nodded. "Well firstly I have to ask about what the Custodian meant when he was talking about the Vessel?"

"At present, the Crown's intelligence is only in spiritual form. If it is to manifest in physical form it needs a host body to dominate," the Professor answered.

"A host body - you mean a human?"

"That is correct."

"So, what happens to the Vessel?"

"We don't know for certain. However, if the Crown reforms, its intelligence will inhabit the Vessel's body and it is possible that the Vessel's soul will be evicted and perish."

Tom shuddered. "That's awful."

"Indeed."

"So, who is the Vessel?"

The Professor arched his fingertips, not meeting Tom's gaze. "I would rather not say. I am not yet certain."

That did not ring true. Tom was certain the old man was keeping something from him, but that was not exactly new so he let it pass - for the moment.

"So, we don't let the Crown reform," Tom said.

The Professor shook his head. "No, we do not."

Tom got up and paced around the room. It was getting dark outside, the street lights had come on and were casting an orange glow into the garden. He turned back and asked the other question that was on his mind.

"What about me? The Custodian spoke of me being a potentate. What is that?"

"What makes you think he was talking about you?" The Professor half stood, leaned across to his desk lamp and switched it on so that for a moment his face was lit from below, his features ghoulishly shadowed until he sat down again.

"Because to the best of my knowledge I am the only schoolboy currently in the employ of the Institute," Tom snapped.

"Ah – you heard that, did you?" The old man sighed. "Then I must tell you that at any given time there are Walkers who transcend the normal talents that our kind posses. They rise above the others and manifest powers that are almost godlike. Potentates have it in them to dominate their world. Their powers are so awesome they could be corrupted to terrible effect."

Tom thought about that. "Like Thielmann?"

"Yes, like him. The victory of the Nazis over the allies in the Twisted Reality was due in no small part to his actions. In his reality, he is totally dominant."

"Then, if he is a potentate, Professor, so are you?"

The Professor nodded. "I am, as is the Custodian - and you are well aware of the powers he has."

"Then you each have the same strengths and powers?"

The Professor shook his head. "Not exactly. When we were divided, aspects of our personality separated and each of us inherited only some of the abilities we once possessed as an individual. As it happens, both the Colonel and I are human - more or less - but the Custodian is something else: more a creature of energy and thought than flesh and bone. We each have powers that are somewhat different: the Custodian is able to exert a much greater influence on time than I, but he can interact less with the real worlds - either of them - than I or the Colonel can."

"So that is why he could not trigger off the sword to change into the fragment in the tomb?"

"Just so."

Tom wandered over to sit on the chair opposite Neoptolemas and faced him across the desk. For some reason his legs were wobbling. He screwed himself up to voice the question to which he feared he already knew the answer, reluctant to have it confirmed. The only sound in the room was the incessant hollow ticking of the mantle clock.

"So am I a potentate?" he asked at last.

"Well, not yet ... but you are becoming one, Thomas. Let us

just say that you have the potential. And each contact with a fragment of the Crown seems to accelerate that process as the touch of them awakens dormant powers. It is why you have been experiencing bouts of dizziness and nausea lately. You have, haven't you?"

Tom nodded: each contact with a fragment ... so that was what was happening when he felt dizzy and the Clock and Map went wild. It had occurred in the Museum and again in the tomb when he had touched the sword. Did the stone tablet have the same effect? Is that why the Professor was storing it in a lead-lined strongbox? But, if that was so and contact with fragments was causing him all this disorientation, what had triggered the problem when he had Walked from Fort Bellam? There had been no contact with a fragment then, had there? He put that question aside for later and asked another.

"The Custodian said that a time was coming when I had to stand beside you. What time is that?"

"The Custodian was getting ahead of himself. But what he means is there are other dangers beyond the likes of Knossos and Redfeld. However, there will be time to find out about them later. Let's just deal with the immediate problem shall we?"

"What must I do?" Tom leaned back in his chair and gazed intently at the Professor.

"Firstly, please remember your promise not to mention what we have discussed about Dr Midas to anyone. It will be hard I know, but it will not be for long." He paused, took out his hand-kerchief and again polished his specs. "Tell me, Thomas, how much of what you overheard did you tell the others?"

"Not much," Tom said, feeling vaguely uncomfortable.

"I thought not," the Professor smiled. "That is good. It is as well to keep it to yourself for the time being. Agreed?"

Tom nodded. "OK ... I guess."

"Now, I want you to try to master some new talents. This ability of yours to be inside the head of others and to see them in other places and times - that is what we would call a 'Potentate Talent'. I want you to learn to use it."

"How? The dreams just come when I am asleep. I have no power over them," Tom replied with a puzzled frown.

"That must change. You must learn to control the ability so we can use that talent when we need to." The Professor looked pensive for a moment and then nodded his head vigorously as if making a decision.

"Yes, it is time indeed to learn that talent and for you to learn the truth of what happened during the Event. Tonight I want you to direct your own dream."

Tom blinked. "How?" he asked again.

"There must be a moment at the start when you are aware the dream is beginning, but you are still conscious of the fact."

"Yes," Tom said slowly.

"Then tonight, in bed, think of that dream you had a few days ago - the one of Titus and Knossos. Keep thinking about it and then exert your will, much as you do when you are Walking, to carry on where the dream left off. Then we shall see what happens. You may not succeed the first time, but keep trying ... and do not worry about what we have been discussing, Thomas. I have every faith in you, and you in turn must trust me to protect you until you are strong enough to protect yourself."

There was a knock at the door and it opened. Dr Midas stood there peering in at them. "May I come in, Professor?"

"Yes Dr Midas, Thomas here was just leaving. Come in and sit down Doctor. Let me order some tea and then let us examine the tablet together. I think you will find it very interesting ..."

Tom got up, walked to the door and strolled thoughtfully down the corridor towards the library to say his goodbyes. Mary was sitting at the table darning a hole in her jeans; she looked up and smiled as she saw him. Charlie was drinking a mug of tea and seemed to be thinking about something, judging by the faraway look in his eyes. Edward was in one of the armchairs, reading The Times and Septimus was in another, apparently dozing, although he opened his eyes as Tom entered.

"Well," Septimus asked, "What was that all about?"

"Oh, nothing much," Tom replied evasively. "I got told off for eavesdropping."

"Bad luck, boyo; not much gets past the Prof does it?"

"You were in there for a fair while if that is all you spoke about," Edward observed, looking up from his paper.

"He wants me to try and direct my dreams - thinks it would be a useful talent to master. We talked about that for a while." Tom exaggerated a yawn. "Sorry, I am really tired. Look, can I tell you later? I am off home to bed now."

"Suit yourself," Edward replied coldly.

Knowing he had been less than convincing, Tom avoided Edward's stare and without further discussion, waved at Mary and Walked home.

He did feel guilty about Edward, but he had promised the Professor. Besides which, Tom had things on his mind. The enormity of what he had learned about being a potentate was just beginning to sink in and if he was honest, Tom was as excited as he was terrified. After all, the Custodian had hinted that dangerous times lay ahead and that he - Tom - would be at the centre of it. Compared to that, Edward's sulking did not seem important.

Later that night, as he prepared for bed and then climbed un-

171

der the sheets, he pondered the dream in the Temple of Knossos. So how had it ended? He recalled Titus discussing with that officer, Xanthus, what they would do to deal with Knossos. It seemed that Titus had a plan but he was afraid to go through with it. Yes, that was it. Now, his eyelids heavy, Tom felt sleep coming and willed himself to revisit the dream. In his mind he summoned the image of the inner sanctum of the Temple. There he saw Xanthus and his soldiers and the sorcerer, Titus, staring in horror towards the figure of Knossos and his crown. Knossos was the key. He, Tom, needed to change the dream and get inside the head of this man and then follow events from this point forward. He must know what happened next and what became of Titus' enemy.

"What are we going to do?" Tom said, drowsily repeating the words of Xanthus. Again, "What are we going to do?" and a third time, "What are we going ..." Finally, sleep took him.

"What are we going to do?"

Titus shrugged. "I don't know ... I have an idea but ... but..."

"Come on man! We must act now!"Xanthus shouted above the chanting, the gruffness back in his voice.

"Yes, yes I know but ..."

"But what?"

"But, I am ... afraid ..."

Now, thought Tom, only barely aware that he was slipping into the dream: move on, he instructed his mind. What comes next?

CHAPTER SEVENTEEN
THROUGH THE EYES OF A MONSTER

"*N*o Will, No World But Mine," Knossos chanted. "No Will, No World But Mine," he repeated and carried on reciting the incantation. All at once he became aware of a chilling sensation descending from the Crown, through his limbs to his fingers and his toes. Meanwhile, above him, the emerald gem shone brightly; exuding an aura that Knossos could sense, could feel ... could see. The aura spread outwards, carrying wave upon wave of his darkest thoughts. Out there, the universe he hated remained in existence and it offended him. How dare it? A world that did not worship him; did not recognise all that he was and all that he had done. A world that he and Titus had once saved and now rejected him. Well ... it would pay. He focused his will through the Crown and felt the energies that would destroy everything building towards a crescendo.

Meanwhile, Knossos could see that in the anteroom the lights were growing dim.

No, more than the lights. The very walls were fading, so too the roof and the floor beneath the feet of those accursed soldiers and that traitor he had once called a friend. To think that he, Knossos, had once looked up to Titus. Together they had destroyed monsters and an ancient evil. After that men had believed that he and Titus were gods, but Titus had told them that he was as mortal as they were. What an idiot: they should have taken that adoration and used it to set themselves amongst the Olympians. But no ... that would offend Titus' sense of truth and honour. Now the fool with his pathetic ideals and beliefs would perish.

Whilst Knossos looked on, he saw Titus turn to stare at the officer Xanthus, then heard him cry out in shock.

"Xanthus!" Titus gasped at him and pointed. The soldier's armour, sword and shield, and even his flesh were becoming translucent. Then Titus looked down at himself and his expression became one of abject horror as he realised that the same was happening to him.

"NOW Titus, you must act now!" Knossos heard Xanthus implore the sorcerer.

Titus gulped and then nodded, raising his hands in preparation to channel the energy of time itself. Knossos watched and waited. Would his barrier hold against his former friend's powers? He had told his followers that he, Knossos, was the greatest sorcerer ever to have lived. Yet in his heart he knew that Titus was stronger than he - but how much stronger? They had never been certain ... they had never tested each other before today. Knossos felt the beginnings of doubt. That said, he was powerful too, and his barrier was surely almost impenetrable. Almost ... but not quite. Indeed there was a weakness and it was now that Knossos realised his own arrogance had permitted it.

He observed dryly that Titus had been right when he told Xanthus that he, Knossos, liked an audience. It was true; he had wished them to hear him and to hear in turn what they were saying about him. For that to be the case, he had permitted sound to penetrate the barrier in both directions. It was a needless risk to have taken because it meant that now his barrier had a flaw.

As Knossos struggled to focus his will through the Crown, he kept a part of his concentration on what Titus was doing. So he was aware that Titus was now focusing on that weakness, that opening in the barrier, and Knossos knew the very moment that Titus reached out for the particles that made up the air about him - minute and invisible to them

174

both, but present nonetheless. Through his talents, Titus was able to feel them, see them and move them. Today, Knossos sensed it as Titus sent a rhythmic vibration through the air, towards the barrier and then through the channels Knossos had left open within it. With all his focus directed on the Crown, Knossos was unable to intervene, he could only observe as Titus accelerated the vibrations. Around him now he could hear a buzzing noise, which grew louder and louder as his enemy sped up the movement of the particles.

Inside the frozen wall of time Knossos had created, the agitation of Titus's particles battled with the stubborn resistance of the dark sorcerer's barrier. Then, suddenly, the force was too much and the structure shattered with an explosion that threw Titus, Xanthus and his soldiers, along with half of the Black Robes, onto the ground.

Knossos stopped chanting for a moment, glared at Titus, and then bellowed out an order to his followers. "Kill them all! Keep them away for a few moments more."

It was an order from their leader, but Knossos knew that to the Cultists it was more than that. Through the power of the Crown, an order became a compulsion. For them, there was no choice but to obey, no option but to yield all, body and soul, to their master. The Black Robes got to their feet, drew out long daggers and advanced on Titus and his companions.

"Warriors attack!" Xanthus shouted and his men spread out and readied shields and spears.

As the two parties converged, Titus cried out, "Stop this, Knossos, please. I beg you as a friend. You alone can still prevent this bloodshed. It need not be this way. We can make the world better, you and I."

Knossos snarled with contempt: the man was as pathetic as his viewpoint. "What world would that be Titus?" he shouted. "A world where Titus is stronger than Knossos? A world where men do not respect me?"

175

"Knossos, men will respect you for the good you can do."

"That is not enough! I will make a world where men worship me for the god I am!"

"No Knossos!"

Now though, Knossos was not listening. The emerald jewel shone again and he was chanting. "No Will, No World But Mine! No Will, No World But Mine!"

Xanthus' warriors moved to meet the fanatical charge of the black robed Cultists. Knossos heard the clash of blades, the grunt of effort and the screams as weapons plunged into flesh, but he paid no heed. These men and women were nothing more than tools. Does a carpenter shed tears if his hammer breaks? Not at all. He merely discards it and picks up another. So too with his followers. As they threw themselves onto the swords of Xanthus' warriors and as they cried out, whimpered and perished, he ignored them and closed his eyes to focus all his thoughts and will on the Crown. Not long now and none of this would matter. He would make a new world where Xanthus and Titus were his slaves and all men bowed to him.

But whilst he ignored the deaths of his followers, he could not ignore the strength of feeling he felt radiating from Titus. What was it now that the fool was feeling? Compassion? Sorrow for those who died? No - more than that. There was anger there too. Anger directed at him - at Knossos.

Knossos' eyes snapped open as he felt that anger being brought into focus - directing his enemy's actions against him. He saw Titus' hands come up, palms held outward, facing straight towards him. What was Titus doing? Surely he would not have the gall, the guts to contemplate ...

"AGE!" Titus shouted.

"Stop him!" Knossos screamed.

More of Knossos' followers - this time including the child - surged *towards Titus, to be cut down in their turn. Did the child survive? Knossos did not see; did not care. His gaze was on Titus. One of the Black Robes, blood streaming down his side, had reached Titus and as he died he fell into the sorcerer, knocking him backwards.*

Knossos felt the power in the Crown reach its peak and with all his will, he directed the destructive force on the world he hated. The gem pulsated with energy, but at that very moment Titus discharged his attack - the full force of the blast hitting the gemstone head on.

Searing pain shot down through the Crown. Knossos screamed in agony, his hands clawing at the Crown in a desperate attempt to pull it from his head. Then the pain reached new depths and he felt his body torn asunder. With a final cry ... oblivion came.

Darkness - eternal. Drifting forever. No past ... no present ... no future. Years passed ... centuries ... millennia.

Then he heard it calling. Something familiar. Something intimate. Ah yes ... of course. It was the Crown. But it was not just one Crown. It was divided, shattered into fragments and now, above all, it wanted to be whole again. So it had sought him out. Found his spirit adrift in forever. Found it and linked with it and offered it life and form again. A name once more. A name he had once owned: the name of Knossos.

The time had come to return ...

Far away a voice was calling.

"Tom! Tom wake up!"

Whose was the voice - and who was Tom ...?

177

"You must get up now," the voice - a female voice, urged him. Then he felt someone shaking him by the shoulders. Anger welled up inside him and his eyes snapped open. He glared at the women bending over him. Who was this creature? Was this one of the Cult? Where was her Black Robe? How dare she touch him? He would make her pay for the affront. Did she not know who he was? He was a god; Knossos. She should be on her knees before him.

He blinked and looked again at the woman. Then in an instant he recognised her. This was no servant ... no Black Robe. This was ...

"Mum ... it's you. What time is it?"

"Of course it's me! And it's time you were up and out the door. I was just telling your sister to get in the car when I saw you had not eaten your breakfast. You've overslept; come on sleepy head, get dressed."

She glanced at her watch and hurried towards the door. "Look, I can't wait for you. I have to take Emma to school and get off to a meeting. You will have to get the bus."

Tom pulled himself out of bed and as he heard the front door slam, he tried to gather his thoughts. For a fleeting moment, he was aware of that consciousness in the void and its desire to have form again: to be whole again. Then, at last, he was fully awake. He stared at his alarm clock as he pondered that dream. It meant, of course, that things were far worse than they had believed until now. Knossos had not been destroyed during the Event. His body was gone, but his soul lived on and was in contact with the Crown. That meant that if the Crown reformed then it would be Knossos in the body of this Vessel - whoever that might be. Tom thought he should tell the Professor, but he had to go to school. Maybe he could Walk to the Institute and re-

178

port this and then Walk back in time for school. Then again, the way his talents were playing up, he was reluctant to test them too far. Maybe safer to ring the Prof later in the day.

He rolled out of bed and tugged on his school uniform. It struck him that protecting reality and time would be a heck of a lot easier if he did not need to go to school. Then he thought of Persephone being there and realised that he was really quite happy to go after all. He checked the time on his alarm clock. Eight-thirty! Blast; he had forgotten to set the alarm last night and now he had missed the bus and would be lucky to get there on time. There was no other choice: he would just have to Walk and hope for the best.

He focused on the Map, located the school in his mind and then tried to Walk into the gymnasium. As lessons had not yet started, it was a safe place to appear at this time in the morning. That was the theory but, as he stepped out of the Walk, he realised at once that all was far from being alright. He had not - as he had planned - materialised in the empty gym from where a short cut through the main hallway would lead him to his classroom. Instead, he had appeared on the top of the balustrade of the stairwell that led from the staffroom down to the main entrance area.

Overbalancing, he fell backwards on to his behind and then slid forwards down the slanted balustrade. As he slid, he picked up an alarming amount of speed so that at the bottom of the staircase he was catapulted off and with a cry of alarm, went tumbling through the collection of teachers standing around in the entrance hall. In just the same way that a well placed Yorker blasts the stumps out of the ground and scatters them in all directions, he knocked the three nearest teachers flying.

With a groan, Tom picked himself up and realised that

the usually noisy hallway was suddenly silent as the pupils stared in amazement at the carnage and the teachers disentangled themselves. Glancing across at the crowd of school kids, Tom could see Andy and the Desperadoes standing with their mouths open. Next to them, the face of Kyle Rogers had taken on a look of awed respect. Behind him, Persephone's face was oddly emotionless - stunned into silence maybe, Tom thought with a sinking feeling.

"OAKLEY," bellowed the all too familiar voice of Mr Beaufin as he came hurtling down the stairs after Tom. "Headmaster's room, NOW!"

Tom groaned again and stomped off towards the Headmaster's office. As he walked that way he pondered what had occurred: again he had experienced the disorientation. Yet, he had not been in contact with any fragments of the Crown. Was the Professor's theory wrong then? Was something else affecting his ability to Walk?

An hour later, after Mr Beaufin and Mr Singh had lectured Tom about his behaviour, AND after he had been given two weeks' detentions starting the following evening, Tom joined his class in Chemistry lesson.

"Wow, mate. I mean *wow!*" Andy said and the other Desperadoes nodded as if that pretty much summarised the situation.

"You OK, Oakley?" Rogers asked. "Have to say that was pretty cool. You ever want to dump these losers and join a real gang the offer is there."

"Er thanks ..." Tom was no longer looking at Rogers, but at the approaching figure of Persephone. Her face wore an expression of concern.

"That was, er ... a very interesting display there, Tom. But are you hurt? I was afraid you might have twisted something when

180

you fell."

"It's nothing. I just got a bit lost and ... ended up on the staircase ..." he stumbled to a halt as he realised how unlikely that sounded.

"Right ... " She raised a disbelieving eyebrow.

"Anyway ... you were going to come in for a drink last night, but you vanished once my, er, family friend turned up."

"Yes, sorry about that. I remembered I had promised to be home earlier. But how about tonight?"

Tom nodded. "Yes ... that would be nice."

"Alright. I have History now, so I will see you after school."

"After school, sure!"

Persephone ran out of the room.

Andy chuckled. "Nice going Romeo. Mind you, I still don't know what she sees in you!" he said ruefully. "I mean, not when she could choose a hunk like me."

Tom frowned in response, unable to think of a suitably rude riposte with Beaufin's ears flapping a short distance away.

Later that day, Tom waited for Persephone outside the school gates. When she appeared they set off to walk the twenty minutes to his house. Tom chatted about music, showed Persephone his iPod, which she seemed oddly hesitant to touch, and waffled on about the teachers. It was only as they approached his street that it struck him the girl had hardly said a word. Had he been talking too much?

"You said that your folk run a delicatessen shop. Where is that?"

"Oh ... on Windsor Road," she answered vaguely.

"Where's that?" Tom asked. He had never heard of it.

"Other side of the city."

"So why did your folk get a house here, then?"

181

"My uncle was living here already, so we moved in with him."

"Yeah? Whereabouts?"

"Huh?"

"Which street do you live on?"

Persephone blinked. "Nightingale Drive," she eventually replied.

"Oh ... nice. Some big houses along that road - which one's your uncle's?" They had arrived outside his house and he fumbled for the key and opened the door.

Not answering the question, she followed him inside. "So, what do you have to drink?"

"Oh, coke, squash, water, milk shake," he answered. "What do you fancy?"

"Oh, er, milk is fine."

While Persephone looked around the living room, Tom went into the kitchen and poured them each a glass of milk. When he returned she was examining a picture on the wall.

"Is this old?"

Tom looked at the painting. It was a modern copy of the *Mappa Mundi*, the famous medieval depiction of the world, which his father had bought from an art student a few years before.

"Not really. Just a reprint. They made it at the local college."

Persephone seemed to have lost interest and moved aimlessly to the bookcase. Her gaze ran across the titles. "Your parents read a lot, do they?"

"Yeah." Tom shrugged. "They like to read on holiday and Dad usually has a couple of murder mysteries on the go."

Pulling a few books off the shelf, Persephone rifled absently through the pages, then replacing them, she moved away from the shelf towards the door. "So, can I see your room?"

"Erm ..." Tom winced. "It's in a bit of a mess, I'm afraid."

"No matter."

He led the way upstairs to his room. "Do you like music?"

"Yes," Persephone nodded.

"OK, I'll put some on."

He walked over to his desk and dropped his iPod into his speakers. Then he tapped on the screen, scrolling down it. She came across to look at the listing then nodded without comment as he selected an Eminem track.

Persephone listened for a moment and smiled, then drifted over to Tom's bookshelves and perused the volumes, running a finger along the spines. After a moment she turned around and held something up so he could see it.

"What is this doing here?" she asked. She was holding the acorn the Professor had given him earlier in the year. It was a bit of a joke between them, but the old man had used it as a symbol to illustrate a serious point and to persuade Tom that he could be trusted. Tom had kept it as a souvenir of his first adventure.

"Oh nothing, just ... found it one day," he answered as he absently dropped the acorn into his trouser pocket, feeling under his finger the slight ridge, a fault in the otherwise smooth shell.

She shrugged and then asked, "What time is it?"

"About four-thirty, I guess," he answered and turned to look at his brass alarm clock. "Yes, four-thirty just gone."

Persephone glanced over at the clock. At that moment Tom's mobile phone rang and he checked the screen. "Oh, sorry, I'd better take this," he grimaced.

She smiled. "It's OK, go ahead."

"Won't be a tick," he said, turning his back on Persephone. "Yes?" he said into the phone.

"Tommy, it's me, Septimus," a crackly voice replied.

"Right ..."

"Can you come straight away? The Professor has found the location of the next fragment."

"What now?" Tom replied, peering over his shoulder at Persephone, "I'm kind of busy."

"It's urgent, boyo!"

"Well ..." Tom started to reply, but he noticed Persephone shaking her hand at him. "Hang on a minute, Septimus," he said, lowering the phone.

"It is alright," she said, "I need to go anyway."

"Oh ... must you?"

Persephone nodded.

Glumly, Tom lifted the mobile again, "It's OK, Septimus. I will be there soon," he said and rang off, turning back to Persephone. "Oh well, maybe we can meet up again tomorrow night?"

"Maybe," she replied drifting towards the stairs. "Your friend has an unusual name."

"Yeah, he's an unusual guy." Tom grinned. "Outside the gates after school then? P'raps we can go to the milkshake bar?"

Persephone nodded. "Alright ... whatever you say."

When she had gone, Tom reached for the Map, crossed his fingers and Walked to the Hourglass Institute. This time there was no problem and he stomped into the library glaring at Edward and Mary, who were sitting side by side with a book open on the table. They looked up as they heard him enter.

"What is it with you lot - you determined I will never get to meet a girl?"

CHAPTER EIGHTEEN
KOHINOOR

Tom went through to Mr Phelps' office, grunted at him and walked towards the Professor's door.

"Wait a minute, Master Oakley. The Professor is busy."

Tom paused and then frowned. "Yes, I know. They called for me to come join them."

Mr Phelps shook his head. "Septimus Mason sent for you, but he is in with the Professor having a private meeting with Mr Hawker at present."

"What private meeting ..." Tom began to ask and then stopped because at that moment, raised voices could be heard coming from the study.

"I don't care, Professor!" Charlie Hawker's voice boomed out loud and clear, despite the closed door.

"Mr Hawker, please calm down."

"Why should I? I asked for help starting my career and all you and Septimus here give me are refusals and obstacles."

"Charlie boy, it's not that we don't want you to go your own way. It's just that right now is not a good time," Septimus protested.

"Huh, you said the same thing a couple of days back when we met Tom in the park."

"Well yes, I did. But I have my reasons for not being keen to

185

promote my old lifestyle - believe me I do. Let's just get through this present job and then I will see what I can do."

"See what you can do? Like a master throwing a dog a bone after he finishes his meal, you will see what is left on your plate and maybe spare me some time?"

"Mr Hawker ... please," the Professor pleaded.

Tom heard a footfall in the hallway and saw that, attracted by the row in the study, Edward and Mary had come to join them. He frowned at Edward and tilted his head towards the study. "What's going on?" he asked the lieutenant, but before Edward could answer they heard Charlie's voice raised in anger again.

"Are you going to help me or not?" he demanded.

"What is it exactly that you're after, Charlie?" From his tone, Septimus was trying to be reasonable.

"What do you think? The same as you: I want to make some money; get on in the world you saw fit to bring me back to naked. I had nothing on that day and I still have nothing, except what the Professor here throws me. I do not want to be a charity case! I want to use my talents to better myself. Is that too much to ask?" Charlie was almost sobbing out the words.

"Charlie ... lad, can't you see there are more important things going on just now. Just give us a few days."

The answer was clearly not satisfactory to Charlie, for a moment later he replied: "Ah, forget it. If you will not help me, maybe Mr Lapace will ... yes, maybe he will."

"No! You will not approach Rolf. I insist!" Septimus said.

"You insist ...YOU insist. Who do you think you are? That's it. I'm off," Charlie shouted and with that, the door flew open and the sailor stomped out of the room past Tom and into Mr Phelps' office, where first Septimus and then the Professor pursued him.

"Wait a moment, Mr Hawker ... ah Thomas, there you are ... I

186

was about to tell you all when we are all here, that I know where the next fragment of the Crown is to be found."

Charlie paused, turning back. "Really?"

"Yes Mr Hawker, I do. So please help us with this crisis and then I promise to help you. Now, come on back in. Let's put this to one side for a moment and get this job done."

Chewing his bottom lip for a moment, Charlie studied the Professor. Finally he shrugged. "Oh, very well ... but I won't let it drop."

"We will return to it after the business with the Crown is resolved. Be assured of that."

As Charlie nodded and then moved silently back into the study, the Professor glanced around at Tom, Mr Phelps and the others and placed one finger to his lips. "Say nothing ... let him calm down," he whispered then crooking his finger he beckoned them all to follow him back into his room.

Charlie was sitting in one of the chairs at the Professor's desk, his arms folded and an expression of grumpy acceptance etched across his features. Reluctantly and with hesitation, Tom went and sat next to the sailor, but said nothing and Charlie did not look at him. They all found a seat and the Professor returned to his own chair before picking up the stone tablet and examining it. Everyone was a little tense, with no one, it seemed, wanting to be the first to speak.

To break the oppressive, embarrassing silence, Tom told them about his dream. They all listened intently as he revealed the terrifying news that the Crown's creator had not perished during the Event, but lived on, eager to return. He did not mention the Vessel since he had promised the Professor to keep this secret, but the threat inherent in what he was saying was obvious to them all.

187

"So it is not just a matter of someone using the Crown to change history," Edward observed. "It is possible that Knossos himself could come back. If he is as evil as you say, Professor, we have an even stronger reason for preventing the Crown re-forming."

"Indeed," the Professor agreed. "That being the case, let me show you this. Don't touch it, Thomas – er, you know why."

Septimus glanced at Tom, his eyes narrowed as if he was about to ask why, but Tom just shook his head and looked away.

The Professor passed the tablet round so all could see it. Tom avoided contact with the artefact and kept well away from it. It was clearly connected with the Crown and he was now certain it had affected him in the British Museum, causing the confusion and disorientation he had experienced during the fight with the Black Robes. When Tom looked, he saw that the image it now portrayed was that of a strange shape. It was roughly oblong but multifaceted. It looked like some sort of crystalline rock.

"A diamond ... it's a diamond isn't it?" Edward observed.

"What does the writing say?" Mary asked tentatively.

"K-o-h-i-n-o-o-r," Tom read out the word. "What does that mean? What's up with you?" this was to Septimus. A strange choking noise was emerging from the Welshman's throat and judging by his bulging eyes, he seemed to be having a fit.

" Kohinoor..." he muttered.

"Yes, that is correct," the Professor confirmed.

"Who or what is Kohinoor?" Charlie asked.

"The 'Mountain of Light'," Edward said with a dreamy expression.

Tom glanced at the lieutenant and then back at Septimus, who seemed to be recovering from his initial shock. "Will someone tell me what all the fuss is about?"

"The Kohinoor is a diamond, Thomas. Not just any diamond, you comprehend. It was once the largest and most valuable stone in the world," the Professor explained.

Mary sighed. "The largest diamond in the world?" Her eyes were glittering with excitement.

"Indeed, Miss Brown. One legend said that if a man had five pebbles and threw four in different directions as far as he could, with the fifth going straight up in the air, and he then filled the space between the pebbles with precious stones - that would be the worth of the Kohinoor."

"Wow!" Tom muttered.

"That is not the only legend. Many follow the diamond. According to the Hindus, the God Krishna once owned it. Some say that if a man ever possesses the stone, death and destruction follow, but that if a woman does she could rise to rule the world. More reliably, we know that for five hundred years the princes and Kings of India, Afghanistan and what is now Pakistan fought over it and it passed back and forth as the booty of many bloody wars. Finally, at the end of the Sikh wars in the 1850s it was given to Queen Victoria. When she was declared the Empress of India it was placed in her crown." The Professor paused and grunted. "So I guess the old Indian legend might be true."

"Perhaps the song is right and diamonds really are a girl's best friend," Septimus commented with a grin, having finally recovered enough to speak. The Professor nodded.

"Yes indeed, Victoria did rule a huge chunk of the world. Anyway, after her death it was placed in the crowns of the Queen consorts of Edward VII, George V and George VI. That last one being Elizabeth the Queen Mother, who died a few years ago."

Tom nodded; he had been too young to recall much about it at the time, but not long ago he had seen a bit of the funeral in a documentary on TV and remembered that the Queen Mother's crown had been carried on top of her coffin to her place of burial at Windsor.

Septimus grunted. "Since then, it has resided along with the greatest and most valuable treasures amongst the Crown Jewels in the Jewel House of the Tower of London," he said. They all stared at him.

"Don't look surprised that I know that little titbit. I make it my business to know where treasures are to be found... I mean, I used to make it my business, of course," he said, avoiding the dirty look Charlie threw at him.

"Oh heck!" Tom said. "We have to break into the Tower of London and steal a diamond in the Queen Mother's crown?"

"That is not going to be easy," Edward commented. "Not to say that it sounds a bit iffy."

"Actually it won't be necessary either," The Professor said and pointed at the date below the image of the great diamond. Tom peered at it and read the date and time.

21st August 1851
22.01- 22.15

"Oh, I see. We have to go get it in 1851. Well that should be easier. No burglar alarms or laser detectors about," Septimus commented.

"It will not be that easy, Mr Mason. You see, between May and October 1851 the diamond was one of the star attractions of Prince Albert's Great Exhibition."

"Gah!" Septimus said and started choking again.

"That was only a few years before I was born," said Edward. "My parents often used to talk about how splendid it was." He sat back in his chair, his eyes distant and sad.

Tom actually knew what they were talking about for once.

190

Last term he'd had to do a history project. Mr Morgan, his teacher, had asked them to write an essay on the Great Exhibition. "I remember something about this," he said. "Prince Albert had a huge glass exhibition hall built in Hyde Park. The idea was to show off the newest inventions and the most amazing works of art in one vast exhibition. Countries all around the world sent machines and statues and other things. Something like," he squinted as he tried to recall a fact, "something like 100,000 items were on show, from tiny jewels to giant machines. I think six million visitors went over the five months it was running. It worked too - I mean it made a profit."

The Professor beamed. "Well done Tom, you do learn something from that school of yours.. So then, one night, in the middle of the exhibition, you have to get in and steal the most precious stone in the world. Yes Lieutenant, what is it?"

Edward was holding up his hand like he was a pupil at Tom's school. "Assuming for a moment we do this, won't we cause a problem?"

The Professor was nodding but Tom did not see why.

"If we go back and wait for the diamond to form a fragment of the crown and then we bring the Kohinoor back here, how will it be present the next day at the exhibition or become part of the crowns of four queens?" Edward elaborated.

"A good question. Can anyone give me the answer?"

Tom looked at the faces of the others. Each wore a blank, puzzled expression and he knew that they, like he, had no idea – unless the existing diamond was a worthless copy; but that was not possible, surely? Someone would have noticed over the last hundred and fifty years. It would have created an enormous scandal. Thoughtfully, Tom gazed at the old man and waited for the answer.

"No one? Oh well, that's a shame. I was hoping you would, because I haven't got a clue," the Professor said despondently. They all stared at him.

"Sorry!" he said at last. "I will have to work out the implications, but for now let's concentrate on the job in hand and worry about that later."

"So then, what do we do?" Edward asked.

"I suggest you change into mid-19th century costume - the wardrobe department is on the top floor; it should be able to furnish you with everything you need - and I will supply you with sufficient funds for you to gain admission."

"Admission? Why don't we just Walk there?" Charlie asked.

"My dear Mr Hawker; THIS is the Great Exhibition of the Industry of all Nations. It was the first great World Fair. I have been three times. I even met Queen Victoria in the opening ceremony. You deserve a treat once in a while. So ... go as visitors. Enjoy a day at my expense. Then you can locate the Kohinoor. After dark you can return and remove it. But enjoy the day first."

"I must admit, I did always wish I had seen it," Edward said. "My father and mother went to see it on their honeymoon. Yes, that would be nice ... er, I suppose ..."

"What, Lieutenant?"

"Would it matter if I were to go and see them while I'm there?"

"It is inadvisable, Edward. You will be a total stranger to them and something you say or do could change history. You might not even be born! Best to stay well away; I'm sorry, I can see you are disappointed, but you will just have to trust me on this one."

"Very well," Septimus broke into the awkward silence. "Let's do it. Come along Tom, everyone."

They left the Professor studying the tablet and went upstairs. The Institute not only contained a library, the Professor's study,

Mr Phelps' office, kitchens and a dining room on the ground floor, but a basement where technicians and computer boffins merged technology with the world of the Walkers and time travel; a first floor full of bedrooms and a second floor with Dr Makepeace's little hospital and rooms full of costumes. The latter occupied five whole rooms and amongst the many hundreds of assorted garments were included Roman togas, 1960s miniskirts and Napoleonic uniforms. Anything and everything any time traveller could possibly want was here. Mary, her eyes sparkling, went into one room and Tom and the men into another.

When they opened the door, a tiny woman with grey hair piled up in a knot on the back of her head and wearing severe looking horn-rimmed spectacles bustled over in a manner that reminded Tom of his English teacher.

"Hello there." She spoke in a Scottish accent as she peered up at Tom. "I am Mrs Mackay and you must be Master Oakley. The Professor tells me you are off to 1851 so need appropriate garb."

"What is wrong with what I'm wearing?" Tom asked.

Mrs Mackay sniffed and looked Tom up and down. "Och! Jeans and a T-Shirt that says 'I am a Cookie Monster' are not going to fit in well in the Victorian era. They'd have you arrested as a vagrant." She smiled. "Now, go over there" she instructed, pointing at a series of adjacent curtains that led into small changing rooms, "and take off your trousers."

Before Tom could answer, the little woman scuttled away to the racks of clothes that hung on the other side of the room.

"Now ... let me see, let me see," she muttered to herself, rootling (There's a new word for me to look up!) through various garments and either nodding her head or shrugging as she examined each one. Finally, she gave a little 'aha!' wrenched several items off a coat hanger and thrust them at Tom.

193

"Put these on," she ordered, and somewhat intimidated by the tiny lady, Tom nodded and retreated behind the curtain. He yanked off his T-shirt and jeans and then turned to the pile of clothes Mrs Mackay had given him. First was a pair of smart grey trousers, a bit like ones he had once worn as a page boy at his aunt's wedding. Then he put on an equally smart, well-starched white shirt. The third item was a bright yellow waistcoat. Over the top was a stylish jacket, not unlike his school blazer. Finally there was a strip of cloth: a cravat. Tom had no idea how to tie one of those so he emerged from the changing room to ask Mrs Mackay. When he did so he stopped in his tracks and gawped.

His three companions were all dressed like him and looked - for want of a better comparison - like a trio of butlers. All three wore brightly coloured waistcoats: Edward in yellow, like Tom; Charlie in blue and Septimus in conspicuous looking bright red. (how does bright red look conspicuous?) But what had really halted Tom were the hats each of them wore: tall black top hats. Edward was also twirling a walking cane and grinning at Tom.

"Ah ... it feels good to be properly dressed again," he said with a satisfied sigh.

Mrs Mackay came over, helped Tom to do up his cravat and then thrust a hat on his head.

"Great ... now I feel like a real idiot." He looked down at his Adidas trainers, which now looked entirely out of place. "What about these?" He held up a foot for Mrs Mackay's inspection.

"Mm, afraid you will just have to make do. I am a bit short on footwear of the period."

You look beautiful," Septimus grinned. "You are going to be the real jewel in the Great Exhibition, not the Kohinoor!"

"Pardon?" Tom asked, slightly alarmed.

"Not you, you idiot: Mary."

194

Tom looked at the doorway and saw that Mary was standing there, blushing slightly. She looked utterly different to whenever he had seen her before. She was wearing a deep green bodice and skirt. The finely embroidered skirt was enormous and seemed to balloon out at the hem.

"I feel like a doll. I hope we don't need to run. It would not be easy," she said simply, but seemed pleased with the reaction her appearance had caused in the men. Suddenly her face dropped and she gestured across the room.

"Redfeld!" she screamed, pointing towards the window.

Tom turned and saw - plain as day - the man who had caused him so much trouble a few weeks before. The thin figure had dark hair and wore a black uniform: the uniform of a Nazi Captain in the German army that occupied Britain in the Twisted Reality. Redfeld stepped forward, his gaze passing across them.

"Hello, everyone ... how nice to see you once again. I have so missed your company!"

CHAPTER NINETEEN
THE GREAT EXHIBITION

The Nazi officer took a few steps into the room and then examined the racks of jackets, trousers and shirts with interest.

"Impressive collection, I must say," Redfeld observed and then turned to look at them all. "Your Institute is well organised and apparently prepared for all eventualities and yet ... it appears you did not anticipate me." Then he smiled: a smile full of cold threat and malice. "To be totally frank, this is a little bit of a surprise for me also. Do you know what this building is in my world - what its function is in the true reality?"

No one answered, everyone watching the captain cautiously.

"No one?" he asked. "Well, I will tell you. This is a laundry. I have never been inside the Institute, of course, so out of a sense of curiosity I went to visit the equivalent building in my London to see what fate had determined for it. There I was, just moments ago, examining rooms full of dripping shirts and undergarments. Imagine then, my surprise when I find myself here: in *Die Andere Welt* as we call this Earth - 'The Other World' in your language. I have to say that I cannot believe my luck. Can it really be as easy as this to step from my world to yours and into the heart of your precious Institute: to simply enter a room and to be here? It seems too good to be true. Doubly so because I have this," he reached into his pocket and produced a Luther pistol which he now pointed at Tom.

"Time to complete what I tried to do before," he added with a menacing smile as he cocked the weapon. "So, young Thomas, I imagine you believed or at least hoped that I was dead! You should have made sure at Tintagel," he sneered.

Tom's feet were glued to the spot and it seemed this was true of the others, for no one moved, though he could feel Charlie tensing as he prepared to Walk. Redfeld felt it also - or so it appeared - for he glanced across at the young sailor and sneered.

"No, I really would advise against rash action, Able Seaman Hawker. You are fast, but I wager that the bullet is faster."

"Master, look at the walls," Mary hissed quietly to Tom, but the Nazi captain still heard her.

"What? I have not put up any walls, child," he snapped at her, but Mary was shaking her head.

"No, no not you: the walls of the world."

"Was gibt?" Redfeld asked, "What do you mean?"

"It is why you are here, Captain: the walls between here and your world are fading. I can see it now," Mary said. "I can see your world and this world and the walls between them and the holes that are within those walls."

"Mary, I think he knows that. Indeed, he must, for he caused it ..." Tom said, but then trailed off as he noticed Redfeld's bemused expression. Then he remembered the French soldiers in the Welsh Fort and how none of his companions, not even the Professor, could explain why Redfeld would have brought them, nor indeed how he could transport them in the first place. Only a few weeks before, Redfeld could not move between realities without intervention from the Custodian, so was it likely he could now pull down the walls between here and his own world?

197

Tom's eyes narrowed as he stared down the end of the Luger. "No, you didn't, did you, Captain?"

Redfeld shrugged. "I could claim to have done so, of course ... but no, I did not."

"Liar!" Septimus exclaimed.

"Why ... why would I lie?"

"I think he is telling the truth, Septimus," Tom said. "He doesn't have that kind of power, he never did. He's just a corrupt, evil puppet; a bully, but a puppet all the same." He spat out the words, a sudden surge of anger and contempt overcoming his fear and making him careless of Redfeld's reaction.

The Welshman put a restraining hand on Tom's arm. "That's as may be, but you are forgetting one thing, boyo: he still has a gun."

"Indeed I do." Redfeld's face reddened at the insult, a vein throbbing on his forehead. Levelling the barrel at Tom, his finger curled round the trigger and squeezed.

"WALL!" Mary shouted, the instant Redfeld discharged the pistol. The bullet struck her barely visible wall just inches from Tom's face and ricocheted away. Flinching, Tom stepped to one side.

"WALL!" Mary shouted again, but this time there was not the gentle shimmering they had all seen when she created her barrier of frozen time. Tom, wondering what she was trying to achieve, assumed she had failed.

"Look at Redfeld," Edward shouted and they all turned to stare at the captain. Where before he had stood, plain as day and horrifyingly real, now only a faint outline remained.

"What are you doing?" Redfeld's voice asked, only this time it was indistinct and weak.

"Wall!" Mary commanded again, her features pale and tense

with strain, and now the shadowy image of the Nazi captain disappeared completely.

They all stood in silence for a long while, staring at the spot where Redfeld had been and then, awestruck, at Mary. At which point Mrs Mackay gave a sigh and fainted with a thud onto the floor. They all looked down at her.

After a moment and with a roll of his eyes, Septimus said, "Oh, bother. I guess we had better fetch the doc. Charlie, will you go and tell him please. We should also tell the Professor about Redfeld," he added as the sailor left the room. However, before they could move, they heard footsteps and Neoptolemas entered the wardrobe room.

"I am already aware, Mr Mason. I came as soon as I detected a strange disturbance in the Flow of Time. I was just in time to witness Miss Brown's timely intervention; well done, my dear, your powers are growing by the day." The old man crossed the room and looked down at the place where Redfeld had stood only moments before. "So, it seems we have had yet another incidence of the walls between the realities becoming porous. Furthermore, it seems that Redfeld is not behind it after all. So then, the question we still need to answer is, who or what is?"

Tom had a good idea, but was not quite certain if he should suggest the name that had sprung into his head. "Don't you have any ideas, Prof?" he asked. "I mean, Professor," he corrected himself as the old man glared at him. They were interrupted as Dr Makepeace and Charlie came in and the doctor produced smelling salts to revive Mrs Mackay.

Neoptolemas turned back to Tom. "No, I do not. Another mystery we must answer, eventually. That said; you should be about your business this day. Now that we know that Knossos is alive and trying to return, the Crown is the priority. That is the biggest danger. So then, are you ready ... Map and Clock in working order Thomas ... yes? I must say you all look very smart. Well, good luck."

They left the Institute and walked to where Albert Gate led off Knightsbridge into Hyde Park. Septimus guided them to a white Regency-era building, which was now an accountant's office but, he told them, had been a private house in 1851. They occasioned a few amused glances from passersby, who probably assumed they were on their way to a fancy dress party, thought Tom. A sheltered rear entrance under an overhanging porch provided a reasonably hidden spot to Walk back to the 19th Century. Tom found that he could move them all back without any difficulty; there was none of the disorientation that had accompanied these journeys over the last few days. At least the Professor seemed to have discovered what caused it and avoiding contact with the tablet had paid off, thought Tom. However, the problem at the fort and his sudden arrival in the battle at Ypres remained a mystery.

Tom took them to 10 a.m. on August 22nd 1851. When they arrived, he discovered that it was a warm day: the formal Victorian clothes seemed rather heavy for summer. He wished he had been allowed to remain in his jeans and T shirt after all and remarked on the fact to Edward.

"My dear Thomas." Edward smiled and shook his head. "One is not seen out of doors without the proper attire. I am afraid it simply isn't done. Lady, gentlemen: shall we take a constitutional?" he said, crooking his arm for Mary, who winked at Tom and placed her white-gloved hand gingerly on Edward's forearm. The lieutenant seemed suddenly at ease as he led the way towards the park, jauntily swinging his walking cane. Tom was not surprised. They might be visiting London a few years before Edward was born, but it must still be a lot more familiar than the one the Victorian officer lived in now - one hundred and sixty years later.

As they emerged from between the buildings, Tom saw a sight that took his breath away. Rising above the mature oaks and beech trees that populated Hyde Park was a colossal structure. Made of glass and steel, which caught and reflected the summer sun as it climbed the southern skies at their backs, Tom got the impression of a gigantic greenhouse. Indeed, in terms of style if not size, the building did look a little like the one his grandfather owned on an allotment a few streets from Tom's house. He almost expected to see the old man pottering around with pruning shears. This, though, was not a greenhouse. This was a vast exhibition hall hundreds of metres long and so tall that Tom could see that its roof actually arched above one of the Park's ancient oak trees. No wonder they called it the Crystal Palace, he thought.

A road ran across their path and following it was a mass of humanity, everyone laughing and relaxed as though enjoying a public holiday. Men dressed like Edward rode proudly by on tall stallions, tipping their hats as they passed the many open, horse-drawn carriages, in which ladies sat wearing elaborately coloured and decorated dresses, a little like Mary's. Some carried gaily painted parasols, others wore hats topped by plumes of ostrich feathers. Mary gazed at them all, her mouth slightly open, a flush of pink staining her cheeks. "They are beautiful are they not?"

"None as lovely as you, Miss Brown," Edward replied with a bow, which made the young girl blush and giggle.

"Pass me a bucket someone, I'm going to be sick," Septimus murmured to Tom, who snorted with amusement, his attention

201

caught by a gaggle of young army officers in scarlet tunics, including one Highlander wearing a kilt and an enormous black Busby. For a tense moment he thought Edward was going to forget himself and salute them, but he walked on by with barely a backward glance.

Next to the soldiers were sailors in bell-bottomed trousers and beyond them, more folk in civilian coats; couples walking arm in arm; children scuttling past as they played with hoops and sticks. Edward was right: not one of them was scruffily dressed. Even the less well off, though not so grand, had apparently turned out in their best clothes. All the men wore ties and hats and Tom could not see any girls or ladies who looked anything but smart. The only time he could remember everyone being so well presented in his own time was at his cousin's wedding. Comparing this scene to that of Proms in the Park made him smile; everyone here was so prim and proper, yet for all that, the atmosphere was just as carefree.

They passed a formal garden that had been laid out around the exhibition hall, complete with statutes of Greek gods dotted around between fountains which played musically. All the people were now heading towards the entrance to the Great Exhibition. Here, carriages and horses were taken away by stewards and parked for their owners. Amongst the crowds, Tom and his friends all joined the queue to enter the Crystal Palace.

When Septimus reached the front of the queue, Tom heard the attendant ask for a shilling for each of them and watched as the Welshman handed over the unfamiliar coins. They looked a little like modern, ten-pence pieces, but bore the image of a young looking Queen Victoria. Charlie eyed them hungrily, and Tom wondered if he was evaluating their worth in the present day. Once they had received their tickets they then entered the exhibition hall.

The interior rose like a great cathedral above them, but whilst a medieval cathedral had arches and pillars of ancient stone, this edifice was made of vast steel girders and huge sheets of glass. A central nave ran the length of the building. Down each side were great alcoves, above which a balcony projected and from which hung dozens of flags from all over the world: France, Britain, America - and many more that Tom could not recognise. As they walked around they found the place was divided into courts, each with a different theme. The Indian Court was gaudily adorned with jewels, exotic fabrics and clothing, which Tom had seen ladies wearing in the Asian supermarkets in his own city. The China Court was full of ceramics, vases, oriental screens, and illuminated lanterns; whilst the Turkish Court was populated by hookahs, curved scimitars and a camel saddle. Not far away was a huge Celtic Cross. These items were surrounded and dwarfed by great machines which puffed and groaned as their pistons pumped up and down and hammers rose and fell.

"This is the height of the Industrial Revolution, Tommy boy," Septimus said as they paused by one vast machine that was punching holes in steel sheets. "The power of this industry is giving all these nations an empire. But it is Britain that is becoming the super power of the Victorian age and whether you think that is right or wrong, the Brits of this day are not afraid to brag about it. To be honest it's quite exciting, isn't it?"

Overwhelmed by the size and number of the displays, Tom nodded.

Edward was nodding too and Tom thought he could hear him whistling a few bars of 'Rule Britannia.' Mary was no longer holding his arm, but lagging behind staring at everything in amazement, her eyes like saucers.

"Still, we are here for a reason, so let's go and find the Kohinoor," Septimus said. "Catch up Mary, no time to linger," he called back to her.

The display of the Kohinoor, along with two other diamonds of great worth, was in a marquee with two entrances: a way in and a way out. Both were guarded by policemen who, Tom noted, were armed with revolvers. Throughout the day there had evidently been no fewer than two hundred people in the queue and so Tom and the others took their places and waited for their turn to see the diamond.

Gradually the line moved along until finally, Tom and the others stood in the centre of the marquee. Here the display cabinet looked a little like a bird cage, with the diamonds elevated on a platform over which rose an iron cage. The three precious stones were mounted at the heart of the cage. Tom squinted at the Kohinoor, expecting to see a blazing flash of light, but was disappointed by the slightly dirty brown rock he saw. From the whispers about him it seemed he was not the only one who thought the title 'Mountain of Light' was hardly justified.

"It does not shine much, does it?" Mary said. Septimus shook his head.

"No and many were disappointed by it. It only shines from a certain angle. Prince Albert has it specially cut next year in Holland and it takes some work before the jewel's true beauty shows," he whispered. Nevertheless, lady and gentleman, that there is our target. Come, let's go eat and think about how we are going to capture it."

When they were outside the exhibition, they looked for a nearby hotel where they could order dinner, intending to while away the time until the moment to retrieve the Kohinoor arrived. They could have just Walked forward three or four hours, but as Charlie put it: "We are supposed to be enjoying our day out on the Prof and I think a nice steak is in order."

As they strolled out through the gardens towards Knightsbridge, Tom was suddenly aware that someone in the crowd behind them was calling out a name. He could not quite make it out at first, but as the caller moved closer to them, Tom realised that it was Edward's surname that was being called out.

"Dyson, Dyson old chap. Is that you? Wait up a moment, there's a good fellow!"

Edward heard it too and they all turned to look back. After a moment a dark-haired fellow with a moustache had emerged from the crowd and was heading straight over to them. He thrust out a hand towards Edward.

"It is George Dyson isn't it?" the man asked, doubt now in his voice.

The lieutenant's mouth fell open. "George ... no George is my father," he said, shaking the offered hand.

"Your *father*? You jest sir. I thought I saw the marriage of George Dyson announced in the *Times* only last week!"

Edward hesitated and it was Septimus who came to the rescue. "Yes ... he meant his father's brother."

"Ah, so you are George's nephew. Splendid to meet you and your friends." He tipped his hat. "Permit me to introduce myself I am ..."

"You are Dr Livingstone are you not ... the famous explorer?" Septimus interrupted.

Dr Livingstone turned to face the Welshman. "Hardly famous, sir. I don't suppose my journeys have generated much interest here at home."

"Ah, but they will," Septimus replied. Livingstone leant forward and peered at the Welshman.

"I'm sorry? You have me at a disadvantage, sir. Have we met?"

"Not yet ..." Septimus muttered under his breath, but the stranger must have heard because he looked ready to reply when Edward, with a warning look at Septimus, distracted him by performing the introductions.

"So, sir, you knew my ... er, my uncle George?" he said conversationally, when Livingstone had kissed Mary's hand with a muttered, "Charming."

The doctor turned back to Edward. "Yes indeed. He and I were in Kolobeng in '47. I was working at the mission station there and your uncle was mapping out the interior of Africa for the army. Rather inspired me to go exploring myself, he did. I am just back here settling the family, then I am off up the Nile. I have heard some rumours of a great waterfall somewhere and thought I might investigate. Anyway, that's enough about me. I need to get some dinner. Permit me to provide nourishment for yourself and your companions. There is a very good chop house not far away that seems adequate."

"We would be delighted," Edward replied and he and Dr Livingstone headed off together, the others trailing behind.

"Who is he?" Mary asked.

"Dr David Livingstone. He is the greatest explorer of the age or will be soon. In the next few years he explores the greater part of Africa, including finding what we call today the 'Victoria Falls'."

"You know him though?" Charlie asked.

"Not until he is much older. He gets lost in about twenty years and an expedition is sent to find him. I used to run vacations to historical periods for Walkers who wished a bit of adventure. The mission by Henry Stanley with the purpose of finding Liv-

206

ingstone was one I did once."

"He's the one who when he found him said, 'Dr Livingstone, I presume,'" Tom muttered, recalling one of Mr Morgan's history lessons.

Septimus laughed. "So it is believed, but I confess I didn't actually hear him say it."

The smile dropped away.

"What's up?" Tom asked.

"Oh, it's just sad sometimes meeting people when you know their future."

"What do you mean?"

"Well, it's not that long after Stanley finds him that Livingstone contracts Malaria and Dysentery and dies."

"That's awful," murmured Mary.

Their spirits somewhat dampened, they strolled across Knightsbridge and into the nearby restaurant where Dr Livingstone ordered lamb chops for everyone, followed by plum pudding. As their food was served, Livingstone regaled them with tales of his journeys to what he referred to as the 'Dark Continent'. Edward listened, becoming apparently more and more entranced by the stories. The explorer finished by relating his plans to explore the limits of the River Nile and to find a route across Africa.

"My family will no longer accompany me," he said. "The children have reached the age where they need an education and furthermore, Mary, my wife, was finding the journeys tiresome. So we agreed to return to England and they will stay here while I am away from home," he concluded as he sipped at his coffee.

Fortunately, beyond polite small talk, Livingstone did not engage Tom and his friends in conversation, which would have necessitated quick thinking had he asked about their circumstances. Listening to the explorer talk, Tom felt a weird sense of anxiety. It was odd to know about this man's future. It was a factor in time travel that Tom had not come up against before and it unsettled him.

Not so Edward, who remained riveted. "I must say, sir, these stories are exciting," he said animatedly. "I had heard about you of course. I had not realised that my fa... ah, uncle knew you and had shared with your adventures."

"Yes, George is a good chap. Level-headed and not easily frightened," Dr Livingstone said, fixing Edward with an appraising stare. "Young man, I find you easy to talk to. I could use a companion on my voyages. George Dyson's nephew would do nicely. Why not come with me when I leave for Africa?"

Edward looked taken aback by this, but, as they made their farewells and prepared to return to the exhibition, Tom noticed that he eagerly pocketed the visiting card Dr Livingstone handed to him. "You can reach me at the Imperial for the next couple of weeks. Have a think about it young man - unless you have a better offer for adventure that is!" Livingstone said with a smile as he departed.

It was almost dark when they wandered back across the road. Edward wore a thoughtful expression. Tom drifted alongside him.

"Nice dinner," he offered by way of an opening.

"Yes, not bad," Edward replied vaguely.

"So, that Dr Livingstone; you are not thinking of taking him up on his offer are you?"

Edward shrugged. "I might. It is not as if I have a better offer at present."

"But the Professor..." Tom muttered.

"The Professor seems to be managing quite well without my

208

counsel, Tom. If Dr Livingstone could make better use of me, why not go? Just imagine ... to be there when he discovers the Victoria Falls. Do you know what the natives call it?"

"No?" Tom replied

"They call it *Mosi-oa-Tunya*: 'the smoke that thunders'. To be among the first Europeans to see it – ah, now that does appeal."

"But how could you bear it? To know what eventually happens to him and say and do nothing? Aside from which, knowing what you now know about everything: history, geography, world events, the great strides in medicine, not to mention new technology – you name it – how could you, knowing all of that, keep schtum? (keep schtum is a UK phrase the US wouldn't recognize)I cannot see how you could not have some impact on the future."

"Ah, I see what you mean," Edward said; then a determined expression crept onto his face. "Still, it is not impossible - if I was set enough on going with him, I mean - I would find a way." He fell into a contemplative silence, leaving Tom wondering just how serious his friend was about it.

Soon they stood outside Hyde Park again, eyeing the Crystal Palace. No one was visible nearby. The Exhibition was closed for the day and at first the building seemed deserted. Then they heard a noise from the direction of the path they had strolled along earlier: the crunch of feet stomping along and the sharp bark of orders revealed that soldiers were approaching. Edward gestured silently and they all withdrew into the cover of some nearby elm trees. A moment later an army patrol came into view. Half a dozen men in scarlet tunics armed with rifles were marching briskly along, led by a fierce looking sergeant with a prominent moustache.

The Walkers waited in silence as the redcoats moved past

209

them and eventually disappeared into the gloom. As soon as they were alone, Tom Walked them all inside so as to appear behind a great Egyptian vase, which was taller and wider than a man. The area was dimly lit, a few gas lamps casting dark shadows around the exhibits. Septimus edged to where he could peer around the vase towards the marquee and then ducked back into cover. He examined his watch and Tom glanced at his. It was a few minutes to ten.

"There is still a guard there," Septimus whispered. "Charlie, Edward can you take care of him? Everyone else keep your eyes peeled for Lapace or the Black Robes. Edward, are you awake?" The lieutenant was obviously still lost in thought; he blinked and roused himself.

"Sorry, Septimus, I was miles away. Come on Charlie."

The two young men circled the vase, Charlie Walking directly towards the guard in his stuttering disco like movement.

"Heh! Stop," shouted the guard, raising a pistol to point at Charlie. A moment later Edward Walked, appeared behind the confused guard and tapped him on the shoulder.

"What ... who?" The man spun round to face the lieutenant, but now Charlie arrived and grabbed him around both arms while Edward disarmed him.

"Keep quiet, there's a good chap," Edward said as the others joined them. Septimus took the guard's pistol and gestured with it inside the marquee.

"Is there another guard?" he asked.

Eyes wide, the sentinel shook his head. "No."

Pushing the bemused man along in front, they entered the tent and reached the central chamber to find that he had spoken the truth: there was indeed no guard inside. . The Kohinoor, though, was visible in the cage and oddly, in the gloomy light, it seemed to catch reflections better than it had earlier. As a result the stone appeared far more attractive than when they had visited in the afternoon.

"What is the time, Tom?" Septimus asked.

To be completely accurate, Tom made contact with the Clock. "10.00 p.m. exactly," he answered. Septimus nodded and walked around the cage until he located a padlock at the rear.

"Key?" he said to the guard.

"I don't have it. It is kept in the Tower for security."

"Search him!" Septimus ordered and Charlie did so, but found nothing except a cheese sandwich which he bit into.

"Charlie - you only just had dinner!" Mary hissed.

"That was twenty minutes ago," he grinned.

Feeling a prickle of unease, Tom looked around. This was all too easy: it was time for the fragment to form and yet there was still no sign of anyone else. No Black Robes and no Lapace. That seemed very strange. Septimus pointed the pistol at the padlock and fired a shot, shattering the steel lock. The sound echoed alarmingly. He quickly freed the remnants of the lock and opened the cage, then glancing at the others, he reached out to touch the Kohinoor. They waited, expecting to hear the high pitched sound that accompanied the fragment manifesting.

Nothing happened. Septimus kept a hand on the diamond and looked up at Tom. "You sure about the time?"

Tom checked and nodded. "It's 10.02 now. Why is it not changing?"

Septimus shook his head. "I don't know ... I really don't know. Can the tablet be wrong?"

Tom shrugged and stared at the Kohinoor: the 'Mountain of Light' and supposedly one part of the Crown of Knossos and yet, here and now it was just an ordinary uncut diamond.

Septimus scratched his head in contemplation. "It has been right so far. I don't understand. Do you suppose someone has switched it?"

In the distance there was the shrill, strident sound of a police whistle. So it seemed that someone had heard the gunshot and raised the alarm. The guard smiled at them nastily.

"Hear that, do you? Soldiers know you are here. Them and the coppers are on the way, chums. The game's up," he said with a chuckle.

CHAPTER TWENTY
THE OTHER GREAT EXHIBITION

Ignoring the still chuckling guard, Tom turned away and stared at Septimus, who looked helplessly back at him. The stone tablet had been correct so far and it had seemed so very precise about the date and time. There in front of them was the diamond. As Tom gazed at it, that little puzzle the Professor had mentioned about the Kohinoor came back to him. How, if they took it today, could it remain here to become part of Queen Victoria's crown? It was surely impossible. Then again, was this the real Mountain of Light? Perhaps this was a fake and had been switched for another stone.

Another stone?

Tom snapped his fingers. Of course! It wasn't a question of another stone. It was the same stone ... in another reality; a parallel world. What was the time? 10.05. He had to move quickly.

"Septimus - everyone come here quickly. Come on move!" he repeated after they hesitated.

"What is it Thomas?" Edward asked trotting over to him.

"It is the Kohinoor we need - only not THIS Kohinoor. The reason it is not transforming is that we need the stone in the Twisted Reality!"

"Are you sure, Tommy?" Septimus asked doubtfully.

"It's the only explanation that makes sense: this stone right here is not stolen this day. History tells us it remains here and one day becomes part of Victoria's crown. This means that the only stone that can become the fragment is our own Kohinoor's twin: the diamond from Redfeld's world."

"Tom," Edward said, "we don't even know if the Kohinoor exists in the Twisted Reality, still less do we know if it is on display in the Great Exhibition. Indeed there may not even be a Great Exhibition there."

Outside the marquee, the sound of pounding footsteps and police whistles drawing near echoed out to them. They all turned at the noise and then back to stare at Tom.

"Do you have a better idea?" he asked. No one replied.

"OK ... let's go. We have only minutes," Septimus said with a note of decision.

Tom reached out his arms and they all moved to touch him. He thought of the Twisted Reality: that other version of the world. The Professor had once told him that at some point in the past it had diverged from the world he knew, splitting away to follow an alternate path where history played out often in very different ways. It was a world where France had occupied Wales at some point in 1805, and where Britain lost the Second World War; Tom's own world as it might perhaps have been, but thankfully was not. But it was always there, just out of reach, like a ghostly image of the Earth, which the vast majority of people believed was the only one.

Several months ago, when Redfeld had captured Edward and Charlie and taken them through a portal to the Twisted Reality, Tom and Mary had followed in the hope of staging a rescue. It was Edward who had discovered there was an alternative Map: one of the Twisted Reality that lay behind the normal one, shadowy like a sheet of tracing paper over a picture. Once Tom had learned how to access this he was able to move his companions between the worlds. It was why he had been sought after by Redfeld, who did not have this ability. Tom, recalling that everything felt strange in the Twisted Reality, like he was wearing his shoes on the wrong feet, connected with the Flow of Time and then brought that other Map into sharp focus. And suddenly they were there.

As they appeared, before he even took in his surroundings, the first thing Tom became aware of was a high pitched screeching noise: the noise of the fragment of the Crown manifesting itself. He turned to look in the direction of the sound and took in the view. They were indeed in a building that looked remarkably similar to the Crystal Palace they had just left. Here too there rose a vast steel and glass structure high above them. Just as in their world, there was a plethora of exhibits and a myriad of flags lining the hall. Yet, as was always the case here, Tom saw at once that there were distinct differences. The Great Exhibition created by Prince Albert in his reality had seemed to Tom a magnificent showcase of the heights to which man's ingenuity could reach, celebrating at the same time the peace and prosperity of the era in which it was built and the indomitable human spirit. Looking about him, it was clear that here in this parallel world, very different motives were at work.

One entire side of the central nave was occupied by statues, paintings and flags that seemed to depict the history of the last fifty years in this world. There was an image of Wellington leading an uprising that threw the French out of Britain. Next there was a picture of the crossing of the channel and joining with German allies to defeat Napoleon. It was odd the way history seemed to come together and then diverge again - that battle was labelled 'The Battle of Waterloo'. Then Tom saw how the British went on to embark on a series of campaigns across Europe and the rest of the world. Each war, each battle won, brought with it trophies, treasures and finally slaves - shown here as statues in native costumes, chained together. Tom knew that many of these years in his own world were not exactly Britain's finest hour, but his own Britain had abolished slavery, whilst in this world, the Empire seemed to stand upon the bodies of a hundred slave nations.

This was not the 'Great Exhibition of the Works of Industry of all Nations', this was an exhibition of the glory of the British Empire and its supremacy over all others. Somehow, Tom felt Redfeld would approve.

Amongst the trophies of a hundred wars was a large gilded octagonal display stand, built up in several layers rather like a wedding cake and full of booty brought back from the Sikh wars. At its pinnacle - clearly intended to be literally the jewel in the crown - was the Kohinoor. It was glowing with an intense bright light that was almost blinding to look at.

"Well, that's hardly fair, theirs is shinier than ours!" remarked Septimus as they crept closer.

The screeching noise was getting louder and it was obvious that it was not a more skilful cut that had made the diamond shine, but rather that it was already transforming. If so: who had touched it? It was only then that Tom became aware of people moving about on the far side of the display stand and it seemed that a battle was about to begin. "Look over there!" he hissed at the others.

The first figures Tom saw were ten soldiers clad in scarlet jackets, black caps and smart, well starched white trousers, very similar to the patrol they had just avoided in their own world. They were armed with rifles fixed with vicious looking bayonets. At the far side of the soldiers, their officer stood with a sabre held up in the air. He had lined up his men in a single rank and had them level their rifles so they pointed at a target, which now, as Tom and the others moved around the stand, came into view. There, instantly recognisable despite the hooded cloaks they wore, stood Lapace, Orme and three of his companions, their hands held up in the air. The other big brute, Jez, was balanced awkwardly on the lower level of the stand, his hand reaching up towards the Kohinoor. He had evidently already touched it - hence the screeching noise - but had withdrawn his hand when these soldiers arrived and threatened to fire a volley at them all.

"The noise," Mary gasped, "it's getting louder."

Tom could hear that she was right. He checked the time: eleven minutes past ten; that meant the fragment had to be seized in the next four minutes. By the intensity of the sound and the increasing brilliance of the light shining forth from the Kohinoor, the fragment was almost here. The soldiers were staring at the diamond now - their eyes wide and faces pale. They clearly had no idea what was causing the noise, but were unnerved by it. They had not yet spotted the newcomers.

"We have the advantage of surprise," Septimus murmured, having realised this too. "We'll have to rush them." However, as the other four bunched around him, there was a cry from one of the red-coated soldiers. He pointed at them, yelling, "More intruders!"

"Ah; no surprise, then," Edward drawled as rifles swung to point at them.

"Halt!" the officer ordered. "So there are more of you. You are all under arrest!"

Lapace glanced towards them. "Ah; Septimus my old partner, there you are. How nice of you to join us ... but as usual, you are a little late." He smiled and then drew a lungful of air and yelled, "Now!"

As one, Lapace's men moved: Orme and the others Walked, fists flying, right up to the soldiers who, startled, could not react before four of them were felled. They went down, faces bleeding and out for the count as the mercenaries fell on their companions.

"Fire!" bellowed the officer and the rifles cracked and belched forth smoke. Lapace, however, was no longer in the soldier's sights, having apparently vanished. There was a yelp from Jez, who was once more reaching for the Kohinoor when a bullet hit him in the right calf. He fell back off the platform with a choice curse.

"WALL!" shouted Mary in the nick of time, as three of the bullets spun toward Tom and his friends and then ricocheted off her barrier.

The officer glared at them all for a moment, puzzled by the negligible effect of his volley and then, recovering quickly, shouted an order.

"Charge!"

Several soldiers broke away from the skirmish around Orme and headed towards Tom and his friends. Charlie moved towards them in his peculiar stop start staccato motion and soon was running around one poor lad, who was getting dizzy as he tried to follow the sailor with his bayonet.

Edward Walked behind another solider and kicked his legs from under him, sending him sprawling to the ground. Septimus made a bee line for the display, hopped up on the lower tier and reached up towards the diamond. Just as his finger touched it there was a final burst of incandescence and the blast of energy tossed the Welshman back off the stand. He landed heavily on his back and slumped unconscious. Tom glanced at him and then back up at the diamond. Now that the light was dying down, it was no longer a gemstone. Instead, as before with the sword and the pearls, he could see that it was a curved piece of iron and bronze. He checked the Clock: it was 10.13.

"The fragment is here! We don't have much more than a minute. I'm going to get it," he shouted.

Just then, a soldier bellowed out a war cry and charged straight at Tom. He leapt to the side and then Walked back ten feet. The soldier gasped in amazement, spotted Tom, growled at him and then came on again, recoiling as he walked straight into the invisible barrier that Mary had erected.

Charlie glanced over at Septimus and then at the others who had been scattered by the charge. He then flashed out with a hand and chopped it down onto the back of the soldier's neck. As the man collapsed to his knees, the sailor made a dash for the display stand, jumping over Jez who was rolling around clutching his leg in agony.

On the far side of the stand, the fight was going badly for the soldiers. Overwhelmed by the strength of Orme and the agility of his companions, they were now all stunned or unconscious and mostly piled in a heap. Lapace was fighting the red-coated officer who jabbed forward with his sabre. As the blade lunged at Lapace he Walked a yard to the right, let the man stumble past him and then stuck out a foot to trip him up. The sabre spun away and Lapace put one foot on the man's back as he sprawled full length on the ground. Now, standing like a triumphant hunter over his kill, he looked up at the display stand to see Charlie clambering up.

When he had climbed to the top, Charlie reached out and seized the fragment holding it aloft like a trophy, mirroring

219

Lapace's display of victory.

"That's it, Charlie," Tom shouted. "Well done. Now come here and let's get away."

He moved towards where Mary was helping a groggy Septimus up off the ground. Edward ran over to the soldier who was still probing Mary's wall with his bayonet and, like a rugby forward, he shoulder-barged him into the barrier. The man gave a grunt as he hit his head, slid down the invisible wall and then neatly folded up into a heap on the ground. Now, Tom, Edward, Mary and Septimus were together and Tom glanced over to the display stand to see that Charlie had not budged. Septimus had noticed it too.

"Come on, Charlie boy: it's time," he shouted.

Charlie glanced at Septimus and then across at Lapace. Tom checked the time. 10.15. He shook Septimus by his shoulder and tapped his watch. By the look on the Welshman's face, he was fully aware of how little time remained.

"Charlie, NOW!" he urged the sailor.

Charlie nodded at Septimus and then gave a little smile. "Yes, it is time," he said, "time for me to start my new career!"

With those words still hanging in the air, he leapt down from the display stand, but not on the side nearest Tom and the others. Instead, he landed right next to Lapace.

"What are you doing Charlie?" Tom asked, aghast at what he was seeing.

Charlie stepped up to Rolf Lapace and held out the fragment. "I think THIS is a suitable qualification to apply for a job," he said, handing it over.

Lapace looked into his eyes and then over his head at Septimus, a sly smile creeping across his face.

"Oh dear, it seems you are lacking in manmanagement skills,

220

Septimus old friend. I told you before that you are a fool to trust in sentiment and human nature. Men will do what comes naturally - they will always act for their own best interests. So now, today, we have another item that I have taken from you," he leered at the Welshman.

Tom wondered what exactly Lapace meant by that, but Septimus just glared at his former partner, for once apparently at a loss for words.

Mary gave a broken cry, "Charlie, oh Charlie, how could you?" The sailor, looked at her for a moment, appeared to hesitate then shrugged and turned away.

Lapace pocketed the fragment and placed a hand on his shoulder.

"Good lad, welcome to the team," he said and then, with a faint pop, he and his mercenaries, accompanied by their new recruit, were gone.

CHAPTER TWENTY ONE
TRAITOR

"What just happened?" Tom asked, staring in disbelief at the spot from which Charlie and Lapace had vanished.

"Charlie just left with Lapace and took the fragment with him," Edward said in a hollow tone.

"I cannot believe it," Mary said, her face screwed up in distress.

Around them the soldiers were stirring and slowly staggering to their feet.

"Nevertheless, we all saw it," Septimus said, his mouth tightening into a grimace. "I suggest we get away before this little lot figure out the Kohinoor is gone."

Tom had not moved. He seemed paralysed by the shock of what had just occurred. The officer gave a shout of outrage and was pointing to the location where the diamond should be. Then his gaze snapped across to Tom and the others.

"Tommy ... please!" Septimus implored, and finally Tom stirred, reaching out for the link to the Flow of Time. Bringing up the Map he saw as usual the two images, one above the other, and flicked across to his own world. Then he connected with the image of the brass alarm clock in his mind and Walked them forward one hundred and sixty years.

"So then, will you tell me exactly what occurred this time," the Professor asked in an almost resigned tone a few minutes later.

They were sitting in his office, the stone tablet lying on the desk in front of him. Tom was staring in disbelief at the single empty chair where only a few hours before, Charlie had sat as they discussed their plans. He shook his head and then glanced across at the faces of his remaining companions. Mary and Edward wore expressions of shock and horror as they stared at Neoptolemas. Septimus, however, looked grim, resolute even.

"We solved the puzzle of the Kohinoor," Tom said despondently, "it was duplicated in the Twisted Reality."

The Professor started forward in his chair then slowly he nodded. "Of course. Well done, Tom. I should have realised. So what happened?"

"Charlie took the fragment and ... gave it to Lapace," Septimus said.

"So, Lapace was there as we suspected he might be? It is curious how your partner seems to interfere with our affairs a little too often."

"Former partner, I think you will find."

"As you say Mr Mason."

"Are you suggesting differently?" Septimus asked in an icy tone.

"Not at all," the Professor replied and although Tom was at first certain that was exactly what he was suggesting, his tone was softer when he continued. "I am sorry if my words the other day were harsh, Septimus. I do, of course, trust you. I meant that we were right to worry about Lapace. We must be sure to deal with him. "

"There, at last, we are in agreement. Believe me Professor, if I have my way, Rolf Lapace will get his comeuppance very soon."

"But what do we do now?" Mary asked, her face streaked with tears.

The Professor glanced down at the tablet. He studied it for a moment and then looked up. "Something is forming here, but I cannot tell what it is. But ... but, bear with me a moment," he said, lifting up a hand. "Ah, yes... oh ..." he went on and then stumbled to a halt.

The other four stared at him, expectantly.

"Erm ... Professor?" prompted Tom.

Neoptolemas looked up, a startled expression on his face. "Ah, sorry; I got distracted again. It is just that the tablet only shows one thing. It's the date. It's Saturday: this Saturday I mean - the day after tomorrow, at noon. But I can't see the object that will become the fragment."

"Saturday?" Tom said.

"Indeed. So I suggest we reconvene just before that time unless something else presents itself."

Edward looked up sharply. "What do you mean, reconvene? What are we going to do about Charlie? We can't just sit back and do nothing."

"That is exactly what I propose doing," The Professor said in a calm, seemingly disinterested voice.

Edward blinked and then he glanced across at Septimus, before turning back to Neoptolemas. "You cannot be serious. Surely ..."

"I assure you I am quite serious. Trust me Lieutenant, and the rest of you, I know what I am doing."

Tom grimaced. "Forgive me for saying so, Professor, but the last time you refused to tell us what you were planning it led to no end of trouble," he pointed out. "We thought you were in league with Captain Redfeld, if you remember."

Neoptolemas nodded. "Yes, I admit that I gave you reason to doubt my wisdom then, but in the end you trusted me and accepted that there were things I could not tell you at the time. Please allow that this might also be the case now."

Tom's fingers drifted down to his trouser pocket where he was carrying the acorn. Feeling its reassuring presence he simply nodded, accepting the old man's point. Edward, however, was not convinced. He looked from Neoptolemas to Septimus and frowned.

"You seem to be keeping very quiet about all this, Septimus. Rather unlike you, I would say. What would you do in this situation?" Edward asked him.

"I would keep very quiet," Septimus answered, noncommittally.

"Oh; very well!" Edward waved his hands in the air. "Have it your way. But I hope you know ... I hope you both know what you are doing."

"So then," Tom said, as much to break the brooding atmosphere as anything else, "back home it is I guess. See you all soon."

When Tom arrived home he felt shattered. This was hardly surprising. The trip to the Great Exhibition had taken twelve hours. He had to Walk back to five p.m. - to shortly after he had left, but still before his parents returned. He then collapsed on to his bed and fell asleep. When his mum found him some time later, he had only enough energy to drag himself to the kitchen table and pick at the dinner she had cooked, before heading back to his room.

"I'm worried about him," he heard his mum say as he staggered up the stairs.

Tom grinned to himself as he overheard his father's stock

reply. "Ah, he's almost a teenager now, love. You know how much sleep they need."

Back in his room, Tom scribbled his homework and shoved it in his school bag and then thought to set his brass alarm clock to wake him the next day. Unable to immediately locate it, and by now too tired to care, he instead activated the one on his mobile and flung himself onto his bed, falling quickly asleep.

The next day was Friday and Tom kept an eye out for Persephone in order to confirm their agreed date for that milkshake. He had not seen her around school all day and as the end of it arrived he mentioned it to Andy. "We're supposed to be meeting up."

"Nice going, Romeo," Andy chuckled, adding ruefully, "Mind you, I still don't know what she sees in you!"

"Yeah, so you said: 'when she could choose a hunk like you,' I believe your exact words were," Tom retorted dryly.

Andy grinned. "Wait a minute, though. You say you've not seen her all day. Well, there you are then: must have scared her off!"

Tom frowned in response. "Bog off Andy, I'm sure she'll turn up."

"Hang on; don't you have detention after school today?" Andy's grin grew wider.

"Oh blast!" Tom swore, his heart sinking.

"Don't worry, mate. I'll look after her for you!"

"I'm sure you will," Tom grimaced. 'Oh well,' he thought, 'after detention I will just Walk back the hour or so and then I can meet Persephone after all. Andy will be surprised.' He smiled to himself, 'Actually, Andy will be livid!'

"What's so funny?" Andy asked.

"Oh, nothing ..." Tom said airily.

At the end of school he reported to Mr Beaufin's classroom for detention, switched off his mobile in case it rang and old Beaufin confiscated it, then settled down to write an essay on health and safety on staircases. When he was finally released the school was empty. He made his way to the gates, looked around to make sure he was alone and then Walked back an hour.

As he did so, he felt as if he was walking through a muddy field that kept tugging and pulling at his feet. Then he remembered what the Professor had taught him about Walking and how it was impossible for Walkers to visit the same point in space-time more than once. The reasons for this were bound up with the laws of the universe. Damn; he had forgotten. That meant, because an hour ago he was present in the school just starting his detention, he could not go back to it. He tried again and once more felt a resistance. Right, maybe further away from the school it would be easier. He imagined the café a couple of blocks away from school where the kids went for milkshakes in seventy different flavours. They even had drinks with boys' and girls' names. Tom's favourite was a 'George'.

Fixing the place in his mind he Walked. Yes, even now there was still resistance, but it was not as strong as before and with an effort, he forced himself back one hour in time. He appeared near the back door of the café and stood there for a moment, pondering what he had just done. He was sure, from what the Professor had implied, that it should be harder than this to bend one of the fundamental laws he had been taught about time travel. Had the Professor been mistaken or... was there another explanation? Was this a potentate power he was using, just like in the dreams? If so, what exactly was he able to do? What were his limits? It was a heady thought, but what might be the price of these new talents?

"Hey kid!" a voice called out. Tom stirred from his thoughts and saw the café waitress pointing at him. "You coming in for an 'Albert'? It's today's special; banana and custard flavour. Fancy one?"

He checked his watch, but it appeared to have stopped, so he switched his mobile back on to check the time. "Er, not right now. Maybe later."

"OK kid. Whatever you say," the waitress turned away. Tom ran up the road towards the school. As he approached he heard the bell ringing and through the fences saw the kids pouring out of the doors on their way home. He thought he caught a glimpse of Persephone amongst them. Then he frowned when he spotted that she seemed to be walking along next to Andy. His best friend was talking animatedly, but the girl was just nodding vaguely and looking around: 'Looking for me perhaps?' thought Tom hopefully.

It then occurred to him that he needed to be especially careful to avoid seeing himself - it was dangerous and one of the main reasons Walkers were not supposed to revisit the same space-time - so he had to keep well away from Beaufin's classroom, where right now he was sitting in detention. The thought was mind boggling!

Tom scampered along towards the school gates, losing sight of Andy and the girl when they were obscured by the bus stops. He reached the gates and searched the crowd for a moment. He then turned and saw Andy walking away, down the street in the middle of a crowd of school kids. There was a girl next to him; Tom could not quite tell, but he was sure it was Persephone. He started to walk after them to find out, but just at that moment his mobile phone rang.

"Tom?" It was Septimus.

228

"What?"

"I've been trying to get hold of you. Doing anything important?"

"Apparently not," Tom replied with a final glare up the street.

"Pardon?"

"Oh, never mind. What is it?"

"Come quickly. We have received a message from the Custodian. He is calling us to a meeting in The Office. He wants to talk about the Crown of Knossos."

Tom gulped. 'The Office': a place that existed in the gap between his world and that of Redfeld; a place outside Time, but which observed time pass by. Its occupants, those 'Men in Suits,' who under the control of the Custodian had one purpose: to see that each reality survived, remained in balance and did not destroy the other. A summons to The Office was unprecedented and could not be ignored.

Persephone forgotten, Tom reached for the Map. "I am on my way."

Tom had never been here as himself, but he recognised every corner of The Office. Just months before, he had dreamt several times that he was the Custodian and through the Custodian's eyes had seen the marble floor tiles, the wooden wall panels and the tall glass windows that looked out from the tower block onto a world of nothingness. For here, only The Office existed - and the sun. That was curious and Tom wondered about that feature, when outside the tower nothing else existed, for it was solely this building that defined the Custodian's reality. At its heart was the table: the long, wooden boardroom table with chairs on either side for a dozen to be seated. Upon that table was the sandbox: a large, high sided, silvery white box made from tungsten and filled with sand that rippled and writhed to match the fluctuation in time; the goings on in and between the two realities that the device had been created to observe.

Now, as the Professor, Tom and his companions materialised simultaneously in The Office, Tom could see the ever-changing surface of the sandbox. As he watched, the lines showing the Flow of Time of both realities converged into a swirling whirlpool: a maze of probabilities and possible futures, beyond which the sand showed no future, no predictions of what might be ...

Only oblivion.

At the head of the table in his customary place, looking extraordinarily agitated, sat the Custodian in his grey suit. He was flanked by a pair of the Men in Suits standing like grim gargoyles, silently observing the room from behind their dark glasses. The Custodian waved the Institute members forward to take seats down one side of the long table. Tom looked up to see who was opposite him and jumped when he saw that it was Charlie. The sailor looked down at his hands and did not make eye contact with him. Next to Charlie, lounging rather theatrically and with his feet up on the table was Rolf Lapace, and beyond him were Orme and Jez.

Unlike Charlie, Lapace looked straight at Tom and winked. "Hullo Tommy lad, Septimus my old friend, lady and gents. Professor, I am so pleased to finally meet you. Of course I have offered my services to you more than once ... somehow you don't seem to want them."

"I find I prefer a more reliable employee," the Professor replied.

Lapace made a mock display of horror. "I am wounded to the heart old man. But, reliable you say?"

"Indeed."

230

"Strange then that it is I who have two of the fragments while you have what? One?" Lapace sneered. "And in fact the tablet was given to you, was it not? My employer has been quite happy with my reliability I can assure you."

"So, Mr Lapace, will you now tell me who you are working for. Is it Knossos?"

"Knossos?" Lapace snorted. "Are you mad? Knossos is dead these five millennia."

"Are you sure of that?" The Professor looked disdainfully over his spectacles at the mercenary.

Lapace sniggered and made to reply, but perhaps he saw something in the Professor's expression for doubt flickered into his eyes and he remained silent.

"So, if you are not working for Knossos who are you working for?" Edward asked.

Before Lapace could answer, Tom felt that strange movement in the Flow of Time that told him someone was Walking. A moment later, the fourth side of the table was occupied: one chair filled by Captain Redfeld and the other by his superior, Colonel Thielmann. The senior officer glanced coldly at Tom and the Professor, inclined his head towards the Custodian and then turned to look at Lapace.

"Do you have them?" Thielmann asked in a deep voice, which carried none of the vibrant warmth of his 'brother' Neoptolemas, nor the slightly wheezy tones of the Custodian. To see the three of them round the same table made the hairs stand up on the back of Tom's neck. Physically they were identical. He had been right: the Nazi Colonel was behind the mercenaries. He wished now that he had voiced his suspicions to the Professor.

Lapace nodded. "I do," he answered and reaching beneath his chair, brought out two curved pieces of the crown of Knossos and placed them on the table. Tom flinched back in his seat, his head swimming, nausea rising in his throat.

"You have got to be kidding, Rolf?" Septimus exploded. "Working for them! You really have no morals at all, do you? Is there no one you wouldn't work for?"

Considering this for a moment, Lapace shrugged. "To be honest, if the money's right, probably not. Indeed I certainly can't think of anyone ..."

"I'll bet you can't! Work for ... or betray," the Welshman snarled, looking from Lapace to Charlie, "it's all the same to you."

Lapace did not respond, but just coloured and looked away. Tom thought he was actually embarrassed.

"See who you ultimately betrayed us for Charlie?" Edward eyed the sailor coldly. "The very Nazis you almost drowned fighting to defeat – and all for a few pounds."

Charlie glanced up at him, then across at the Professor. He did not respond, but his face was scarlet.

"Quite a few pounds, actually," Lapace retorted, turning back to glare across the table.

"Gentlemen, please," Redfeld's crisp voice cut in. He turned to Septimus. "Can I remind you that you worked for me in the past, Mr Mason?"

"Only until he found out what type of man you are," Mary cut in fiercely, coming to Septimus' defence. She seemed to have done that a few times lately, Tom thought.

"Touché, Miss Brown," Redfeld responded.

There was a loud bang as the Custodian rapped his knuckles on the table. "If we can perhaps get to the business at hand," he said, drawing everyone's attention.

"Please do," Thielmann said. "Why have you summoned us here?"

"It was not I who summoned you here," the Custodian replied.

Again, Tom felt the strange sense of disorientation and of dizziness that indicated someone was Walking. Slowly the Custodian lifted one finger and pointed it towards the window where, silhouetted against the sunlight, a group of figures could now be seen. Squinting, Tom could see that each of them wore a black robe with the Crown of Knossos emblazoned upon their chests.

One figure, shorter than the rest, detached itself from the group and stepped forward. Even though Tom could see no features beneath the hood, there was something familiar about the person's stance: he was sure it was the Black Robe from the Museum, the one who had seemed to be the Cultist's leader. Frowning, Tom watched as the figure came to stand a few feet behind Thielmann, who craned his neck round to stare. Motionless, for a moment the Black Robe seemed to study each of them in turn before reaching up to pull back the hood.

When he saw the figure's face, Tom let out an involuntary yelp of surprise:

"You!"

Returning his gaze, a faint smile rolled across the Black Robe's lips.

"Hello Tom."

CHAPTER TWENTY TWO
PERSEPHONE

"Persephone!" Tom cried, "I ... don't believe it." There was a shocked silence in The Office as all but the Custodian stared at the girl standing before them. Like all the Black Robes she wore a silver necklace, the pearl pendant visible as she smiled at Tom. It was a mocking smile, which said clearly that she had used him - certainly had not fancied him. He felt his face colouring; what an idiot he had been!

"You know this girl?" the Professor asked. "A member of the Cult of Knossos, and you did not tell me?"

"I ... I didn't know who she was," Tom stammered.

"You have met me too ... old man," Persephone spat, as her eyes narrowed with loathing.

"I have met you?" The Professor asked, peering over his glasses at the girl. Then his face lit up in recognition. "Of course ... the attractive girl Thomas was talking to a few days ago outside his house."

Persephone snorted with derision at that reply. "Oh, further back than that ... much, much further."

The Professor started, his eyes narrowing, but before he could respond, the Custodian interrupted.

"Why did you call us to this meeting, girl? In your message you mentioned it concerned the Crown and a chance for one of us to obtain all the parts."

Persephone looked up at him and her expression of disdain did not flicker for a moment. "My master knew you would all come given bait such as that," she said and started to circle the table, slowly examining them each in turn.

"So, all the players are present: the Custodian and his beings of order and balance; the Professor and his hallowed Institute - preservers of the true time line ..." She hesitated as she stopped by Mary, flinching slightly at the glare the other girl had fixed on her, then moved on. "Colonel Thielmann and his officer, hoping for a chance of conquest, and the soldier of fortune, who would do anything for money, even betray his friends. What brought you all here was this," she tapped the image of the Crown on the front of her robe. "The most powerful artefact ever created. Given the abilities of those in this room, possession of the Crown would make any of you invincible. All your dreams and all your fears lie in the ownership of this one object."

"Not if we prevent the Crown from reforming," barked Thielmann.

Persephone laughed and the peals echoed around the room. "You expect me to believe that you would forgo the chance to use the Crown - even just the once - to bring down the barriers between your world and his," Persephone pointed at the Professor. "To open up that world for your armies to conquer - is that not what you desire most?"

Tom felt he was being watched and looked across to see Redfeld's dark eyes staring at him, glinting with just that desire. He glanced away and found he was speaking to break the tension. "Not the Professor ... or the Custodian."

Persephone turned to glare at him. "Not the Custodian? With the Crown he could achieve the everlasting balance and stability he craves. You of all people should know what steps he will take to achieve his goals."

"How do you know about ...?"

"Not your precious Professor you say," the girl went on, ignoring the question. "Let me tell you that so called altruistic men are the worst of all. They will do anything for the 'good' they serve - and the gods preserve those who get in the way of their crusade."

That was an odd expression, Tom thought. 'The gods preserve?' Now that he thought about it, so too was her language: formal and elaborate - not exactly commonplace amongst the teenagers he knew.

"So then, you all have motives. You all too have parts of the Crown. The Custodian has that which was the sword; Thielmann's mercenaries the former pearls and the diamond, the Professor the tablet itself. Yet five it takes to make the Crown whole. My master knows where the fifth part is, the last part: the part that connects all the others - the key indeed to the Crown. He invites you all to meet - to meet tomorrow."

The room was silent as they all watched the girl.

"Come then, tomorrow, and the last part will present itself. Then one party will take all the items and make it whole again. Why should you come? I will tell you why: for power, for order, for duty or simply for fame. Well then, my master proposes one game: one play and winner takes all."

Still no one spoke until Tom glanced around The Office and asked the question on all their minds.

"Where - where do we come?"

Persephone looked up at him and smiled. She was extraordinarily attractive, her smile bewitching and for an instant Tom forgot that she was a leading member of an evil Cult.

"Where? Why, where it all started. The temple of my master: the Temple of Knossos. All must come. The Custodian will permit Thielmann and his entourage to travel this once to your world, Tom. Noon tomorrow, just like it was when this happened before."

Persephone walked back down the far side of the table, behind Rolf and his associates, and rejoined the other Black Robes. With a final glare around the room the girl and her fellow Cultists were gone.

Lapace coughed, breaking the silence. "Does she think we are all fool enough to fall for that?"

"Indeed, it seems unlikely that anyone would go along and help her master complete his task of uniting all the parts," Edward agreed.

Tom noticed, however, that the Professor and his counterparts were exchanging worried glances. Reaching into his voluminous pocket, Neoptolemas pulled out the stone tablet and squinted at the image and the writing around its edge then looked up thoughtfully at Tom.

Warily, afraid that the effects he was already experiencing from the other fragments might be magnified, Tom leant over and peered at it.

The image, which had been blurred the night before, was now coming into focus. It showed not one, but two objects. One was an irregular oblong shape with writing and engravings upon it. It was, without a doubt, the stone tablet itself. When Tom looked at the other object, he at first did not recognise it. Then he gave a gasp of shock. It had three legs, two forward and one back. The shape was large and round with numbers around the edge and projections emerging from the centre pointing at the numbers. It was ... it had to be...

"It's my alarm clock," Tom blurted out and then recalled that he had not been able to find it last night. Now he thought back, he realised he had not seen it since he and Persephone had been in his room the previous afternoon. So then, had Persephone stolen it? She had been so very keen to see his house, eager to look around it and then just as suddenly, disinterested and wanting to leave. She had found what she was looking for and had then departed. He felt an even bigger fool - tricked, used and discarded.

"That explains a lot," the Professor said, disturbing Tom's bruised pride.

"Why?" he asked, conscious that all the other people in the room were gazing at him. Did they know what a fool he had been? Probably, Tom thought, colouring.

"Your strange symptoms of disorientation, those that started only a few days ago, I mean. One possibility I had never considered is that you were being exposed to a fragment of the Crown of Knossos."

"But I have had that clock for years. It belonged to my father. Why should I be experiencing these things now?"

"I suspect the part of the clock that was the fragment was dormant. It only became active when Dr Midas first touched the stone tablet and so awoke it. It was then the tablet started calling to all the other parts of itself. "

"That must have been Persephone's doing," Septimus said, "or maybe someone else in the Cult? Remember what Dr Midas said about someone suggesting where to dig - this sponsor he had never met?"

The Professor nodded. "Yes, I imagine you are right - it must be them."

Tom was studying the stone tablet. Both objects were now depicted above a series of numbers as usual. "Saturday at noon EEST - that is the time on the tablet," he read out. "What's EEST?"

"Eastern European Time, boyo. That fits as it's the time zone for Greece and is about three hours ahead of the time in London," Septimus remarked.

Tom did a quick sum in his head. "So that's er ... nine tomorrow morning, our time?"

The Welshman nodded, but then as he studied the tablet he gave a puzzled frown. "What is that over there?" He pointed at an area of the tablet, to the side of the central images, which previously had always been blank. Now Tom could make out that an image was forming, getting sharper until he could see it clearly.

"It's a depiction of the treasures, all of them in a circle," he said. Then he noticed that in the centre of the circle was a tiny picture. It was a sphere with shapes on it and was cracked and slightly opened up. It took a moment to see that it was the Earth: the planet Earth; shattered and cracked open like a walnut.

"What does it mean?" Mary asked.

"Miss Brown, it suggests to me that if the five parts of the Crown are brought into proximity: that is to say, if they unite and form a Crown, then the world will be destroyed," the Professor said.

Thielmann gave a hoarse sigh. "We know that already. That is what Knossos wanted to do at the start - destroy the universe. That girl – what did you call her," he glared at Tom, "Persephone? - is attempting to make it happen. She is endeavouring to bring the pieces together and is trying to make us do it for her by offering us these temptations. I suggest we depart and go our separate ways and take with us the fragments we own and keep them in our three realities. Let her have the boy's clock and be

239

damned to her."

Tom looked at the Colonel in surprise; perhaps after all he was not so different from the Professor. Even Thielmann, it seemed, had a line he would not step beyond, even for ultimate power - unless ... did he mean to con them? Tom glanced at Redfeld, eyes narrowed; nothing would surprise him with those two. Lapace was looking at him too, his brows arched, lips twisted in a wry smile.

The Custodian was nodding. "I agree. Let us not be drawn in by her deception. Brother, what do you say?"

Neoptolemas stared at the tablet, a frown etched deeply on his face. Then, he gave a slight shrug and nodded. "I suppose you are correct. So be it. I imagine that concludes the meeting?

The Custodian gave a curt nod.

The Professor pocketed the tablet and looked around at his Institute members. "Right: Tom, Mary, Edward, Septimus, I suggest we go home."

CHAPTER TWENTY THREE
THE VIKING

*H*arald *stood at the foot of the stairs feeling dizzy. He dropped his battleaxe and reaching up, removed his helmet then rubbed his closed eyes. The dizziness slowly subsided and now he opened them again. In Thor's name where was he? A moment ago he had been attacking a farm full of plump pigs ripe for the pillaging. He and his fellow warriors had arrived at dawn, slaughtered the Saxon family that lived in the house and then started scouring the place for booty. He had gone into the barn and was searching for a way up to the hayloft when he was suddenly no longer there. There was a moment of blackness and he felt like he was passing out and then he was here ...wherever here was.*

The building was in darkness, but as Harald's eyes adjusted he looked around him in awe. He realised that this could only be a palace: the floor was covered with something that felt soft and warm under his feet, the walls with what looked like a strange tapestry of flowers and leaves. Ahead of him a stairway led to a second floor, perhaps hinting that the Lord of the land lived up there. If he could kill him, maybe he could claim this place as his own. A grin of anticipation slid across his face as he took up his axe and replaced his helmet. Then he placed a foot on the bottom step and started to creep upwards.

Once he reached the top, he could see that several strange looking closed doors led off on either side, but at the far end a light glowed from one that was half open. Perhaps an accursed monk was awake and at his studies? Maybe he had a silvered candlestick or a richly decorated bible - both worth a princely sum? Harald crept along the passageway to the door and peered quietly around it. What he saw was a chamber, illuminated from the light cast by a strange enchanted picture, which moved and swirled. 'What sorcery is this?' he muttered. The light revealed a shelf filled with at least a hundred books - a vast library indeed. Surely the room must belong to a scholar or a wizard. If he could kill him, he could take all his wealth.

Carefully, Harald pushed open the door and searched the chamber. Ah - there was the bed. A shape lay under the blanket and he heard a slight snore as the wizard rolled over. Shifting the haft of his axe to his right hand, Harald stepped closer then slowly lifted the weapon back over his shoulder in readiness to strike. He must act quickly before the wizard awoke and enchanted him. Just as he was about to bring the blade down into the man's torso, the figure moved again and the bedclothes slipped a little. Now, in the glow from the strange moving picture, Harald saw that it was just a boy. Ah, the wizard's apprentice and acolyte mayhap? If so, behind one of the other doors might be the sorcerer himself. But what to do about the boy? Who knew what powers he had already learnt? He must die now.

With that thought, Harald lifted his axe again to crash it down on the boy.

And Tom woke ... and gaped in terror at the warrior he had dreamt he was: now solid flesh and poised to strike down at him.

With not an instant to waste, Tom Walked. He vanished from in front of the disbelieving eyes of the Viking and materialised behind him. As he appeared, he saw the warrior's blade cut deep into the mattress. Grimacing as he imagined trying to explain that away to his mother, he leant forward and slapped a hand on the warrior's shoulder.

Then he Walked.

Too rushed to consider the consequences, Tom made contact with the Clock and spun the hands backwards. It seemed to be working OK. He kept the Map fixed in the location he was in, but Walked them both back twelve centuries. When they materialised they were standing in a field near the edge of a wood. The warrior screamed once and then turned, fixing Tom with a baleful stare.

"*Swa scealta leoh life samod beloran weodan*" he shouted, raising his axe.

Tom gaped at him. "Nope, no idea what that meant, and I'm not staying to find out," he replied and Walked himself back home, leaving the warrior standing there.

Legs wobbling with relief, he stared around the bedroom for a moment. Yes, it had been his room in the dream. There was his computer still switched on with the screen saver active - what the Viking Harald had believed was an enchanted picture. Tom was used to experiencing life through the eyes of others in the past or the present. It was unnerving, though, for a person in his dream to appear here in his house. That was worrying enough, but what also concerned him was that this was yet another example of someone from another time or another reality crossing between worlds.

Lately, stories about ghosts had started cropping up in the newspapers and on the TV news and even though most of the media considered the reports dubious hoaxes, the world in general was aware that something strange was going on. Nobody had a clue about the truth, of course, but the rumours were flowing and chatter about it was all over the internet. Two days ago, Andy had sent him a link to a You-tube video of a Viking longboat being rowed under London Bridge and then vanishing.

It occurred to Tom that all this may not be a coincidence, but might be linked to the Crown. But how? He yawned and, aware he still felt tired, climbed back into his damaged bed to catch what sleep he could.

He was woken by the phone ringing on the bedside table. He fumbled blearily for the receiver, picked it up and croaked, "Hello?"

"Tommy ... at last, there you are." Septimus' voice was urgent.

"Eh? Wa... what time is it?"

"Eight a.m. I'm sorry to say. But, can you come now? The Professor says it's urgent."

Tom blinked and stared again at his room and then down at the carpet where a muddy boot print could be seen. "Oh heck ..." he gulped. It had been real!

"What is it, boyo?"

"Septimus, last night one of those things happened where someone from another time, or maybe from the Twisted Reality, was here."

"What? Where?"

"Here in my room. I think ... yes, I am sure he was a Viking and was about to kill me. I dreamt it but in the dream he was going to hit me with his axe and then I woke up and ..."

"Whoah; slow down. Just get dressed and get here and then tell us all."

"OK, fine." Tom rang off, got dressed, scribbled a note for his parents to say he was out with a friend and would be back later, then Walked to the Institute.

"Sorry to wake you so early on a Saturday, Thomas," the Professor said, looking up from his desk as Tom walked into the study. The room was full of Tom's friends - apart from Charlie of course - as well as the archaeologist, Dr Midas, who was spreading marmalade onto a slice of toast. The Professor gestured at a plate on the table. "Have you breakfasted Tom? Help yourself; have a pain au chocolat or something. I wouldn't have called you were it not urgent. It is what Persephone said last evening that had me worried."

The smell of food made Tom's stomach rumble. He reached over and helped himself to a croissant, bit into it and then asked a question, crumbs flaking onto his sweatshirt.

"What was that, Professor?"

"Hum ..." The Professor sipped at a mug of coffee and thought for a moment before answering. "She worried me, that girl did - firstly what she said about us having met before, although I cannot recall where. Then it was that bit about the final part of the Crown - your battered old alarm clock oddly enough - being the key part.

That phrase bothered me and I have been up all night thinking about it. Not long ago, I found something written here in the tablet that I felt was relevant and I asked Dr Midas to join us and help me decipher it. As you know, his knowledge of Cuneiform is unsurpassed and I wanted to check I was right. Doctor, can you tell everyone what we found?"

Midas nodded, crunched on his toast and gestured with his little finger at some tick marks on the side of the tablet. He swallowed and then spoke.

"There are two sections that I am sure are new. I am still working on the second part, but the first part we have both been able to read. It suggests that when the Crown was shattered and scattered across time and space ... and from what the Professor tells me, we now know into this alternate 'Twisted Reality' ... two special fragments were created. One was the tablet, destined to be the guide and to show the way to the others. The other was the clock: 'the key part' as Persephone apparently called it. Its role was to be pivotal. You see: the sentience – that is, the state of consciousness - at the heart of the Crown perceived that others opposed to his master's plan might seek it and might locate fragments. A single fragment out of the Crown would prevent it reforming. Thus, a key component was created that would be the beacon for the other parts to home in on."

"So we can use the tablet to locate the other parts?" Edward suggested.

Midas shook his head. "My apologies, my English is sometimes incorrect. What I meant to say was that the fragments would then behave like homing pigeons."

"Homing pigeons are trained to always find their way home," Septimus said. "Are you saying what I think you're saying?"

"Yes, the script here talks of the key fragment calling to the other parts and that when that happens they will come to it."

Tom dropped the half-eaten croissant onto his plate. "I still don't understand why - or how - my alarm clock comes to be a 'key' part. It's not that old. And by the way, Professor, battered or not, my dad is NOT going to be happy about his clock going missing! But anyway ... that said, the clock will manifest as a fragment in less than an hour!"

Neoptolemas nodded. "Indeed; I was not understating the urgency, Thomas. So you see, my friends, our plan to stay away from the Temple is futile. According to the tablet, in the next sixty minutes the clock will become the key fragment. Once that happens, Persephone will be free to use it to summon the others from wherever they are, the Crown reforms and Knossos is free."

Dr Midas cleared his throat and said into the horrified silence, "Then, according to the tablet, he will use the Crown to destroy the world!"

CHAPTER TWENTY FOUR
THE TEMPLE OF KNOSSOS

"Persephone again! She seems so pivotal to all that is transpiring." Mary frowned, saying, "And yet we know nothing about the wretched girl."

"Mary is right," Septimus said. "We must find out why she is involved in this."

"We don't have time," Neoptolemas replied.

"Is there something you know that you're not telling us Prof? And before you answer, don't just tell me you are a Professor for a reason. You know what I mean," demanded Septimus.

Tom smiled faintly and looked at the old man, but he was staring into space, frowning. "Professor?" Tom prompted.

Neoptolemas got up and paced across the room to the patio windows. He peered through the glass at the sundial that stood upon a stone pillar in the garden. Eventually he turned back to the others.

"That is the problem. I can't remember. I mean, when she said that about knowing me, I had the feeling I should be able to recall it ..." he shrugged, "but if I have met her before either she has changed ... or I have."

"Maybe I can find out in a dream?" Tom suggested.

The Professor shook his head and returned to the desk. "As I just said, we don't have time." He pulled from his waistcoat pocket a watch on a gold chain and examined it. "Your timing is not quite accurate, Thomas. In fact the clock manifests as a fragment in less than thirty minutes."

"Ah ... oops," muttered Midas through a mouthful of toast, and they all turned to him.

"Doctor?" The Professor asked, but Midas did not reply. He picked up the tablet he had been examining, put it in the lead case that was also on the desk, closed the lid and then took the case and put it over near the door to the garden. When he returned he spoke in a whisper.

"I have just deciphered the second inscription," he explained. "As we suspected, there is intelligence in the Crown and that passage also confirms what Tom dreamt: the consciousness of Knossos is indeed present. However, we have always assumed that it was waiting for the Crown to be reformed in order to get free." He turned and looked towards the back door and all their eyes followed his gaze.

"That is not the case," he said after a moment, "or not entirely the case. It seems that the consciousness is aware of its immediate surroundings. In other words ..."

"It can see us, hear us?" Mary gasped.

"Well, maybe not in the way we do, but it is aware of us. Perhaps some form of telepathic link or sense. If so, maybe Persephone and her companions maintain some link to the spirit of Knossos also."

Tom saw in his head the pearl pendant around the neck of Persephone that first day at school and then later in his dream around the necks of the Cult of Knossos and finally again in The Office just last night.

"It's the necklaces. That's how he enforced his will upon them in my dream."

Edward grunted. "Perhaps then, that is how he still does."

"But in that case every discussion we have had in front of the tablet, any of the other treasures or the clock ... all our plans ... every one of them has been known to them all along."

"I have been a fool," Neoptolemas said despondently.

A thought occurred to Tom.

"Hang on, if the treasures were like a webcam, why did the Black Robes attack us in the Museum? I thought it odd they never came again. After all, we were chasing after the fragments along with Lapace and so on and there was not even a hint of them."

"It's almost as if they wanted us to do the work and find the treasures," Mary suggested and the Professor nodded.

"Yes, that is it. We are like a toy that they wound up and let go."

"So they were using us all along?" Tom said.

"Not just us," the Professor said, "but my counterparts too. The Custodian and Thielmann were also in pursuit of the treasure - Thielmann just used Lapace to do it. All along the Cult knew that once they had the vital fragment - the clock - it could summon all the others to it."

"But why make us do the work?" Tom was puzzled. "Would it not be safer to get all the fragments for themselves?"

"Revenge!" The Professor said. "Knossos wanted revenge on me for what I did to him back then."

Tom gasped as another piece of the puzzle fell into place. "You ... you were the sorcerer? Titus?"

The old man nodded. "Yes, I was Titus. Or rather, more accurately we were Titus - the Custodian, Thiemann and I. Titus was the man we were, who got split between the realities just as the realities themselves split."

"Wow," Septimus whistled. "If Titus shattered the Crown in the first place, then that would explain why Knossos has it in for you and would want to get his own back."

"Yes; by using me to do his work for him. Even that charade at The Office was part of the act. He put temptation in our way, knowing that we would reject it. Then he could summon the fragments and when the Crown was formed again he could destroy the world and laugh at us. Finally, Knossos would triumph."

"What should we do?" Mary asked.

Tom checked his watch: a few minutes to nine o'clock. "Mary, quickly - put up a wall around the strongbox!" he ordered.

Mary glanced at the Professor, who nodded encouragement, then she closed her eyes and her face took on an expression of profound concentration. In the air around the strongbox there was a shimmering and a silvery globe of almost translucent energy formed around it. Without opening her eyes, she gave a barely perceptible nod and a faint smile of satisfaction.

Suddenly the smile dropped into a frown. A moment later, Tom could feel a surge of power in the room and a disturbance to the Flow of Time. Someone was Walking or ...

"It's happening!" Mary hissed through teeth clenched in effort. The sphere's smooth surface suddenly jumped, heaved and rippled. Mary groaned and then slumped forward onto the desk. As she fell, the sphere vanished. A moment later the sensation of disturbance of temporal energy abruptly ceased and Mary came to her senses. "I'm sorry," she gasped. "It was too strong."

"Oh dear!" Septimus rushed over to the strongbox and tentatively lifted the lid. His expression grim he looked up at them.

"It's gone!"

There was a moment's horrified silence before the Professor

spoke. "The Temple: we must go at once. Come!" he ordered and suddenly Tom felt a monumental shift in the Flow of Time. The Professor was Walking them all. There was no reaching forward to make contact with them - he just willed it and suddenly the study in London was gone and they appeared instantly in another place ...

... another place where the noonday sun beat down upon them from high up in the cloudless sky; and where they stood like Olympian gods on a plateau way above the plains of Greece. Nearby, the steeply pitched roof of a temple lay upon its colonnaded supports. Some had fallen over or were cracked; all were weathered with the passage of fifty centuries. Yet to Tom, who had seen it before, there was no doubting where they were. If the crown carved into the stones and defacing the front of the structure was not enough, there was a feeling to this place - a sense of power and an echo of death. They had arrived at the Temple of Knossos.

"My word!" exclaimed Dr Midas, "I had not realised how exhilarating it would be. You are lucky people to be able to travel thus at will."

"I apologise, Doctor, I had not asked permission to bring you along, but I wanted you close and I was in a hurry. Now, spread out everyone. Let's find the Cult members."

"Professor!" shouted Septimus a moment later. He had wandered to the edge of the plateau and was pointing down the path, which curved around the hill to reach the hilltop close to where he was standing. A moment later, the Custodian and a dozen Men in Suits strolled off the end of the path and stood right next to him.

"Good heavens, Professor!" Dr Midas exclaimed. "That man

is the spitting image of you. Twins, are you?"

"Not exactly," The Professor muttered.

"Oh, I see," Midas said absently, looking with a puzzled frown from Neoptolemas to the Custodian and plainly not getting it.

"It seems the Doctor has not understood what the Prof said about his relationship to the Custodian," Tom murmured to Edward.

"Clearly not; but can you blame him?"

"I guess not," said Tom, watching as the Custodian and his Directorate heavies strolled towards them. "Wait till he sees Thielmann!"

Edward grinned.

"I see that we have come on the same mission, brother," the Custodian addressed Neoptolemas. "As has he ..." he added, pointing towards the other side of the hilltop where twenty men had suddenly materialised. Half were dressed in the black, red and silver of the Twisted Reality guards and included Redfeld and Thielmann. The other half comprised Lapace and his party, together with a wild-eyed Charlie, who had the look of a man who has not quite understood what he is getting himself into.

Dr Midas's eyes appeared about to pop out of his head as they fixed on Thielmann then swivelled back to Neoptolemas and the Custodian. He opened his mouth to speak, but no words came out.

Every one of the newcomers, even Charlie, was armed. Two of Redfeld's men were carrying a heavy machine gun and ammunition boxes; another had a bazooka-like device.

"It seems we're all here then," Septimus remarked dryly as he examined the weapons at Redfeld's disposal, "but we did not bring an entire arsenal with us!"

"Is all that strictly necessary?" the Professor demanded of the

253

Nazi captain.

"Indeed, Captain Redfeld," Edward commented, "it does seem a little 'over the top' as you say these days." He gestured towards the Temple. "Those who oppose us are mostly fanatics with knives, not well-armed soldiers."

"Strange to hear that coming from you, Lieutenant," Redfeld sneered, "coming, I mean, from a man who was once part of an army that took rockets, artillery and rifles along to invade a country defended only by primitive Zulu spearmen!"

Edward coloured. "Well maybe my views have changed, sir," he said stiffly.

"You mean you've gone soft," Redfeld retorted.

"Leave him alone," Mary shouted, moving to Edward's side and glaring up at Redfeld.

"Ah, how touching: the baker's maid coming to the aid of the soldier. Poetic even," he sniggered.

"That will do!" snapped Thielmann. "We have little time for such bickering. We must put our differences to one side ... for today anyway."

"Agreed," replied the Custodian.

Neoptolemas gave a curt nod of assent.

"My men will attack the Temple," the Colonel declared. "We will find the fragments and prevent the Crown from forming," he squinted up at the sun. "Come, we don't have long." He turned to Redfeld. *"Setzen Sie ihre Männer, Hauptmann. Jetzt!"*

Redfeld snapped his heels together. *"Ja, Herr Oberst!"*

Responding to the Colonel's command to ready his men, Redfeld roared out orders to his guards, who moved forward. One pair set up the heavy machine gun, whilst the others continued towards the Temple, rifles at the ready. To begin with there was no sign of resistance. Then, as the soldiers closed in on the pillars, Tom heard a curious whirring sound in the air. It tugged at his memory. Then, eyes widening, he remembered where he had heard it before.

"They have sling shots, Captain! Watch out!"

Redfeld opened his mouth to respond when half a dozen stones flew out from the darkness between the pillars and towards the soldiers. Two of Redfeld's men gave yelps of pain and another just collapsed without a sound, blood pouring from his scalp.

"*Feuer!*" Redfeld bellowed and with a 'snap-crack', the rifles opened up. A moment later the staccato 'rat-a-tat-tat-tat' of the machine gun joined in and the side of the Temple was assailed by a hail of bullets.

"Not terribly subtle, is he," remarked Septimus.

"Maybe not, but it is certainly effective," Edward commented, observing the battle with the professional eye of a soldier. "Those slings have been silenced."

Grimacing at the machine gun, Mary clapped her hands to her ears. "It's so much louder than musket fire," she complained.

Septimus grinned. "Wait till they fire the rocket!"

"*Ruhe die Waffen!*" Redfeld yelled, "*Vorwarts!*"

As commanded, the soldiers stopped firing and advanced again. This time there was no response from the Temple. The Professor led his Hourglass Institute along after them, whilst the Directorate brought up the rear.

"Professor." Tom caught up with the old man. "Isn't the Colonel breaking the rules? I mean, if people get killed, won't we be altering the future?"

"Ah, Thomas, in this we really have no choice. Unless we can defeat Knossos, there will be no future. It is, you might say, the lesser of two evils."

Tom gulped and nodded glumly, falling back to walk between Edward and Mary.

Once they had passed between the pillars the light was poor and the shadows closed in. Nevertheless, as they moved towards the inner temple, Tom spotted one black-robed Cultist in a crumpled heap on the floor, a spreading pool of blood beneath him. Tom grimaced: he could not see the face, but he did not think it was Persephone.

As they passed between yet more pillars and reached the door to the inner temple, there was a blinding flash of light as a torch ignited and flared up. It burned alone for a moment before several more joined it and suddenly the entrance to the antechamber was bathed in light. Illuminated by the torches, Tom could see no fewer than twenty Black Robes. They were standing in a circle just outside the door, their hands linked to form a chain.

"Move or we fire!" Redfeld ordered. There was no response.

"Wait!" Neoptolemas shouted. "Don't shoot!"

"Too late, old man!" Redfeld snapped out the order, "Feuer!"

Tom closed his eyes. An instant later he heard the terrifying fusillade of rifle shot and waited for the screams of agony from the Black Robes. To his surprise the only sound he heard was Redfeld cursing.

Tom opened his eyes. Given how tightly packed the Black Robes were and the extreme shortness of the range, he would have expected half a dozen casualties at the very least. Yet, not a single figure had flinched or fallen.

"*Mein Got, wie Kann es Sein?* My God, how can it be?" Redfeld repeated in English, his eyes wide and staring.

"They must have a wall," Edward suggested to Mary.

"Aye, I can see it. It comes from all of them."

"Some form of collective barrier my bullets cannot penetrate,"

Redfeld scowled, "so it seals them in? Hence we cannot get to them and bring it down." He swore. "Clever - if irritating."

"Then, let us try," the Custodian said. "Move your weapons back, Captain, and do not interfere," he ordered Redfeld, signalling his Directorate forward. The Men in Suits shuffled along like automatons, faces identical, expressionless and cold. As they reached a point a few metres from the Cult members, they made contact with the invisible barrier. There they halted and then as one raised their hands and pushed against it.

At first, there was no response and for the first time tension showed on the faces of the Men in Suits and was mirrored on that of the Custodian.

"It is strong," he gasped. Then he gathered himself and thrust his hands forward. Around him his men did likewise. Suddenly there was a shimmering in the air and the Men in Suits staggered forward a few steps as the wall collapsed under the strain.

"But not strong enough!" the Custodian added grimly as his men advanced on the Cultists.

The men and women in black robes drew their curved daggers from their sleeves and rushed at the Directorate. Each of the Custodian's men was outnumbered three or four to one, but the Cultists were mere flesh and blood, armed with puny blades. Useless against the creatures of energy the Custodian had created. The Black Robes attacked fanatically, screaming and yelling and swinging their blades to left and right, but the Men in Suits had fists of steel. As each Cultist came in range, a fearsome smash from a fist connected with a face or belly and the Black Robe crumpled to the ground, stunned or dead.

"It's madness. They are just sacrificing themselves for nothing!" Tom overheard Rolf Lapace say to Charlie, who stood at his side. The Professor heard it too.

"NO! Not for nothing," Neoptolemas shouted back at them from where he was peering round a pillar towards the antechamber door. "They are buying time. We must get inside NOW. Tom, can you remember the layout of that room?"

Tom nodded. "It is simple enough."

"Then, you must take us because for me it's been a while! Right, let us go. Bring as many as you can, Tom. The rest must occupy the Cultists. My brothers and I will follow your lead. Now Tom!"

Whirling round, Tom reached over to grab Septimus' arm. Mary and Edward were close by and touched him as well. Then he Walked.

He, Mary, Edward, Septimus, the Professor and both of his doubles materialised in the antechamber. It was lit up - just as it had been in Tom's dream - with fires in braziers and torches in sconces on the walls. Beyond this chamber he could see the inner sanctum. There, upon the altar, were the treasures: the fragments of the Crown of Knossos separated all those centuries ago and scattered across time and reality, now brought back together. Someone had arranged the fragments in a ring, waiting for the moment when they would reunite.

Yet the inner sanctum was empty. Were all the Cult members outside, fighting the others? Tom wondered.

"We must hurry. If I can separate the pieces then they will not reform," the Professor shouted and started forward towards the door. As he did so, Tom saw a movement from behind a pillar. He opened his mouth to shout a warning - but he was too late. Persephone stepped out; her dagger held aloft, seized the Professor and thrust the blade into his chest. With a groan, Neoptolemas collapsed to the ground, blood spurting from his wound. The Custodian and Thielmann cried out, clutching their chests

258

as though they too had been struck.

"Die, old man," Persephone screamed at the Professor as he and his doubles fell. "Do you remember me now? Do you remember the child? A little girl whose parents died in this Temple? I blame you the most of all, for it is you who were the conscience in the sorcerer, Titus. Anything good was yours. The other two were cold logic and evil. It is you who should have made a difference!" she shouted, spitting at the crumpled body on the floor.

The Professor lay on the flagstones, blood pouring from his wound. He gazed up at the girl and a look of horror flashed on his face. Through his agony he managed to speak.

"You? That was you? I did not know. I am sorry."

"Sorry? You think 'sorry' is enough? You will pay!" Persephone raged, swinging the blade up again ready for the killing blow.

"WALL!" Mary shouted and Persephone was thrust violently away from the Professor. Mary stood in front of her, face tense with concentration, her outstretched arms radiating energy and pinning Persephone to the pillar.

Panicking, Tom ran forward and knelt down next to the Professor. Blood was gushing from his wound and Tom pressed his hand on it to try to staunch the flow.

"Professor! Professor," he gasped. The old man opened his eyes, looked at Tom and then pointed at the altar. He opened his mouth to speak, but no words came out. He tried again.

"Quickly ... quickly, you must separate the f ..." he managed before collapsing.

"Come on! Edward! Septimus! The fragments," Tom shouted and the three of them Walked to the altar.

"Take all the pieces!" Septimus ordered. He and Edward

seized two fragments each, and Tom the remainder.

"Now! Split."

They Walked to the far corners of the room. As they did so, Tom felt an intense heat radiating from the fragment. With the heat came a dragging sensation as it tugged at his hand and seemed to be pulling towards the other fragments. He swayed, his head swimming as nausea surged into his throat. The dragging grew more and more intense, becoming a searing pain as though his fingers were immersed in a fire. "I cannot hold it!" Tom gasped in agony, gritting his teeth.

But hold on he did until, suddenly, the heat dissipated and the tugging ceased, the fragment rapidly cooling and as it did he felt it change in his hand. A moment later, he was holding his father's alarm clock.

"We've done it!" he cried. Shaking with the effort, he looked across at the others: Septimus had the stone tablet and the diamond, whilst Edward held the sword of Alexander and the pearls. It appeared that all the fragments had transmuted back to their original forms.

"Is it... is it over?" Tom asked.

The answer was a violent shaking of the room. Tom was tossed onto his hands and feet, the clock tumbling away from him with a clatter.

"What is happening?" he shouted.

The next noise he heard was a total surprise. It was the sound of Persephone laughing. "Fools - you are fools!" she shouted.

The shaking grew more violent and stones started to fall from the ceiling and smashed on the ground next to him.

"Everyone out, it's an earthquake," Septimus yelled. Tom and Mary ran towards him as he and Edward reached down to the Professor. Dragging him between them, they stumbled out of

260

the antechamber, the Colonel and the Custodian shuffling behind. Outside, the remaining Black Robes had ceased attacking
the Men in Suits and fallen to their knees, hands lifted in prayer.

The sound of laughter pursued them out of the antechamber
and soon Persephone emerged. Triumphantly, she thrust her
hands in the air. "I am the Priestess of the Temple! Behold, I
have my revenge and now I am glad. For Knossos has won!"

The Temple shook again, but this time Tom could see that
the whole hillside trembled. Out on the plain the shaking olive
groves revealed that the tremor was manifesting over a huge
area. It was like Alexandria all over again.

Persephone, still laughing, now started dancing, swaying
back and forth, her robe billowing out behind her, a fanatical
grin of ecstasy stamped on her features.

"She's insane!" Mary gasped in horror as the priestess cackled
and screeched.

"The end of all the worlds comes," Persephone taunted them.
"Death awaits us all!"

CHAPTER TWENTY FIVE
MESSAGE IN A BOTTLE

"What is she going on about?" Charlie muttered. "Just an earthquake ain't it?" he asked Lapace. Everyone turned to face him. The same thought was on all their minds it seemed: was it just an earthquake or something more?

"The end comes, behold your doom. You have brought this on yourselves!" Persephone shouted.

Redfeld snapped an order and three of his soldiers scampered over and seized her, binding her hands and ankles and depositing her next to the other Black Robes, who had been roped and were huddled together.

"What is going on, Custodian?" Tom yelled. Around them the shaking of the pillars intensified. There was a sudden ear-shattering noise and a huge chunk of stone sheared off the roof of the Temple, came tumbling down from high above them and pulverised a statue of a Grecian warrior on a plinth only yards from where they stood. Everyone took a few steps backwards.

"I ... I don't understand," the Custodian stuttered, staring around him.

"They did not expect this eventuality," Redfeld said, looking intently at his superior and then at his duplicates.

Tom looked too and noticed the confusion on the faces of Thielmann and the Custodian. The Professor, meanwhile, was still unconscious: his breathing shallow. Mary was kneeling by his side. "Is(Are) any of your soldiers a physician?" she gasped. Thielmann shook his head, but beckoned to one of the guards carrying a first-aid box. The man rummaged inside and held out a field dressing to Mary, who took it and held it against the old man's wound.

"The Crown has not reformed. Knossos is not reborn. Why then is this world ending?" the Custodian asked.

"It is not only this one," Colonel Thielmann said, "but my world, too. Look ... the wall has shattered."

He pointed and within the Temple, Tom could now see the soldiers from Theilmann's parallel world. The shadowy outlines of troops from Redfeld's army, which presumably occupied Greece - including the Temple - in the Twisted Reality, were gawping open-mouthed as the world shook about them.

A pillar tumbled and a soldier's scream of terror was cut off as he was crushed beneath the falling stone. His comrades scattered like startled birds and then hung around outside the Temple, studying the Walkers - obviously uncertain who they were. Redfeld sent one of his men over with orders for them and they withdrew, away from the disintegrating building towards the edge of the plateau.

"There, too ..." The Custodian cried in a hollow, emotionless voice that still somehow suggested fear.

He was looking at a nearby pillar that was lying on the ground. Part of the stone appeared to be a table: a sand table standing on a marble floor. It was the table from The Office. The three worlds: Tom's, the Twisted Reality and The Office, were all present, overlapping and intruding on each other.

"At least now we have an explanation for all those visits from other times and worlds," Edward commented. "If the realities

263

are overlapping and intruding on each other, then men can pass from one to the other. Just like Redfeld did in the Institute or your Viking from the past, Tom."

Tom nodded, but he had noticed something else. He could see that the sand table and Redfeld's soldiers were in fact getting clearer and closer. It was as if the worlds were merging; coming together, collapsing into each other in some cataclysmic event that would end everything.

"The stone, Septimus, get out the stone tablet!" Tom shouted.

Septimus did not respond, but instead just stared in disbelief around him. "I...what?" he muttered. Tom tried again, rushing to stand in front of the Welshman.

"The stone tablet. Get it out!"

Septimus blinked. He stared at Tom then finally nodded. He brought out the tablet from inside his jacket, where he had thrust it earlier in the inner sanctum. He glanced at it then frowned, holding it up so that they could all see. There on the surface the image of the Crown lay in fragments. Beside it were depictions of disaster and destruction, but more striking than before. The scene was clearer and more vibrant. The stones and pillars it portrayed shaking and tumbling to crush the terrified men and women under them.

"But, Colonel," Redfeld said, "we came here to prevent this. We came here to stop the Crown re-forming so that this destruction would not occur, so why ..."

Thielmann shook his head. "Unfortunately, Captain, it seems that we were wrong. The tablet does not show the destruction that would result if the Crown were to reform and Knossos rise again. Quite the reverse: it shows what will happen if it does not reform! We have been tricked."

"Ah, what fools we have been. I comprehend now," the Cus-

264

todian said. "When the Event occurred and the universe was divided it was inherently unstable. Because it was also shattered at the moment the realities were created, the Crown is needed to stabilise them. Otherwise we have ..."

"The end of everything," Thielmann completed his sentence.

"What are you two saying? That we came here to prevent the Crown reforming, that the Professor lies dying there," Tom pointed at Neoptolemas who was sitting, slumped against the base of a statue, his breathing getting shallower by the moment, "but you got it wrong! We should not have even tried?"

The Professor coughed, opened an eye and looked at Tom. "That ...," he began in a weak voice, "... is just what they are saying."

"On the whole, it would have been better to have learnt this earlier, don't you think?" Septimus commented.

Around them the Temple juddered and beyond the pillars it seemed the whole world was shrinking as the realities collided. Tom stared gloomily out of the ruins. A mile or so away he could see a range of mountains. One of them - taller than the others - had a flattened top from which acrid smoke seemed to be rising. As he gazed upon it the smoke grew thicker and he could now see that the peak was beginning to shake. Suddenly, with a tremendous boom, the top of what he now realised was a volcano exploded, filling the air with the stench of sulphur. Molten rock spewed forth, hurled high in the air and fiery lava came sliding down the mountainside straight towards them.

"Is there nothing you can do?" he asked, aware that his voice was high-pitched with fright, but really not caring. "At this rate it will all be over very quickly unless we can do something!"

The Professor's face knotted up in sudden agony and he let out a cry of pain. Blood was now speckling on his lips as he

265

answered. "There is only one chance. We must change what has been. This timeline - this series of events -must never come to be."

"You are saying we go back and do it again ... but I thought no one could live through the same moments twice," Tom said, "at least, not without great difficulty."

The Custodian came over to look down at Neoptolemas then nodded. "That is true, Thomas, but if we sent a message back to the past ... to one of us ... then that person could try to prevent this future by allowing the Crown to reform after all."

"Like a message in a bottle?" Charlie suggested, moving to stand near them. No one mentioned his betrayal. It seemed irrelevant now when around them the world was ending. Even so, Tom saw that Edward's expression was cold as he regarded their former friend.

"Exactly so ... Mr Hawker," the Professor answered and his voice, though weak, was friendly and welcoming as if he had forgotten the incident, or it did not matter to him.

"Is that even possible?" the sailor asked incredulously.

"It takes great amounts of energy to do such a thing. To generate a message that would change the past we must tap into a different future," Thielmann explained.

"You mean different to this one?" Tom asked, looking around again. There was a loud crack from over near the edge of the plateau where a group of Redfeld's soldiers stood in a small huddle. Tom saw terror stamped on the face of one young trooper as he realised, too late, that the cliff face was giving way. A massive chunk of rock sheared off and fell tumbling into the valley below, carrying the doomed men with it.

Thielmann grunted and Tom saw that he was looking in the same direction. "Indeed," he answered, "for there is nothing but death here: no empires to conquer; no hope of one day invading your world after all. Not even your pathetic desires will survive ... such as they are. Nothing ... nothing, forever. Ironic don't you think that Knossos gets his wish after all? The end of our worlds," he added with a hollow laugh and then shook his head. "Of course, boy, I speak of another future. One in which this does not happen."

"One in which none of us dies, you mean?"

The Colonel nodded. "Perhaps ... or maybe ..." he started to answer, but it was the Professor's weak voice that completed the sentence.

"Maybe some will live who were already dead. You see, I now remember why Persephone hates us, why she did this to me." Still lying on the ground, he pointed to where Persephone and the captured Black Robes sat tied up with their backs to a pillar.

The Custodian stirred. "You cannot suggest promising what I think you are! I also recall what happened to her parents. Tragic, I am sure, but you risk changing everything."

"Now, just think a moment about what you are saying," the Professor responded breathlessly. "Look about you, Custodian. Everything is changing. We cannot risk not doing it."

Thielmann looked at his brothers and shook his head. "But are we not both forgetting how we three feel ... felt about Knossos and the Crown? None of us would believe a message telling us to ensure that the Crown reforms. All of us have the strongest motivation to ensure exactly the opposite."

The Custodian nodded and then tilted his head as another thought occurred to him. "You are right, besides which, we ... that is, none of we three ... can do it. We were already here all those years ago, brother - you know that. And only a potentate could do what you suggest."

"That is exactly what I am saying, Custodian. If you recall it was you who suggested who that might be."

Tom gulped. "Are you talking about me?" he asked. "If so, maybe you would like to explain what it is you are saying."

"There is energy in the diff ..." the Professor's voice died away as he groaned in pain, wiped his forehead with a handkerchief and tried again. "The difference ..." he gasped, shook his head and waved at Thielmann to go on.

"What my brother is trying to say is that there is energy in the difference between one future and another future, and the greater that difference the greater the energy. Redfeld here can create a hypothetical alternative to this timeline: an illusion in which Persephone is alive and living with her parents, the man and woman who died millennia ago when Knossos fell and the Crown was shattered. We will show her the possibility that they are saved and ask her to help us. That difference would be enough to generate the power we need to send a message back."

Tom looked across at the girl, sitting with her hands and ankles tied, face peaceful as she awaited the end.

"But that would be a lie!" Tom flung out his hand in a dismissive gesture at Redfeld. "His power is to make illusions. They are not real. You would be promising her nothing."

"Ah, but we would promising her just what she sees, Tom," the Professor said weakly, "for a potentate could make that happen: a potentate with his power enhanced by the Crown of Knossos. You, Tom - you will change the past so that her parents live."

Thielmann stirred again. "Indeed you must, for as you imply, an illusion is not real and will not generate the power we need. We will use it merely as a tool to show her what we intend if she will be our messenger and help us. That alternative future must occur though, or we will fail and the worlds will end."

"I don't understand." Tom said.

The Colonel frowned then held up a hand, counting out the points of the plan one finger at a time.

"One: we get Persephone to agree to send a message back to you. Two: the potential energy of the future YOU will eventually create will be enough to deliver the message. Three: You get the message a few hours ago - we cannot manage to fling the message back very far. Four: you ensure the Crown reforms and then somehow defeat Knossos. I suggest your meddlesome friends will be of help here because we," he pointed at his duplicates, "will not. Five: You ensure Persephone's parents live and so complete the loop."

Tom blinked; his mind boggling as he grappled with the concept. "Is that all? I thought it would be something difficult," he muttered, but nobody smiled, not even Septimus.

He looked around him: beyond the Temple it was becoming dark. Right now, in the middle of the day. Where was the sun? Were the fumes from the volcano obscuring it, or had it also been swept away by the imploding realities? If so, the end could not be far away.

Then another thought occurred to him. "But are we not forgetting that I will have no reason to believe Persephone? If she turns up telling me that the Crown must be allowed to reform, I would just reject it as a trick by Knossos wouldn't I? Wouldn't that be your reaction?"

Septimus, who had been following the conversation closely, scratched his chin. "The lad has a point and if he must persuade me and the others, our reaction will be just as sceptical," he agreed.

"So then, we must include in the message something to per-

269

suade Tom and Septimus and we must think of it quickly," Edward commented, with an anxious glance towards the oncoming darkness. "But what?"

The Welshman snapped his fingers and kneeling down whispered into the Professor's ear. Neoptolemas nodded. "Yes, that is a good idea Mr Mason and should convince even a sceptic like you, but what of Thomas?"

"Would it be possible to send a small object back with the message?" Tom asked, a thought coming to him.

Thielmann shrugged. "You could, but it will not last more than a few moments when it arrives - it will vanish along with Persephone after she delivers her message."

"Then I also have an idea," Tom said. Reaching into his pocket, he retrieved the acorn and passed it to the Professor. The old man looked at it solemnly then looked up at Tom, his blood-stained lips lifting in a weak smile.

"Perfect," he said.

"Very well gentlemen," the Custodian muttered. "We can delay no longer so I suggest we put the plan into action. Can I ask everyone else to step away? I will fetch the girl. This conversation must be private. Redfeld, we will call you when we need you."

They moved a little distance away, although not so far as to be too close to the edge of the plateau; nor did they approach the tottering structure of the Temple. Tom glanced round at Charlie, Septimus, Edward, Mary and even across at the Captain. Everyone looked frightened.

Mary, as she continued with shaking hands to press a blood soaked dressing to the Professor's wound, looked despairingly out at the raging chaos that threatened to engulf them, her face pale and streaked with tears. The volcano continued to boom and belch out fire in a spectacular eruption, black smoke billowing into a great mushroom cloud above it, the smell of sulphur intensifying and catching in their throats. "It is God's wrath visited upon us with fire and brimstone, like it says in the Bible," she cried, her voice trembling. "Is this the apocalypse? Is this judgement day?"

Edward crouched down beside her and placed his arm gently around her waist. "If it is, my dear Mary, then you have nothing to fear from the wrath of the Almighty."

Tremulously, Mary smiled up at him, but her hands still shook. She was right to be afraid, thought Tom. This could well be the end of them all. He wondered how it would feel to die. He imagined his family, probably still asleep in Britain. At home it was about 9.30 a.m. The household might still be slumbering: enjoying the lie in of a weekend. He pondered the thought that maybe he should go and wake them. He could warn them that in little more than minutes the world might end. He just as swiftly dismissed the idea. To begin with they would hardly believe him and if they did, they would surely try to stop him returning to the Temple or be a distraction and worry. Secondly, what good would it do? All he would achieve would be to scare them. If they must die along with everybody else in the rest of the world, why not make it swift, perhaps even without them knowing. Twice this year the people he loved had been in terrible danger. If he and his friends succeeded in averting this disaster then it would be the second time that his family had known nothing about it.

They all watched in silence as the Custodian led Persephone over to stand near the Professor. She wore an expression of profound scepticism as she listened to whatever he was saying. Slowly, though, it was replaced by puzzlement, then something

271

like a hint of hope lit up her sullen features. After another moment she nodded once.

"Septimus?" Tom asked as they all watched.

"Yes boyo?" The Welshman replied.

"How will we know if we succeed?"

"That is the strange thing, Tommy boy. None of us will remember this moment, for if we succeed this will never have occurred. But Tom, whatever happens you must still save Persephone's parents. You understand that don't you? If you don't save them, then even if the message is delivered and the Crown forms and is used to stabilize the realities and stop all this ..." he waved around him at the dark, disintegrating landscape, "... well, then there will be a paradox and in the end, it will all rebound like an elastic band and we will be back where we started, staring down into the abyss."

"Well fine, Septimus. The only problem is that there is not much point in telling me this is there. The Tom that will get the visit from Persephone won't remember this conversation!"

Septimus grimaced. "Hum; I see your point. We had better hope those three can get that message across to you then."

Thielmann waved Redfeld over. The Nazi captain reached out a hand and placed it on Persephone's head. She looked frightened but did not flinch. Redfeld started talking to her, but the words were soft and Tom could not hear what he was saying.

Around them darkness flowed like a flood across the plain beneath the plateau. Tom could see nothing out there now except the volcano's river of fire. It was as if the world was confined to the immediate area upon which they stood. With a gasp he realised that if this were so, his family was already dead: swept for a second time into oblivion. Then, the pillars of the Temple began to rattle and shake again and even the fire was disappearing into

272

blackness. Tom could see that the world had mere moments left before it was gone ... perhaps forever.

"I hope they get it across to me as well, Septimus, but more than that; I just hope I know what to do about it when they do..." he said grimly.

Then they stood in silence, staring fearfully out as the darkness closed in upon them ...

CHAPTER TWENTY SIX
A SECOND CHANCE

Tom and Harald, the Viking warrior, materialised in a field near to the edge of a wood. The warrior screamed once and then turned, fixing Tom with a baleful stare.

"Swa scealta leoh life samod beloran weodan," he shouted, raising his axe.

Tom stared at him.

"Nope, no idea what that meant, and I'm not staying to find out," he replied and Walked himself back home, leaving the warrior standing there.

When he materialised in his bedroom, Tom stood for a moment examining the room, reliving the frightening encounter in his mind. He checked his watch. It was still early - some hours before he was due to join the others in the Professor's study to talk about the meeting in The Office last night when Persephone had been revealed as a Black Robe. Yawning with fatigue, Tom was about to climb back into his bed when he heard something strike against the outside of his window. He assumed it was just the wind, but again there was a clatter of something hitting the pane. He scuttled over to it and peered down.

Outside in the back garden a shadowy figure was huddled under the apple tree next to the swing. He could not make out the face, but whoever it was gestured that he should join them.

Too short to be Septimus or Edward; that left Mary, but why was she here alone? Puzzled, he dressed quickly and crept out of his room, holding his breath past his parents' bedroom, down the stairs and out of the back door. Once outside he went over to the apple tree. The moonlight flashed over the figure's face and now he saw who it was, he froze.

"*Persephone!* Is that you?"

"Of course it's me. Were you expecting someone else?"

"Er ... no. I wasn't expecting anyone and certainly not you," he retorted. "You already have my alarm clock so what are you doing here?"

Persephone did not reply at first. She studied Tom for a moment and then suddenly put a hand on his shoulder. "My time is limited ..."

Tom flinched away for her. "What do you mean? What are you after anyway? You made your intentions pretty clear last night in The Office ...." Tom trailed to a halt because Persephone was shaking her head.

"You do not understand. I am not the Persephone who met you in The Office. She is even now ... elsewhere," the girl said enigmatically.

"I don't understand ... you are Persephone."

"Oh Tom, wake up. I am not that Persephone because I have come from the future ... I have come to give you a message."

"What?" Tom replied, aware that his mouth had just dropped open.

"I am a message sent back in time by the Professor to warn you about the future."

"Eh? I don't believe you. This is just some trap you and Knossos dreamt up, isn't it?"

"I don't have time for this, Tom. I have only a few moments

here. The Professor said you would not believe me and I am not surprised. So he gave me this ..."

She held out her hand. In it was an acorn. Tom blinked and took a second look. It was not just any acorn. This was identical to his keepsake, given to him by the Professor months ago; he recognised the slight ridge in the shell. Reaching into his trouser pocket he retrieved the acorn he had put there a couple of days before. He placed them both side by side in his hand and examined them under the moonlight. They were like two peas in a pod or two identical twins. He looked up at Persephone. Could she be speaking the truth? He would never have believed it except that only the Professor and he knew of the significance of this item the girl had brought him. It had been enough to convince him to trust the Professor once before - earlier in the summer - and he realised it was still as potent now.

"Wow ... I don't know what to say...," he mumbled.

"Then don't say anything. Let me talk. You see, we are about to enter a Nexus."

"A what?"

"A Nexus ... oh get the Professor to explain it - but not tonight. He said that under no circumstances were you to discuss any of this with him or his duplicates! None of them must know of this conversation yet. They simply won't accept what I am about to suggest."

"But a Nexus?" Tom asked, now thoroughly confused. "And anyway, if he sent the message in the first place, he must know ..."

"Oh wake up, Tom!" she repeated. "I told you, it is not from now, it is from the future."

"Sorry, er ... I forgot. So what are you about to suggest?"

"Well, as far as I understand things we are at a decision point in time. Soon you will go to the Temple. Then, in the next few hours a moment will come when a choice will be made and that choice will select one of two possible futures. In one future you and I are friends and the world survives."

Tom stared at her in disbelief. "And the other?"

"I kill the Professor, the universe is destroyed and we will never be friends!"

"Gah!" Tom replied. Was she mad? Or could this really be true?

"You kill the Professor? How?"

"I hide in the antechamber behind a pillar nearest the inner sanctum. When he passes by I leap out and stab him," she explained.

Tom gawped at her. "But wait a moment, you are here today telling me this ... so it must be OK. I mean, we must win. Don't you see?"

Persephone shook her head. "That is not how a Nexus works, Tom. We are at a decision point that could go either way. That means there are two potential futures floating out there. In the end, one of them will collapse and one will survive. I am a projection of the Persephone that would exist if we win. The Professor created me from that potential energy and sent me back to tell you this. "

Tom felt like the girl had started talking Chinese. "Potential what?" he muttered.

Persephone tapped her foot impatiently. "I am a fragment of what MIGHT be, but not necessarily what WILL be. It all depends on that decision."

Tom blinked. "So why are you telling me this?"

"Oh, don't you realise? It's you and those close to you who are going to make the decision."

"What decision?"

"The Crown, Tom. It's all about the Crown."

"What do you mean?"

"You will find this hard to believe - especially coming from me, BUT the Crown MUST be allowed to reform. The future of the universe depends on it doing so."

Tom stepped away from her, suspicion jumping back into his mind.

"Oh come on, Persephone, the Professor has been adamant all along that the Crown should not reform, whilst you are blatantly keen that it should. Why has the Professor now so suddenly changed his mind?"

Frowning, Persephone tapped her foot again. "I don't have long to convince you. The Professor was wrong as were his brothers. The Crown reforming is a risk - for it means Knossos lives again. BUT, only the Crown reformed can be used to stabilize the worlds. The worlds are collapsing. That is why you are seeing visits from other times and realities and if it is not stopped the worlds will collide and destroy each other."

Tom considered that. Was that at last the explanation? Was that why these visits were getting more frequent - accelerating as the realities collapsed in on themselves – enabling a Viking to walk into his bedroom?

"How long before the end?" he asked tersely.

"Only hours. You must act now. Go and rouse your friends. Together you must find a way to stop this happening. I can only say a little more. Firstly, if Septimus Mason needs persuading that all this is true, just ask him what it feels like to betray a woman."

"Eh? I don't get it."

"No, but he will. It will convince him."

Tom shrugged but let it pass.

"Finally, the Professor said that you had to consider one question."

"What is that?"

"You need to think about what happened to my parents and prevent it. They must live - that was the deal he and I reached."

Tom blinked and stared at Persephone for a moment. "Can't you tell me what happened?"

Suddenly Persephone looked away and then back at Tom. "I don't have long enough. The potential energy is collapsing."

"Oh.. so ... how do I find out what happened to your parents?"

"The Professor just told me to say he hoped you did not have any nightmares."

Tom stared at her and then feeling suddenly tired, lowered his head in his hands and rubbed his face, the fingers of one hand closing over the acorns.

"Nightmares? What did he mean?"

The girl did not answer.

"Persephone ...?"

He took his hands away from his face and looked up, his voice trailing away as he realised he was alone. "Persephone?" he repeated, looking into the shadows, but there was no reply. She had gone.

Uncurling his fingers, Tom glanced down at his palm where the two acorns had been only seconds before. He could only see one there now: its twin had vanished just as Persephone had. Shaking his head he heaved a sigh. "I have a seriously weird life!"

Back in his room, Tom thought about what the girl had told him. According to her the world was going to end in just a few hours. She was sent back from a future which he and his friends had apparently lived through; at least for long enough to get a message to him in his past. They had experienced all that, but he had not; not yet. How was he expected to change what he had never seen? Persephone had hinted that it was a choice that was made by him and his friends. If they had succeeded in preventing the Crown from reforming, maybe he could change that. He could see to it that the Crown reformed after all. But if he did that, Knossos would return and with the power of the Crown at his disposal, could destroy the world anyway. Tom stood up and walked across to his mirror and stared at himself in the glass.

"This is crazy," he said to his reflection. "Whether the Crown reforms or it does not, Knossos wins and he knows it. So the question is: IF I allow the Crown to reform, what then? What can I do?"

Tom turned away from the mirror, his brain working overtime. How could he and his friends tackle Knossos? The man was a god! Persephone had not been forthcoming about that, had she? Why had the Professor and his brothers not come themselves or maybe sent Septimus to deliver the message. Was it just some limit to the energy needed to transfer the message ... or was there something more? By choosing Persephone, was the Professor sending him a message within the message? Thinking about it, Tom realised it could well be the case that Persephone was the key to all of this. So, was it something to do with her ... but if so, what? What happened at the Temple all those years ago? Why had Persephone attacked the Professor? Why did she hate him and his brothers so much?

"Nightmares ..." Tom muttered, "a message within a message ...?" Yawning, he turned to look at his bed. There was only one way to find out.

The sounds of the clash of daggers on shields filled the air as the Black Robes attacked and Xanthus' soldiers hewed at them. This was no battle though. Xanthus and his men were killers - trained warriors in armour. The Black Robes, whilst fanatical, were untrained and unarmed; this was a massacre.

As Titus watched, several of the Cultists screamed in agony and fell in a pool of their own blood. Titus felt his anger rise at Knossos - this man who believed he was a god and now sacrificed his own followers to give him the time to finish his incantation.

He could not let it go on. Bringing his hands up, Titus held them palm outwards towards Knossos and shouted, "AGE!" As the word left his lips, he felt the power of his anger flooding through him and building towards his outstretched hands.

"Stop him!" Knossos screamed.

Three black-robed figures moved towards Titus. He could not see their faces, shrouded as they were within their hoods, but they seemed to be a man, a woman and a child. The child could not have been more than six or seven and Titus realised these other two were its parents. As the adults ran forward the gem on top of the crown pulsated and for a split second, the two figures seemed to freeze in mid-stride. Then they rushed on again, hurtling toward Titus. Xanthus and two of his warriors moved forward to intercept them.

"NO!" Titus shouted as the swords went back and stabbed into the black-robed couple. The taller of the two, blood running down his side, stumbled past Xanthus, grasped Titus and fell forward, dragging the sorcerer backwards. At that moment, the energies Titus had summoned exploded with the full force of the anger he had felt. But because he had been tugged backwards the blast was directed not at the body of Knossos as he had intended, but with vengeful wrath directly at the Crown. At that instant, the gem atop the Crown flared in intensity as Knossos' incantation reached its climax. The energy driven through the Crown by Knossos, coupled with the power of Titus' own blast, overwhelmed it and in an instant, it shattered.

Titus gaped in horror as he watched the gem stone explode with a vibrant burst of light. Now a slowly expanding globe of incandescent energy was formed. With a final terrible scream, Knossos was annihilated - his body just vanished, consumed by the force of the explosion. The Black Robes that clustered around him were sucked in and disappeared. Those further out, who had not yet been slain by the warriors, fell to the ground, their faces twisted in fear. Titus saw the small figure of the child turn his or her head towards him. Then the hood fell back and Titus saw the face of a young girl, tears running down her cheeks. The expression she now directed towards him was one of hatred, terrible in its intensity. With a final glance full of spite, the child picked herself up from the body of her mother, ran towards the globe and leapt into it.

Titus held out his hands. "Stop!" he shouted, but the sphere was still expanding. He realised that nothing he could do would stop it now.

"Xanthus! Run. Get your men out! I will hold it back ..."

But it was too late for him. The force of the explosion he was containing overwhelmed him. It erupted outwards and as it reached him he felt an excruciating, tearing sensation as though his body was shattering in the same way the Crown had shattered. The pain reached a crescendo of unbearable agony and then ... he passed into oblivion.

How long did he tumble through the endless void? How many years did he spend alone in the infinite blackness? He would never know. But, in that eternal solitude and oblivion came two feelings. Firstly, there was sorrow and regret at the lives that were lost that day. That face - that terrible face of the girl whose parents had been slain haunted him and gnawed at his soul. Could he have prevented it? Maybe. Should he have tried to? Definitely.

Terrible feelings of guilt and self accusations of failure flooded his being and did battle with the other sensation that was his sole companion

282

through the limbo in which he drifted: the sensation of anger.

He was angry at that monster Knossos. Well, at least the man was dead now. At least he could never again turn his mind to the domination of others ... unless, somehow, he had survived. Was that possible? It was not very likely. What of the Crown - he had seen it shatter. But was it destroyed or like Titus - the man that he had been - had the fragments drifted down the millennia? Would they emerge at some point? Could they ever be brought together and the Crown resurrected? He hoped not; he felt a compulsion to prevent that at all costs.

When consciousness returned he was lying on a hard surface. His head was spinning and as he opened his eyes, the sun above seemed unbearable and he could not focus on his surroundings. He closed them and then opened them once more. The light was gone; indeed it was dark here. Above him stars shone in the night sky. He was not lying on a hard stony surface any more but on grass. He felt dizzy again and so he closed his eyes a second time. When next he opened them, this time he focused on his surroundings. He discovered that he was not lying down anymore. He was sitting in a chair. The chair was at a table and he was in a room. In front of him was a long tray with sand in it. It ran the length of the table. It was the last thing he registered before he passed out.

When he woke again it was in the place with the grass, beneath the star-strewn heavens. He looked around and now saw that he was sitting in a field. There was a cow in the corner lying on the grass, sleeping. Nearby, smoke rose from a house. He climbed to his feet and as he did his vision blurred and he saw, for a moment, a road in a strange city and then an instant later that room with the table. The images came fast and furious as though he was in several different places at once.

"Where am I? Am I here or there?"

Then he felt himself answer. No, it was not himself. The voice was his, or almost his, but the man behind the voice did not sound quite like him. It was a calculating voice that replied.

"The I that we were is no more. Titus is gone. We are divided. Just as the world is divided; the realities split. Let us see what we gain from the world we are in."

"Wait!" he said, getting to his feet in the grass. "We need to be careful. If the world is divided we must find out about it, protect it and see if we can heal it. Make it whole again."

But the man in the city did not respond and the man in the field could feel him no more.

"He is gone. Into his world to make of it what he will," a third voice replied; the voice of the man in the room ... The Office.

"But that is not right. We protect and we preserve. We do not conquer."

"I suggest you look to your reality .... Everything has changed and we each have a role. Goodbye for now ... brother."

Titus was left alone. No - he thought - that is not my name. That is the man I was. I will need a new name now. The Titus in The Office - whatever his name will now be - was right. I must look to this reality and protect it. I will take my father's name. I will be - Neoptolemas.

Tom woke and sat up in bed. So then, that is what happened. Titus had caused the Event. It was an accident, well sort of, but he had caused it. Was this why the Professor had not wanted to talk about the circumstances of the Event in the past? Or was there more going on here? Well yes, Tom thought, answering his own question. There were the feelings over Persephone - plainly the little girl in the dream. That guilt over her parents' death, coupled with a feeling that it was his fault that Knossos - once long ago a friend of his - had turned evil and that maybe he, Titus, should have done something about it, had burnt into the Professor's soul and left a strong determination that the Crown

284

should never be reformed.

This was why Persephone had said the Professor and his brothers would never accept a plan to allow the Crown to be reformed, and why she had told him not to discuss the message with any of them. In the future, the Professor, the Custodian and the Colonel had known that and sent the message back trusting that he would use it, and even with their opposition prevent the Crown reforming. But, the Professor had buried something else inside the message. He had sent Persephone because the old man knew she was the answer. She was the key to everything and Tom knew that only if he could get her on his side, only if he could manage to save her parents, did he have a chance of saving the world.

CHAPTER TWENTY SEVEN
THE FORT

Tom checked his watch. It was five a.m. now. Just over four hours before he was due to return to the Institute. So what to do? Find Persephone and try somehow to persuade her to help him? To do that he would need Edward: Edward, with his unique ability to sense people's whereabouts, could track Persephone wherever she was and in whatever time period. He picked up his mobile phone and dialled a number.

The Institute was dark. For just about the only time that he could recall, the omnipresent Mr Phelps was not at his desk. Tom mused idly about what type of home Phelps had. Was it orderly and neat like his office or a chaotic untidy opposite? That was hard to believe: Tom imagined that Phelps' house was in a pristine state and yet it was difficult, surely, for a man to be so obsessive all the time?

Edward, like Mary and, until recently, Charlie, had rooms in the Institute although Edward had told Tom that he was keen to find a flat nearby. He wondered if it was anything to do with Edward's wanting to distance himself, maybe to take Dr Livingstone up on his offer. Tom hoped not; they had already lost Charlie. If Edward went too, the team of Walkers he had assembled would be cut by half. He crept up the gloomy stairs to the second floor and knocked on the lieutenant's door. Edward was at (the) threshold in a flash - years of army life making him a shallow sleeper, able to come to the alert in mere moments.

"Tom? What is it? What is the time?"

"A little after five, Edward - sorry to wake you but there is something you need to hear - Mary too. I think we should get her up as well."

Edward's eyebrows rose in shock. "Wake a lady; disturb her in her chamber? I think not!"

Tom blinked. "You really are a Victorian aren't you?"

"I suppose I am." Edward shrugged and then smiled.

"Come on, this is urgent!" Tom insisted and carried on along the corridor a few paces before stopping at another door and tapping on it. This time it took a little longer to get a response, but eventually a bleary-eyed Mary peered around the door.

"Wha ..." she started and then coughed, cleared her throat and tried again.

"What is it ... Master Thomas, is that you?" she asked and then, eyes widening, she added, "Who is hurt? Is Edward injured?"

"I am here, Miss Brown," Edward replied.

"Mary, no one is hurt ... yet. But we must talk - downstairs in the library. Hurry – and for goodness sake, don't start calling me 'Master' again!"

Mary looked doubtful but then nodded and shrugging herself into a dressing gown, followed the other two down the stairs. Septimus Mason was already in the library, as was a steaming pot of tea and four mugs.

"Alright Tommy boy, thanks for the call. I'll be mother and pour the tea and you can tell us what is going on ... and why you are not telling the Professor about it."

Surprise must have shown on Tom's face at this comment because Septimus smiled and nodded in response. "I'm not as

287

stupid as I look, boyo. Something is afoot and the Prof not being here suggests he is right in the middle of it."

Grimacing, Tom did not reply.

"One lump or two?" Septimus asked jauntily, holding up a pair of sugar tongs along with a bowl of rock sugar.

"Alright, alright," Tom surrendered, "I had better explain what happened after I left that meeting in The Office last night."

So, he told them of the encounter with the Viking warrior, Harald, and how, after returning to his house, Persephone had appeared. Ignoring their expressions, which grew increasingly doubtful, he related what she had said about being a message from the future. How the Professor had used her to inform them about what would happen IF the Crown did NOT reform. Finally, he described what the connection between the Professor and Persephone was: how the old man was tormented by guilt over her parents' death at the hands of the soldiers that he, as Titus, had guided to the Temple. Tom concluded by describing the overwhelming drive the three brothers had that the Crown of Knossos should NEVER be allowed to reform.

"That is why the Professor sent a message to me and not himself. He and his brothers knew that they would never believe it was not a trick by Knossos."

There was silence for a full minute after he had spoken as the others absorbed what he had said. Edward sipped at his tea, whilst Mary stared out of the window at the hint of dawn that hung in the air. Septimus broke the peaceful scene by drumming his fingers on the table.

"Well, well. If I had just heard all that from anyone but you, boyo, I would say they were as mad as a hatter. But we all know the value of your dreams, don't we," Septimus added with a stare at the others, who just nodded, for it was only because of

Tom's past dreams that they sat there at all.

"Indeed," continued the Welshman, "you have never been wrong, Tommy boy. However, I am very uneasy about this. Only a few hours ago we all met this Persephone and saw how deeply loyal she is to her master and how much she hates the Professor. This could still be a clever trick by the enemy to make us do exactly what they want us to do."

"Indeed, I agree, Septimus. I wish we had proof," Edward said.

"There is the acorn," Tom pointed out. "Except that it has now vanished, so I cannot actually show it to you. Nevertheless, it was pretty convincing; to me anyway."

Then Tom remembered the message he had to give Septimus. "Oh ... there is something else. Persephone said I should ask you ...," he hesitated for a moment.

"Ask me what?" the Welshman asked.

"I had to ask ..."

"Come on lad, spit it out."

"What it feels like to betray a woman?"

Septimus' eyes bulged at the question.

"Thomas, how could you?" Mary gasped.

Tom looked at her and shook his head. "I am sorry - but that is what she asked. I don't know what it means."

Silent for a moment, at last Septimus nodded. "Whereas I do - Mary does too - I told her. I will explain what it means another time, Tom, but apart from Mary, only two other men know the significance of that question: Lapace and the Professor."

"Which means this can only be a message from the Professor," Edward summarised.

"Yes," Septimus agreed.

"So then," Edward continued, his military bearing coming to

the fore. "Let us assume all is as you say it is. In that case we must ensure that the Crown reforms and we must do so *against* the wishes of not just the Professor and Thielmann, but also the Custodian which is not going to be easy. Then, assuming we can do that, we must deal with the spirit of Knossos reborn and prevent him from destroying the world."

There was a click as Edward opened up his fob watch and examined it. "And ... all in less than three and a half hours - that is the time that the final fragments are revealed."

"How will we do all this, Master?" Mary asked, turning to Tom.

"Tom, Mary; it's Tom, as I keep telling you. I'd hoped you'd lost that habit! But as to how - I thought Edward could find out where Persephone is and we can Walk to there and try to persuade her to help us."

"That will be hard, Tommy," Septimus commented. "She seems completely under the domination of Knossos. Even to the point that she is willing to die for him."

Tom nodded. "Yes, and the difficulty is, she will have no recollection of delivering a message to me. But we have to succeed somehow. And then we must return to retrieve the fragments ..." He broke off as, unbidden, the image of Persephone's necklace of silver and pearl came into his mind.

"Yes it will be hard ... but I have an idea."

Ten minutes later the four of them appeared in the shadows around the pillars of the Temple of Knossos. Tom glanced around. The sun was already rising above the eastern horizon, the local time being three hours ahead of that at home, but the Temple seemed quiet and there were no signs of any of the black-robed Cultists. He gestured to the pillars and the four of them slipped between them into the roofed area outside the inner sanctum. Septimus turned a questioning face towards Edward, who closed his eyes, his face screwed up in concentration. After a moment he opened them again and pointing along the back of the Temple, led the way. On the far side of the building - the eastern side - he halted just inside the outer row of pillars and lifted one finger to his lips. Then he peered carefully around the pillar before gesturing with one crooked finger and heading out into the sunlight.

There - on the eastern side of the plateau - they found Persephone. She was standing facing the rising sun, arms stretched outwards as she appeared to bask in the gentle heat of the sunrise.

The four Walkers exchanged glances and nodded. Edward kept watch on the Temple whilst, as one, Septimus, Mary and Tom acted as they had agreed earlier. Septimus Walked to just behind the girl and slapped one arm across her shoulders to pin her to him and the other over her mouth to silence her. Tom materialised by his side and reached round to pull the necklace away. He gave it a huge yank and snapped the silver cord and then stepped back, still clutching the pearl in his hand. He turned and tossed it towards Mary so that it landed on the stony ground at her feet. With a single word of command: "Wall", she flung up an impenetrable barrier around the pearl, which they hoped would sever the connection Persephone had with her master.

Tentatively, Septimus took his hand away from the girl's mouth and then released her from the vice like grip in which he held her. Persephone staggered forward and then turned slowly around. Her face, when it came into view, was blank: eyes staring and confused. Tom glanced at Septimus.

291

"What is wrong with her?" he whispered.

Septimus chewed at his lower lip as he considered the question. "I guess she is disoriented. If the pearl is used as a link between the mind of Knossos and the Cult members and if - as you believe - she has worn it for aeons, then she may not be able to think straight without its control."

Tom glanced over at Edward and the Temple. "If there are as many Cultists in there as I saw in the dream, it won't be long before someone comes out here."

"Yes I know, I ..." Septimus began, but just then Persephone spoke.

"Where am I?"

"The Temple of Knossos - don't you remember?" Tom asked. Persephone stared at him and then blinked twice.

"I remember you. You are Tom Oakley. I ... oh, it's coming back to me now. The Temple, Knossos - my parents..." she trailed off as tears appeared in her eyes. Near to where she stood were the cracked and broken remains of a statue; its body long gone, but two pearly white feet still remaining on a small pedestal. The girl stepped over to the plinth and collapsed onto it, arms over her head, her body turned away from them. Her shoulders were heaving and Tom could hear heartrending sobbing.

"I'm sorry," Septimus said.

"Me too," Tom said, turning at the sound of voices on the far side of the Temple. He stared anxiously at either end of the building, fearful that at any moment Black Robes would appear.

"My parents loved me once you know," Persephone said, drawing Tom's gaze back towards her. He did not reply - unsure what to say.

"We had a little farm not far from here. Down there in the valley," she pointed. "We had an olive grove, some sheep and goats

292

and a wheat field. Not much perhaps and it was a hard life, but my mother and father were content and I was happy growing up there." Looking up, her eyes were distant as she struggled to recall the past.

"I was only five when my parents joined the Cult of Knossos. He gave a talk in the village and invited people to receive gifts of necklaces and then to follow him. He offered them all great wealth and comfort. My parents came home and told me we were leaving the farm. When I argued my father slapped me across the face - the only time he ever hit me. Then they dragged me up here and Knossos gave me a necklace too."

She got up off the statue base and drifted across to where the necklace lay, surrounded by a tiny shimmering sphere. Persephone tilted her head as she regarded it. "Putting it on was like falling asleep. Everything became dark and distant - unreal somehow. I was aware of all that was going on, but all the time there was a voice telling me how to think, what to feel and forcing me to obey his orders. All that mattered was obedience. Nothing else - not pain, not loss and not suffering."

Tom frowned. "But you did feel pain. The day your parents died?"

Persephone looked at him in surprise. "Yes ... yes I remember I did. The shock I suppose. But that day was full of confusion. There were the soldiers and Knossos' followers fighting - happy to sacrifice themselves. There was that sorcerer, Titus, weaving his magic. Then there was the explosion when the Crown was destroyed and suddenly I was here - still in the Temple, but thousands of years later. Knossos was still there - in my mind. Still talking to me and instructing me. He told me I would avenge my parents' death if I obeyed him and I agreed. It was like a compulsion. That was eight years ago. In all that time the

293

real me has been here inside my head. I was aware of it all, but I could do nothing."

"And now?" Septimus asked.

Persephone glanced again at the necklace before replying.

"Now it is as if I have just woken up. That is why I cried just now," she explained as her face screwed up again and her eyes moistened. "You see, I never cried for my parents ... not ever, and I do so miss them."

Tom shot a questioning glance at Septimus and saw the Welshman nod back at him.

"Well, now. We might be able to do something about that ..." Tom started.

The girl looked up at him. "Do what? They are dead. That can't be changed."

"Well it's funny you should say that," Tom smiled, "but actually you are wrong. It is exactly because the past CAN be changed that we - our Institute - exist. We exist to keep history on the track it is on, to prevent anyone meddling and changing what has been."

"Which is why we know exactly how to go about doing just that," Septimus commented with a hint of irony in his voice.

"So what are you saying?" The girl asked, with the slightest edge of hope in hers.

"I am saying we might be able to save your parents."

"How?"

CHAPTER TWENTY EIGHT
LAPACE AND CHARLIE

Tom spoke quickly, describing to Persephone the Hourglass Institute and its purpose. He explained how everyone feared that if the Crown of Knossos was reformed then Knossos himself would return and would use his Crown to destroy the world. Persephone nodded.

"That is exactly what he wanted you to fear so that you would do everything you could to prevent it. In so doing you are playing right into his hands ... "

Before she could finish, Tom butted in, "Yes, because no one realised that the realities are collapsing and spiralling towards each other. If nothing is done they will wipe each other out. So the Crown has to be allowed to reform and then used to fix that. Only it - the thing that caused the Event - can be used to prevent disaster."

"How do you know that?" Persephone asked. "Knossos is convinced that your Professor and the others would never agree to such a plan."

"Ah well, Knossos is right - they never would agree."

"You have not told me how you know."

Tom hesitated before speaking.

"Well?" Persephone prompted, tapping her foot.

"You told me."

"What?!"

"You brought me a message from the future. Another you who had lived through these next few hours and saw the world end and agreed to carry a warning back in time."

Persephone scowled at him. "That sounds like madness. Why would I have done that? What would be strong enough to break my loyalty to Knossos?"

"The love you had for your parents and the hope that you might see them again. You told me the Professor promised you I would save them. I can ... and I will, Persephone - IF we survive these next few hours. Firstly, though I MUST reform the Crown."

"But if you do that Knossos will return and he will take the Crown and destroy everything." Persephone stared at him. "You lose either way."

"That is why we need you."

"Me?"

"Yes, you are going to give me the Crown. Only you can get close enough to Knossos to get it off him."

Persephone let out a gasp of humourless laughter. "You are asking me to take an enormous risk. Why should I do that? When I wore the necklace, all I thought about was vengeance. To destroy the world would be revenge on Titus and the universe he cared so much about. You speak of saving my parents. How do I know I can trust you?"

"If you help us, I will go back and stop them dying."

"How do I know you are capable of doing that?"

"You don't - but I tell you that I am."

Persephone nodded and then seemed to have thought of another question. "Wait a moment, there is a problem. If I don't put on the necklace, Knossos will know something is wrong. But if I do ..."

"You become the evil teenage girl again! Yes, I know."

Mary caught hold of Tom's sleeve. "Master ... sorry, I mean Tom, I have an idea that might help," she said.

"Mary? What is it?"

"I will teach Persephone to make a wall. That is, a wall around her mind. Or part of it at least. I believe I can show her how to block her mind from knowing what her soul feels."

"What?" Tom asked, but it was Septimus who answered.

"I think she means that Persephone's conscious mind will not be aware of her inner thoughts. This Persephone - the one with us here - can still be in there," he tapped Persephone's head lightly, "and hopefully, the evil teenage girl version, as you put it, will not know and nor will Knossos."

Persephone shrank back. "You are asking me to put that thing back on again - to go back into the nightmare?"

Tom nodded. "I'm sorry, but it's the only way you can be free of Knossos or see your parents again."

She barely hesitated. "Then I will do it. Just make sure you do your part in this and ensure that the Crown forms again. So, Mary, what are you going to show me?" Persephone moved to stand beside Mary and the two girls went into a huddle. Observing them, Tom was relieved to see that Mary's dislike of the girl appeared to have vanished now that she knew Persephone's heartbreaking story.

Just then, Edward turned his head sharply and disappeared into the forest of pillars. A moment later he returned and gestured violently, waving them over to him.

"Oops ... trouble. Come on," Septimus said and he and Tom ran towards Edward.

"Mary, come along!" Tom hissed from the edge of the Temple. She did not look up, still engrossed in her conversation with

297

Persephone. Through the pillars, Tom heard voices and a moment later saw two of the Cult members strolling towards the east side.

"Mary – *now*," Septimus urged.

Tom glanced desperately towards the Black Robes and back at Mary. It was no good. If she ran now, she would be spotted and have no chance of escaping. They must get away without detection.

Then, suddenly, Mary vanished and an instant later appeared next to Tom.

"Wow, Mary ... I did not think you could Walk on your own."

"Edward has been teaching me," she said simply.

"I'd say you were a quick learner, but it's time to go," Septimus said and nodded at Tom who stretched out his arms for them all to latch on to.

A moment later they were once again in the library of the Institute.

"Very well, that is part of the plan carried out," said Edward. "But how the blazes do we ensure the Crown reforms against the will of Thielmann, the Custodian and the Professor?"

Septimus rubbed his cheek and then fiddled with his short goatee beard. He fixed Tom with a stare. "We cannot ... not alone anyway. They are too powerful," he sat down heavily.

"Your expression suggests that you have something on your mind," Mary observed.

"Aye lass, I do," Septimus nodded. "Trouble is, I don't like where my mind is taking me," he replied, falling into silence again.

"Which is ...?" Tom asked.

The Welshman tapped his fingers on the table before answering, "Which is that we need Lapace and Redfeld."

"Are you out of your mind?" Edward gazed at him in astonishment.

Nodding emphatically, Tom agreed with Edward. "Redfeld can't be trusted - we all know that. And ever since this started you have been avoiding talking about whatever your problem is with Lapace, and now you want to go talk to him, to bring him in on this. Isn't he the man you said you'd never trust again?"

Septimus opened his mouth to speak, closed it again then nodded.

"So then, in the name of all that is holy, why do you contemplate such an alliance?" Mary asked.

He looked at each of them in turn. "Because of all the Walkers we know, whether we like it or not, those two are the most capable - save perhaps the four of us. Do you doubt that?"

Tom considered this and had to accept that Septimus had a point. He might loathe Redfeld. He might distrust his motives and even fear him ... but the man had so very nearly succeeded with his plans earlier in the summer. He was ruthless and able. If anyone could help them with the task ahead he was the one.

"OK, I'll buy what you say about Redfeld, but what is the deal with Lapace?"

"I thought you knew, boyo; he and I were partners. Whether I trust him or not, he is as able as they come. As the Prof told you, we ranged up and down the time line. There was no object too precious to steal, no artefact too holy to plunder.

"Until this summer," Mary said, with a heavy emphasis that suggested she was hinting at something.

Septimus glanced at her and then sighed. "Aye lass, it is perhaps time to talk about it and thank you for keeping it secret till now."

He stood up, walked across to a book shelf and stared blankly at the spine of a book. Tom glanced at his watch. Time was passing and they did not have an abundance of it - Walkers or not. Yet he did not feel he could interrupt. Eventually Septimus turned back to look at them and took a deep breath.

"Very well: 'Septimus and Lapace' were once a partnership who robbed their way across history. That was until we met a woman in the past: a woman who was both beautiful and charming. The worst thing happened - we both fell for her in a big way. In the end, Julia - that was her name - chose Lapace and I accepted her choice and went away. Then there came 'The Job': the last one we did together. We accepted the commission and then found out that the job was to steal something valuable and irreplaceable from Julia. It was a priceless heirloom left to her by her father. Lapace accepted without question. To him, the pursuit of wealth was always his drive and his passion, at whatever the cost. I ... I refused. I tried to dissuade him, but he just laughed at me."

The Welshman paused for a moment, his eyes suspiciously moist as he recalled the past. He cleared his throat. "I still loved her, you see, and would not betray her even for money. Lapace did not see it that way. He completed the job without me. When Julia found out, she assumed we had done it together and tried to have us arrested and thrown in jail. We escaped, naturally, but she was badly hurt and refused to talk to either of us again. Lapace laughed about it ... though I think he regretted losing her in some way. You see, to him she was a prize. Another trophy he had won."

"And you, Septimus, how did you feel?" Tom asked.

Septimus glared at him. "What do you think, Tommy? I was devastated! I told Lapace that I would never work with him again. Indeed, I told him that I would never do a job again. Not that sort, anyway. I had never realised until then how much distress I had caused by stealing. It was just a game to me until I witnessed Julia's grief. It was not about the money: to her the heirloom was a last link to her beloved father. I tried to get it back for her, but I failed ...." his voice trailed away and he flung himself into a chair, his head bowed.

"So is that what the Professor's message was about - when he asked how it felt to betray a woman?"

"Exactly; he knew the truth - I told him only a day or two ago when Lapace popped up again and the Prof all but accused me of double dealing. I needed the old man to understand why that could never happen. So I guess he must have believed the question would convince me."

That explained a lot, thought Tom: why Septimus was so keen that Charlie did not take up his profession; why he reacted so violently when the Professor suggested that he and Lapace were in cahoots. But now he was suggesting an alliance with the man he had sworn never to work with again.

"So ... you see, I have reasons to distrust Lapace," Septimus said, seemingly aware of Tom's thoughts. "Furthermore, the very idea of cooperating with him fills me with disgust. Yet, outside of those in this room and Redfeld himself, I can think of few more able to oppose the Professor and his, er, charming brothers!"

Tom glanced across at Mary and Edward. Mary nodded without hesitation. Edward looked thoughtful: the professional officer appraising the risks and benefits. After a moment's consideration he agreed as well. Then he slipped his watch out of his pocket and popped open the lid. "It is almost seven. We don't have long."

The sudden sound of Septimus' mobile ringing out made

301

them all jump. He answered it. There was a brief exchange and he rang off.

"That was the Professor. Turns out he has been in his study all night studying that tablet. He has found out something and he wants us to meet him about half eight."

Edward frowned. "Hope he has not heard us talking. But it means we have less time than I thought."

"I agree," Septimus muttered. "So I suggest that you and I, Edward, go and find Lapace and try to persuade him to help us. He must have a means of contacting Redfeld if he is working for him."

Tom bit his lip. "But why would he help and how will you persuade him that this is not just a trick by Knossos? I mean, you might trust my dreams but why would Lapace?"

"You leave Rolf to me, I have an idea."

"What about Charlie then?" Tom asked.

Septimus shrugged. "I expect he will be with Lapace. I will try and talk to him, but I think he's a lost cause."

"What about Tom and me?" Mary asked.

"Mary, you stay here in case the Professor comes looking for us. Try to keep him occupied until we all return. Tom, you push off home. If the Prof sees you here before he's asked for you he will get suspicious. Come back later, just around eight, OK?"

"Right," Tom replied.

"Very well." Mary nodded.

Septimus got to his feet. "Well good luck, everyone. If we succeed, the beer is on me - or in your case, Tom, the milkshake!"

CHAPTER TWENTY NINE
UNLIKELY ALLIES

When Tom arrived in the Professor's study an hour or so later, he tilted his head questioningly towards Septimus and Edward, who were already there along with Mary. The Welshman glanced at the Professor and then responded with a faint nod of the head. So he had apparently been successful with his mission. Tom smiled briefly at that but then felt suddenly gloomy again. As he had set off for this meeting he was aware of the disturbing knowledge that he had already lived through the events that were about to occur. However, he could not, of course, recall any of it. He felt a bit like a puppet with someone pulling his strings. So, as the conversation over breakfast that Saturday morning ranged on, he said little. Even the Professor's revelation that he had once been the sorcerer Titus was no surprise; he knew that already from the dream, so it failed to distract Tom from his anxiety. Whenever he spoke he could not help but wonder if he had said the same thing the first time around. He was unsure how to act, whether he should suggest a course of action or whether his suggestions would backfire and change the future. It was an unnerving sensation and he soon fell into silence and instead brooded on the problem of ensuring that the fragments of the Crown were reunited.

After a while, Neoptolemas and Dr Midas moved on to discussing the markings on the stone and explained to everyone just how the clock fragment would summon the other fragments to it. Tom glanced across at Septimus and saw the relief on his face. He too realised that this would make their job of retrieving all the pieces of the Crown a great deal easier.

He felt a moment's alarm when Midas pushed the stone into the lead box, worried as to whether this would prevent it being summoned to join its fellows at the Temple. Then, moments later, there was a tremendous disturbance in the Flow of Time. It became apparent that the clock was calling to the stone and with an edge of panic in his voice, the Professor ordered Mary to put up a wall around the lead box. Mary hesitated and looked over at Tom, silently asking what she should do. Tom shook his head. 'No, Mary,' he said to himself, 'you must let it go.'

"Now Mary!" the Professor ordered. "You must do it now!"

With a helpless expression on her face, Mary raised her hands and closed her eyes. After a moment, there was a shimmer in the air around the box. The disturbance in the Flow of Time grew more pronounced. Mary's forehead wrinkled in concentration.

"I can't hold it," she said through clenched teeth and with a quick glance at Tom, she sighed and slumped down onto the desk.

The disturbance immediately dissipated. Dr Midas rushed over, checked the box and announced that the stone had vanished. The Professor cried out in horror and without any warning they were all unceremoniously swept away from the study and en-masse Walked to the Temple of Knossos. So then, thought Tom, here we are and the fragments are here too. So far so good, but what comes next?

Soon after they arrived they were joined firstly by the Custodian with his automaton-like Directorate men, then Lapace and his mercenaries with Charlie in tow, and finally Redfeld and his guards. Tom thought back to his visits to the Temple - both the ones in his dreams and then again just now in real life. When and where would be the right moment to seize the fragments and how should he go about doing it?

A sudden feeling of panic jumped into his chest. What was he doing? Was this after all a huge trick by Knossos? If he was wrong he could be handing the universe to the enemy of the Professor and his brothers. He looked over at Neoptolemas striding forward besides Midas and wondered whether he should have told him, after all. The Professor seemed to feel Tom's gaze upon him and turned to glance his way. Then the old man shifted his focus across to the figure of Charlie. The sailor returned the gaze and his expression grew determined, resolute even. Had he imagined it, Tom wondered, or had something just passed in the air between them? His thoughts were racing nineteen to the dozen and he felt suddenly dizzy. With effort, he pushed the doubts he was feeling away from his mind. He had no time for them. He had to trust his instincts and hope they were right.

They reached the Temple and as they stood upon the plateau and studied the structure before them, Tom moved across to Septimus and asked in an undertone, "Well? Did you reach Lapace?"

Septimus looked about and then, certain now that he was out of earshot of the Professor, he nodded. "I did. We agreed that when you give the signal he will move to us together with Charlie and Redfeld and then we all Walk together inside the Temple, create a cordon around the Crown and keep everyone away until it reforms."

"I'm impressed. So are you going to tell me how you managed to persuade them?"

Septimus shrugged and nodded across to where Lapace, Red-feld and Charlie were walking along side by side.

"Them? It was not hard. Think about it, Tommy - Lapace will do anything for money and to win the game. Redfeld will risk anything for his ambition."

Tom thought back to the meeting in The Office and that expression on Redfeld's face. He nodded.

"Neither was keen on just preventing the Crown from forming," Septimus continued. "What gain is there in that? Redfeld was following orders and Lapace doing what he was paid for. But the Crown reformed? Ah, now that is a much greater prize! To hold that even for a moment is worth any gamble as far as my former partner is concerned. As for Redfeld, the Crown is the key he needs to open our reality to him and mould it as he sees fit. It is what he has always craved. That was the carrot I dangled before them."

"What!" Tom shouted and froze on the spot. Several heads turned towards him. Mary and Edward drew closer.

"What vexes thee, Master?" Mary asked.

"You mean aside from the fact that you keep calling me 'Master'? Oh nothing much. Just that Septimus here promised Lapace and Redfeld the Crown of Knossos in payment for helping us today."

Septimus was shaking his head. "No, Tommy boy, I did not ... I might have implied that, but that was the bait to get their help. Clearly WE must control the Crown."

No one answered.

"Look - you said yourself, Tom." The Welshman sounded exasperated. "Why would they help? Why even trust us? When the objective was merely to stop the Crown reforming then they were happy to help because everyone gained equally in the little matter of the universe surviving. But now the Crown must re-form and be used to save the universe they are thinking - as are we - about who controls it at the end. That means that they see a gain. They see a win and are willing to help us to allow that possibility. But you can be certain they intend controlling it in the end."

Edward cleared his throat. "So, there is another game going on here. It's not just us against the Professor and his brothers. Not just us against Knossos and the Cult but, assuming we win through that far, we then have a final battle against Redfeld - again," he summarised and Septimus nodded.

"No one made any lunch plans for today did they?" the Welshman added with a wink.

Tom opened his mouth to say something rude when the quiet of the Temple was shattered by the rattle of machine gun fire. Redfeld's men had set up their weapon and were firing it into the gaps between the pillars, whilst his riflemen skirmished forward. The Custodian, the Professor and Thielmann were watching the engagement from the far side of Redfeld's soldiers. Meanwhile, Redfeld, Lapace and Charlie had drifted closer to the Institute members and stood just within earshot, observing the soldiers but also keeping an eye on Tom.

"This is it!" Septimus said. "Tommy you are up. You have the ball boyo. Don't muck it up lad."

Tom stuck out his tongue at the Welshman but bit back a re-tort. He checked that the Professor and his brothers were not listening and then laid out his plan.

"Very well. Redfeld, get us through the pillars. Once we are near the antechamber entrance I will raise my arm up. Everyone who wants a lift get to me fast and we zap inside. Let's go," he said and started forward behind the soldiers. Redfeld joined him and barked out some orders to his men.

"*Schnell, schnell! Gehen Sie in den Tempel hinein!*"

Led by a sergeant, Redfeld's squad ran between the pillars and the sounds of fighting and screams of wounded men echoed out to those standing outside. A moment later, Tom and the others entered the stone forest of columns and followed the soldiers through the outer temple until they reached the antechamber. Tom watched as the Directorate's heavies engaged the Cult members. 'Good, that should occupy the Custodian,' he thought. Finally, when the battle was at its height, he thrust his right hand upwards. As one, Edward, Mary, Charlie, Septimus, Lapace and Redfeld joined him and he Walked them the twenty yards or so to the antechamber.

To where four men waited.

The first man, Dr Midas, stood off to one side, looking both excited and bewildered.

The Professor, the Custodian and Thielmann, however, did not look excited or bewildered. Instead they looked angry.

"Well then, gentlemen and lady. What exactly is your intention today?" The Professor asked them, stepping forward and fixing them all with an intense glare.

CHAPTER THIRTY
KNOSSOS RISING

Tom stepped up to the Professor. "Sorry, sir, but it's important that the Crown of Knossos is allowed to reform."

The Professor's face darkened. "What talk is this, Thomas? You of all people have seen the mind of Knossos. You know what he will do if he returns; what wanton destruction he would rain down upon us all. Surely you cannot wish that?"

"You believe that is what will happen because you know Knossos. Because you three were his best friend: you were Titus."

"You think you understand, young man," Thielmann now spoke, "but this is not something that concerns you. We know what we are doing. We are acting through knowledge you do not have and following a logical plan."

"Rubbish, there is no logic here. You are acting out of fear and hatred. Knossos betrayed you," he pointed at Thielmann. "That angers you, for you will not be beaten. You must defeat him so that you will be the ultimate victor." Thielmann's eyebrows bristled in anger but he did not reply.

"Enough, Thomas Oakley the time approaches to act," the Custodian objected and now Tom turned on him.

"As for you, Knossos threatened the order of things. He brought chaos and that offends you. You must remain in control at all times, is that not so?"

Tom turned back to the Professor. "Finally, Professor, I have seen into your mind. I have seen the moments after you were split from the others. I felt your anger at Knossos for all the blood that was on his hands, but in particular at his murdering a young girl's parents. You will do anything to stop that evil coming again ... but in your case there is more. There is guilt. You blame yourself, don't you, Professor?"

"We don't have time for the boy's ramblings. We only have moments," Thielmann snarled, spinning on his heels as the sound of a pistol being cocked interrupted him.

"I am sorry, sir ... but I must insist that you listen to the boy. It is in our best interests," Redfeld ordered and Tom noticed how he emphasized the word 'our'.

"What are you doing, Hauptmann? This is treason. I will have you shot!"

"If the Crown does not reform you will not have the opportunity. You see, when I learnt that the boy had received a warning from the future - supposedly from yourself and your brothers - directing that the Crown MUST reform, I was sceptical, but I did not dismiss it. The thing is, when Oakley defeated me only a few months ago, I decided then that I would not underrate his abilities again. So I tried an experiment. I used my own talents to project the future and I tell you, he is correct. If the Crown remains splintered, the realities collapse and everything ends."

"This is madness. You are making a guess based on the boy's day dreams and your illusions. None of that is fact - none of it real," Thielmann spat, stomping up to his inferior so that their noses almost touched."But what is fact is that if it does reform, Knossos will destroy everything."

"The Crown must be allowed to reform. We will deal with

310

Knossos if he returns!" Redfeld insisted.

"It is too great a risk, Thomas. Surely you see that," the Professor said, although an element of doubt tinged his voice.

"Sir, you sent me a message back to tell me what to do. You even sent my acorn as well, to prove it came from you."

"Enough!" boomed the Custodian and as he spoke everything in the ante chamber froze. The flames in the braziers became like the plastic in some modern electric fires. The air seemed to cool and took on a thick, syrupy texture. Meanwhile, every person in the room was motionless apart from four people: Neoptolemas, the Custodian, Thielmann and Tom himself. The other half dozen occupants of the antechamber had become statues, immobile and frozen like waxwork dolls. Tom glanced again: half a dozen? Six? Someone was missing: who was no longer there?

"How did you think this would end, Herr Oakley. Did you think that you alone could stop us?" Thielmann sneered, breaking Tom's train of thought. "I have wanted a chance to get even with you. My department never lost a campaign you know. Not before a certain day in Tintagel. How pleasurable it will be to crush you here today."

"Leave the boy alone, Thielmann," the Professor snapped.

"The Colonel is right though, Oakley," the Custodian stepped forward. "How do you, a mere boy, expect to overcome us?"

Tom clenched his fists and ignoring the Custodian, looked with rising despair into the Professor's doubtful face. "I hoped that you would see reason, sir. I am telling you, Professor: you all sent me a message. You must believe me. This has happened before. We lived through this day, but we made the wrong choice and the world was doomed as a result. We MUST allow the Crown to form."

Shaking his head, the Professor looked away. "Sorry, Thomas,

311

you may believe you know something, but I can't take the risk." He moved towards the inner sanctum, his path taking him closer to a pillar.

A pillar ... Persephone had said something about a pillar. Without thinking, Tom Walked to the other side of the pillar. As he materialised he thrust out his hands just as Persephone jumped out of the pillar's shadow, dagger in hand, and made a lunge towards the Professor. Tom latched on to her and held on tight.

Persephone gave a cry of outrage and struggled in Tom's arms. The curved dagger was knocked loose and with a clatter went flying across the chamber. Tom shook her and stared into her eyes.

"It's me, Persephone – Tom," he whispered.

But Persephone's eyes burned with malice. Tom sighed. There was no hint, no clue that the rational girl was in there. All he could see was a creature of anger and vengeance.

"Stop!" the Custodian ordered and the girl froze, her rigid, snarling features etched with rage.

"Thomas, you saved me," the Professor gasped, his face suddenly pale. "But how did you see her?"

"I didn't. The message you sent back was brought by Persephone herself. She told me that she had attacked you and also where she had been hiding. Thank God I somehow remembered that just in time to stop her. Please sir, do you believe me now?"

"That changes nothing," the Custodian said. "I will not risk everything on this gamble. He is just a boy."

Tom scowled at the Custodian. He'd had enough of this. He had thought it would be hard to convince them, but now it seemed the Custodian was being deliberately stubborn. A spike of anger uncoiled in his chest, as if a spring had been suddenly released.

"No!" he boomed. "I am more than that. You said so yourself ... I am a potentate!" And with that statement, Tom clicked his fingers and the air in the room again became warm, the torches flickered in their sconces. Leaving Persephone frozen, Tom released the other six statues from captivity and as they animated, he counted them again. Yes there were only six - Septimus, Mary, Edward, Charlie, Lapace and Redfeld. That left Dr Midas. So where was he?

As if to answer his question a voice called out to them from within the inner sanctum. "You fellows should leave off arguing and come in here: something extraordinary is happening."

The Custodian threw an angry glance straight at Tom. "See what you have done, foolish boy. The Crown is reforming!" Still shouting at Tom, he started towards the door. "Stop them!" he bellowed over his shoulder as he moved. From nowhere, a half dozen Directorate men appeared and formed a cordon across the doorway. Tom tried to Walk to the inner sanctum but felt a barrier in his way.

"The Custodian has created a wall, Tom," Mary cried from across the room. "It is too strong, I cannot penetrate it."

Tom appealed to the Professor. "We must get inside now!" he said in desperation.

The old man grimaced and Tom could imagine the conflicting emotions he felt as he struggled with the overwhelming desire to oppose Knossos and to never let him return.

"Please, sir, trust us this once," Edward implored. Neoptolemas stared at him and, oddly, a faint smile came to his lips as if he was enjoying a private joke. He nodded and turned to Thielmann. "Come, Colonel. We must do this."

Thielmann stared at Tom with an expression of hatred and

revulsion.

"Colonel, sir, he speaks the truth," Redfeld insisted. "We must help!"

Thielmann glared at his subordinate and then finally, with a snarl, hissed, "Very well. So be it!"

As one, Thielmann and the Professor turned and flung their hands outwards, projecting their palms forward towards the Men in Suits. The Directorate men were bowled over by a ferocious burst of energy.

"The wall is down!" Mary yelled and everyone sprinted towards the door.

In the inner sanctum, the five fragments of the Crown of Knossos were glowing intensely. A tremendous screeching noise was emanating from them all and Tom could see that the pieces were moving towards each other as if by a magnetic attraction.

The Custodian had reached the altar and was stretching out to grab one of the fragments. Suddenly, Lapace materialised on one side of the old man and Septimus on the other. A glance passed between them as, simultaneously, they seized him and Walked. What then followed was a most peculiar optical effect as they both disappeared whilst still holding one of the Custodian's arms apiece. It was as if the man was standing in front of a novelty mirror at a fun fair: one moment he looked normal and the next he was stretched sideways.

Then, there was a burst of lightning followed by a horrendous explosion. It shook the room, throwing everyone off their feet. The next instant, Septimus smashed against the wall next to Tom and slid down it to lie groaning on the flagstones. Meanwhile, Lapace materialised about six feet in the air just behind Midas and crashed to the ground from where he did not move.

The Custodian himself had been flung backwards and ended up slumped down between his duplicates, near the antechamber door.

As Tom picked himself up he wondered what on earth had caused that explosion. Was it because they had tried to Walk when close to the fragments as they were coming together?

It seemed likely, for the energy and disturbance to the Flow of Time was now immense. He was aware that the noise coming from the fragments had reached a crescendo and then, with a blinding flash of light the fragments were separate no longer.

Now, upon the altar stone, there sat an exquisite crown of bronze and silver, at the top of which was mounted a jewel of surpassing beauty. There was utter silence in the inner sanctum as everyone gazed upon it. Then, without warning, Dr Midas picked up the crown.

"My word, but it is wonderful. What an artefact ..." he began to say. Then he gave a sudden cry of pain, staggered backwards and slumped to the ground, momentarily out of sight behind the altar stone.

"Doctor! Are you alright?" Edward shouted and led the others around the stone. As Midas came into view everyone halted. The doctor seemed fine and indeed he was even now rising from the ground, still holding the Crown in one hand.

"My dear Lieutenant I am quite well, I assure you," Midas replied. But his voice sounded strange. He now turned to face them and fix them all with a glare, which held none of the benevolent vacancy of Dr Midas. This expression was full of calculating malevolence and something else - something chilling.

Triumph.

"But you are mistaken about one thing. I am no longer that fool Midas," he said and as he stepped towards them his hand came up, the Crown still clutched in his fingers. With one swift movement he held it up high and then placed it on his head.

"No indeed ... I am Knossos!"

CHAPTER THIRTY ONE
CHARLIE

Knossos in Midas' body raised both hands above his head and thrust his legs apart so he now stood like the statue of a god; or like some colossus. As he adopted this pose, Tom felt a sudden surge of energy, which tugged at the Flow of Time, tearing and distorting it.

"To me all my followers, my apostles - come worship at my feet!" Knossos cried.

Tom felt a sensation of many people all Walking at the same time. Then, suddenly, all the black-robed Cult members appeared in an arc around Knossos, with Persephone at the very centre, apparently released from her frozen prison. As one they fell to their knees, their faces lifted up towards their master, hands help out in supplication. It seemed to Tom as if all their thoughts and desires were focused around Knossos and they worshiped him like the god he wanted to be.

Yet, Tom noticed something else. The body language and posture adopted by the Cult members did indeed speak of veneration, but he could see that their eyes and faces appeared blank. As he had seen before, every one of the Black Robes wore a silver necklace with a single pearl suspended from it and now, as Tom watched, the pearls began to glow, pulsating rhythmically; the pattern of the illumination matching the pulsation of the great

317

jewel mounted atop the Crown of Knossos.

"He is controlling them!" Tom shouted across to his companions.

"Yes ... yes he is," the Professor replied. "His greatest talent is the ability to dominate minds - his will is magnified by the Crown. Dr Midas is the Vessel! I suspected it but I could not be certain ..."

Around them the Temple began to shake. Small flakes of stone detached from the roof above them and floated to earth. The shaking grew more violent and this time a stone came loose and fell, shattering on the flagstone floor, sending splinters and dust flying in all directions. Flinching back against a pillar, Tom could see that in places the Temple walls around them were becoming transparent, and in those gaps he caught glimpses of The Office with its oak panels and marble floor tiles.

"The realities are still collapsing," Tom shouted to make himself heard over the rumbling of the disintegrating structure of the Temple. "Only the Crown can stabilise them now."

Stepping over the rubble, the Professor rushed towards Dr Midas. "Knossos, please listen to me," he pleaded, hands outstretched.

Midas squinted at him. "Titus? Is that you - part of you anyway?"

"It is I, old friend. Please give me the Crown. If we don't use it soon, the universe will destroy itself – and what use will your power be then?"

Knossos laughed - and again it was not the archaeologist's jovial little chortle, but the cackle of a deranged man. "Titus, you old fool, all of you in fact - three fools give me thrice as much pleasure." Knossos fixed Neoptolemas, Thielmann and the Custodian with a baleful glare.

318

The gem upon his Crown suddenly burst into light. The Professor and the Colonel each gave out a groan and fell to their knees beside the slumped form of their duplicate. As Tom looked on, helpless to intervene, he could see that both were struggling to get back to their feet, but they were unable to move and remained kneeling in front of their old enemy. The Custodian stirred at last; he also tried to rise, but he too was helpless under the power of the Crown.

Knossos laughed again - a laugh full of spite and triumph. "I have bested you at last, Titus. I have proved I am a more powerful sorcerer than you. What gives me even greater satisfaction is the knowledge that you – all three of you - did the work for me. How I laughed to see your minions galloping around history locating the fragments, knowing that Persephone could summon them all here whenever I commanded."

"We might not have succeeded, Knossos. The fragments might not all have been located." Thielmann pointed out. "Did you think about that?"

"Yes I did ... Colonel is it? Ah, another Titus, but this one in uniform. That would not matter either, for in that case the universe would end. You see, either way you lose; you all lose!" Again he cackled like the madman he was. "And I have brought you all here to witness my triumph!"

Tom glanced at the Professor and the Custodian. The Professor gave a nod of acknowledgement, whilst his brother the Custodian showed no emotion, although Tom was sure that he detected annoyance in the man's eyes.

"Please, Knossos. Do not do this," Neoptolemas implored. "You cannot want the world destroyed. No sane man would."

"No World, no Will but Mine. Remember that, Titus?" Knossos said, walking over to stand near the altar. "What am I? You

319

think I am insane: a consciousness forever adrift in eternity? Well no longer," he boomed. "Now I have form. I could choose to undo the damage that is done. I could elect to prevent the realities colliding. Maybe I can still be God here. It is my choice. MINE, do you hear me?"

The Custodian, struggling from the ground and onto his knees, now spoke. "Do it then," he urged Knossos. "Use the Crown and stabilize the universe. It need not end today."

Midas studied the Custodian. "Ah, but you above all here know that I will not," the voice of Knossos said through the doctor's lips. "That is the risk you took when you started this. You are the Custodian aren't you - the logical thinker; the one who balances all things? You should understand more than anyone else that what you sow ye shall reap."

"What do you mean?" Tom asked, puzzled now, looking from Knossos to the Custodian.

"I mean," Knossos boomed, "that I choose not to save this miserable universe. I choose to let it end. I have the Crown. It is the Crown that started this and the Crown that will survive it. And I? I will begin again. This time it will be a universe fresh born. It will be a universe I create and I rule. I truly will be God."

"The Professor's right, Knossos," said Tom. He spoke conversationally, stalling for time. "You are a wee bit mad you know ... just thought someone should mention that."

Knossos laughed and around him the world shook. As Tom stared in horror he could see that just like in his dream of the ceremony all those millennia ago when all this started, the walls to the inner sanctum were now paper thin. Reality was breaking apart around them: fragmenting even as they spoke. There was little time left. The Professor and his brothers were immobile, as were the Men in Suits, still locked outside the inner sanctum.

320

Persephone seemed in the thrall of Knossos and so it was down to him and the others to act.

He focused on the Crown. That was the key. Yet, if he and the others made a move to reach it then the Cultists would block their path.

Stalemate!

Unless ... unless the control Knossos had over the Cultists could be disrupted. That control was focused through the enormous pulsating gem – so, destroy the emerald and the mind control was gone. BUT, if they did this, would the Crown still be able to stabilize the realities? Tom knew he had no choice; he would have to take that chance.

"Mary," Tom hissed, "we need to destroy the gem on the Crown. Can we Walk to Knossos ... to Midas?"

Mary closed her eyes for a moment and concentrated. After a moment she opened her eyes and shook her head. "Sorry Master, the Crown is projecting some aura."

Tom made a decision: "Then if we can't Walk there, we will have to force a way through them." He turned to where Redfeld, Charlie and Lapace were standing with Septimus and Edward near the altar. "Get the Crown," he shouted. "Fast: we don't have long!"

As if to emphasize the point the roof shook once more and now Tom could see great gaping holes in the walls. Beyond them the soldiers of Redfeld's army were visible in the Twisted Reality. They were glancing to and fro, staring with fearful incomprehension at the scene unfolding within the Temple.

"Now!" Tom bellowed, his voice rising almost to a screech in desperation.

Septimus nodded at him and he and Edward set off around the altar stone in one direction whilst Lapace and Redfeld went in the other. Charlie, in the middle, glared at the figure of Midas from across the altar itself.

"Destroy them!" Knossos commanded and the Black Robes divided. There seemed to be dozens of them. Half went towards Septimus and the rest towards his former partner. The Cultists drew their curved daggers and launched themselves at the Walkers. They came on, swinging and hacking with their wicked blades. Tom could see Lapace dancing elegantly around, avoiding the knife attacks then tripping his opponents up and so scattering the Cultists. There was a repeated loud 'crack-pop' as Redfeld fired shots from his Luther into the crowd and Tom heard the screams of the Cultists as the bullets slammed into them.

On the other side of the room, Septimus had brought his hands up in fighting stance. Closing his fists he jumped away from an attack and then, quick as a flash, darted in a left hook, caught one Cultist on the chin and sent him hurtling into his companions so they went down in a heap. Edward was alongside him now and the pair were weaving and dodging, retreating and then counter attacking. Several Black Robes were now lying wounded, unconscious or stunned on the flagstones, but more came on and threw themselves on Tom's friends.

"It's no good, Master," Mary said. "There are too many - they can't reach Knossos."

Tom tried Walking, but sure enough he felt the barrier, invisible but impenetrable, emanating from the Crown. He saw Charlie move forward, heading straight for the altar stone, beyond which stood Knossos.

Knossos saw him coming and the gemstone flared once. The air in front of the altar took on a syrupy consistency and Charlie seemed suddenly to be moving through treacle. Knossos had slowed time down in front of him. Charlie was fast, but even he seemed to be taking an age to reach the far side. Tom cried out in despair: this was not working, they could not reach Knossos and time was running out.

Unless ...

"Master – look!" Mary pointed at Persephone. Alone of all the Black Robes she had remained apart from the fight. She was behind Knossos and until a moment ago her face had been wearing the same vacant expression as the other Cultists. Now, suddenly, her eyes shone and she focused them on Knossos. She reached up and tore off her necklace, tossing it in revulsion to the floor. From her robes she produced a knife and moved towards Knossos.

"No, Persephone," Tom screamed, "you will kill Midas!"

Knossos frowned and turned to stare at his acolyte. "You ... but why?"

"You took everything from me ... my parents, my childhood. That is why," she replied and back went her hand, ready to strike.

It was at this moment that Charlie attacked. Distracted by Persephone, Knossos had not spotted that the sailor had reached the far side of the frozen air. Freed from its impediment, he launched his assault. He jumped up onto the altar, seized Midas by the collar, heaved him forward and rammed his face into the stone altar. The jolt dislodged the Crown from the archaeologist's head. The magnificent bronze and silver circlet rolled forward, teetered for a moment then tipped over the edge. Charlie jumped full length and caught it an inch from the ground.

"Howzat!" he shouted as he rolled over and popped back up on his feet.

"Well caught, sir!" Edward yelled breathlessly, felling anoth-

323

er Black Robe, his animosity towards Charlie forgotten in the heat of the moment.

There was a great crack that echoed across the inner sanctum. A pillar swayed this way and that and then came down with a crash only a foot from where Charlie had caught the Crown. Narrowly missing Tom's head, it cannoned into Persephone, knocking her to the ground.

"Blimey!" he said and stepped back, looking around. Near to him the Professor, Thielmann and the Custodian were struggling to free themselves from the mystical bonds that Knossos had placed upon them. Beyond the altar, Redfeld and Lapace on one side and Edward with Septimus on the other were now surrounded and outnumbered by at least five to one Black Robes. The archaeologist was beginning to stir. Tom had hoped that Knossos's spirit had been released from Midas' body when he had been stunned by Charlie's attack and lost the Crown, thus losing control of the Black Robes - not to mention the entrapment of the Professor and his brothers - but apparently this was not so.

"The Crown, throw me the Crown," yelled Lapace, gesturing wildly from within the mob of Black Robes.

Midas, the embodiment of Knossos, jumped over the altar and jabbed Charlie in the throat with rigid and outstretched fingers. Choking, one hand jerking to his throat and the other still holding the Crown, the sailor fell to the ground. Knossos lifted up a foot and kicked Charlie in the ribs. He staggered to his feet, backed away from Knossos and looked across to Lapace.

Lapace was waving madly. "Now Charlie - give me the Crown!"

Charlie lifted it and pulled back his arm, preparing to throw it across the room. It was then that a calm voice spoke from just behind him.

"Mr Hawker, now's the time," the Professor said.

Charlie smiled. "Yes sir, you took the words right out of my mouth!" He turned and threw the Crown. It spun gently, glittering in the firelight as it flew across the room, but not towards Lapace. Instead, it flew unerringly towards Tom.

Startled, he leapt upwards, raised both hands and plucked it out of the air.

There were cries of outrage from Lapace and Redfeld. "What have you done, boy?" Lapace yelled at Charlie.

"Done? I have done exactly what I was expected to do!" Charlie said with a wink at the Professor.

Redfeld shouted an incomprehensible curse in German, and levelled his pistol at Charlie. There was a crack and the sailor screamed, spinning backwards, blood spouting from his shoulder. Knossos, meanwhile, was advancing on Tom.

"Give me the Crown! Do it now, boy!" The archaeologist's eyes glittered as he reached towards Tom, spittle flecking on his lips, his face a mask of fury.

Tom backed away, his mouth suddenly dry. Then Mary was behind him. Her hand touched his shoulder. "Master, we are losing the battle and time flies from us. We have no choice. You must use the Crown. Do it now!" she urged.

Tom glanced down at the circlet of bronze and silver in his hand and swallowed hard. He had heard it called the most powerful artefact in history: the source of Knossos' power and the device that had corrupted him utterly. He felt the power radiating from it, suffusing his body, making his head swim. Was he strong enough to use it and not lose himself in it as Knossos had done?

Tom heard a scream and saw that Knossos had stepped back

325

to where Persephone was sprawled on the ground. He had pulled her to her feet and now held the girl in one arm and with the other had a knife across her throat.

"Drop it boy, or she dies!" he ordered.

"If I drop it we all die," Tom answered and without hesitation he thrust the Crown onto his head.

For an instant no one moved as everyone turned to stare at him.

Then ... Tom screamed.

CHAPTER THIRTY TWO
END GAME

The instant Tom put the Crown upon his head his mind was filled with an intense sensation of the vastness of the universe. He was immediately and terrifyingly aware of every star; every solar system; every planet. No ... he was more than aware. In contact - yes that was the phrase - for he now had a contact with it all. He felt the worlds spinning about each other, sensed the vastness of life in all its infinite variety; sensed all the feelings, hopes and fears of every living soul. He felt as though he was caught in the fury of a monsoon, or standing with his head pressed against the speakers at a rock concert. His senses were overwhelmed and his head was about to explode. Screaming, his fingers fumbled for the Crown, intending to fling it far away - anything to be rid of these sensations that beat upon his consciousness.

"No Master!" a voice implored him. He opened his eyes to look for the speaker, but he could see nothing apart from a kaleidoscope of colours bursting in front of him. His fingers touched something metallic and he was dimly aware that it was the Crown. He started to lift it off his head.

"Master, you must use the Crown," the voice urged him. Mary; yes ... that was her name. He remembered her, but through the haze she and all the others seemed so distant as to be unimportant; insignificant as bugs he could squash beneath his thumb.

Use the Crown? Was she mad? "I ... can't. I can't stand it. It is too intense."

"If you don't use it now it will be too late. Everything is collapsing," another voice said. Tom remembered him too: it was ...Septimus ... that was the speaker's name. He tried to see him but could see nothing, blinded as he was by the brilliance of colours.

"It is too much," he replied. "I am too weak."

"Too weak indeed mere boy that you are - did you really imagine you could defeat *me*?" A voice boomed, coming not like the others from outside himself. No, the voice was here. It was in his head. That meant it was sharing the Crown. Tom put his hands to his ears in an effort to block out the sound that could only be ...

"Knossos?"

"That is right, weakling. I am here within you."

"But you are in Midas too."

"Fool. I have spent fifty centuries divided and yet still whole. Once that ridiculous archaeologist put on my Crown it was easy to dominate him. Yet I am still part of the Crown on your head."

Tom gasped. "Fifty centuries in here - with those feelings, how did you cope?"

"It is my Crown. I made it and I control it."

"I am not so sure," Tom said. "I think it controls you. I think after you built it and put it on, when you felt what I am feeling and saw what I just saw, you went mad. This thing you created to be your tool, to dominate others and to change the world ... in the end you became its slave."

"What nonsense is this? I know what I am doing. Even now your destruction races towards you."

Tom cursed himself. Knossos was right - he was a fool. Even whilst they spoke and traded insults, the realities were colliding. Tom knew that ... but he also felt it. The Crown projected his mind and was in contact with all worlds everywhere. Tom could see the planets hurtling towards each other. He could see that other world - Redfeld's world -overlapping into his own world and both of them merging with The Office. And out there - beyond his own solar system - there were still more stars and planets imploding. He knew that it was just moments from the end of everything.

He had to act. He had to take control of the Crown and there was only one way he knew how. He would have to embrace his full powers; the full powers of the Potentate he now knew that he was. These last few days he had feared to do just that. Ever since he had overheard the Custodian and the Professor talking about him he had not wanted this. He feared he would lose himself; that it would change him more than he had ever wanted or imagined. Then there was that dream when he had been inside the mind of Knossos and had seen and felt the madness. Did that insanity come from contact with the Crown? Tom believed so. He could feel the almost irresistible temptation that it offered him.

Yet, Tom reasoned, he was not Knossos. He had not acted on some selfish whim. He was not seeking domination of all things. Maybe that would protect him. He had to hope so, for time was up and either he acted or everything that he knew; everything that he was, ended.

Closing his mind to the monster of Knossos within him, Tom reached out in the way he usually did to make contact with the Flow of Time and the Map. Yet here, in the Crown, he instead embraced the full ferocity of the sensations with which the artefact bombarded him. He pushed through them and now he, Tom, was touching the very fabric of reality. He could see the Twisted Reality, his own universe and The Office. He could feel them overlapping and intruding and now he perceived the cause of that attraction. Like a magnet drawing iron filings towards it, it was the Crown itself that pulled at them. It had always been the Crown. No, more than that: it was Knossos himself. In the Event, split apart by the blast that Titus had flung, the Crown, Knossos and the realities had separated. The very presence of the fragments across all of time and space had kept it apart like tent pegs holding up a tent. But the pegs had been pulled out of the ground and the tent was falling down. Here and now it was the presence of the fragments, all together in this one place and reformed, that was sucking the universe inwards.

So then, that was the solution. The Crown must once again be split up. It must be shattered and with it Knossos. Once more the fragments must be flung across the eons and the realities to act as anchor points, pinning the realities apart. This time, though, they must never be united. Tom, not Knossos, would decide where they went. There would be no guide to what was where. But something else was needed. Knossos must not be able to contact his followers, he must be unable to influence others and lead them to the fragments. Knossos must be imprisoned forever in the fragments - abandoned and alone.

Tom reached out and seized the universe and channelled his will through the Crown. With a supreme effort he wrenched the realities apart.

"Stop! I command it," boomed Knossos, his voice rising to a scream.

"Your days of giving orders are finished, Knossos."

"This is my Crown. I am all powerful. You cannot do this. I

am a god."

"No, you are not! You are merely a madman." Tom opened his eyes. No longer was he blinded by the swirling colours. He could see that the Black Robes had broken off their attacks and were gathered in huddles, arms around each other looking up at the Temple that had, until moments before, been threatening to collapse. Redfeld and Lapace were standing next to the altar. Redfeld still had his pistol trained on Charlie, who was back on his feet although holding his shoulder tightly - blood seeping through his fingers. The Professor and his brothers were watching Tom with interest, while close by the Institute members were studying him with expressions of concern on their faces.

Across the room, he locked gazes with Knossos who, within the body of Dr Midas, still held the terrified Persephone in his arms, the knife at her throat. But now fear was showing in his eyes.

"No ...," Tom repeated, walking slowly towards him. "You are not a god, Knossos. You could have been a great man, perhaps ... but it is too late for that now. Also, you are wrong: I can in fact do this. For it is not you who are the Potentate ... it is I!"

That said, Tom projected a burst of energy that crackled from his fingertips. Seizing the Crown, he flung it from his head and across the room. As it spun, it shattered with an earth-rending crack. The fragments spiralled away and vanished. All save one. It fell to the ground by Tom's feet and as he looked at it, it transformed and became once more his father's alarm clock. He bent over and picked it up.

"No!" Midas's mouth opened in a scream and from his lips there issued a blood-curdling cry. It shrieked to a crescendo then gradually diminished, trailing away into silence. For a moment nobody moved then the archaeologist dropped the knife

331

and collapsed to the ground behind the altar. Tom felt a sudden wave of vertigo pass over him and slumped to his knees. His head swam for a moment and then, finally, his eyes cleared.

"Tom!" Mary shouted and bustled over to him, knelt down and laid a hand on his forehead. "Are you injured?" she added.

Tom blinked and focused on her and shook his head. After a moment, he smiled. "You called me Tom. Not Master ... at last!"

"Well, as I see it we are friends, are we not?" She returned his smile.

"Yes Mary ... we are indeed."

"Are you alright, boyo?" Septimus asked, coming over to join them. Blood ran from a half dozen nicks and cuts; one eye was bruised and he was limping slightly, but he looked otherwise well.

Tom considered the question. Even now, the fragments were spinning away into space, drawing the imploding realities apart and with them went Knossos, sent into eternal oblivion. The universe had survived. All around him lay the Black Robes, no longer a threat; those who were conscious were motionless, some were weeping. Tom lifted a hand to probe his head. It felt as though a herd of buffalo had stampeded through it and his limbs were trembling, but ... he was alive and this time his family had not been obliterated.

"You know, yes ... I'm fine," he said with a smile as he struggled to his feet. Then the smile dropped as he glanced across the room and saw that Midas was also back on his feet and that an expression of terror was in his eyes. Held close to his neck, the curved blade pressing on his skin was a dagger in the hands of Persephone. Loathing and anger were written plainly upon her face.

"Don't kill me," Midas pleaded and the voice of Knossos was

gone. This was the archaeologist once more.

"Kill you, Knossos," she hissed, "why should I not kill you for what you have done?"

"No! Persephone, please wait. Let me explain," Tom said.

"Ja ... well that is a good idea, Mr Oakley," Redfeld said with an ominous flick of his Luger. "However, I think I too am owed an explanation about what just occurred."

Tom turned and glared at the Professor and his brothers.

"Actually, Captain; Persephone, I think there is someone here who owes us ALL an explanation!"

CHAPTER THIRTY THREE
POTENTATE

"What explanation is that?" Persephone snarled. "Knossos is the reason my parents died. Tom, I ... I did what you asked. I did it to betray him and for him to know that I had, and now that he knows, I will kill him."

"I am not Knossos," Midas gasped as the knife pressed deeper into his throat.

Persephone sneered. "I heard his voice through your lips, deceiver. His soul is in your body. Now I will rip it from you."

"No ... please don't. He was here but he has gone. He took me over when I put the Crown on my head. That was stupid of me: I could not resist ... such a nice looking Crown. But he left. I swear to you, he has gone."

Tom stepped closer, both hands held out to show he was no threat. "Persephone, believe me that Knossos is gone. I have banished his soul. He is in the past again - along with the fragments. Hidden forever where no one will find them. So trust me. I made a promise to save your family - or at least to try - and I will do that today. Just release Dr Midas."

"You can do that? You can bring them back?" The girl gazed at Tom, her voice soft, begging even.

"I will try, that much I promise. Just give me a moment to ask a question or two."

Persephone smiled thinly and slowly lowered the blade. "Very well," she answered and then by way of an afterthought turned to the archaeologist. "Sorry, Dr Midas."

"Not at all," he said vaguely, stepping away, one hand going up to rub his throat then finger his bruised, swollen face. "Honest mistake," he added bravely, although his voice was high pitched and shook with nervousness.

"Well, I am still waiting for an explanation of what occurred here," prompted Redfeld, swinging the pistol around to face Neoptolemas, Thielmann and the Custodian.

"Put the gun away Hauptman!" roared the Colonel. "How dare you point it at me!"

"Not until I have an explanation of exactly what happened here today, sir," Redfeld replied in defiance. Thielmann bristled but remained silent.

"I too am curious," Lapace drawled, pulling out his own revolver, "but my interest is in your actions, Mr Hawker."

"Me?" Charlie replied weakly. Mary had joined him and was rolling up his sleeve to examine his wound.

"Yes, Able-Seaman, you: you came to me bearing the gift of a fragment of the Crown. I take it that all the time I thought you were a turncoat, you were in fact working for Septimus here?" Lapace flicked his weapon towards his former partner. "Revenge, I assume, for a certain grudge between us?"

The Welshman stared at Lapace for a moment and then a bright smile broke across his features. "Much as I hate to say it, Rolf, it wasn't entirely my idea. Oh, using Charlie was my idea alright, but the overall plan was not mine. Actually, it was first suggested that I be the one to give you the fragment. But let's face it, you would never have believed that I'd had a change of heart, would you? Not after what you did to me."

Lapace snorted. "You got that right, but whose idea was it then?"

Everyone now stared at Charlie. "Well erm ... you see," Charlie hesitated.

"It was my idea, actually," the Professor admitted cutting across him.

"What?" Tom, Edward and Lapace chorused simultaneously.

The Professor strolled across to Charlie and placed a hand on his shoulder. "I asked Mr Hawker to assume the role of a defector from my Institute, initially because I wanted to establish who Mr Lapace was actually working for. Then, when we had discovered who his employer was," he turned and glanced at Thielmann, "... and given the reluctance of the Colonel to inform me, I decided to leave him undercover as security. Just in case everything went wrong, the Crown reformed and Redfeld tried to do just what in fact he did - take it for himself."

"Why did you not tell me?" Mary asked.

"Or me," Edward put in grumpily.

"Or me!" Tom added.

"Well in your case, Thomas, because I hoped that in your ignorance, you would react just how a betrayed, outraged colleague should react. I needed Lapace convinced that Charlie had defected and you played your role perfectly in that regard."

"Thanks," muttered Tom with a wry smile.

"What about me?" Edward repeated impatiently.

"Well much of that goes for you ... and for Mary too. In both your cases I felt you would not be comfortable with deceit, although in your case Lieutenant, I did have an ulterior motive."

Edward's face grew quizzical. "May I ask what that is, sir?"

"Oh this is all very interesting I am sure," Redfeld interrupted, tapping his foot. "So the Professor sent the sailor as a spy and we were taken in by him. Well done and so forth, BUT ... I am no fool. I heard what Thomas here said about Knossos, '*He is in the past again - along with the fragments. Hidden forever where no one will find them,*'" he quoted. "So then, this means, does it not, that he knows where the fragments are to be found. Am I right?" Now the steel gun barrel was pointing at Tom.

"If you kill me, you will never know," Tom pointed out.

"Perhaps, but you will still be dead, boy!"

"We have been here before, Captain, and at Tintagel you did not have a bullet in the gun. How about now?"

"Care to try me?" Redfeld replied with a snarl. "Tell me where the fragments are to be found: tell me now, or you will die!"

"Enough, Hauptman! Put away your weapon," Colonel Thielmann ordered. "The quest for the Crown of Knossos is over."

"But, sir, we can still retrieve it."

"No, fool, we cannot. For Oakley has reset the universe using the fragments. Take them away and the whole thing will collapse. It is over. We did what we came to do."

"What was that, sir, if I may be so bold as to ask," Redfeld sneered.

"For one thing we saved the universe "

"For one thing?"

"The other need not concern you, Hauptmann, just call it a happy accident," the Colonel added, his gaze flicking across to Tom. "Go get your men. We are leaving."

"Before I go, I can settle a score. Why not kill them all?" Redfeld waved the Luther at the Institute members, "Less to get in our way in the future."

"Not today."

"Why not?"

"That is an order, Hauptmann. I am your superior officer for

337

a reason! *Klar? Klar?"*

"*Ja wohl!"* Redfeld shouted, snapping his heels together. He cast an evil look at Tom and the others. "Until next time, my *dear* friends," he added and then marched out of the anteroom towards the outer temple to round up his men.

"Ah well, it was fun while it lasted," Lapace said, putting away his pistol. "You sure you don't want those fragments retrieved, Colonel? I can do you a decent deal for all of them. One of them is right there in the boy's pocket."

"No, Mr Lapace. Our business is concluded. Your account will be credited the agreed fee for work so far. You may go."

Lapace wandered over to Septimus. "Well, there you go, mate. You don't have the Crown and neither do I. I will give you a few points for pulling that little trick with Charlie, but overall I think we will have to call it a draw."

"So it seems, but I was not aware there was a competition," Septimus replied stiffly.

"Oh, come on now, Septimus. There is always a competition. This time neither of us won. Neither of us has the prize." His face cracked into a grin. "Bit like Julia really."

"Julia is not a prize," Septimus snapped.

"Oh, but she is, she is. She is angry at both of us right now. Me because I stole from her and you because I said you had helped."

"That really was a dirty trick, Rolf."

"Oh yes, of course it was. But if I was going to lose her I was not going to lose her to you, was I?"

"Just go, Rolf, before I get my friend here to send you into oblivion with Knossos. And don't forget to pick up your associates on the way out!"

"I will, I will," Lapace answered hurriedly with a swift glance at Tom. Then he sketched a theatrical bow to them each in turn,

338

said, "Till we meet again," and was gone.

Tom grimaced at Septimus. "He's the reason you stopped your freelance work. Are you going to let him get away with what he did? Don't you think you need to sort him out?"

The Welshman nodded and his eyes glinted darkly. "I will sort out Rolf Lapace one day, boyo, believe me I will, but now is not the time."

"What about Julia?" Mary asked.

Septimus stared at her. "Yes, lass, her too one day."

Thielmann stamped his foot and looked with irritation at his brothers. "Enough of all this nonsense! I will leave too."

"And I," the Custodian agreed.

"Just wait a moment, you two. I have not finished with you yet," Tom said.

"YOU have not finished with us?" The Custodian said in tone of outrage.

Thielmann was also shocked. "Your little hero needs to be taught manners and how to respect his betters, Neoptolemas. If not, how much use will he be to us when the time comes?"

"That is what I am talking about," Tom said, "when the time comes. What do you mean? The time for what exactly?"

"You will find out soon enough, boy. Just you learn obedience."

"I don't think so!" Tom snarled. Thielmann stepped forward, eyes blazing.

"Do you want to take me on boy? Well do you?"

"Back off," the Professor urged him. "All will be well. I will explain."

Tom shook his head. "Oh, it is not you who needs to explain, Professor; at least not everything. Thielmann can go if he wishes because it is not him either. It is the Custodian."

339

"I?" the Custodian answered.

"Yes you. There are a few pieces of the puzzle here that are falling into place."

Tom walked towards the Custodian and his brothers. "Something Knossos said just now. What was it he said? *'Ah, but you above all here know I will not...That is the risk you took when you started this. You are the Custodian aren't you. The logical thinker: the one who balances all things. You should understand more than anyone else that what you sow ye shall reap',*" he quoted. "Tell me, Custodian. What did he mean by that?"

"Ah ... he was deranged," Thielmann said. "He did not know what he was saying."

"He was mad alright, but I think he was saying something to the Custodian. Tell me, what *did* you 'sow'?"

All eyes turned to the Custodian. But the Controller of the Directorate did not reply.

"The stone tablet did not present itself by chance did it, Doctor, can you remind us?" Tom asked Midas. "Why did you choose to dig where you did?"

Dr Midas shrugged. "It was a grant. The university was short of finance for the summer season and this anonymous benefactor came forward and offered funding if we would dig in a specific spot."

"It would have been one of the Black Robes, surely," Thielmann argued.

"It wasn't any of us," Persephone replied. "We were swept away when the Crown shattered. We woke and heard Knossos telling us that the tablet would one day be found and that the time would soon come to rise again. But it was another eight years before he called us. We hid ourselves, got used to your strange world, learnt your language and waited for the time to

340

come. When the stone was found, we rallied to it."

"I get it," said Septimus, "the tablet acted like a beacon, drawing you to it through time. That is why you and the Cultists were able to locate us in the Museum and attack us."

"Sounds plausible," the Professor said.

"Then if it was not a Black Robe who told Midas where it was to be found, who was it?" Mary asked.

"Oh, very well. It was I," the Custodian replied with shrug.

"You?" gasped Thielmann and the Professor in unison.

"Why are you so surprised? I did what was necessary."

"You risked the destruction of everything, all that has been and will be, for what?" the Professor asked in shock.

"We needed a potentate. We need the boy to be ready. You two both know why. You know what is coming. That is why. I was confident we could prevent the destruction of the universe. It was worth the risk to bring him into his power."

"But you nearly didn't succeed, did you?" Tom pointed out. "You all got it wrong. You assumed that the Crown reforming would be used by Knossos to destroy the universe and so tried to prevent that. You guessed wrong, Custodian, and it was I who saved everything."

"Oh? And how did you save everything?" the Custodian asked innocently.

"Well you know how." Tom clenched his fists, "Because ... because I am the Potentate," he replied then realised that he had been led into a trap.

"Yes, because the Crown made it so. All that has happened has been part of that. Even as far back as the shattering of the Crown I knew this day would come. So the part of Titus that I became - what Knossos called the logical thinker - ensured that the stone tablet came to manifest in a place and at a time of my

341

choosing. So that one day I could send someone to retrieve it."

"I cannot believe how rash you were!" Thielmann said.

"Rash? Rash! You say that to me. When YOU abandoned greater concerns for petty empire building and he," the Custodian gestured at the Professor, "bothers about just one time line, one world. Have you forgotten the greater threat? Have you forgotten who we once were?"

"I have not forgotten it, Custodian," Neoptolemas replied, "and when the time comes you will not find me lacking in resolve. But it was still reckless to go about things in this way. Suppose the boy had been killed? Suppose Knossos had won? You might have consulted us at least."

"Would you have agreed?" the Custodian asked.

"Of course not!" Thielmann replied.

"Then what would have been the point?" the Custodian commented, strolling towards the door. "Now, with or without Thomas Oakley's permission I am leaving – and I will also collect my men as I leave," he gave the ghost of a smile to Septimus. "Good day gentleman," and with a final piercing gaze at Tom, he was gone.

There was silence for a moment after he had left. Then Thielmann glanced at his double. "Well, what is done is done. The ends perhaps justify the means."

"Let us hope so, Colonel. We came perilously close to disaster."

With a nod of the head, Thielmann vanished and now all that remained were the Hourglass members, the Black Robes, who still lay about looking terrified, Dr Midas and Persephone.

"Is it time now, Tom?" Persephone asked. "Time to save my parents?"

Tom glanced at the Professor who nodded.

"Yes it is time. But neither you nor the Professor may come. We," he waved his arms at his friends, "we alone will go."

"I will take care of her, and the others," the Professor replied. "But be careful, what you are attempting is dangerous. If you succeed, go straight back to the Institute. I will have Dr Makepeace on standby."

Tom nodded and reached out his arms. Septimus, Edward, Mary and the newly bandaged Charlie all latched on.

"Good to have you back, Charlie," Tom muttered.

"Good to be back, Tom mate!"

"So what do you think about life as a mercenary?" Septimus asked him. "Still want to follow that career?"

Charlie shrugged. "Oh it has its attractions and I may dabble once in a while ... care to give me some pointers?"

Septimus shrugged. "Why not, I've missed the life these last few weeks. Yes, why not indeed. Fancy a trip to Leonardo da Vinci's workshop, Charlie boy?"

"Gentlemen, please! Behave yourselves," Edward muttered.

Septimus stopped talking abruptly, but Tom caught him winking at Charlie and grinned to himself as he turned his focus to the Clock.

Then he Walked them back five thousand years. He knew exactly when to appear, for he knew in the dream when Xanthus and his men attacked Persephone's parents, just before the Crown shattered.

So it was that they materialised in the outer part of the Temple, where the sounds of battle could be heard all around them.

"What now, Tommy boy?" Septimus asked.

"The Custodian's motives were decidedly dodgy," Tom said, "but the net result of my contact with the fragment and the Crown is that I have gained more talents than I had before. I am

343

not sure about all that I can do yet, but what I am going to do now is to use Redfeld's trick. I am going to create the illusion that Persephone's parents die. I have to do that because Persephone, Knossos and Titus all saw it happen and to change things so they see something different will change the future and muck things up a lot. So gather round; this is what we shall do ..."

Within moments they were shrouded within a wall that Mary had created - a transparent barrier that bent the beams of light around her, rendering them invisible. They crept through the antechamber into the inner sanctum. Mary was grunting with the effort of maintaining the illusion and sweat was running down her face.

There, in the anteroom, a battle was raging between the armoured warriors of Xanthus and the Black Robes. The Cultist fanatics were flinging themselves at the soldiers, careless for their own lives and desperate to obey the urgings of their master.

"That is Knossos", whispered Tom, nodding at the dark-haired figure who wore the Crown, which even now was glowing with the pulsating light emanating from the gem. In a huddle that reminded Tom a little of a rugby scrum, the Walkers manoeuvred around the outside of the room so they now faced down the battle line.

"Evil looking so and so isn't he?" Charlie commented in a hiss. "We could do for him now and save us all a heap of trouble later."

"Tempting though that is, boyo; that would really muck things up," muttered Septimus. "Let's just do what we came here to do."

"There is Titus." Tom pointed to the young sorcerer, who was even now raising his palms to face Knossos.

"That's what the Prof and his brothers used to look like, is it?"

344

Charlie asked. "Handsome-looking bloke when he was younger. What do you say, Mary?"

Mary's answering smile was distorted by strain. "Please finish this quickly," she gasped, "I cannot hold it for long."

"AGE!" shouted Titus. Energy was weaving round his hands, becoming quicker and quicker in readiness to strike.

"Stop him!" Knossos ordered. Tom was waiting for this moment and as the two black-robed figures and their child moved towards Titus, he acted.

Reaching out for the Flow of Time, Tom seized it and became one with it. Then as it was raging through him, he envisaged the Flow being not his old brass alarm clock, but a tightly bound rope with hundreds of strands wrapped around each other. He unpicked a thread and looped it out from the rope and then placed another thread in its place. To any observers in the inner sanctum there was a moment when the child's parents seemed to hang in the air, and then they came running forward to be struck down by Xanthus' warriors.

What only those within Mary's barrier saw was that as the two Black Robes hurtled onwards, two duplicates were left frozen in the air. Frozen just for the split second it took Mary to open her barrier and bring them inside.

Edward, Charlie and Septimus leapt forward, clamped hands onto their mouths and dragged them back to Tom and Mary.

"Walk now!" Tom said and in an instant, they were gone - passing through fifty centuries in the blink of an eye and across a continent, coming to rest in the small ward of Dr Makepeace who, alerted by the Professor, was awaiting their arrival.

Two hours later, they were sitting over a cup of tea in the Professor's study. An emotional Persephone had gone up to see her parents and they had thought it best to let her go alone.

"She is keen to remain in Britain and at your school, Thomas," the Professor said, busily polishing his spectacles. "She told me she is hoping that once her parents have recovered, they will buy a house in your neighbourhood in order that she has a legitimate reason to continue at Parklands Comprehensive." Neoptolemas perched his glasses back on his nose and smiled at Tom. "She seems quite attached to you, lad."

Colouring, Tom looked down at his feet. So, Persephone would soon have a home and now had parents to live with her - presumably she had lied about having an uncle with a shop. He wondered how she had got that past the school authorities. He tried to remember the first time he had seen her - had the teachers even been aware she was there? Perhaps not. Not that it mattered now. He hoped it all worked out as she planned, although he would not have admitted that to a soul. Looking up he saw that Mary was watching him with a big grin on her face and his colour deepened.

He coughed. "What about the Black Robes, Professor?" The remainder of the Cultists, whom the Professor had Walked back to the Institute, posed a greater problem. Over twenty had survived the battle in the Temple and it was only now Tom realised how difficult the next few days would be for them. He voiced the thought and saw Septimus and Edward nodding in agreement.

"You are indeed right, Thomas," the Professor said, sipping at his tea. "For the past eight years they have been held in thrall by Knossos, unable to think for themselves - the necklaces, incidentally, have disintegrated. For the Cultists, the shock of coming back into consciousness and finding themselves here and now, so many years beyond their time, can only be imagined ..." he paused, his expression distant and thoughtful.

346

"Is that what happened to you, Prof?" Tom asked. His fingers curled around the acorn in his pocket and he pulled it out, looked at it and placed it on the desk.

The Professor glanced at it and smiled up at Tom then shook his head and seemed for once not to notice the 'Prof'. "Not really Thomas. For me it was ... different."

"How?"

"That is a tale for another day perhaps. As for the Black Robes, I have already thought of that. Dr Midas is keen to help the Institute further. He is due to return to Greece in any event as his sabbatical at the British Museum is coming to an end. He volunteered to settle the Cultists in out of the way parts of his homeland. Maybe they will adjust better living back in farming communities just like those they came from. They will, of course, receive psychiatric help whilst they are here. It will be hard for them to adjust, but Midas is a clever man and can keep an eye on them for us."

"I must see him before he leaves," Edward said. "I misjudged that man. Turns out he was just an honest man being used as a pawn by the Custodian. So then, how does he feel now, after all that happened to him?"

The Professor shrugged. "Shaky, rather bewildered, but he is a good man. He will pull through and I hope we will see him again. In fact I am sure we will. Lest you forget, he is also a Walker," he added then seemed to drift away into his own thoughts again.

"Good of him to help out. The Cultists will have it tough adapting to modern life," Septimus commented. "That said, it will be worse for Persephone's parents. To them it is as if their daughter went from seven to fifteen in an instant."

"Could you not have brought Persephone forward too, Tom -

347

I mean the younger one?" Mary asked.

"No, he was right not to," the Professor said, stirring from his thoughts. "If he had done that there would be two possibilities: one, there would be two Persephones and that, as we know, is impossible, so the older Persephone would have ceased to exist. Had that happened there is a distinct possibility that all the events that occurred might have unravelled, pivoting as they did so much on her."

"She is not the only girl around here who was pivotal to what went on this last week or so," Tom said.

Mary blushed and looked away.

"Come on Mary ... you must realise that too. All that talk about being useless and not fitting in. You know that is rubbish. Surely you know that by now?"

"I suppose so. It's just that ...," Mary began.

"Just that what?"

"It's just that ... I feel so ignorant," she said in a rush. "I want to be able to read. Properly I mean. I can't read and you all can. Even children can, and I can't. I want to read, can I learn?" The words came tumbling out in a tone of desperation.

"My dear Miss Brown," the Professor said, "I should have arranged a tutor for you months ago. Of course you can learn. And quickly too; you are as bright as any of the Walkers I have known. Does that answer your question my dear?"

Mary beamed and then nodded, but it was Edward who now spoke. "It answers her question, perhaps, but what about mine? I still want to know why you kept me in the dark about Charlie. Why, indeed you have kept me in ignorance of most of what has gone on."

"You have found it frustrating, Lieutenant?"

"Of course I have," Edward replied. His gaze flicked towards

348

Tom. "In fact, so frustrating that I have given serious thought to leaving here. Dr Livingstone invited me to join him on an expedition. I am tempted to do just that, unless you can perhaps give me a reason to do otherwise?"

The Professor did not answer at first. Glancing down at the acorn he looked thoughtful, as though choosing his words with care before he spoke.

Eventually he said, "I wanted to see how you would react to being excluded from my trust for a while, Lieutenant."

"Why on earth would you do that, Professor?" Edward asked indignantly, his face colouring with anger.

"Call it a little test. This job requires of us a certain degree of wisdom in how we deal with uncertainty; it requires a fair degree of trust when being asked to follow a leader down a dangerous path, but even more so when that path is clouded and uncertain." The old man chortled before carrying on. "You know, the strange thing about this test is that it got turned on its head. In the end it was I who had to show trust in you, because the rules had changed and you were leading me down a path I was not sure about." He looked up at Edward and smiled. "I do hope that you will stay because I would say you passed the exam, whichever way you look at it."

"Exam? What exam was that?" Edward looked mystified.

"Oh, did I not make myself clear on that matter?"

"No, sir, you did not."

"I apologise. I meant that I wished to see if you were up to the task of replacing me as Secretary of the Hourglass Institute."

Edward dropped his teacup - it landing with clatter on his saucer.

"What?" he asked.

All eyes swivelled to the Professor. He sat back in his chair,

349

pursed his lips and looked at each of them in turn, steepling his fingers.

"The Custodian was reckless in what he did, but it was a calculated risk. He was right in that we do need Thomas to be as powerful as possible - all of you too - but Tom in particular; so much so that we could not wait for him to come into his powers naturally." He turned to Tom. "I have suspected since even before we first met that you possessed potentate powers, Thomas - or at least that they were lying dormant just waiting for the stimulation to trigger the changes and awaken your abilities. In fact it was the Custodian who spotted you first ..."

"Why is it so important and what does it have to do with you leaving?" Tom asked.

"Oh, I did not say I was leaving. Edward will replace me if I die."

"Well you are not that old are you, Prof? You are pretty healthy too, for an old bloke," Septimus pointed out.

"I am older than you think, Mr Mason, but it is not death through old age I am preparing for. The Custodian was quite right in saying that a time of danger is fast approaching and we need our best warriors to be ready."

The Professor reached for the acorn, rolled it in his fingers then handed it back to Tom. "The thing about warriors, my friends, is that they have a nasty habit of not coming back."

Pocketing the acorn, Tom gave the Professor a sharp look as the implications of the word sank in.

"Warriors? You mean you are preparing for ..."

The Professor nodded.

"Yes that's right, Thomas - preparing for war!"

The End

"Thomas Oakley, a time always comes when you have to ask yourself this question: are you fighting on the right side?"

Read on for a sneak peek at the third volume in the Hourglass Institute Series.

TODAY'S SACRIFICE
CHAPTER ONE
THE STUFF OF LEGENDS

"War? What war?" Tom asked, breaking the silence that had descended upon the Professor's study.

He gazed across the room at the old man sitting behind his antique desk in front of the French windows, which were open to allow air to circulate. The noise of the London rush hour had subsided and the evening was cooling quickly after the hot September day. Feeling a draught, Tom shivered. The Professor felt it too and walked across to close the windows before returning to his seat.

"What War, Professor?" Tom repeated when the old man was seated again.

He did not reply at first. As was his habit when pondering how to broach a difficult subject, Professor Neoptolemas slipped off his glasses, retrieved a handkerchief from his breast pocket and vigorously polished the lenses. Finally he popped them back onto his nose and peered over the top of them at the five individuals who sat across the desk from him. It seemed to Tom that the Professor was weighing them up - perhaps seeing if they were ready for the answer to his question.

Tom glanced around the room at his companions - like him, all 'Walkers' or time travellers - with whom he had now shared two terrifying adventures. Next to him was the Welshman,

351

Septimus Mason, a mercenary adventurer who had first taught Tom how to travel through time. Together they had journeyed back through the years and rescued his other friends from certain death. These were Mary Brown, a baker's maid from Pudding Lane, just sixteen when she was plucked from the fires that destroyed London in 1666; Edward Dyson, the young Victorian lieutenant, whom Tom had saved from the sharp spears of the Zulu warriors in the battle of Isandlwana, and finally, Able Seaman Charlie Hawker, who had almost drowned during the Second World War having boarded a sinking U-boat in the Mediterranean sea.

The five of them had battled evil men from other worlds and hurtled through history on a treasure hunt that almost ended with the destruction of the universe. After all that, Tom was certain they were ready for anything else the Professor might care to throw at them. Not, of course, that he wanted any more adventures anytime soon. But if they came along, surely they could cope? If so ... why was the Prof so hesitant to answer?

Professor Neoptolemas was the head of the Hourglass Institute, whose role was to protect history. In the last few months his organisation had been busy doing just that and Tom had hoped that the troubles were now behind them. The Professor, however, seemed to be aware of yet another danger looming, and judging by his manner, one even more challenging than the last. Suddenly, Tom felt like a mouse caught in the open fields with an owl swooping down from the skies, its talons open and ready to seize him.

"Professor? What War?" asked Edward, his tone impatient and eager; a soldier wanting to know where his next battle lay and which enemy he must face.

At last the old man answered.

"I speak of a struggle from long ago: a conflict that was ancient even when Titus and Knossos walked the Earth."

"So you were not involved in this war then?" Tom enquired.

The Professor's response was a loud snort. "Oh, I was involved in it, Thomas, as Titus of course. In fact we both were - Titus and Knossos I mean. Actually you might say that we were up to our necks in it. But it is old ... so very old that now it is the stuff of legends, myths and - even - religion."

"Legends," Septimus put in, fingering his goatee beard, "which legends?"

The Professor's reply was to walk across to one of the many oak bookshelves that lined the walls of the room. There were books on science, history, collections of maps and, Tom knew, old stories and legends: anything in fact that might help the Institute in its mission. He ran his fingers across the leather spines of several volumes before selecting one and tugging it off the shelf. Returning to his seat he blew the dust from the top of the book, opened it and flipped through a few pages until he found what he was looking for. Turning the book around, he pushed it across the desk towards them, tapping his fingers on a picture that filled the double spread of pages.

There was a creak of chairs as all five of them craned forward and peered at the image. They studied it in silence for a moment before Septimus spoke.

"You are having a laugh aren't you, Prof?"

Neoptolemas' response was to treat the Welshman to an intense glare.

"You're serious then?" Septimus asked, his gaze flicking back to the picture and then up again to the old man.

A curt nod was the only answer.

Not understanding the unspoken conversation, Tom frowned

and bent again to look at the picture. The image showed a battle raging. Some of the figures were humans - or at least they seemed to be. Others were far from human and he could see ferocious looking creatures with wings, others with tentacles and still more made, or so it appeared, from water, fire or ice. It was hard to see who was fighting whom. He glanced at the writing at the bottom of the page. It read: 'The Titanomachy. Led by Zeus, the Olympians defeat the Titans and become the gods of Greece.'

It did not mean much to Tom. Puzzled, he looked up at the Professor and saw that the old man was now studying him.

"I don't understand," Tom shrugged.

"Nor I," mumbled Mary, "what is this a picture of?"

It was Edward who answered. "Before Zeus and the other Greek gods came to power, the ancient world was ruled by a race of powerful beings of immense strength. They were the Titans. Let me see now ... there was Cronus, Hyperion, Oceanus ...er ... Lapetus, Rhea and some others. They each had different abilities, such as control over minds, the elements, the oceans, life and death and so forth."

As he paused to gather his thoughts, the others, used to Edward's seemingly limitless knowledge of arcane subjects, grinned and rolled their eyes.

The Professor shook his head at them. "Please continue, Lieutenant."

"Well anyway," Edward said, unruffled, "as you might expect from legends, their rule was cruel and harsh and their own children, led by Zeus, overthrew them and became the Olympian gods. The picture depicts the final battle between the Titans and the Olympians."

"Impressive," Septimus muttered.

354

"Learn that in the army did you," asked Charlie, "cos they never taught it to me in the navy."

Edward grinned. "I told you before - the benefits of a classical education in a Victorian grammar school." His grin faded as he turned back to the Professor. "But surely this is just myth. All religions have tales of a war in heaven, or a war of the gods - the Vikings, the Babylonians ... even the Christian Church. What are you saying, sir? Are you saying that it actually happened?"

The Professor drew in a deep breath. "Yes, Lieutenant, that is exactly what I am saying. Or rather, what I am saying is that a war did occur, involving great and powerful beings that men called 'Titans'. The war raged for years and the Titans were defeated in the end."

Now Septimus spoke, his voice filled with incredulity. "Defeated by Zeus, Poseidon and Hades, if I recall correctly," he said and then winked at Charlie. "We did have schools in Wales too you know, boyo." He threw Neoptolemas a challenging look. "That is what you are saying, Professor, isn't it?"

"No."

"No? What do you mean, no?"

"I mean, Mr Mason, that the Titans were certainly defeated, but not by the Olympians."

"Then by whom?"

There was silence again.

A flash of memory came to Tom. One of his unique abilities as a Walker was to inhabit the minds of others in dreams and not long ago, when he and his friends had been battling the black-robed Cultists from Ancient Greece, he had dreamed he was their master, Knossos. Something had struck a chord. What was it? Narrowing his eyes Tom thought back, trying to recall Knossos' thoughts. Then it came to him: Knossos had been thinking of the time when he and Titus were friends and together had destroyed an ancient enemy of humanity. Another memory surfaced - this time from his dream of being Titus when he had been approaching the fateful confrontation with Knossos, who had become his enemy. Titus had been thinking about how they had once been the saviours of Greece and had defeated Hyperion, Coeus and their brothers.

Tom gasped as all the pieces came together: Edward had said that Hyperion was a Titan which meant that ...

"It was you, wasn't it Professor? Before the Event changed you, you were Titus: so it was you; you and Knossos who fought the Titans and destroyed them."

Neoptolemas eyed Tom with a glint of approval. "That is right, Thomas. Or rather, we defeated and imprisoned them. You saw that in your dream of being Titus I take it?"

Tom nodded. "And also something that Knossos was thinking when I was him. But Knossos believed he had destroyed the Titans."

The Professor barked a harsh laugh. "Knossos sometimes believed what it suited him to believe. But yes, he and I battled the Titans and in the end got the better of them. But I fear they were never destroyed ...."

Stunned by this news, no one spoke as they all gazed back at the image in the book. Now he looked more closely, Tom thought the picture of Zeus with a thunderbolt in his fist did look a little like a young Neoptolemas - a little like how Titus had looked, in fact. With a nasty feeling in his gut he stared up at the Professor. Was the old man implying that the forthcoming war was against the Titans? Tom dared not ask, in case the old man confirmed it - and there he was, only moments ago, thinking they could cope with anything!

Finally, Septimus coughed. "Wow, Prof, that's ... er ... quite a story."

"Oh it is, it is," the Professor replied, staring at the Welshman over his spectacles before adding, "so, would you like to hear the tale?"

To find out what happens next read
Today's Sacrifice
ISBN 978-0-9568103-0-4
Published by Mercia Books
Find out more at:
www.richarddenning.co.uk
Follow the author via Facebook:
www.facebook.com/RichardDenningAuthor

The Northern Crown Series

Book One - The Amber Treasure
ISBN: 97809568103-1-1

"I will take care of the body of my lord and you can carry the sword, story teller. For all good stories are about a sword."

6th Century Northumbria: Cerdic, the nephew of the great warrior Cynric, grows up dreaming of glory in battle and writing his name in the sagas.

When war comes for real though, his sister is kidnapped, his family betrayed and his uncle's legendary sword stolen. It falls to Cerdic to avenge his families' loss, rescue his sister and return home with the sword.

Winner of a B.R.A.G. Medallion

Book Two - Child of Loki
ISBN: 97809568103-2-8

A divided land ... a divided family.

The Battle of Catraeth has been won and Cerdic's homeland is safe ... but for how long?

The Northern British were crushed but yet more enemies have risen to replace them.

Soon Cerdic and his friends must go to war again - against the Scots and Picts north of Hadrian's wall. He goes to help his country's allies - the Bernicians - under their great warlord, Aethelfrith.

But what is Aethelfrith's true design? How ambitious is he and how far will he go to fulfil his dreams? And what is Cerdic's treacherous half brother, Hussa up to in these fierce wild lands?

The Praesidium Series

Book One - The Last Seal
ISBN: 9780956810397
Gunpowder and sorcery in 1666…

17th century London - two rival secret societies are caught in a battle that threatens to destroy the city and beyond. When a truant schoolboy, Ben, finds a scroll revealing the location of magical seals that binds a powerful demon beneath the city, he is thrown into the centre of a dangerous plot that leads to the Great Fire of 1666.

"an awesome array of characters which definitely included the good, the bad and the ugly, and an amazing plot!"
" This young adult historical fantasy had me totally engrossed and I would recommend it to anyway who loves historical fantasy/fiction (especially British) whether you're a teen or an adult. "
FIVE STARS
The Slowest Bookworm

"Denning has a real thirst for historical knowledge and this certainly shines through in his books, with his descriptions of London in 1666 making you feel as if you were in the middle of the raging fire."
YA Yeah Yeah

Winner of a B.R.A.G. Medallion